'Forget the detail, just hear this, we are predicting a fall in the global population from 9 to 5 billion – from 9 to 5 – in just a hundred years.

From 9 billion to 5 billion.

And this momentous, planet saving, change is all going to happen because of the decisions of ordinary people around the world, from Nairobi to New Delhi to New York.

It is you people sitting right here who are going to save the planet, just by having smaller, happier families. Nothing else.

From 9 to 5. Tattoo it on your forehead, or even write a song about it.'[1]

---

1   Isarebe, S, 2053, Eye-Ted Talk: *Saving the world with pills, coils and condoms*, 17th June 2051, www.eye-ted.com [accessed 17th June 2149]

This is a fictional biography, written by a fictional author living in the 22nd century.

The quotes, characters, events, incidents, forecasts and analyses are also fictional. Any resemblance to actual persons (living, dead or yet to be born), events and facts is purely coincidental. Photographs of characters in the book are played by actors and models who have no link to the characters described in the book or their opinions. Certain long-standing institutions, agencies, and public offices are mentioned or made reference to, but the references are wholly imaginary. Although its form is that of a biography, it is not one. The opinions expressed are those of the characters and not of the author or publisher.

Published by Coil Press 2023

Copyright © Coil Press Limited 2023

ISBN: 978-1-7395139-0-0 (paperback colour)
ISBN: 978-1-7395139-1-7 (paperback black & white)
ISBN: 978-1-7395139-2-4 (e-book)

ANNE WYETH is an economic historian, curator and commentator. Her books include: *The End of Christian Monetarism*, described by *The New Technonomist* as 'a book on economics that bears reading to the end'; *Isarebe and the Myth of Genius*, which was runner-up in the biography section of the McKellick Prize in 2136 and *As easy as 1-2-43*, an introduction to economics for the under 14s, which won the Eileen Hammer Award for Children's Non-Fiction in 2142. She is also the author of a well-received collection of poetry, entitled *Crows Circling the Bell*. A former Vice-President of the British Economic Society and a Distinguished Fellow of American Economics, she has been a contributing editor to the Pan-American Economic Review for the past twenty-eight years. She is Professor of Economic History at Cambridge University and a Fellow of St Aubrey's College. She has co-curated many exhibitions on economics and prominent economic figures, including shows at the Sovereign British Museum, the American Revel-Smith Institute and the International Harmony Museum in Shanghai. Married to the sculptor Michel Harring, she received the NAA for services to economics in 2148. She spends her time between her homes in Pennsylvania, USA and Cambridge, England.

First published to accompany the exhibition:

From 9 to 5

The Arem Johns Gallery, London, England: 6th June – 22nd November 2150
Organised in collaboration with Kizz Living History Productions

The exhibition was supported by The Anscott Foundation

Published in Great Britain by Harper Willams in 2150

WALC 978-0-00-811821-2

World Archive Library Cataloguing in Publication Data

A catalogue record for this book is available from The World Archive Library

Printed and bound in Finland by Maisie Day Productions
EID7584A453, Helsinki, Finland

Design by Maisie Day Design

Front cover: Solomon Isarebe, 2083, courtesy of The Isarebe Trust

Photographic credits: All photographs printed by kind permission of The Isarebe Trust, Christian Bortelli, Lambeth Art School and The Arem Johns Foundation.

Paper made from 98% recycled waste tissue and papers

From 9 to 5

The life and work of Solomon Isarebe: 2008-2093

ANNE WYETH

The Anscott Foundation   Harper Willams

Contents

Foreword by Dora Mann

Chair of The Isarebe Trust

In his lifetime, Solomon Isarebe was seen by the public as a rebel, a genius, a villain and finally a figure of pity. Among those few who knew him, he was revered as a man of shining and sometimes bewildering brilliance, but also a man with many deep flaws. He was a complex man, often in psychological turmoil, but also a man capable of extraordinary kindness towards the small group he trusted and relied upon; first among these was Arem Johns, the celebrated British artist and Solomon's great love, whom he tragically lost after just eleven years together.

In the exhibition and this accompanying book, we are thrilled he is being celebrated 100 years after the publication of his greatest work, *Future Perfect*. It was a book that shook the world and created political shock waves that reverberated for many decades after its publication. It was arguably the catalyst for a global consensus on the path we needed to follow to peacefully co-exist with the fragile planet upon which we live.

I think Solomon would give a small, bewildered smile if he knew he was still being feted for his work, but would perhaps be quietly pleased that we are also remembering his love for Arem Johns.

Much of the exhibition looks at the predictions Solomon and his sister Isabelle made in *Future Perfect* and compares them to the world as it is now. On the whole, the forecasts were remarkably accurate and Solomon and Isabelle's concerns about how politicians would manage this dramatic fall in the population were sadly prescient.

There never was going to be a 'Future Perfect' and we certainly don't have a 'Present Perfect', but things could have been a whole lot worse, and Solomon Isarebe played a small but significant part in ensuring we have managed to muddle through this, 'the most momentous change in the history of Humankind'.[2]

I hope you enjoy the exhibition and this accompanying book, written by the incomparable Anne Wyeth.

3rd January 2150, Amsterdam.

---

2   Isarebe, S and I, 2050, *Future Perfect*, Cambridge and Oxford University Press, Cambridge, p. 437

I never would, but I long to be brave enough to join you in whatever oblivion you are in. There seem to be so few worthwhile sensations left in me. I feel changed and I've hardly the strength to make it from the bed to the bathroom. I'm glad you can't see me like this— I don't know where the man you said you loved has gone. Twice last night I thought I heard you coming down the hall. Both times I sat bolt upright, ridiculous in my hope that you would come in a slip beside me in to bed. But it wasn't you, of course, and I was left in a silence so overpowering that I had to shout out just to make sure I still existed. I sat in the workroom for an hour or so this morning, but couldn't do much except sit. I kept looking up in the mirror, without thinking, expecting to see you there, but there is just your work. It's all so dusty now and I've not one wish to do with it. I think I'll leave it for Barbie to sort out. The workroom, to me, doesn't smell the same any more and it's made me realise the smell of our house was the smell of us, not the smell of me and you. It is killing me. I put my head in your chair almost every day and try to catch some smell of you but I think the faint scent of you I think I catch is just my imagination. The police and the press and the idiot public won't leave me alone. I got 43 calls today and didn't answer any of them. Rita has given me a new phone, just for her and Casey and the lawyers to use. I get thousands of messages everyday, from strangers who claim to know and love you. They accuse me of hate, of some private grief. I'm full of malevolence, I always have been, but for fools like them, not for you. I mean, how fucking senseless are they?! Tomorrow, they are locking me away pre-trial. I am now 'a flight risk' apparently, but the logic of the law says I'm a flight risk tomorrow, but not today. I feel some gratitude for their sympathy, because I don't want to leave Sylvie. Rita and Casey are busy doing something legal, to set me free Rita says, but part of me just wants to go, to just get on with the process of rotting away. And then even suddenly, out of the despair, I find the unexpected saviour of hate. Someone did this to you and to me. Someone took you away from me. And that hate momentarily makes me want to live, just to find the person who killed you and to rip their heart from their chest. I want to feel their blood running over my wrists and to be deafened by their screams. It's not a grand thought, but it persists and it's the only thing that makes

The lion strikes with throw-away courage.
The fox's conscious deceit before genocide in the coup [*sic*].
The hawk nodding aloft the trembling rabbit.
And Me! A pitiful, frit mouse.
Flayed in the air. Held by his foolish tail.
Ga ava geerichonty hlaja meeka sti, I cry!!

I never would, but I long to be brave enough to join you in whatever oblivion you're in. There seem to be so few worthwhile sensations left in me. I feel drugged and I've hardly the strength to make it from the bed to the bathroom. I'm glad you can't see me like this – I don't know where the man you said you foolishly loved has gone. Twice last night I thought I heard you coming down the hall. Both times I sat bolt upright, ridiculous in my hope that you would come in and slip beside me into bed. But it wasn't you, of course, and I was left in a silence so overpowering I had to shout out just to make sure I still existed. I sat in the workroom for an hour or so this morning, but couldn't do much except sit. I kept looking up in the mirror, without thinking, expecting to see you there, but there is just your work. It's all so dusty now and I'm not sure what to do with it. I think I'll leave it for Barbie to sort out. The workroom, the house, doesn't smell the same anymore and it's made me realise the smell of our house was the smell of us, not the smell of me or you. It is killing me. I put my head in your chair almost every day and try to catch some smell of you, but I suspect the faint scent of you I think I catch is just my imagination.

The police and the press and the idiot public won't leave me alone. I got 43 calls today and didn't answer any of them. Rita has given me a new phone, just for her and Casey and the lawyers to use. I get thousands of messages every day, from strangers who claim to know and love you. They accuse me of hate, violence towards you. I'm full of malevolence, I always have been, but for fools like them, not for you. I mean, how [expletive] senseless are they? Tomorrow they are locking me away pre-trial. I am now 'a flight risk' apparently, but the logic of the law says I'm a flight risk tomorrow, but not today. I feel some gratitude for their stupidity, because I don't want to leave Sylvie. Rita and Casey are busy doing something legal, to set me free Rita says, but part of me just wants to go, to just get on with the process of rotting away. And then Arem, suddenly, out of the despair, I find the unexpected saviour of hate. Someone did this [to] you and to me. Someone took you away from me. And that hate momentarily makes me want to live, just to find the person who killed you and to rip their heart from their chest. I want to feel their blood running over my wrists and to be deafened by their screams. It's not a proud thought, but it persists and it's the only thing that can make my heart beat strong. I know I am too cowardly to do it, but the dream gives me a moment of pleasurable revenge.

I worry about Sylvie. She is sitting at my feet right now, looking disapprovingly at my untouched whisky. Does she want me to drink more or less? I'll walk her along the river for a while before I go to bed. Barbie and Nola are coming for her tomorrow at 8, just before the police come for me.[3][4]

---

3   Isarebe, S, 2068, single page of loose-leaf notebook, undated but assumed 7th October 2068, The Isarebe Trust Archives, Cambridge, England (Box 482, Folder 3)
4   'Sylvie' was Solomon Isarebe and Arem John's dog, a black Labrador, which they shared with their neighbours and good friends Barbara French and Nola Sharp. Barbara French was joint executor of Arem Johns' will, along with Solomon Isarebe.

Introduction by Anne Wyeth

Solomon D. Isarebe was a man who was to become more famous for something he didn't do, than for the many things he did.

Named by Time Crake Media in 2100 as one of the 100 most influential figures of the 21st century, he was pilloried and reviled for much of his later life as the convicted murderer of his lover, the artist Arem Johns. His good name and reputation were eventually restored, but only after nearly twelve years of imprisonment. After his release he became a recluse, wanting nothing to do with the world that as a younger man he had seen so worthy of redemption.

His work is now held up as a paragon of academic rigour and the pursuit of truth. His novel methods, of placing individuals' decision-making at the centre of analytical models in both demography and economics, are now common practice and iterations of some of his modelling and research techniques are still in use today.

Solomon Isarebe and his sister Isabelle were the discoverers of 'Cheerful Nihilism', now referred to as Will Suppression Syndrome, but his most celebrated achievements were his forecasts of demographic change over the period 2050–2150 and in particular his prediction of a near 50% decline in the global population and the implications of this for the economy, land use and climate change. He received the Nobel Prize in Statistics and Economics[5] in 2055 for the research and modelling techniques he developed in the course of his work.

In 2050, these demographic, economic and climate forecasts were published in the book, *Future Perfect*. It was an extraordinary success, combining groundbreaking technical achievements with a populist accessibility. His gift as a communicator, in particular his ability to explain complex concepts in simple language, meant his ideas became known to many around the globe in the second half of the 21st century, with his work on population change featured within the curriculums of high schools in 165 countries by the turn of the 22nd century. His ideas were perhaps so widely propagated because they insisted the world had the potential to be a better place, whatever the media, politicians, influencers, cultural commentators and religious leaders might say. This optimism comes through in this excerpt from the original preface to *Future Perfect*:

---

5   This had previously been known as the *Sveriges Riksbank Prize in Economic Sciences in Memory of Alfred Nobel*, but was changed in its name and scope in 2039.

I do not believe these forecasts will come true. In fact I am certain they won't.

New unexpected technologies will emerge and the cultural pressures that influence individual decision making will subtly change. But all the evidence suggests directionally I will be correct and in order of magnitude I will not be far out. In this sense, the results of our work are irrefutable. You could argue about which year we will reach a certain stage of development, or the odd percentage here or there, but that would be to miss the point. We are on the verge of the most significant and dramatic change in the human realm that has ever been seen. At the end of the forecast period in 2150, the world will barely be recognisable as the place we know today.

Food poverty will be largely gone. The conditions for long-term reversal of global warming will be in place and it is likely the world will already be cooling. Housing costs in the developed world will be a fraction of what they are now. Congestion will be confined to the heart of our major cities. Women around the world will be free of the pain and economic and personal confinement that accompanies large families and multiple pregnancies. It will be the decisions made by billions of ordinary families over the next century that will have ensured our collective survival.

The future won't be perfect. Societies will still bemoan their lot. Politicians will still foment hatred. The media will still rely on tragedy for their daily bread. But, many of the existential threats to humanity and the rest of the biosphere will have started to recede. In that very limited sense the title 'Future Perfect' is perhaps not inappropriate.

Within a further hundred years, by 2250, who knows, maybe the global population will have dwindled to less than a billion people, maybe the population will have stabilised, maybe it will be rapidly growing again. We should never underestimate our potential for collective stupidity and our inability to learn the lessons of the past.

Some people on reviewing this book have labelled me a hopeless optimist. I am not. I lie awake at night imagining the many ways in which politicians might mess this up. It literally stops me sleeping. But, if we collectively insist this decline in the global population is truly wondrous, then perhaps our vision of a better future for the planet will be realised. It is up to all of us to stand up and say no, when politicians tell us this is the end of the economic world, or try to coerce women into having more children. We must shout loud and clear that this simple freedom, to have small and happy families, is essential for the survival of our planet.[6]

Solomon Isarebe has been a towering presence throughout my adult life. First, as a lowly undergraduate, struggling to understand Continual Inference Revision, his and Isabelle Isarebe's poisoned gift to undergraduate economics students throughout the world. Then, as a slightly more confident PhD student, examining the economic impact of the social uprisings and military conflicts of the late 21st century: events that were a direct result of population decline; events Isarebe spent many years forewarning world leaders about. Then in my post-graduate life as an economic historian I became fascinated by Solomon Isarebe, the man, and in particular his relationship with Arem Johns, one of the great British artists of the 21st century. The mythology around them as a couple is extraordinary, fuelled by their fame and brilliance, their unlikely love for each other and her murder, aged just 43, in 2068.

In 2136, I wrote a biography of Solomon Isarebe, but I now see I was guilty of terrible deceit in this work.[7] I had fallen in love with him and Arem Johns, you see. And love is the most terrible disease for a committed academic. It renders you blind to the truth. That the book was well received reflects how much Isarebe's reputation had recovered, but also that I was not alone in my love for him and Johns.

Fourteen years later, I hope that first flush of love has passed and I can now look at Isarebe's life and work with a little more detachment, but more importantly I have now been given access to his private photos, letters, notes and files, the first time anyone has been granted such access. That he is more complex than I once thought is a given: he is just a man after all, so how could the truth not be more complex than the myth. Perhaps surprisingly, I now realise how much I underestimated him and how much I like him too.

I would like to thank Dora Mann and the Isarebe Trust for the access they gave me to this archive and for the free rein they gave me in preparing this book. I would also like to thank the Lambeth Art School in London and The Arem Johns Foundation for their permission to use material from their respective Arem Johns archives.

---

6   Isarebe, S and I, 2050, *Future Perfect*, Cambridge and Oxford University Press, Cambridge, pp. 17–18
7   Wyeth, A, 2136, *Isarebe and the Myth of Genius*, Throwers Publishing Company, Boston

Writing about Solomon Isarebe is always a challenge. Which aspect of his life should you focus on, and which aspect of his life do people want you to focus on? Many know he published a quasi-academic book in the middle of the 21st century about the impact of a falling population on the future of the world and that it became the best-selling non-fiction book of the 21st century. Even more people know he had a long and passionate love affair with Arem Johns and was convicted of her murder. Fewer know that he was acquitted of her murder after twelve years in prison, but I suspect many of these still think or hope that he was really guilty, whatever the courts said. We all love a real-life Bollywood tragedy.

Like everyone else, I pretend to be most interested in the academic side of Isarebe's life – it is the mark of a good education, after all – but secretly I want to know more about him and his life with Arem Johns. Their love is the one we all secretly want. His pain is the one we all think we have felt. The tragedy of their romance sucks us all in with a hopeless voyeurism.

I was relieved of the terrible responsibility of deciding how to write this biography by the forbidding wonder that is Jonathan Ward, curator of the exhibition *From 9 to 5*. He remained impervious to my poetic, romantic pleading and insisted our primary focus must be Isarebe's work, showing where he got it right and where he got it wrong, without fear or favour. That remained my goal during my research for this book, but even when looking through Isarebe's academic papers and private musings on technique and method, the person always came through. In reading his diary entries, I sometimes felt I could smell the man, his aura was so strong. I would literally hold the pages to my nose and breathe deeply. No one who could write such heart-rending diary entries deserves to go unheard. In the end, it became clear to both Jonathan and me there could be no separation of the man and his work.

So 100 years after the publication of the first edition of his most famous work, *Future Perfect*, we look back at both his life and his work, examining the man and the predictions he made. This book has been written as an accompaniment to the touring exhibition *From 9 to 5* which contains many items from his archive, including photographs and videos of Isarebe and Arem Johns and a reproduction of their studio where they worked together for over ten years. Many of the photos and images from the exhibition are reproduced in this book.

Anne Wyeth, Concordville, February 2150.

CERTIFIED COPY OF AN ENTRY

1. No. of entry		
2. Date	451007	
and place		
and	Unknown, assumed 19/05/2008	
country of	XXXXXX	
birth of child	XXXXXX or	
	XXXXXX	Registration District
3. Name and surname		Southwark
of child	Solomon Isarebe	Sub-district
4. Sex of child		Peckham
	Male	
5. Name and surname	Juuri Isarebe	
	Riko Isarebe	
address	Örje Bogvvägen 427, 12634 Hägersten, Stockholm, Sweden	
and occupation of		
the parent(s) of the	Engineer	
adopted child	Poet	
6. Date of adoption order or date on which the adoption was effected		
	28th February 2018	
and description of court or by whom effected		
	London High Court of Justice Family Division	
7. Date of entry		
	16th March 2018	
8. Signature of officer deputed by Registrar General to effect the entry		
	Michael Marego	

CERTIFIED to be a true copy of an entry in the Adopted Children
Register maintained at the GENERAL REGISTER OFFICE. Given at
the General Register Office, under the seal of the said Office.

on .... 23rd July 2015 ....

CERTIFIED COPY OF AN ENTRY
Pursuant to the Births and Deaths Registration Act

BIRTH

Registration District	Southwark	
Sub-district	Peckham	CHILD

1. Date and place of birth
   Unknown, assumed 19/05/2008
   Unknown, streamed outside of the U...

2. Name and surname
   Solomon Denamed ISAREBE

3. Name and surname
   Unknown

Place of birth
   Unknown

Name and surname
   Unknown

Place of birth
   Unknown

Maiden surname
   Unknown

Usual address
   Un...

PART 1
The creation of Solomon Isarebe

1.1 Isarebe starts a family

Solomon D. Isarebe knocked on the door of The National Poetry Library on London's South Bank on 12th June 2017, demanding to see Reba Desalli. He was 9 years old.

The librarian, Ella Delatrange, explained to him that Reba did not work there and she thought she was living in Sweden at the moment. 'He was visibly startled, but he looked me right in the eye and said, "Well, you should tell her she needs to get here as soon as she can, to pick up her new son." How do you respond, when a kid says something like that? He wrote down his name and explained to me that Isarebe was pronounced Is-are-be, as in 'it is', 'you are', 'just be'. He said he got very angry if people pronounced it wrong and I believed him. He gave off this sense of enormous power.'[8]

Ella Delatrange knew Reba Desalli, a largely unheralded poet with a small but fanatical fanbase, having met her at a poetry festival in 2015. Thinking that maybe Desalli could shed some light on what was going on, she telephoned her in Stockholm.

Reba Desalli had never heard of Solomon Isarebe, but Delatrange said she did not sound surprised by the phone call. Desalli got on a plane to London three hours later. In the meantime, the police and social services had arrived at the library and were trying to make sense of the situation. Solomon refused to speak to anyone 'until my mother gets here.'[9] This strange, gangly, pre-pubescent boy had hints of a slight Australian or New Zealand accent and diplomats from their Embassies were competing to feed him when Reba Desalli arrived at 8.30 p.m.

She greeted Isarebe with a brief, un-returned hug and explained to the now proliferating authorities she was Solomon's aunt and following the unexpected deaths of her sister and her sister's husband she was in the process of adopting Solomon. Isarebe nodded as Desalli spoke. She told them Solomon was currently staying with some of her extended Romany family and he had come to the library because he was getting frustrated, waiting to start his new life with her and her partner in Sweden.

What Reba Desalli said made no sense and the authorities were not taken in, but neither Desalli nor Isarebe would change their stories. Isarebe refused to say who his biological mother and father were, where he had come from,

---

8   Isarebe, R, 2054, *Chosen Poet*, O'Daley's, London, p. 24
9   Isarebe, R, 2054, *Chosen Poet*, O'Daley's, London, p. 25

or where he was staying. Reba refused to say where her sister had lived, when she died, or how Isarebe had ended up in London.

PIXELLATED IN ACCORDANCE WITH CPA GUIDELINES WEF83THU (2147)

Solomon Isarebe and Reba Desalli, Festival Hall, London, 12th June 2017

In his unpublished autobiography, Isarebe recalled these early moments with Reba Desalli and her unquestioning acceptance of his arrival in her life:

> Almost from the minute I met Reba, mum, I realised she would do anything for me and in my imagination at least, I believed I would have done anything for her. I knew she would die for me. I used to fantasise about it. Even now I don't understand how I could have been so sure; how I could have such a conscious and certain sense of my own security when I was with her.
>
> It gave me a sense of enormous power and I knew I could misuse that power and she would always forgive me. I suppose it is the power children with doting parents feel as a normal fact of life. I think I abused this power for a while, perhaps for a long time, but I have come to forgive myself. Even if my demeanour insisted I was in command, I was just a small mundane messed-up kid. It took me

a long time to realise I didn't need to always get my own way just to stop people hurting me.

I now know this power is just plain old love. I know where my love for my mum came from, but I have never understood why she loved me. Why would she? I am not and was not lovable. Why did she decide to embrace this unpleasant boy, who demanded she turn her life upside down and look after him for ever more?

Perhaps because of this power, this love, mum never asked me where I came from or why I was there in London, or why I had asked for her. If she'd asked, I maybe would have told her, but if she'd asked I don't think I would have trusted her, so I probably wouldn't. In any case, soon after I arrived in London, my 'life-before' disappeared from my mind; I couldn't or wouldn't recall it.

Memories of my early life were to eventually return to me, but I'm not sure I felt better for it and I was glad I never told mum. She would have been so cross with everyone and it wouldn't have made her love me more. She couldn't.[10]

Five months later, Reba Desalli, now living in London, was awarded temporary custody of Solomon Isarebe, after a fruitless world-wide search for his parents and extensive lobbying from the Romany community. Reba's grandmother had been a British Romany and they were a group the UK government were wary of upsetting.

On 19th March 2018, Isarebe moved to Stockholm to live with Reba and her partner Jannik Nieminen, a Finnish-born nuclear engineer. Isarebe agreed to move to Stockholm under one condition: that Reba and Jannik, who had never married, change their name to Isarebe. Reba and Jannik agreed, organising a ceremony in front of friends and family when they formally became 'Isarebes'. Reba Desalli explained their decision to change their name and not to question Isarebe on his past, in her memoir *Chosen Poet*:

We found so many scars on his ██████████████████████████[11] They looked like tiny razor cuts and cigarette burns. He claimed he was born like that. How anyone could do these things to a special

---

10   Isarebe, S, 2067, typed notes for an unpublished autobiography, manuscript dated 24th September 2067, The Isarebe Trust Archives, Cambridge, England (Box 448)
11   Redactions in accordance with Child Protection Agency Guidelines MGJ3/23 (2147)

piece of brilliance like Dizzy was literally unimaginable to us. He showed no sign of fragility or trauma, in fact he was quite dauntingly self-confident, so we decided to let it be, for fear of smashing the façade and finding nothing but a trembling mass of tortured flesh inside.

I will always remember the day he asked us to become Isarebes. It was like a strange marriage proposal. We were so proud to have been chosen by this rare exotic creature, that we immediately said yes, like two blushing brides-to-be. People thought we were mad, giving in to such an extreme demand from a 9-year-old boy, but it was an honour, not a sacrifice, and it helped us all cement our sense of family.[12]

A year later, the Isarebes moved to Egypt, where Jannik Isarebe had signed a two-year contract to work for the Egyptian government, advising on the early stages of the country's first nuclear plant at El-Dabaa, 200 miles west of Cairo. El-Dabaa was a largely Russian-financed and Russian-constructed project. Jannik Isarebe was fluent in Russian and spoke a little Arabic, as well as being a well-respected engineer, specialising in nuclear safety systems.

Solomon was home-taught by Reba in El-Dabaa, but every afternoon, whilst his mother napped, he would wander into the compound where many of the people working on the site lived with their families. He never played with the other children, but would sit watching them.

On 14th January 2020, Solomon walked in to the Isarebe's house, holding the hand of a small girl with milk chocolate coloured skin and the biggest brown eyes Reba had ever seen:

Izzy's arrival in our life was beyond a shock.

I can still see Dizzy's eyes, unblinkingly boring into mine, when he announced Izzy was going to join the family. He was daring me to defy him when he said: 'This is my new sister and she is going to be called Isabelle Isarebe. Her mum is not well and her dad is an alcoholic, so I've decided she should live with us. I've talked to her mum and dad and they are quite happy about it.' Isabelle stood still as a little mouse beside him, her eyes down, determinedly holding his hand. I remember staring at their two hands, Izzy's deep brown, Dizzy's white from the pressure of Izzy's grip.

---

12   Isarebe, R, 2054, *Chosen Poet*, O'Daley's, London, p. 46

When he made this announcement I think I laughed at first, but then I realised he meant it and from the corner of my eye I saw Janni looking intently at the two children, his head leaning towards them. I panicked, because I realised Janni was carefully and seriously thinking about what Dizzy was saying. I couldn't blame Janni for being drawn in, because even when Dizzy was a small child there was some sort of entrancing sincerity about him. It made you feel foolish not to trust him, even when he was on some flight of fancy. For once though, I was immune to Dizzy's words, because alarm bells were ringing and I sensed some enormous danger to our little family.

Janni and I walked to Izzy's house at the far end of the compound and found her father asleep on the floor, behind a small sofa, one of the few bits of furniture in the sparse living room. Janni recognised him as one of the structural engineers working on the design of the administration block, a man who had been sent home the previous week after he had appeared drunk at a meeting with local planning officials.

Janni woke him and found Leo Denikin was no raging drunkard, but a mild-mannered educated man, in a clean white shirt and tie, albeit deeply inebriated. Leo was grieving the loss of his wife, because Izzy's mum was not ill, she was dead, having been involved in a fatal car accident on a shopping trip to Cairo. In broken English, Leo whispered to Janni he had been afraid to tell Izzy, whose real name was Inessa, that her mother was dead, so he had told her she was ill and in the hospital and would be home soon.

I took the children back to our house while Janni stayed with Leo. Leo was unable to face life without his wife, Rima. Rima had been a doctor in Damascus before escaping the Syrian Civil War and seeking refuge in Egypt. She had met Leo in Cairo six years earlier, on his first journey to Egypt, when he had been part of a delegation meeting officials in the Egyptian Atomic Energy Authority. They had fallen in love and within a year had married and Inessa was born shortly afterwards. The way Leo spoke it was a marriage of love and some happiness, only shadowed by Leo's periodic bouts of self- destructive drinking, for which he had no explanation.

He kept insisting to Janni, over and over, in the way drunks do, that he couldn't look after Inessa and she needed a proper family, not a broken drunk pretending to be a good father. Janni persuaded him and Inessa to come and stay with us for a while. I welcomed Leo and Inessa into our home, but in my mind I knew I was going to do everything I could to push them away. I was determined not to let these strangers in to our lives and ruin all we had built. I wasn't going to let them reverse the recovery we had witnessed in Dizzy's wracked mind.

I suspect many people think Janni is an almost invisible presence in the Isarebe family; that he is under the loud persuasive thumbs of me and Dizzy. It is true he is quiet and he is undoubtedly the most tolerant man I have ever met, but he also has the super-human powers of a man utterly sure of what is good and right. He carried Izzy's dad back to our house that day, like a parent carrying an injured child, and was nurse, father and best friend to Leo until he recovered his sense of himself. That first night he told me Inessa and Leo would stay with us for as long as they wished. I shouted and screamed and argued with him, but he said nothing in reply, until I found I had run out of things to say. He then told me again, they would stay with us for as long as they wanted to. The next morning, he told Dizzy to be his kindest best self to them and that he would not tolerate any bad behaviour – none. I think both Dizzy and I quaked in our sandals and felt the most loved we ever had.

They stayed for over two years and we became a family, all through the Covid-19 pandemic, which barely touched our lives. We loved them both. On Dizzy's insistence, everyone started to call Inessa 'Isabelle' and then of course 'Izzy'. Dizzy and Izzy, only separated by a single letter. At the end of those happy years, Janni's contract finished and we were headed to Germany, where Janni was to work on the decommissioning of three nuclear plants. Leo was calmer than he had been, but still had occasional alcoholic blackouts. Two days before we left, he presented us with a sheaf of papers stating we were now the parents of Inessa Denikin. I don't know how he did it, but perhaps the Russian authorities had more on their mind than the fate of a five-year-old girl.[13] When we became official parents to Izzy, Janni held Leo in his arms and said Leo was now an Isarebe and would always be welcome, wherever in the world we were.

---

13   Russia invaded Ukraine on 24th February 2022

We arrived in Bremen in May 2022, two days before Dizzy's 14th birthday. We were now a family of four. Dizzy had got his way, as he nearly always did and proudly held Izzy's hand as he pushed his way to the front of the passport queue.[14]

PIXELLATED IN ACCORDANCE WITH CPA GUIDELINES WEF83THU (2147)

The Isarebe family, Egypt, 25th October 2020

---

14   Isarebe, R, 2054, *Chosen Poet*, O'Daley's, London, p. 84

PIXELLATED IN ACCORDANCE WITH CPA GUIDELINES WEF83THU (2147)

Solomon and Isabelle Isarebe, Egypt, 25th October 2020

Solomon and Isabelle Isarebe were inseparable. In Egypt they had shared a bedroom, but with Jannik's new position in Germany came a large four bedroomed house and the two children were given separate rooms. Solomon fumed at this injustice, but Jannik and Reba seemingly decided they had to stand up to him on some matters. The bedrooms were located under a tall, chalet-style, gabled roof and there were cupboards in each bedroom that ran under the eaves of the house. On the second night in their new home, Solomon was woken by the sound of scratching from inside his cupboard. Solomon was frightened, but crept along the floor with his reading torch, tentatively opening the cupboard door. There inside was Isabelle. Blood was dripping on to her white pyjamas from what had once been her fingertips. She had realised Solomon and she had identical cupboards under the eaves and had concluded there must be a way through from one room to the other. She had scratched and scraped at the plasterboard cupboard walls until she had made a space bigger enough to slip her tiny body through and then crawled along to Solomon's bedroom.

Jannik and Reba realised they were never going to be strong enough to keep their children apart and said they could share a room, but Isabelle insisted on sleeping in Solomon's cupboard, which she did for the one and a half years they lived in Bremen.

Solomon was now at high school, where he soon picked up enough German to survive, whilst Isabelle sat silently in her 'Grundschule'.[15] Reba recalled their loneliness and unhappiness at school:

> Solomon sat at the front of every class, so he wouldn't have to interact with the other children. They were all bright kids in the Behringer Gymnasium and from good homes, but kids cannot bear the child who stands out and Solomon did and knew he did. He seemed to understand how children worked and decided to adopt a strategy of self-isolation. So he sat at the front of the class, taking no notes, saying nothing unless asked and spent the day looking at his hands. In breaks he sat in the library, refusing to eat with the other children, garnering protection from an ever-present adult.

> Izzy meanwhile was slowly disappearing, becoming the mouse we think she dreamt of being. She decided not to speak once we arrived in Germany and she insisted on sitting under the desk she had been given in her classroom. Her teacher, Diemut Weber, was a sensitive and caring woman and she let Izzy be.

---

15   Primary school

At the end of the school day, Izzy would scuttle out of school before the other children emerged, run straight past me and on to the Gymnasium. She had a duck-like gait and if I hadn't been so worried it would have been funny trying to catch up with my little mouse-duck each day. At Dizzy's school she would put her head through the railings and stare at the door where five minutes later she knew her brother would emerge, trying to keep ahead of the braying mob – the time of day when he said he felt most vulnerable to attack.

They seemed content at home, locked away in their bedroom, but it wasn't a happy school life for either of them, or me.

It came to a head one day when Izzy and I were called in to the principal's office after school, to discuss Izzy's silence. It was a brief and fruitless meeting (as Izzy didn't say anything), but it meant we were late picking up Dizzy. When we got there, we immediately knew something was wrong. Dizzy was standing against the wall of the main building with a group of about fifteen boys around him. It looked like it was just verbal bullying, but from Izzy's perspective it must have looked like Dizzy was being beaten to death.

She shook off my hand and ran over to the group. She picked on the biggest boy, who was now poking Dizzy in the chest and she kicked him in the knee with all her small might. It doesn't matter how big you are and how small your attacker, if you are kicked in the knee it hurts. She then turned to the rest of the group and shouted:

[Expletive] dich! Erdnuss gehirn [expletive]!

I burst out laughing. It was the first thing she had said in over a year. We didn't even know she understood any German, let alone insults such as these, however meaningless. The encounter could still have gone either way, but this little monster mouse was steaming in front of this crowd of adolescent boys, and they collectively decided there was no way they were going to come out of it well and rapidly evaporated.

Dizzy announced that night we were moving to England and he had found a school where he and Izzy could be together and where all the kids were odd so they would be left alone.[16]

---

16   Isarebe, R, 2054, *Chosen Poet*, O'Daley's, London, p. 107

The Isarebes did eventually move to England, but not until December 2023, after Jannik had been made redundant.[17] It was to be a tough time for Jannik and Reba, living off a small pension and Reba's meagre earnings from her poetry and readings, but after nearly twenty years of roaming the earth together they felt the urge to put down roots and to focus on raising their family, which had been so unexpectedly gifted to them.

Solomon was 15 and Isabelle was 7 years old when they moved to England. Solomon had intended that he and Izzy would go to a Weber-Seed school, but Jannik and Reba could not afford the fees and they had in any case discovered Solomon and Isabelle would still be taught in separate classes, so the idea was abandoned.[18] They moved instead to a small house, Hilman Cottage, near Garway Hill in Herefordshire, a hundred metres from their nearest neighbours and many miles from any shops or entertainments. It was perfect for Solomon and Isabelle: nothing to keep them apart, no school, no other children, and parents who had committed to staying at home and teaching their strange children all they knew.

Until this point in their lives, Solomon and Isabelle Isarebe had effectively had no schooling. They had chosen not to listen and not to learn. Reba said it was like they had never eaten before and were put in front of the grandest feast that had ever been prepared: they could not get enough. Within a year of their arrival in Garway Hill, Solomon had taken three A Levels[19] and got top results for all of them and Isabelle had taken GCSEs in Mathematics, Russian and German.[20] Solomon vowed to wait for Isabelle to catch up and so took a further three A Levels with similar results in the following year. At 17, Solomon had A Levels in Physics, Mathematics, German, Economics, Statistics and Latin, whilst Isabelle, aged just 9, had eleven GCSEs.

Jannik and Reba eventually abandoned trying to formally teach them and just left them to read.

> We couldn't keep up with them, particularly Dizzy. He was a phenomenon. He seemed to understand the next step before we had even mentioned it. Janni said there was nothing more he could teach him and I often had little idea what Dizzy was talking about.

---

17   Reba Isarebe had joint Swedish and British nationality.
18   Weber-Seed schools were independent schools that took a liberal, individual approach to education. They were often labelled as 'alternative' or 'hippy'. The last Weber-Seed school closed in 2134.
19   A Levels were examinations normally taken at 18 years of age.
20   GCSEs were examinations normally taken at 16 years of age.

The only area in which Dizzy struggled was poetry. He just couldn't get it; couldn't seem to understand what anything meant. He would cry every time I encouraged him to try and read something, even a simple nursery rhyme. He found it very hard being unable to do something. It gnawed at the fragile roots of his ego.

Izzy never cared if she understood something or not, she just kept reading and writing and laughing quietly to herself. She couldn't stop writing poetry, which she illustrated with the most exquisite drawings.[21]

It was only after Solomon Isarebe's death that it was discovered in his notes and diaries that he had written poems his entire adult life. From the marks and scrawls and crossings out they were sweated over, but they had an odd beauty to them that revealed someone far from the cultural philistine many thought him.

The Isarebes' life in rural Herefordshire was one of relative poverty, social insularity and solitary intellectual pursuits. It may seem an utterly alien way of life from the perspective of someone living in urban comfort in 2150, but the Isarebe's lifestyle was also highly unusual in Britain in the 2020s.

Solomon Isarebe started writing his diaries around this time, a habit he maintained throughout most of his life. These diary entries were initially a simple record of what he and Isabelle had done each day, but they seem to suggest a contented if unusual family life. Reba was the happy place the children ran to first, but it was Jannik who seemed to define their behavioural and moral boundaries. Isabelle Isarebe wrote about one instance of his quiet moral and behavioural insistence, when she was an 18-year-old student:

Traceeeeeeee!!!!!!

Sorry to bother you so early in the morn, but I need to dump some thoughts and you seem the perfect receptacle!

I had a dream last night so vivid it woke me up in a puddle of sweat. The dream quickly went pop, but for some reason I started thinking about this really weird day I had when I was about 8, so Solly must have been 15 or 16ish. It was a very very very clear body parts tingling memory.

---

21   Isarebe, R, 2054, *Chosen Poet*, O'Daley's, London, p. 145

Solly had had a temper tantrum – spectacular of course – because Dad had told him he was too young to drive, even around Garway. I remember slipping into Mum's bed and hiding down at the bottom of the duvet, brave little mouse that I was, while Solly raged. I heard Solly stomping up the stairs and then the front door quietly closing and the car starting and Dad driving away.

Dad was gone for nearly 8 hours and I became more and more upset. I thought he was never coming back to us. Mum laughed at me and said Dad wasn't cross and we would know it if he ever was. I think that frightened me even more – the idea that he could be really cross, because then what would happen? Something worse than this.

He didn't come back until the evening and when he did, he came in with the strangest-looking dude we had ever seen (yes, stranger than Michael Young, before you ask). He was about the same age as Dad but this man only had one good arm, the other a stump, neatly tucked away behind a pinned folded shirt sleeve. I remember it was really well ironed. He also had a series of deep vivid liverlike (word?) scars on one side of his face, like a badly ploughed and bloody field. He worked his way expertly around the kitchen in a wheelchair. He was strangely handsome and was made even more romantic by the eye patch he wore. I know, I always fancy the truly weird ones – you inc – but in my defence I was only 8.

We sat down for dinner and this man, Sunny Joe, told endless slightly risque stories about his childhood in Finland, where he lived before his parents brought him to England when he was 17. They were good stories – really funny sunny stories – sunny with the threat of thunder. He had known Dad when they were little and he teased Dad, saying how straight and boring he had been – a true nerd – a totta nörtti (better in Finnish, yes?). Sunny had raced cars through the forests from when he was a little kid, using blocks tied to his shoes so he could reach the pedals. When he was a teenager he stole cars from his neighbours at night and then returned them in the morning, covered in mud, but with a note on the front seat promising to clean them at the weekend. Why was he never arrested? Finns are decidedly odd – Dad sort of excepted.

There were no stories of when he was a grown man and he never talked about losing his arm, or what happened to his eye, or how he got the scars on his face, or why he was in a wheelchair and we were too scared or too polite to ask.

Dad took Sunny Joe home later that night and we never saw him again. Mum told us the next day Sunny lived in a sort of hospital in North Wales and had lived there since he first came to Britain. She also said Dad had never mentioned him to her before, and no, she had no idea how he got his injuries and no, she wouldn't ask Dad and neither would we.

Solly and I talked about Sunny Joe for years and made up endless stories about him. Sunny Joe was a big figure in our young, admittedly just a teeny weeny bit sheltered lives, even though we spent no more than a few hours with him. It was the first time I fell in love I tink [sic] – I know I said it was you, but I lied to get my evil way and anyway you never loved me back.

Solly never asked Dad if he could drive the car again. In the end, when we arrived in Boston, I had to insist Solly learnt to drive, because your country is ridiculous if you're a pedestrian. He is the world's second most cautious driver, after me.

Thanks. Dump done. Possibly a bit tedious. Possible unintended and unwarranted suggestion of weird sexualised childhood. Anyway, go back to sleep Oxton. Izzzzzzzzzzzzxxxxxxxxxx[22]

In Reba Isarebe's memoirs, *Chosen Poet*, there are many references to the closeness of her children, but also the sharp differences in their characters, even when they were youngsters in Garway Hill. She recalled: 'One day Dizzy came running into the house visibly upset and said there was a rabbit in the garden which had been attacked by something and was bleeding to death. Isabelle, who was eight years old, immediately picked up my rolling pin and disappeared into the garden. She came back two minutes later, washed some blood and animal tissue off the rolling pin and went back to the sculpture she was making with eggshells. Solomon stood there, nose running, staring at his miraculous baby sister.'[23]

---

22   Isarebe, I, 2034, email to Tracee Oxton dated 8th February 2034, The Isarebe Trust Archives, Cambridge, England (Box 61, Folder 5)
23   Isarebe, R, 2054, *Chosen Poet*, O'Daley's, London, p. 65

By early 2026 Solomon understood he needed to sit at the feet of people other than his adoptive parents if he was to continue his intellectual journey. He sent a hand-written letter to Professor D. Kamil at Cambridge University,[24] criticising a paper Kamil had written on tax competition between governments for Foreign Direct Investment (FDI).[25] Professor Kamil wrote back to him, thanking him for his comments, and saying he had already considered the points Solomon had raised, before explaining in eight pages of dense, hand-written text why Solomon was wrong in his assertions.[26]

Solomon Isarebe, First day at St. John's College, Cambridge, 29th March 2026

24   Isarebe, S, 2026, letter to Professor Kamil dated 9th March 2026, The Isarebe Trust Archives, Cambridge, England (Box 23, Folder 9)
25   Kamil, D, 2025, *Tax competition and its impact on global growth*, American Quantitative Economic Review, 17, 1, pp. 342–387
26   Kamil, D, 2026, letter to Solomon Isarebe dated 16th March 2026, The Isarebe Trust Archives, Cambridge, England (Box 23, Folder 9)

Solomon Isarebe, Matriculation Day, St John's, Cambridge, 9th October 2026

Solomon had rarely had anyone tell him he was wrong before. It startled him, and in response he wrote back an even longer letter to Kamil, explaining in more detail the flaws in Kamil's arguments.[27]

Two days later, Solomon wrote another brief letter to Kamil saying he had looked at the problem again and realised that he had been wrong and Professor Kamil was right. He awkwardly, painfully apologised to Kamil.[28] The letter was returned to Solomon Isarebe on Kamil's death, along with many of the papers they subsequently worked on together.

On 27th March 2026, Kamil rang the Isarebe house and asked to speak to Solomon. He invited Isarebe to come and visit him at St John's College, Cambridge to discuss his work and to see if there was any way they could work together. Two days later, the 17-year-old Isarebe, 6 feet 5 inches tall, and with a cruel bout of acne, turned up at St John's. He was to spend the next four years at Cambridge working with Kamil.

There is little evidence of the more personal aspects of Isarebe's life as an undergraduate at Cambridge. His diary entries read more like technical records than emotional exposés and differ little in style from his academic notebooks, which were still largely hand-written at this stage of his life. He rapidly became obsessed with his academic pursuits and made few friends and rarely made contact with his family back in Herefordshire.

During the spring term in his first year at Cambridge, Solomon received a letter from Jo Kesonyu, President of the Economistas, an exclusive private debating and dining club. In the letter, Solomon was informed he had been chosen as one of only four undergraduates to join their society that year. The letter asked him to attend an initiation dinner and said that he was required to wear formal dress. Solomon hated the idea of exclusive societies and even more the idea of humiliating initiation ceremonies, but Isabelle told him in an admonishing eLetter that he must go and it was a great honour. She said the Economistas had probably received a recommendation from Professor Kamil who would be very upset if he refused.

27   Isarebe, S, 2026, letter to Professor Kamil dated 20th March 2026, The Isarebe Trust Archives, Cambridge, England (Box 23, Folder 9)
28   Isarebe, S, 2026, letter to Professor Kamil dated 22nd March 2026, The Isarebe Trust Archives, Cambridge, England (Box 23, Folder 9)

On the evening of 1st March 2027 Isarebe set out in a badly-fitting tuxedo he had found in a charity shop and navigated his way to the address he had been given, where he was supposed to find St Ronald's House. He was guided to a small alley, where there was little except a side entrance to a burger restaurant. There was no sign of St Ronald's House and he repeatedly checked the address on the invitation. He then looked up at the restaurant and saw his 9-year-old sister, smiling, sitting at a table next to the window. She was wearing a home-made badge: 'President Jo Kesonyu'. He laughed and gleefully made his way into the restaurant, where she told him he should have guessed the letter was from her by the name of the President and this was his punishment for not writing to or calling Reba and Jannik as often as he promised. From then on, he rang his parents every Sunday and wrote to them on Wednesday evenings, and he began daily written exchanges with Isabelle that would continue throughout her short life. There is no record of Reba and Jannik Isarebe's reaction to their 9-year-old daughter making the 7-hour journey from Garway Hill to Cambridge and back again under her own steam.

Isarebe was in theory an economics undergraduate, but was already spending much of his time working with Professor Kamil on what was to become his much-lauded doctoral thesis on the long-term impact of government incentives on personal decision making. It was only when Isarebe submitted the first draft of his thesis to Kamil that it was suggested to him he might want to focus on completing his undergraduate degree for a while.

Isarebe completed his undergraduate degree in June 2029. After he had finished his final exams and the results had been published, Solomon had a few days before his family were expected in Cambridge to see him graduate. The weather was perfect as only early English summer days can be and on the Tuesday afternoon he lay by the side of the river in the grounds of St. John's. He had shut his eyes against the sun when he was leapt on by a four-foot-four-inch duck, making the loudest and most unconvincing duck noises he had ever heard. He claimed to have known it was Isabelle from her smell and they rolled around together in a tangle of legs and feathers. Behind Isabelle were a laughing Reba and Jannik.

Isabelle wore the duck costume the whole time the three of them were in Cambridge. There was not a single student in St John's who did not know who my sister was by the end of those three days, even though most of them had no idea who I was. She was refused entry into the Senate House for the actual ceremony, but PDK [Professor

D. Kamil] intervened and made them put an extra chair for her at the end of the line of Members of the Senate. 12 stuffed shirts and a duck. It was totally brilliant.[29]

Solomon Isarebe, Graduation Day, River Cam, Cambridge, 28th June 2029

In the following year, Isarebe completed his doctoral thesis[30] and aged 22, became Doctor Solomon D. Isarebe.

---

29   Isarebe, S, 2067, typed notes for an unpublished autobiography, manuscript dated 24th September 2067, The Isarebe Trust Archives, Cambridge, England (Box 448)
30   Isarebe, S, 2030, *Understanding long-term behavioural responses to governments' social, educational and health policies*, PhD thesis, University of Cambridge, Cambridge

Solomon Isarebe, Graduation Day, St John's College, Cambridge, 28th June 2029

1.2 The Garway Hill papers

Many have an image of Solomon Isarebe as a hard man: a ruthless, soulless, loner; a man with an unshakable sense of his intellectual superiority. Whilst there are many anecdotes that support such a view, there are as many that dispute it, not least those illustrating his undoubted love for his family and Arem Johns. What has not been in the public domain before was throughout his life Isarebe suffered repeated mental crises and periods of depression. One of these episodes was meticulously logged by Isarebe in his diary entries, just after he completed his doctoral thesis in 2030.[31] They painfully document a period of sadness, self-doubt and almost overwhelming existential anxiety:

26th July 2030

I'm imagining madness and I like the thought. My mind is working without my volition anyway. I repeatedly feel myself being dragged back to the days before Isarebe. I can't remember much, or won't let myself remember much, but I feel something from then sucking at me, dragging me down. It's petrifying. Truly [expletive] terrifying.

27th July 2030 maybe 28th?

I don't know what happened last night. It feels like drugs, but it wasn't, I don't think. I woke up by the side of the punt pool – one leg in the water. Some drama I was cooking up, the porter said. I think he was kind, maybe. I'll be labelled mad, by the servants anyway.

Death is so easy to think about. It's almost the one thing that isn't confusing or scary. It seems like a beautiful place – a beautiful, long, silent blackness, a perfection of unbeingness, where we all happily lived before we were born into this [expletive] world ...

---

31   Isarebe, S, 2030, diary entries dated 2nd – 30th July 2030, The Isarebe Trust Archives, Cambridge, England (Box 42, Folder 1)

think I'd better call home. But I don't think I can. I
can't get it back in the car.

26th July 2030

This imagining madness will I like the thought. My mind
is working without my volition anyway. I repeatedly feel myself
being dragged back to the days before Isarebe. I can't remember
much, or won't let myself remember much, but I feel something
from there sucking at me, dragging me down. It's petrifying.
Truly fucking terrifying.

27th July 2030   maybe 28th?

I don't know what happened last night. It feels like
drugs, but it wasn't, I don't think. I woke up by the side
of the punt pod — one leg in the water. Some drama I was
cooking up, the porter said. I think he was kind, maybe. I'll
be labelled mad, by the servants anyway.

Death is so easy to think about It's almost the one thing
that isn't confusing or scary. It seems like a beautiful place —
a beautiful, long, silent blackness, a perfection of
unseeingness, where we all happily lived before we were
born into this shithole world.

Mum comes in to my head as I write this, telling me of my
perfection, my wonderfulness. Why she loves me like this I don't

Solomon Isarebe diary entries, late July 2030

46

The diary entries from this period include some of the few written references Isarebe ever made to his early childhood: 'the days before Isarebe'. Some of the diary entries from this period are particularly harrowing. That such an exceptional man found it impossible to escape the black hole of his early years is saddening; haunted by so hurtful a place he could not even name it or think of it.

These depressive episodes were sporadic and mercifully brief, but Isarebe at this time was also experiencing the normal pains associated with the transition from boy to man. For whatever reasons, Isarebe's adolescence was exceptionally late or perhaps prolonged. His private papers show his awkward longings to be accepted: to be one of the boys; to find love with the girls; and his desperation for the secrets of life to be revealed to him. Isarebe was destined not to find romantic love until much later in his life, but he found ways to negotiate the complexities of everyday life and social interactions, albeit in a 'clumsy learnt-by-rote manner'.[32]

The norm in the 2030s was for young people, either pre- or post-University, to have an extended holiday of six months or more, in far-flung exotic locations set up to offer a safe form of adventure. This was also a period when many recreational drugs were still illegal, which enticed some young adults into drug experimentation. Isarebe was not the average young adult and had never previously expressed any interest in travel or drugs, so his family were astounded when three months after receiving his doctorate he announced he was going to Australia and New Zealand, by way of Bali and Thailand, and was hoping to try a range of drugs on the way.

> Izzy looked at him open-mouthed, visibly trembling. "You're leaving me? Again?" she said, her voice catching on the rough edge of Dizzy's words. Dizzy looked down at his startlingly new walking boots and shifted his empty backpack around on his shoulders. "For a bit," he said, so quietly we had to hold our breath. Isabelle looked at him, blinked, swallowed and blinked again and then said "Okay" before turning and going up to her room. I thought she was smiling, but it seemed so unlikely.[33]

The archive of Isarebe's notebooks, diaries, letters, messages, eLetters, photos, soundies and emails provide some patchy evidence of his travels. There are photographs of the locations of his journey, some showing groups

32   Roberts, D, 2059, *The Secret Life of a Master of the Universe*, 10th November 2059 [Blog]. Available at http: www.ukblogarchives.org [accessed October 2148]
33   Isarebe, R, 2054, *Chosen Poet*, O'Daley's, London, p. 168

of happy young people, although none with Isarebe in the frame. There is a trail of messages to his parents, methodically telling them of his adventures. Reba Isarebe, in her memoir, recalls how on his return he would tell stories of danger, wild parties and drug-fuelled orgies, although 'he told these stories with a strange look in his eye – like he was reading a pre-prepared script.'[34] Reba also noted that shortly after Solomon departed on his travels, his 14 year-old sister Isabelle made friends with someone who lived some miles away from Garway Hill, a friend she visited every weekend, a friend who no one else had heard of, a friend who never came to Hilman Cottage, a friend she lost touch with as soon as Solomon returned home.

In his diary, many of the pages from this period have been torn out, but in his notes are detailed descriptions of his experiences taking drugs. He appears to have tried everything: from the mildest of marijuana, to natural and artificial hallucinogens, heroin, crack cocaine and opioids, most of which were illegal at the time. His diary reads like a science experiment. Only the hallucinogens seemed to really appeal to him, but as a one-off experience, rather than the beginning of a drug-fuelled lifestyle.

In April 2031, Isarebe returned to Hilman Cottage with an uneven tan. The Isarebes, so unusually close and open as they were, seemed to display an almost negligent lack of curiosity about Isarebe's six-month 'travels', just as they had with his early childhood. Perhaps this apparent disinterest could be better characterised as respect for the failings of a damaged and much-loved son.

Whatever the true story of this period in Isarebe's life, it was to be the end of a short dalliance with the norms of late adolescence. He came back with his confidence temporarily shaken, but with a strong desire to work. On the recommendation of Professor Kamil, he started work as an analyst at Forecast Dynamics, a small economics forecasting consultancy in London. Isarebe was both horrified and enthralled by the way they worked:

I sat in the conference room today with my jaw on my knees, listening to our almighty boss 'Billy Boy' Mather delivering the results of a project to the people from GeeMuck. He was amazing – I could barely resist being taken in by what he was saying and I knew most of it was rubbish. GeeMuck lapped it up like he was the Messiah.

I can't help thinking that although FD are charlatans to a wo/man, their work is somehow better for it. Billy Boy is completely shameless, but he's not the only one – they cut corners, work with scarily crap

34   Isarebe, R, 2054, *Chosen Poet*, O'Daley's, London, p. 169

data, exaggerate the significance of the most insignificant 'fact', but despite all that some of their work is brilliant. They seem so free to think. It makes me feel like some repressed Supernerd. And they do everything so freakily quickly and they never seem to bother justifying what they've done. It's genuinely exciting as a spectator sport. PDK must have thought I needed to see this.

I think it works because we all want to be told a story – we're programmed for it. When people are continually bombarded with tedious information and have no way of judging what's good or bad, they fall back on how good the story and the storyteller are. People listen to Billy Boy Mather, even though they shouldn't and probably know they shouldn't.[35]

Isarebe only worked at Forecast Dynamics for a short time, but it influenced his approach to the presentation of information. There is no evidence he ever took significant shortcuts, or was cavalier with the truth, but he did become a good storyteller. Many think it was his greatest strength.

His final decision to leave Forecast Dynamics was precipitated by a meeting with Billy Mather, Forecast Dynamics' CEO, who perhaps sensed Isarebe was unsettled:

Billy Boy had me in his office today to tell me how wonderful I was and what a great future I had and how he reminded him of himself when he was young. He's only 37!

He seemed high to me, but maybe he was just happy. Maybe everyone who loves themselves that much is perpetually happy.

I can't help thinking he somehow knows I've pretty much decided to go. I didn't feel ready to tell him though. I did a lot of nodding and slipped out before he got me to agree to another pay rise. The man literally slapped me on the back as I left. I never knew people actually did that. It hurt a bit.

It's really fun here, but I think I've got to go. I want to do things properly and that takes time and they don't have time. They like me and I know PDK told them I was good, but I have this weird nagging

---

35   Isarebe, S, 2031, diary entry dated 25th July 2031, The Isarebe Trust Archives, Cambridge, England (Box 47, Folder 3)

thought I have something important to do and nothing important will ever happen at FD.

I think I might go home for a bit.[36]

Isarebe did go home, to Garway Hill, and stayed there until Isabelle went to university in 2033. Those two and a half years were not wasted. They have been compared by some of Isarebe's more doe-eyed acolytes to Einstein's time as a Patent Office clerk in 1905, when he produced five papers that changed physics and the world for ever. Isarebe was clever and had a productive period, but not even Isarebe would claim his work or mind were comparable to Einstein's.

The areas that Isarebe worked on during these Garway Hill years were to interest him his whole life. Isarebe produced three short papers during this time, only two of which were published, but each of them broke new ground and they became the foundation upon which his reputation was built.

The first of these, published in May 2032, was particularly provocative, challenging the value and role of politics in economic life. The title of the work was 'The impact of active economic management on economic growth in 52 countries,'[37] although in his notes Isarebe always referred to it as 'How politicians [expletive] things up'.

Isarebe had concluded in his doctoral thesis that many governments' initiatives aiming to alter the social behaviour of their citizens had a smaller impact over the long-term than had previously been understood. Much of this early work examined attempts by governments to encourage citizens to adopt healthier lifestyles, but he also looked at initiatives designed to alter travel patterns, gambling and the take-up of higher education. In his PhD thesis, he had shown that whilst there were sometimes significant short-term changes in citizens' behaviour associated with such policy initiatives, within five years the measurable impact of these policies was often negligible. His work suggested that although the behaviour of citizens may change significantly over time, there was no evidence these changes were being driven by government policy. He concluded that policies may affect the timing of change, but have little effect on the change itself. Isarebe gleefully stated: '... before my eyes treasured government initiatives disappeared in a puff of white statistical noise.'[38]

---

36   Isarebe, S, 2031, diary entry dated 31st July 2031, The Isarebe Trust Archives, Cambridge, England (Box 47, Folder 3)
37   Isarebe, S, 2032, *The impact of active economic management on economic growth in 52 countries*, Borcus Economics, 9, 2, pp. 42-123
38   Isarebe, S, 2030, diary entry dated 27th March 2030, The Isarebe Trust Archives, Cambridge, England (Box 41, Folder 8)

By 2031 he had started to wonder whether this observation on the lack of long-term efficacy of social policy would be mirrored in the economic realm: does a nation's economic policy impact on economic performance in the long-term or does economic success depend on factors largely outside a government's control? The hypothesis he wanted to test was that a nation's economy would perform as well without a government as with one, 'providing the right infrastructure is in place.'[39]

His approach to the problem was innovative. He made the assumption there was a ceiling to the level of economic growth any nation could achieve, which he termed 'maximal economic growth'. He believed maximal economic growth would be different for each country and would change over time. He thought it would be determined by the quality of a country's economic infrastructure, their existing level of economic development and the natural and cultural resources at the economy's disposal. He postulated that the difference between the actual economic growth of a nation and its theoretical maximum was the true measure of economic success; the smaller the difference, the more successful the economy. His ultimate goal was to estimate how much of economic success, so defined, could be attributed to government policy and thus prove or disprove his initial hypothesis.

This approach, whilst novel, was also contentious, because at its heart were estimates of a theoretical 'maximal growth rate' that could never be validated. As one critic later said: 'It is nothing more than Isarebe holding his bony finger in the air whilst claiming to be extremely clever and very profound.'[40]

Isarebe's final models showed that a country's 'economic performance gap' was determined, alongside other explanatory factors, by the number of economic policy changes being made each year.[41] It was this that was to bring him to the attention of economists and politicians around the world. What he showed was that after a certain point, the more actively a government tried to manage its economy the more it 'held it back from reaching its full potential.'[42]

---

39   Isarebe, S, 2032, *The impact of active economic management on economic growth in 52 countries*, Borcus Economics, 9, 2, p. 43
40   James, M, 2032, Economic Review of Books, 7, 3, p. 99
41   In this paper Isarebe first started thinking about the impact of individual and collective decision making on economic performance. He invented and quantified a term called 'cultural norms of economic thinking', using data from social surveys, which he used as an explanatory variable in his models of economic performance gaps. He was embarrassed at the intellectual poverty of this part of the work, but what he saw as a failure represented an important step towards an approach that was to bring him global recognition: giving primary importance to individual and family decision-making in analysing demographic and economic change.
42   Isarebe, S, 2032, *The impact of active economic management on economic growth in 52 countries*, Borcus Economics, 9, 2, p. 55

He showed it did not matter much what these policy initiatives were – taxes, tariffs, employment initiatives, exchange rates, training, bureaucracy, investment incentives – it was largely the quantity of changes that mattered. The analysis suggested that outside of provision of a good economic infrastructure, what an economy needed most from its government was to be left alone; to let organisations and individuals find the shortcuts and legal hacks within a legislative and fiscal system. Even if an existing policy was seen as economically obstructive, businesses and individuals could become adept at dealing with it or finding a way around it. It appeared that in many cases it was better to keep a bad policy than to introduce a good one.

It was a remarkable conclusion. It has since been questioned and flaws in his early models have been identified, but it challenged the way governments managed their economies. It set a simple economic management blueprint: 'get the infrastructure right and then do nothing.'[43] It was a formula that politicians found difficult to follow – after all it's hard to sell to the electorate how well you have done nothing for the previous five years. Although most people took away this over-simplified 'do nothing' headline, Isarebe's paper actually showed that the optimal strategy was to make a small number of rational policy changes each year and to flag them up to businesses as early as possible before their introduction.

This paper, by an unknown economist working from a cottage in rural Herefordshire, was first published in Borcus Economics, one of the less prestigious academic journals, but it was soon picked up by Cambridge and Oxford University Press, thanks to Professor D. Kamil, who was on their advisory board. They asked Isarebe to turn his paper into a short book for their series *Great New Ideas in A Nutshell*. It was published in December 2032 under the title *The Demise of the Political Economy*.[44] It was enthusiastically reviewed by many populist economist magazines around the world and the book achieved a much wider readership after the famously languorous German Chancellor, Karl Schiffer, referred to it in a speech at a European Community summit, when he made a self-referential joke about 'the now proven value of my idleness.'[45]

Isarebe wrote the book in less than six weeks, whilst simultaneously working on two other ideas that had come out of his work on economic infrastructure: the importance to an economy of education provision; and the impact of judicial impartiality on economic performance.

When Isarebe first went to Cambridge University he had deeply resented

---

43   Bryan, F, 2033, *Stay in your box Mr Chancellor,* The New London Times, 27th May 2033, p. 18

44   Isarebe, S, 2032, *The Demise of the Political Economy*, Cambridge and Oxford University Press, Cambridge, England

45   Schiffer, C, 2033, *Welcome to meeting of EU leaders*, 28th February 2033, Brussels

the presence and demeanour of some students from privately educated backgrounds. His mostly rational arguments against the advantages inferred by private schools masked a deeper emotional response to a group whom he believed felt 'they own the bloody world.'[46] Isarebe's sense of grievance about the 'unwarranted access'[47] privately educated students had to the best universities was reflected in top-line admissions data from the period. In 2030, those educated in the private sector were five times more likely than those educated in state schools to get into one of the top three British universities (Oxford, Cambridge and London). This phenomena, part of Lloyd's 'sustainable power transmission,'[48] was evident in most countries, but in Britain this power, culture and wealth transmission from generation to generation was more emotionally charged, given Britain's long history of class sensitivity.

Whether Isarebe's feelings were derived from rational analysis or simple prejudice, his work in this area was of an exceptional quality, leading to the publication of the paper 'The changing impact of education on economic growth.'[49]

His starting point for this work was a question he asked himself after completing his work on economic infrastructure; '... if the economic ideal is for universal access to education, then is universal state provision of education economically preferable to a mixed model of private and public education?'[50]

Many papers on the economic benefits of investment in education had been published in the early decades of the 21st century. These had mostly shown strongly positive results for private investment in an individual's education.[51, 52, 53] There were also macro-economic studies that suggested each additional year a population spent in education added between 0.4% and 0.8% to GDP.[54, 55]

46   Isarebe, S, 2025, diary entry dated 15th April 2027, The Isarebe Trust Archives, Cambridge, England (Box 24, Folder 7)

47   Isarebe, S, 2025, diary entry dated 19th April 2027, The Isarebe Trust Archives, Cambridge, England (Box 24, Folder 8)

48   Lloyd, Z, 2042, *Social immobility and sustained power transmission*, Browlick, Glasgow, pp. 23–24

49   Isarebe, S, 2032, *The changing impact of education on economic growth*, Borcus Economics, 9, 3, pp. 22–58

50   Isarebe, S, 2032, hand-written notes dated 15th June 2032, The Isarebe Trust Archives, Cambridge, England (Box 54, Folder 1)

51   Kali, B, 2024, *Derived economic and social benefits of education 1920-2020*, Economic Prospects, 432, 7

52   Degais, J, 2027, *Educación, formación y economía en América Latina*, The Latin American Economic Journal, 9, 4

53   Smith, S, 2005, *A cost benefit analysis of educational reform in South Africa* (unpublished doctoral dissertation), University of Johannesburg, Johannesburg

54   Halia, G, 2023, *The Economic Opportunist*, Brownside, Chicago, p. 208–215

55   Kali, B, 2024, *Derived economic and social benefits of education 1920-2020*, Economic Prospects, 432, 7

Isarebe undertook a detailed analysis of data collected by Global Education Intelligence, analysing personal rates of return on investment in education at a disaggregated level, as well as building macro-economic models incorporating more granular definitions of education.

The first conclusion he reached was the link between greater provision of education and economic growth was weakening in richer countries. This conclusion had been reached by other economists before him, notably Kali and Halia, but his early work suggested not only was the economic benefit of the 'quantity' of education declining, but the benefit of the 'quality' of education was declining too. He defined 'quality' as the number of people attaining tertiary levels of qualification and above at top universities and colleges. This surprised Isarebe; his assumption had been that with an economy increasingly driven by technology, information and artificial intelligence, tertiary education provision would be of increasing not declining importance to an economy.

It was not until he completed his analysis at a more disaggregated level that he found the error in his initial assumptions. He discovered there was a large and positive economic benefit from education, but only if one considered the number attaining post-graduate and post-doctoral educational qualifications in the sciences, engineering and specialised technical vocational subjects (SESTV subjects). He showed the economic need was for highly qualified technical specialists; exactly the result he had expected.

His work also showed state investment in education at post-graduate and post-doctoral levels in non-SESTV courses had a significant positive rate of return for the individual, but a negative impact on the economy as a whole.

More importantly for Isarebe, his analysis showed investment in private education gave the subject an extremely high personal rate of return, but private education had a small negative impact on the economy: 'It is good for the person but bad for humankind.'[56] Whilst his work was highly detailed and inaccessible to the lay reader, he illustrated the conclusions he reached using simple statistics from Global Education Intelligence; cross analysing access to leading universities by intelligence, for both privately and publicly educated students. The results were clear: for example, 7% of privately educated people in the three lowest I-IQ quintiles attended one of the top 20 universities in the UK, compared with less than 1% of state educated students; and 82% of privately educated students in the top quintile of intelligence studied at one of the top universities, compared with 14% of state-educated students. There were similar results across most developed economies.

---

56   Isarebe, S, 2054, private recording of lecture to MA Students, 14th May 2054, MIT Cambridge Mass., The Isarebe Trust Archives, Cambridge, England (Box 262, Folder 7)

Isarebe just about managed to maintain a constrained academic tone in his paper,[57] but in his notes and correspondence his excitement and sense of vindication jump off the page. He had shown to his own satisfaction that 'privately educated students are denying many of the best people in the country access to the education they need to achieve their potential, something essential for economic growth, and the qualifications some of these people gain gives them an unmerited place in the higher echelons of management, politics and public life, to the detriment of the economy and (probably) cultural life.'[58]

Sustained power transmission is still with us in 2150, but attitudinally Britain is now more like the Sweden of the 2030s:

> In Sweden, we thought of ourselves as having a big fat middle and were quite proud of it. We were nearly all middle class, but it was a label that was rarely used because it had so little political or social resonance. There were richer people, of course, and they were always able to secure the best for their children, but the advantages were small. And there were people who had very little, but most still felt themselves part of the Swedish family.[59]

Isarebe may have found many things to rail against in British society in 2150, but it is unlikely that the fading echoes of the Victorian and Edwardian class systems would be one of them.

This paper did not have the impact of *The Demise of the Political Economy*, but it was seen as an interesting and challenging piece of analysis and was cited many times by other economists, educationalists and social scientists over the following decade.

The third paper he produced during this period of prolific activity also emerged from his work on the ideal economic infrastructure, specifically his conclusion that for strong economic performance there should be 'an efficient and equitable judicial system providing justice to all.'[60] Work by others, including Hargoth and Iska-Dill,[61] had shown that the number of lawyers within a country tended to have a negative effect on an economy

57   Isarebe, S, 2032, *The changing impact of education on economic growth*, Borcus Economics, 9, 3, p. 23

58   Isarebe, S, 2033, eLetter to Professor D. Kamil dated 28th April 2033, The Isarebe Trust Archives, Cambridge, England (Box 56, Folder 12)

59   Isarebe, R, 2054, *Chosen Poet*, O'Daley's, London, p. 91

60   Isarebe, S, 2032, *The impact of active economic management on economic growth in 52 countries*, Borcus Economics, 9, 2, p. 54

61   Hargoth, Z and Iska- Dill, P, 2026, *The economic cost of justice in the USA*, American Economic Principles, 49, 3 pp. 127–198

after a certain level, as did the quality of people attracted in to the profession: '... having the best and brightest go into law stunts economic growth.'[62] In an attempt to understand these counterintuitive conclusions, Isarebe undertook work that led him to conclude that:

> It is the differences in the skill levels and associated cost of lawyers within an adversarial system that distorts outcomes and ensures it is almost impossible to provide justice to all.

> A good advocate is able to build credible stories from a selection of the facts and is able to communicate these effectively. A good advocate will therefore be more successful, irrespective of whether their clients are innocent or guilty. Thus good lawyers distort the market for judicially fair outcomes. These lawyers will receive higher remuneration, such that they will only be employed by people with sufficient income to pay these higher fees, who will therefore be more likely to have a case go in their favour, irrespective of the facts of the case.

> It has been shown that where there is bias in access to justice, then this has a negative impact on economic growth. Thus, adversarial justice systems constrain economic growth.[63]

This last paper is little more than an extended hypothesis, with relatively little data or statistical analysis and it was not published in Isarebe's lifetime. However, Isarebe often made reference to it and it became known as 'Isarebe's greatest unpublished triumph.'[64] Isarebe really had learnt the lesson that good stories can be as convincing as great analysis.

Isarebe's work on education and judicial systems was subsequently seized upon by some sections of the press and academic community as evidence of political bias.[65] However, Isarebe was not easy to pin down from a political perspective, apparently capable of veering from revolutionary socialist to arch capitalist in a single sentence.

Throughout this whole time, Isarebe had been working from his parents'

---

62   Hargoth, Z and Iska- Dill, P 2026, *The economic cost of justice in the USA*, American Economic Principles, 49, 3 p. 128

63   Isarebe, S, 2033, draft paper on *Justice and the Economy*, dated 17th July 2033, The Isarebe Trust Archives, Cambridge, England (Box 60, Folder 1)

64   Unattributed, 2093, *Obituary: Solomon D. Isarebe*, The Independent Guardian, 25th August 2093, p. 34

65   Mishtri, P, 2050, *The Academic Lie*, The Real Daily Mail, 1st October 2050, p. 33

kitchen table and sharing a room with Isabelle, with occasional walks with the family into the surrounding hills. Reba recalled hearing Solomon and Isabelle discussing economics and politics at all times of the day and night, through the cottage walls; the teenage Isabelle able to hold her own with her 24-year-old brother:

> They shared a hybrid language that was not always easy to follow and they had developed an accent over their years together that was impossible to geographically place: Izzy's Arabic and Russian roots and Dizzy's unknown origins, combined with my and Janni's travellers' twangs. I could see that strangers often found this un-rooted accent and occasional forays in to Pidgin disturbing. Izzy and Dizzy never evoked a neutral response from people.[66]

It was Isabelle who brought Solomon's attention to the issue of global population change during this period, which she had been exploring in her own studies. Solomon listened, because it was his beloved sister Izzy, but he did not pick up the baton she was urgently holding out to him. There was seemingly little space in his head for thoughts on the global population. Having completed his three ground-breaking papers he became obsessed with the idea of statistically modelling individuals' thoughts and decision-making, firing off letters to psychologists, social researchers and economists around the world, but receiving back little to encourage him.

It was to be a further nine years before Isabelle Isarebe's interest in population decline and Solomon's interest in measuring individual decision-making would come together, at the start of the *Future Perfect* years.

---

66   Isarebe, R, 2054, *Chosen Poet*, O'Daley's, London, pp. 167–168

1.3 Drifting in the USA

Although Isabelle and Solomon Isarebe shared no genetic heritage, they were equally prodigious as children. Isabelle was possibly even more gifted than Solomon in mathematics and she had a quietly sure and easy way about her that people warmed to. She was still 'a tiny brown mouse with skylark eyes and Chaplin waddle'[67] in her adoptive mother's eyes, but at 17 years old she was an intellectual force equal to Solomon Isarebe's.

Although Jannik and Reba Isarebe were initially distraught at the idea, Isabelle decided she wanted to study at MIT in Cambridge, Massachusetts and she wanted to follow in her brother's academic footsteps, studying Quantitative Economics and Data Science. As is the case for many young people, admiration or love for someone can influence academic and career choices and Isabelle admired and loved no one more than her brother Solomon.

Jannik and Reba had no doubt she would be accepted by MIT, but told her they were worried about her safety in the United States, as she was only 17 years old, and they were worried about how they would pay the very high fees for this four-year course. In what was probably a pre-planned strategy, Solomon announced he would go with Isabelle, that the Department of Quantitative Economics at MIT had asked him to be a visiting lecturer delivering a short series of lectures based on *The Demise of the Political Economy*, and that they had intimated to him that Isabelle, with her outstanding academic record, would be likely to receive a full scholarship. Jannik and Reba's logical legs were cut from under them, when their real concern was simply their youngest child leaving their happy home at such a young age. In one ruthless manoeuvre, Solomon made their loss an inevitable reality and doubled down on the loss with the announcement that he was leaving too.

Solomon and Isabelle were underwhelmed by America in their first few months there, comparing the Cambridge and Boston areas unfavourably with Solomon's beloved Cambridge in England. Isabelle started out in a university residence, while Solomon lived in a small one-bedroom flat in the heart of Cambridge, provided by the university. By the time they flew home for Christmas, Isabelle had moved into Solomon's flat and they had slipped into a routine almost identical to the one they had in Herefordshire.

---

67   Isarebe, R, 2054, *Chosen Poet*, O'Daley's, London, p. 23

Solomon and Isabelle leaving Hilman Cottage for MIT, 2033

Solomon Isarebe soon realised that MIT's Quantitative Economics department had asked him to be a junior visiting lecturer purely as an opportunity to be associated with a rising, if unconventional, economic star. They did not appear interested in his ideas, which Jeanie DeSoto, head of macroeconomics at MIT and a John Bates Clark medal winner, had previously described as 'mere juvenilia.'[68] They told him his only obligation was to deliver six hours of lectures, based on his papers, to first year undergraduates, at a time of his choosing. Somewhat piqued, Isarebe announced his lectures would take place on the last Friday before the end of term and would be open to all. The administration must have either overlooked Isarebe's intention to deliver all six hours of his lectures in one go, or thought it irrelevant, assuming no one was likely to turn up on the eve of winter break. If that was their thinking, they underestimated the appeal of *The Demise of the Political Economy*. Solomon distributed free copies of the book to nearly all of the 500 students studying economics as a major or minor subject. On the day of his super-lecture, 240 students crammed into the lecture room Isarebe had been allocated, comprising almost all of the undergraduate economics majors and a few from other faculties, who came expecting fun and fireworks from the young, unconventional economist with the unplaceable accent.

Isarebe presented for nearly six and a half hours without notes and with only three ten-minute breaks. He forbade students from using phones or computers to make notes or to record the lecture and he turned off the University's ILLF (Interactive Live Lecture Feed) system. It became a throwback to the time before the advent of personal computing, with some students making furious notes, whilst others lay back and listened and a few slept quietly in corners. There were no fireworks, just closely argued explanations of his work interspersed with surprisingly self-deprecating jokes.

Isarebe, the misanthrope, was proving himself an effective and witty lecturer, finding speaking a much easier medium than the written word, which he confessed made him feel 'strangled with anxiety.'[69] These marathon super-lectures, covering his whole syllabus in one sitting, became Isarebe's academic trademark and were the highlight of term for many students throughout his academic career: always the last lecture before the break and always attended by students and teachers from faculties throughout the university. In Cambridge, England, in December 2067, 580 people were at Isarebe's last lecture, given in the new economics lecture hall, the largest in the university. He was given an eight-minute standing ovation, despite leaving the building the minute his lecture was completed.

As his first lecture at MIT proceeded, news of its progress spread through the faculty and by 3.45 p.m., when the lecture finished, the staircases were filled with faculty members looking on in bewildered appreciation at this 25-year-old phenomenon.

68 MIT Internet Radio, 2033, *Interview with Professor Jeanie DeSoto*, Student economic forum, Broadcast and podcast, 16th June 2033
69 Isarebe, S, 2034, diary entry dated 20th May 2034, The Isarebe Trust Archives, Cambridge, England (Box 59, Folder 3)

By January 2034, when Solomon and Isabelle returned to the USA from their Christmas break, Solomon had agreed to take a position as a post-graduate associate, but he found he had little to do and started accompanying Isabelle to her lectures, much to the consternation of her lecturers. Her freshman lectures covered fairly basic ground and Solomon told Isabelle she would be better off staying at home reading. They both started drifting: reading, walking, watching movies and playing endless games of bezique.

Solomon rarely left the little apartment and even more rarely enjoyed the company of others, whilst Isabelle mostly socialised under sufferance. Isabelle was breezing through her assignments and Solomon was half-heartedly reading about decision-making and neuroscience. Neuroscience employed some of the best minds on the planet, but then, as now, they were only able to draw fairly rudimentary conclusions on how the brain functioned and his lack of progress evoked an uncharacteristic intellectual torpor in Isarebe.

Their largely solitary and monotonous life was to change in early spring of that year, when Isabelle was asked to an Easter Ball by Tracee Oxton, a psychology student in her sophomore year at Harvard. Isabelle and Oxton had met in a thrift shop the previous November, where they found themselves fighting over a woollen hat they both wanted to keep out the Boston cold. They were attracted to each other and had a brief uncommitted sexual relationship that soon drifted into a relieved platonic friendship. Solomon records in his diary telling Isabelle she should go and that Easter Balls were a tradition when Americans looked for chocolate eggs and jumped up and down like rabbits and she should probably wear a costume.[70] Isabelle wore a white fluffy rabbit jump suit, white pumps and an enormous rabbit head and brought her date a punnet of chocolate Easter eggs. She met Tracee Oxton outside the ball and was surprised to see most of the other couples in formal wear, with the women carrying corsages not chocolate eggs. Photos of the occasion show Tracee Oxton wearing a turquoise ball gown, but, fortunately for Isabelle, Tracee had also chosen to sport bunny ears, a bunny nose and a little bunny tail.

Isabelle later told her mother that she had wanted nothing more than to go straight home, but Tracee persuaded her to embrace the ridiculousness of the situation and they both ended up hopping up the steps of the grand old building where the ball was being held.

---

70   Isarebe, S, 2034, diary entry dated 22nd March 2034, The Isarebe Trust Archives, Cambridge, England (Box 62, Folder 3)

Isabelle Isarebe and Tracee Oxton outside the Harvard Easter Ball, 2034

The Easter Ball was to be pivotal in Isabelle Isarebe's life; the dance where she was to meet Mooketsi J. Mooketsi, known to everyone as Mooky. Mooky was one of Tracee Oxton's best friends and after introducing him to Izzy, Oxton disappeared with the look of someone with a job well done, taking Isabelle's chocolate eggs with her. Mooky was a Botswanan; a foot taller than Isabelle, with a broad angular face and a smile that 'started small and grew to a spectacular crescendo'.[71] He told Isabelle that Tracee Oxton had asked him to the dance and Isabelle told him the same. By the end of the Easter Ball, Mooky had arranged to meet Isabelle for breakfast. By the end of breakfast Isabelle had asked Mooky to dinner at the apartment. By the end of dinner, Solomon had stormed out of the apartment pledging never to return if Isabelle continued to 'throw herself like a harlot at this complete stranger'.[72]

---

71   Isarebe, S, 2034. diary entry dated 3rd May 2034, The Isarebe Trust Archives, Cambridge, England (Box 63, Folder 3)

72   Isarebe, I, 2034, diary entry dated 27th March 2034, The Isarebe Trust Archives, Cambridge, England (Box 63, Folder 1)

Isabelle Isarebe and Mooketsi Mooketsi, Boston, 2034

Solomon Isarebe was to come around to his little sister being in love, but he insisted Mooky could only come to their apartment on Tuesday nights and Saturday afternoons and could not stay the night. Mooky tried everything he could to charm Isarebe, but he refused to be enchanted. On Tuesday nights, Isarebe enrolled in Kuk Sool Won lessons, a Korean martial art, but after four weeks he lost interest and started going to a bar around the corner from the apartment, where he taught some of the regulars to play bezique. On Saturday afternoons he would sit by the river and watch the anglers pulling crappie, carp and catfish from the water.

Isarebe's self-imposed exile from the apartment whenever Mooky was there and Isabelle's flowering happiness came to an abrupt end in May 2034, when Mooky was called home by his family following the death of his father, who lived in a village some 150 miles west of the Botswanan capital Gaborone. Isabelle was devastated and thought Mooky would never return. She was unable to get out of bed for most of June, despite Solomon's gentle ministrations and assurances that Mooky would soon be back.

Isabelle failed her end of year exams and was asked to attend a department meeting to explain her fall from academic grace, before they made their recommendations to the Committee on Junior Academic Performance. Isarebe went to the meeting in her place and launched into a half-hour tirade on the structure and delivery of the course and how Isabelle had completed most of the four-year course within the first two semesters, showing them essays she had completed but not submitted. They listened to Isarebe with bewildered patience, before explaining to him they had no intention of expelling Isabelle: they realised she was an exceptional student and just wanted to help. Isabelle subsequently switched courses and started as a sophomore on the Bachelor of Science Degree in Artificial and Human Cognition the following academic year.

Isabelle went to see Mooky in Gaborone in August 2034. Most of Mooky's family lived in the city, with his sisters and cousins running a small fabric business on the outskirts of town. It was made clear to her that Mooky was the pride of his large extended family. He was a graduate researcher in the Department of Fertility and Population Studies at the University of Botswana and had been visiting MIT to examine their Fertility Surveillance Research Programme. Mooky showed Isabelle the sights of Gaborone and took her to meet his extended family in the Kalahari. They talked until late each night about Mooky's work and how the world was sleepwalking into a population crisis, as they had done many times before, but somewhere between Boston and Gaborone something had shifted between them; the magic of first love had been lost and both felt an immense sadness for their loss. Isabelle returned to MIT in early September, whilst Mooky stayed on in Botswana, neither of them knowing when or if they would see each other again.

Isabelle and Solomon's relationship changed after Isabelle met Mooky. They spent a little less time together and moved into a larger apartment nearer to the university, as royalties from Isarebe's book sales were now providing a substantial income. They became more like brother and sister and less like a married couple in a sexless but close relationship.

Isabelle, still only 18 years old, started to flower in her second year at MIT, even though her heart lay bleeding in Botswana. Isabelle's was a mix of Russian and Syrian blood and there were hints of her heritage in her passions and tactility with those who were close to her, in contrast to her oftentimes remote and cold brother. She started to go out more with her fellow students and one recalled her 'telling stories that hinted at bawdy double entendres, which disappeared like a chimera once you thought about what she'd said. The stories were wholly innocent, but had people roaring with laughter at their own imagined sexual innuendoes.'[73] There are no records of her having any other serious sexual partners during her time at MIT, but she was as romantic as many others her age, with Solomon recalling in his diary: 'I came home today and found Iz waltzing around the room, with some imagined partner. *Titanic* was playing on her laptop, the old one from the 90s, and she was dancing in sync with the couple in the film. She didn't see me, so I left her to it. It's a bit sad, poor Iz.'[74]

Isabelle encouraged or persuaded Solomon to go on a few dates. He went for a number of coffee-dates with colleagues, on-line friends and even some bezique partners, but whatever their age, gender or sexual preferences, he found none of them attractive according to his diaries and was always desperate for the date to end. He appeared to have little sexual interest and an almost complete indifference to gender, which was a culturally sensitive topic in the 2030s. Isabelle recorded several instances of Solomon's lack of sexual and gender awareness:

4th March 2036

Solly told me a funny story tonight, although I'm not sure he knew it was funny. He had been to a faculty party and had got stuck with a drunk Madden-Joe Adomako – what a surprise, always drunk and he (or hesh, as he would have it) has had the most enormous crush on Solly for months. Madden-Joe told Solly he was the only white, male, cis, Protestant, straight, middle-class, Inter he'd ever met. I expect it was meant as a compliment. Solly was hyperbolically mad, not at Madden-Joe's unwanted sexual advances, nor at being labelled an Inter, but at being called a Protestant! Then he was mad at me for laughing. It took him a good half hour to calm down.[75]

73   Unattributed, 2048, *Obituary: Isabelle Isarebe*, MIT Clarion, 12th May 2048, www.alum.mit/mitclarion [accessed 22nd June 2149]
74   Isarebe, S, 2034, diary entry 3rd October 2034, The Isarebe Trust Archives, Cambridge, England (Box 65, Folder 2)
75   Isarebe, I, 2036, diary entry dated 4th March 2036, The Isarebe Trust Archives, Cambridge, England (Box 74, Folder 1)

29th January 2037

I had to stop Solly constantly referring to Ronja Adhikari-Jones as 'he' today. He's literally gender blind. I asked him if he ever thinks about it or ever has a good look at the people he meets. He said he didn't, on both counts, because he was no good at it and anyway he didn't care. The only thing he admitted was he finds stubble on someone who he thinks wants to be a woman distracting.

I wonder if someone developed special gender glasses he would finally get a boyfriend, girlfriend, it-friend, someone, at least, rather than just me.[76]

Isarebe spent the next three years at MIT living off his reputation as author of *The Demise of the Political Economy*, delivering his end of term lectures and attending occasional departmental meetings. His colleagues at best tolerated him, although Isarebe showed no outward signs of concern. He spent a lot of his time talking to people in the Department of Cognition at MIT and with Rosy Head from the Decision Research Unit within the Department of Psychology at Harvard. He was searching for the switch that would shine a light on the link between neural processes and economic decision making, but by the end of their third year in Massachusetts he realised that neuroscience was decades, if not centuries, away from being able to help him.

He now spent many of his evenings playing poker, 'the first sport after Bezique I am any good at'[77] and it was to prove important in his later work. He wasn't a good poker player, as he was a fidget and never varied his betting strategy, so competent players were able to outplay him over the course of an evening. But he was a good observer and poker was the perfect way to watch people trying to make simple but financially important decisions in an environment with imperfect information. He noticed even amongst the stoniest and most experienced players, that the frequency and direction of their eye movements provided good information on their hands: how long they looked at their cards; which cards they kept returning their gaze to; how they switched attention to the faces of other players. At first implicitly and then explicitly, he developed a way of assessing body and eye movements and relating it to his competitors' play-making. This was his first experience of being able to research and understand aspects of decision-making without

76   Isarebe, I, 2037, diary entry dated 29th January 2037, The Isarebe Trust Archives, Cambridge, England (Box 79, Folder 2)
77   Isarebe, S, 2035, diary entry dated 20th February 2035, The Isarebe Trust Archives, Cambridge, England (Box 67, Folder 4)

relying on the spoken word. In the context of his evolving work on decision-making, it hinted at a way of bypassing the flaws inherent in other available techniques, in particular relying on respondents' answers to conventional questions in survey research, which was known to be wholly unreliable in predictive modelling.

He wrote a short book on his conclusions, called *Improving Win:Loss Ratios in Poker by Observation of External Stress Signals*, but he could not find a publisher, even when he retitled it *The Economist's Guide to Winning at Poker*. As one publisher put it: 'No one could understand it and Solomon Isarebe was one of the worst poker players I have ever seen.'[78] In his diaries, he noted his winnings and losses each week. Between August 2034 and June 2035 he played poker 123 times; he won on fifteen and lost on 108 occasions. His combined stake money was nearly $32,000 and his aggregate losses were over $29,000. Poker was his single biggest expense during this period.

In September 2035, Isarebe started a three-way long-distance conversation: a collaboration which was to intellectually sustain him for the next two years, even if it was to bear no immediate fruit. The two other participants in the conversation were Hetty G. Brown, Professor of Quantitative Economics at Stern School of Business at New York University and Heulwen Gröning, a researcher in the Department of Experimental Psychology at Bangor University in Wales. Hetty Brown was perhaps the world's leading authority on Discrete Choice Modelling, a method of estimating and predicting decision-making through the interpretation of data from research which examined the choices people made when presented with a series of alternatives. Heulwen Gröning was a young researcher who specialised in examining eye and body movements, measured by cameras, body sensors and on-screen tracking devices, to determine how visual information is extracted from the environment and how this manifests itself in body movements. Gröning's work involved statistically correlating her observations with the decision-making choices of participants in simple tasks within a laboratory environment. Isarebe believed these two fields offered potential solutions to his search for a means of reliably assessing and predicting the decision-making of individuals and families in an economic context, but perhaps more importantly these two dynamic academics offered Isarebe a safe yet challenging environment in which to develop his ideas. They were also the closest thing Isarebe had to friends during his time in the United States, apart from Isabelle and his bezique drinking buddies. Although Isarebe spent a number of weekends with Brown in her tiny flat on Roosevelt Island, New York and the three of them were to have marathon online discussions

78   Gabby, G, 2067, *A history of Ebony-Wile press*, Ebony-Wile, Wichita, p. 145

throughout this period, they never met as a group until the launch of *Future Perfect*, when Isarebe generously attributed many of his ideas to the wisdom and inspiration of Brown and Gröning.

Isarebe recognised the strengths and weaknesses of both their approaches, but felt there must be a better solution in the space between them. In retrospect, Isarebe's notes and unpublished models from that period show he was tantalisingly close to a major breakthrough. There was no formal output from their discussions or from the work the three of them completed subsequent to their discussions, but their exchanges sowed seeds in Isarebe's mind which were eventually to grow into ideas that were to be recognised as some of his greatest achievements, most notably in the technical work underpinning *Future Perfect*, for which he was awarded the Nobel Prize in Statistics and Economics in December 2055.

Isabelle Isarebe neared the end of her course in the spring of 2037, winning multiple prizes for her research paper on 'Determinist versus stochastic processes in fertility decisions in the Boston Metropolitan Area'. Isabelle received offers of post-graduate study from universities across the USA and Europe, but she accepted an offer from the University of Botswana to undertake a doctorate programme within their Department of Fertility and Population Studies. Mooky was now Assistant Professor in this department and both were hoping they could rediscover their love for each other.

After a short visit to the UK to see Jannik and Reba Isarebe in Garway Hill, Isarebe accompanied Isabelle to Gaborone, before flying on to Beijing to complete a short tour promoting his book *The Demise of the Political Economy*, which had become a sleeper hit in China. Isarebe surprised his audiences by giving the first ten minutes of each lecture in Mandarin, to great applause each time, claiming to have mastered the language 'on the long journey from Boston.'[79] The reality was he had memorised this section of his lecture and it was on this trip he first used an in-ear simultaneous translator. He caused consternation in the first lecture of the tour, when during the question-and-answer session he quietly spoke into his translator earpiece, which he held in his hand, believing this was how the system worked. Many of the audience thought it was a clever joke and it appeared to do little to dent his reputation as a maverick genius.

Isarebe loved China and was amazed at how its economic progression over the previous fifty years had produced a cityscape, youth culture and media little different to that observed in the West. He vowed to return for a

---

79   Isarebe, S, 2037, diary entry dated 24th July 2037, The Isarebe Trust Archives, Cambridge, England (Box 305, Folder 6)

longer period, but he was only ever to go to China for short research trips. After finishing the tour, Isarebe returned to England, accepting a job as an analyst at the Bates Institute for Economics and Demography in London.

1.4 Rising from the economic ashes

Isarebe started as an analyst at The Bates Institute in late September 2037. His role involved being shifted from team to team as projects demanded, with Isarebe noting, 'I was just one of the many dispensable eggheads for hire.'[80] However, after his relatively unproductive time at MIT, Isarebe applied himself to the work and became friendly with a number of the other young analysts, one of whom he had previously met at MIT. Three of them shared a flat in East Dulwich, a sleepy part of South London, and although none of them seemed particularly sociable, they had some shared interests and it was a relatively happy period in Isarebe's life.

In the spring of 2038, Isarebe was put on a team led by a former academic called Hertha Grün, who worked from The Bates Institute's Berlin office. They were to work together on a project for the EU Commissioner for Environmental Development, identifying the most effective ways to encourage environmentally beneficial behaviour. Isarebe was perplexed by Grün, whom he once described as 'the most pointlessly enthusiastic and cheerful person I have ever met.'[81] She was a statistical anthropologist by training and had proposed a programme of qualitative and quantitative survey research across Europe.

Isarebe strongly disagreed with her approach. He felt that conventional social survey research would generate meaningless results and they needed to undertake 'non-verbal preference research and modelling with individuals and family groups, if we want to even get close to the truth.'[82] Perhaps what he really wanted was an opportunity to test the research ideas he had been developing with Brown and Gröning. Isarebe voiced his concerns in an aggressive diatribe at the first project meeting in Berlin. Despite the nature of Isarebe's unsolicited outburst, Grün noted it with a smile and a thank-you: 'I can't remember ever being so effectively and politely told to [expletive] off. She's one weird and clever woman.'[83]

80   Venessa, 2057, *Modern Lives with Venessa: Solomon D. Isarebe*, National and Regional Public Media / BIBC Media, 16th August 2057

81   Isarebe, S, 2038, email to Professor D. Kamil dated 6th June 2038, The Isarebe Trust Archives, Cambridge, England (Box 85, Folder 1)

82   Isarebe, S, 2038, e-con with Hetty G. Brown and Heulwen Gröning dated 8th June 2038, The Isarebe Trust Archives, Cambridge, England (Box 85, Folder 2)

83   Isarebe, S, 2038, diary entry dated 16th May 2038, The Isarebe Trust Archives, Cambridge, England (Box 84, Folder 14)

Grün did not change their approach and she put Isarebe in charge of the limited amount of modelling they were planning to do. Isarebe was intrigued by some of the early research results, but was concerned, if not surprised, by the stark contrast between the statements respondents gave in the survey research and the historic data they had on actual environmental behaviour. There had for many years been strong public support for environmentally-driven changes in lifestyle, but there had been little observed change in behaviour outside of legally-mandated requirements.

These research results reinforced Isarebe's conclusions on the weakness of the research methods they were employing and he flew unannounced to Berlin one afternoon, confronting Grün as she was leaving the office for the evening. They talked for nearly four hours, discussing Isarebe's concerns that respondents were literally unable to answer the research questions truthfully. He gave her a paper he had prepared, which summarised the academic research on how the unconscious mind made over 99% of day-to-day decisions and that individuals were unaware of how these decisions were reached and were therefore unable to influence them. The paper was entitled 'There's no such thing as free will Hertha Grün.'[84] He also showed her a paper written by Hetty Brown, that showed when people were interviewed individually they gave completely different responses to when they were interviewed as part of a social group, which was where they often made real-life decisions.

Grün nodded and smiled, as she always does, and walked up and down the room while I spoke. At one point she climbed on her desk and stared down at me for a second, before turning her back on me and looking up at the night sky. It was very distracting.

When I had finally finished pontificating I immediately felt embarrassed at having lectured this extraordinary woman, but she jumped down from her desk and kissed me on the forehead and said I was brilliant. I suspected she was just placating me and thought it was probably what I deserved, but next day she arranged for Hetty to fly first class from New York to Berlin (one of the least environmentally beneficial pieces of behaviour I had witnessed in a while) and for Heulwen to be dragged out of a conference in Buenos Aires, where she was the keynote speaker, to talk to her on the phone. It was a masterclass in not being denied.

---

84   There are no physical or digital records of this paper, but it is often referred to in email exchanges between Grün and Isarebe.

By the following week, Hertha, Hetty and I were being paraded in front of a herd of EU bureaucrats in Brussels, where I explained our thinking. They soundly rejected my recommended approach as incoherent, untested and potentially ruinously expensive. This was a masterclass in being denied.

Hertha had anticipated this response and had persuaded the Institute's trustees to fund my alternative approach to the project and run it alongside the conventional research programme.[85]

Isarebe's parallel project was to overrun by months and the results were insufficiently conclusive to be made public. The experiment ended up costing The Bates Institute three times more than they were paid by the EU Commission. Even though the final results were unusable, Isarebe felt able to draw some tentative methodological conclusions from the work: recording non-verbal responses was more powerful in stated preference research than relying solely on verbal responses, particularly when respondents' choices became difficult or contentious; conducting research with individuals when they were accompanied by one or more members of their close social group often produced results more closely aligned with the real world; and these adaptations of stated preference research produced even better predictions of behaviour when used in combination with conventional survey research.[86] The neat and tidy theoretical ideas that Isarebe, Brown and Gröning had developed in their academic huddle had just about survived their first encounter with the enemy of reality. Isarebe was sure with more time and money they could find a workable methodology.

Happy as The Bates Institute had been to fund this experiment, they were not prepared to pay for any further development of Isarebe's ideas. However, they promoted Isarebe to Senior Analyst and moved him to their macroeconomics team, where he was to work on long-term economic forecasts.

Isarebe had been at The Bates Institute for just over a year when the Venezuelan oil crisis struck in November 2038, a global event that was to further advance Isarebe's budding reputation as an economist (see Appendix 1 for more background on the crisis).

Whilst economic downturns are bad news for most commercial organisations, they can represent a boom time for forecasting consultancies,

---

85   Isarebe, S, 2067, typed notes for an unpublished autobiography, manuscript dated 24th September 2067, The Isarebe Trust Archives, Cambridge, England (Box 448)
86   He also noted in this presentation there was a group of older people who were outliers in the research results, a finding that was to be important in his later work.

particularly economic forecasters, as organisations desperately look for a way out of an engulfing crisis to the sound of a thousand stable doors being slammed shut behind them. The Bates Institute was no exception and they won major contracts with the UK and German governments, the BIBC,[87] the EU Economic Advisory Council and several multinational oil companies.

Isarebe was given an increasingly public profile and was to become a soothing voice of calm amongst the many economic calamitists who were claiming a large share of media time. Isarebe and his team predicted that within eighteen months of the crisis 83% of lost economic ground would have been made up, and within five years there would be no measurable impact of the crisis either on economic output or share prices.[88] Although forecasters rarely have their predictions tested, as observers have normally lost interest when the end of the forecast period is actually reached, Isarebe often mentioned in later interviews that his forecasts made during the oil crisis were very close to the actual outcome.

In December 2039, Isarebe was promoted to Economic Research Director at The Bates Institute. He had a short series commissioned by ZDM, the German national media company, entitled *Der Blick über den Horizont* and he delivered three Eye-Ted Talks in 2040. Isarebe enjoyed public speaking and if that had been the full extent of the responsibilities associated with his promotion he may have stayed at The Bates Institute for much longer. However, this was not just a PR role. He had been put in charge of a team of over thirty analysts and made responsible for bringing in work and delivering projects on time. He was remarkably good at selling the company's services and his project management skills were exceptional, but he had no experience of or aptitude for managing people. Within the first month he had brought all six of his senior analysts to tears during their personal reviews, wrongly assuming they would want to know how to be more like him and to be told how badly they were doing in that regard. One of these senior analysts, Rocket Li, was also one of his housemates and within a month Isarebe found himself alone in his large flat above a pub in East Dulwich.

Isarebe started to feel isolated, stressed and anxious, far from his family, in a large city with no real friends. He had a wiry frame as a young man, but lost nearly 20% of his bodyweight during 2040 and his diaries suggest he was experiencing another depressive episode.

---

87   BIBC, The British and Irish Broadcasting Company, was formed in 2030, from the amalgamation of the British Broadcasting Corporation, Saorview and Channel 4
88   The Bates Institute, 2039, *Economic Quarterly*, Issue 96, May 2039, pp. 8–25

ARCHIVE

2000s 2010s 2020s **2030s** 2040s 2050s 2060s 2070s 2080s 2090s 2100s 2110s 2120s 2130s 2140 2141 2142 2143 2144 2145 2146 2147 2148 2

UK Europe India China USA Nigeria Rest of World

Politics **Economy** Global Conflict Climate Business Health Culture Sport Weather Broadca

ISAREBE / GLOBAL RECESSION / 2039 / BIRD

Date:	April 3rd 2039 by S. Bird
Author:	Simon Bird
Channel:	BIBC News Online
Type:	Opinion piece
Title:	Economist tells us to sit tight and think of England
Photo/s:	365-79-342AC-982-SDI
Page:	1/2

Predictions of the end of the economic world as we know it are exaggerated, says maverick economist Solomon D. Isarebe, age 30, from The Bates Foundation.

Despite the global economy shrinking by 6.9% in the first quarter of 2039 - the largest fall since Covid killed our grandparents - and unemployment in the UK about to hit 2 million, Isarebe (strangely pronounced 'Is - Are - Be', who knew?!) says we shouldn't worry our little bamboo socks about it. He predicts that within 5 years the economy will be back to where it would have been had this little political handbags at dawn never happened and our pension pots will be brimming over with cash.

It sounds like he's a crackpot - and to be honest he looks a little mad. When I met him, he was wearing a tangerine shirt that has seen better days, trousers that were made for someone a foot shorter (he's about 9 feet tall, so probs not easy to find trews that fit) and with hair that seemed to defy gravity. But when he speaks, it is like someone is giving your brain a soothing massage, with

ARCHIVE

2000s 2010s 2020s **2030s** 2040s 2050s 2060s 2070s 2080s 2090s 2100s 2110s 2120s 2130s 2140 2141 2142 2143 2144 2145 2146 2147 2148 2149 2

UK Europe India China USA Nigeria Rest of World

Politics **Economy** Global Conflict Climate Business Health Culture Sport Weather Broadcast

ISAREBE / GLOBAL RECESSION / 2039 / BIRD

Date:	April 3rd 2039 by S. Bird
Author:	Simon Bird
Channel:	BIBC News Online
Type:	Opinion piece
Title:	Economist tells us to sit tight and think of England
Photo/s:	365-79-342AC-982-SDI
Page:	2/2

verbal balm reaching places you never knew existed. Like all economists he spouts the inevitable jargon on occasion, but he is so, so, SO convincing.

Now, I'm no economist, but I've talked to some clever folks who are and they have been sucked in by his economic lullabies too. So, it's official, don't try and resist folks, it's inevitable, you just have to believe him. And you know what that means … we should just do as he says and lie back and think of England and wait for it all to pass. What a hoot!

Solomon D. Isarebe, or 'Dizzy' as he is apparently called by both his friends, is the sort of man we need in a crisis - a genius with dodgy teeth and a bed-side manner to die for.

BIBC online article, 3rd April 2039

Isarebe failed to turn up to the Bates Bezique Club on Friday 7th December 2040 and on the following Monday one of the concerned club members alerted Cheffy Bulstrode, the CEO of The Bates Institute in London. Isarebe was the founder of the Bezique Club and had never before missed a meeting. Bulstrode discovered Isarebe had been absent for nearly ten days, with most members of staff assuming he had been filming with ZDM in Germany.

Isabelle Isarebe had been through adventures of her own whilst her brother had been at The Bates Institute. She breezed through the formal elements of her PhD programme in her first year at the University of Botswana and then worked for nearly two years on her thesis, which was based on the development of an AI remote family planning advisor. Her work had been a great technical success and she had presented it at a number of conferences in Africa, but she had encountered one problem she had been unable to overcome: the nature of the programme and interface she had developed meant that it could tailor responses to each individual patient, but it could not account for the views of the patients' family, friends and social group, who she knew were significant influencers of sexual behaviour. Isabelle and Solomon Isarebe were working in different fields, in different parts of the world, but were encountering the same problems with incorporating societal concerns into models of individual decision-making.

After nearly four months of polite and hesitant dating, Isabelle got back together with Mooky in January 2038, but Isabelle found a caution in Mooky that had been absent from their earlier relationship. Isabelle wrote in her diaries that 'the Gabby Mooky'[89] seemed a different man to the one she had known in Boston: no less attractive and loveable, but a man more defined by his culture. Gaborone was the capital of a relatively liberal, fast-growing, mid-income African nation, but had cultural mores and hierarchies that were alien to Isabelle. She found Mooky laughed less than he once had and she believed he was sometimes disapproving when she engaged in debate with his colleagues from the university. He was now in a more senior position and since his father's death was one of the most important people in his family, and she thought he was 'struggling to reconcile his relationship with me and his place in this wonderful smiling rule-bound society.'[90]

She downplayed these problems with her parents and tried to make the most of a place, a people and a person she loved. The most difficult thing for her and Mooky to cope with, alongside their uncertain relationship, was the pressure they came under from his family to get married. Mooky was unsure

---

89   Isarebe, I, 2038, diary entry dated 18th February 2038, The Isarebe Trust Archives, Cambridge, England (Box 83, Folder 4)
90   Isabelle, I, 2039, exText to Beth Williams dated 4th April 2039, The Isarebe Trust Archives, Cambridge, England (Box 85, Folder 9)

about the idea, whilst Isabelle was adamant she would never marry. At one stage she told Mooky she had spoken to Solomon and they had decided Mooky could change his name to Isarebe if he wanted to, hoping this may solve the problem. There is no record of Mooky's response, but they were never to share a name.

Isabelle Isarebe and Mooketsi Mooketsi, Botswana, 2039

Throughout most of her time in Botswana she was in daily contact with her brother. Mooky had always been understanding of Isabelle's unusual closeness to a brother with whom she had no genetic links, but his family berated him over his passivity towards Isabelle and Solomon's relationship. Isabelle told Solomon that Mooky's mother had said she thought Solomon and Isabelle were in a sexual relationship, which she had referred to as 'a perverted unnatural sort of incest'.[91]

---

91   Isarebe, I, 2039, eLetter to Solomon Isarebe dated 25th August 2039, The Isarebe Trust Archives, Cambridge, England (Box 88, Folder 4)

On the day of her viva voce exam, when she was required to defend her PhD thesis to the examiners, Isabelle found out she was pregnant. She told no one, not even Solomon, struggling with the idea of being a mother. She later told Solomon she had spent hours mentally envisaging being with a baby: the hours she would spend exhausted, frustrated and bored and the occasional moments of joy and deep satisfaction.

In early August 2040, just days after she found out she was pregnant, Reba Isarebe called Isabelle to tell her that her genetic father, Leonid Denikin, had died, following a stroke. He had been found lying behind the sofa of his house in Cairo, just as he had been when Jannik Isarebe first found him in 2020. Isabelle was fond of her father, but did not know him well, even though he had written to her once a month and had come to Garway Hill a few times when she was much younger. But his death was an excuse for her to get away from Mooky and his family and she spent the following month in Egypt, slowly sorting out her father's affairs. Isabelle called Reba on 15th September 2040:

> It was the first time she had ever called me 'mum', that's all I can really remember about that call. She normally called me Beba, which is all she had been able to manage when she was little and it had sort of stuck, but it sometimes made me weep that she was seemingly unable to call me mum. Such a silly little word, but one only Dizzy and Izzy had the right to call me.

> She asked me, her mum, to come and get her. I flew to Cairo and we came home on the following Monday morning. She told me she had been pregnant but it was gone now and she never wanted it mentioned again.[92]

Isabelle had decided in Cairo she couldn't be with Mooky, despite her love for him. He was not surprised when she told him it was over and Isabelle found out three months later, through a friend from the University of Botswana, he had married a first cousin from Takatokwane, the town where he had been brought up. As Isarebe said in something close to a joke, 'Obviously an un-perverted natural sort of incest.'[93]

Isabelle Isarebe had inherited a small amount of money from her father and didn't need to work straight away, but she was offered a job by Alpha Meta Research Projects (AMRP) in Dublin and she thought it might

---

92   Isarebe, R, 2054, *Chosen Poet*, O'Daley's, London, p. 103
93   Isarebe, S, 2040, diary entry dated 29th September 2040, The Isarebe Trust Archives, Cambridge, England (Box 96, Folder 2)

be a good, solid, cold, rainy place to make a new start. Her first project for AMRP was developing real-time adaptive models of consumer behaviour, which she found intellectually interesting, although she was ethically and philosophically unsure of its worth.

It was late December 2040, shortly after Solomon went missing from The Bates Institute, that the siblings' lives came together once more.

Isabelle Isarebe was woken by a hesitant knocking on the door of her apartment and found Solomon outside, soaked through, having walked seven miles from Dublin airport wearing nothing more than a mac over his pyjamas, holding a bedraggled cigarette and with a bottle of Jameson's in each pocket. She said nothing, but put him to bed, placing an ashtray on his bedside table, together with a glass for his whiskey. Solomon noted in his diary, 'I felt almost immediately safer, seeing Izzy waddling round the bedroom, saying nothing, just giving me the occasional grin and filling up my glass without asking.'[94]

Solomon Isarebe stayed with his sister during those missing weeks before he informed Cheffy Bulstrode on Friday 21st December that he was having some health problems and would not be returning to The Bates Institute. Solomon had quickly recovered some mental balance after arriving in Dublin and was fit enough to return with Isabelle to Garway Hill for Christmas. When Jannik and Reba Isarebe saw their son they were shocked at his smoking and drinking and skeletal appearance, but what upset them most was that he was almost silent, only speaking to Isabelle after they had both gone to bed.

Isabelle stayed with Solomon in Herefordshire until the end of January, working from his bedroom, with Isarebe slowly starting to take an interest in her work and beginning to chat to Jannik and Reba, albeit with a new tobacco- and whisky-induced gravel in his voice. AMRP were surprisingly tolerant of Isabelle's prolonged absence from work, only a matter of weeks after she had started.

Aside from her main project, Isabelle had been asked to be a junior reviewer of a large study AMRP had recently completed entitled *Project Big Mamma; Reversing the decline in global fertility*, in which they assessed the impact on their business of the accelerating decline in population in Japan and Eastern Europe in particular, and identified ways they could potentially help reverse this trend. Isarebe was appalled when he read one of the early drafts of the report. It was the first time he had thought about the significance of long-term population change:

---

94   Isarebe, S, 2040, diary entry dated 19th December 2040, The Isarebe Trust Archives, Cambridge, England (Box 96, Folder 2)

The work is v impressive, but the ethics are shaky, even for an organisation like them. And if Alpha are getting heated about getting baby's bums on seats, then politicians and the media will soon be on their heels. I need to understand this stuff. I don't understand why Izzy hasn't talked to me about it before? [95]

Solomon with Reba and Jannik Isarebe, Hilman Cottage, Garway Hill, 2040

Isabelle returned to Dublin at the start of February, leaving a message on Isarebe's bedside table that Professor Kamil wanted to see him and she had arranged for him to visit his old mentor in his rooms in St John's College. Isabelle had told Kamil of Isarebe's delicate health and suggested he might be able to help. Kamil duly offered Isarebe a job as his Assistant, a job with no responsibilities, few benefits apart from a room in college and free meals in the college dining room and an absolute absence of stress. 'Do you still play Bezique?' was Isarebe's response to Kamil's offer, 'and have you ever tried Scotch Whisky?'[96]

---

95   Isarebe, S, 2041, handwritten notes dated 17th January 2041, The Isarebe Trust Archives, Cambridge, England (Box 97, Folder 8)
96   Kamil, D, 2041, eLetter to Isabelle Isarebe dated 14th February 2041, The Isarebe Trust Archives, Cambridge, England (Box 99, Folder 2)

Isarebe's room in St John's College was on the top floor of New Court, a 19th century Gothic pastiche. Isarebe's room had a tiny bathroom and an even smaller galley kitchen, together with a bed-sitting room, but it had a desk looking directly down over the river and the Bridge of Sighs and it was perfect for Isarebe's recuperation.

Solomon Isarebe recuperating, Garway Hill, 2040

For the next sixteen months, the 32-year-old Isarebe lived the life of a semi-retired academic, with the mornings spent at his desk, idly looking down at the punters on the river and his afternoons frittered wandering the streets and greens of Cambridge. On Tuesday and Thursday evenings he went up the Madingley Road to Kamil's house, where they played cards or just sat drinking, 'barely saying a word to each other'.[97]

However, it was a time of consolidation of some of his ideas and interests: he read academic papers on population change and fertility and worked on

97   Kamil, D, 2042, eLetter to Isabelle Isarebe dated 1st June 2042, The Isarebe Trust Archives, Cambridge, England (Box 108, Folder 2)

small thought experiments with Brown and Gröning. By July 2042 he felt fully recovered and was keen to do something more than live the idle, idyllic life of an underemployed academic with a very indulgent mentor.

On 19th July 2042, the Isarebes embarked on a family holiday, their first together for many years, staying in a villa just outside the small town of Portoscuso in the south-west of Sardegna. It was to mark a turning point in Isabelle and Solomon Isarebe's lives.

PART 2
The Isarebes take on the world

2.1 Isarebe & Isarebe

The Isarebe family were well travelled: they had each been born in a different country; they were all foreigners in the country they called home; Jannik and Reba had worked on six continents; and Solomon and Isabelle had lived in many countries. However, they were not good holidaymakers, not quite knowing what to do with the time held in their hands and slow to acclimatise to a strange house with a new climate. After a few days in Sardegna, wandering the nearby towns and seeking out the sparse historic sights, they spent a bewildered morning on a local beach, surrounded by beautiful, bouncing, bronzed Italian teenagers. They decided to retreat to their villa for the rest of their fortnight.

> By the end of the first week, Janni and I had been relegated to members of the audience. Dizzy and Izzy sat facing each other, huddled under a sunshade, their sun-dappled noses six inches apart and they would talk, all day. They stopped for meals, because we asked them to, but they were like kids itching to get down from the table to play. They talked on till dawn some days, with only exhaustion able to catch up with them. Twice we found them in the morning sprawled on their beds, clothes on, dead asleep, frozen like Pompeii senators in mid-speech. Dizzy was even letting the ice in his whisky melt some days, although he was never without a cigarette clamped between his teeth. Janni and I watched on in a strange, dazed trance, understanding very little, but realising there was something important happening in that little house in Sardegna.[98]

Solomon and Isabelle's discussions initially focussed on AMRP's Big Mamma report and the direction of the population debate. As Solomon had anticipated, awareness of the potential impact of global population decline was rapidly moving beyond academia and the higher echelons of government and was starting to seep into the broader corporate, public and political consciousness. For many years the consensus had been that the massive population growth seen over the preceding 150 years was not sustainable, although as is often the case with slow, long-term trends, popular passions did not run high, but now the population graph looked certain to start on a downward course people

---

98   Isarebe, R, 2054, *Chosen Poet*, O'Daley's, London, p. 144

were rapidly changing horses. The prevailing reaction to these predictions of population decline was downbeat, with many sagely predicting the end of the known economic world, particularly within the dominant developed economies. Whilst many demographers, economists and populist soothsayers gave small nods to the potential benefits of a shrinking population on global warming, the focus of much of the commentary was on the 'devastating economic impact of reduced human capital'[99] and the 'cloying dead-weight'[100] of the growth in the proportion of non-working older people. Through leader columns, opinion pieces and speeches, there was growing media and political pressure being put on women around the world to 'have larger families for the good of the nation,'[101] a pressure they showed no signs of bending to.

Solomon and Isabelle Isarebe, Sardegna, 2042

There were of course other people beside the Isarebes who could see the benefits of population decline, but whichever side of the debate people were on, it seemed certain that a decline in the world population was going to be of great importance in determining the future of Humankind. Solomon and

99   McKendrick, H, 2037, *Minister for Health statement to Commons*, HC Deb 4th July 2037, vol 420, col 605W

100   Kureishi, B, 2039, *Leader*, The New Economist, 24th May 2039, pp. 23–4

101   Penderley, M, 2039, *Interview with advisor to the Prime Minister*, BIBC News, 19th December 2039

Isabelle Isarebe were terrified that the 'apocalypticos', as they later referred to them in their correspondence, might win the debate.

Solomon Isarebe made extensive and barely legible handwritten notes on their discussions in Sardegna and by night they spent hours producing surprisingly sophisticated 'sketch models' to test and stretch their various ideas, with Solomon looking over Isabelle's patient shoulders as she worked on her laptop, giving her instructions on technical matters he knew relatively little about.

What revealed itself to them during those two weeks was that predictions of an economic collapse at some point in the far future because of population decline could come to pass, but there was no convincing evidence one way or the other and there were so many questions left unanswered that it was impossible to draw conclusions on the economic, social or environmental impact of a large and sustained fall in the global population.

The Isarebes were critical of some of the demographers generating population forecasts at that time. Demographic change is normally slow, steady and predictable in the short- to medium-term, but it is only in the long-term that demographics markedly changes the way people live and the world they live in. The Isarebes felt these population forecasts failed to project far enough into the future, making it impossible to use them to make an assessment of the long-term impact of population decline. They also felt the range of forecasts being given was so wide that it invited people to impose whatever prejudices they may have on the data. They realised the technical and political reasons for the approaches that had been used, but were frustrated by what they thought were 'bizarrely short time horizons and unhelpful statistical caution.'[102]

At the heart of the arguments behind predictions of a decline in the global population were the falls in fertility rates that were being observed all over the world, even in sub-Saharan Africa, where the population was still growing rapidly. In the majority of the developed world, fertility rates had been below the population replacement level for many decades. Demographers thought the reasons for this fall in fertility were well understood, having quantified the impact on fertility of greater access to education, the increased availability and lower cost of contraception, the desire of women to work and be financially independent, the health benefits to women of having fewer children, and the health and economic benefits to children of being raised in small families, among a range of other social and economic factors. Given the quality of the historic data and the reasonable efficacy of the models, the Isarebes were confounded by the conclusion almost all forecasters of population growth

---

102   Isarebe, S, 2042, typed notes dated 26th July 2042, The Isarebe Trust Archives, Cambridge, England (Box 108, Folder 5)

came to that fertility rates in developed countries, which had fallen first and fastest, would start to rise again in coming decades, converging with the falling fertility rates of less developed countries:

> These assumptions are bizarre; beyond heroic. I get a feeling they are being made because these people are frightened, politically pressured or, more likely, intellectual weaklings.[103]

Solomon was certain an important piece of the analytical jigsaw was missing, namely an assessment of the subconscious motivations behind the fertility decisions being made by billions of women all over the world:

> I think I accidentally verbally kicked Izzy in the womb today. We were talking about factors driving population growth – what else – and I slowly got more and more belligerent about the impact of individual decision making on fertility. I've rehearsed these arguments a million times over in my head and I kept bullying Iz into accepting everything I was saying was true. I just couldn't see why she didn't seem to be getting it, so I kept saying it louder and louder, like some drunken Englishman on his hols.
>
> I'd forgotten her pregnancy, mum having spilled the beans. I've never mentioned to her I knew, but I suddenly realised that maybe she was thinking different thoughts to me about babies and I stopped yelling mid-sentence. She looked at me, shook her head and told me she knew I knew, because mum couldn't even keep it a secret that she'd told me.
>
> Wish time went backwards occasionally.[104]

Solomon hadn't needed to bully Isabelle; she was in complete agreement with him that an understanding of the fertility decision-making process was an essential part of any analysis and they started examining how this information could be reliably gathered and incorporated within a forecasting model. As Isarebe biographer Adaline Colvin wrote, 'It is easy to think that Isabelle and Solomon Isarebe went through an extended rational discussion over those two weeks, before coming to a reasoned logical conclusion, but neither of

103   Isarebe, S, 2042, typed notes dated 27th July 2042, The Isarebe Trust Archives, Cambridge, England (Box 108, Folder 5)
104   Isarebe, S, 2042, diary entry dated 29th July 2042, The Isarebe Trust Archives, Cambridge, England (Box 108, Folder 1)

them worked like that. They would circle a problem for days, weeks, months, before making a sudden intuitive, breath-taking leap to the answer.'[105]

It was in their proposed research approach and the modelling of these research results where they made their big breakthroughs. Solomon talked to Isabelle about his work with Hetty Brown and Heulwen Gröning and how they had been developing a technique for using non-verbal cues in discrete choice research. They also discussed his decision-making experiments at The Bates Institute, when he had concluded that it was essential to include the views of family and other influencers in a research programme such as this, whilst Isabelle expanded on her problems accounting for the influence of family in her AI family planning app in Botswana.

The working relationship of Solomon and Isabelle Isarebe was more complex than many appreciated, with no obvious power dynamics and with leadership flowing from one to the other as the situation demanded, particularly as the *Future Perfect* project evolved. Some insisted that Isabelle was the only one able to stand up to Solomon's dictatorial tendencies, but it appears Solomon was a different man with Isabelle. As a mutual acquaintance, Bill Dickson, reportedly noted, they were more like '... two parts of a single, complex organism that recognised no boundaries between them.'[106] This symbiotic relationship characterised every aspect of their life when they were children and it was not until they grew older that their private lives disentangled and their characters became more distinct. In Sardegna, it was Solomon who took the lead on their discussions, but it was Isabelle who made the big initial breakthrough:

Izzy kept tutting today when I told her about my ideas for how we should go about this, with a v annoying smile on her face. She started doing her little duck walk around the pool in her poorly disguised excitement.

The problem with my proposal, she explained with max condensation [*sic*], was that having already looked at my ideas in detail – without asking – she'd calculated it would make any research project so complex it would take between two and three hours to complete a single interview, something that would render the results invalid and would in any case make any research programme prohibitively expensive.

105 Colvin, A, 2099, *The Strange Affair of Isabelle and Solomon Isarebe*, Sheaders, London, p. 212
106 Bortelli, R, 2070, *The Dizzy Digger*, Manchosens, New York, p. 162

I [expletive] HATE it when someone's practical when you've just shared an idea with them and I was ready to be v belig when I realised she had a solution tucked under her wing. It turns out Mooketsi once asked her to help with some research he'd been working on and like a magician pulling a chicken from a cooked [sic] hat, she went on to explain how she had developed the idea of 'Continual Inference Revision for Discrete Choice Analysis' – snappy title Isa-Belle-Belle! She fished out a note she'd written about it from her laptop. Mooketsi hadn't used her idea, but I've no idea why, because it was annoyingly brilliant.[107]

Continual Inference Revision, as it was to be shortened to, was cited in Solomon Isarebe's Nobel Prize nomination. Its design is reputedly still a delight for programmers to explore. It is a modelling program using techniques normally associated with machine learning and variations of it are still employed in social and market research today, allowing observations from individual interviews to be modelled in real time, the results of which are then used to determine the questions subsequently presented to the respondent. At the time of Isabelle and Solomon's discussions in Sardegna, Isabelle's ideas were still in their infancy, but they involved an iterative process of modelling, testing and revision, which improved both modelling results and questionnaire design, ensuring respondents in a study were required to respond to fewer but more relevant questions. This reduced fieldwork costs, but more importantly improved the quality of responses from each individual, which were known to decline rapidly in long repetitive interviews. Part of the analytical engine Isabelle proposed built upon an approach used for many years in analysing and predicting human behaviour called Hierarchical Bayesian Discrete Choice Modelling: the very modelling technique that had also been adapted by Solomon Isarebe, Brown and Gröning.

Solomon and Isabelle Isarebe's professional ideas and interests had finally collided, in what seems in retrospect to have been an inevitable but nevertheless wondrous moment. One feels, if they been different people, they would have set off fireworks and opened magnums of champagne. As it was, they had a family game of bezique and started work again the next morning. The rest of the holiday was spent sketching out a programme of work that would eventually take eight years to complete and would result in the publication of *Future Perfect*, making Solomon Isarebe a household name.

---

107   Isarebe, S, 2042, diary entry dated 31st July 2042, The Isarebe Trust Archives, Cambridge, England (Box 108, Folder 2)

On a badly-written note in both their hands and jointly signed like a pact between two teenage best friends, they determined to work together from then on and outlined what it was they hoped to achieve. Their first goal was technical: to further develop Solomon, Brown and Gröning's research technique (CQR)[108] and to combine it with Isabelle's Continuous Inference Revision programme (CIR). They then hoped to use these tools to forecast global population change over the following 100 years, by taking into account the fertility decision-making processes of women and making explicit assumptions on how and why these may change in the future. Few had ever taken such a long-term view, 'apart from soothsayers, witches and fairground fortune tellers'[109] and no one had formally incorporated women's views in this way before.

In other contemporaneous notes, the Isarebe siblings outlined how they could apply their ideas on collective decision making to migration, another key factor in predicting the future population of individual nations. They knew that most forecasters just assumed 'migration as usual', because of the political sensitivity and complexity of migration, but they thought the collective impact of individual decision making should at least be considered when making assumptions on future migration rates.

The final paragraph in their manifesto outlined how they wanted to examine the impact of population change on economics, global power politics, food supply, land use, congestion, air quality, the climate and ecosystems. It was Isabelle who felt they had to assess the impact of population change on these other areas and that they were as important as the population forecasts themselves: 'If you leave an information vacuum, then it will be filled with conspiracies, hysteria and the media's natural inclination to assume the worst.'[110]

This, the final element of their planned work represented a task so vast that you could argue it could only have been conceived by an egomaniac, genius or dreamer and some have said Solomon Isarebe was all these things. The Isarebes' skills and experience encompassed economics, modelling, AI, demography and to an extent global politics, but Isarebe boasted he was certain they had the basics skills and intelligence to understand these other areas and in any case they could build a team to fill any gaps in their understanding.

---

108   This was the acronym for Collective Quantitative All-Cues Preference Research. Isabelle commented in her diary, 'Snappy title, Sol!'.
109   Isarebe, S, 2042, diary entry dated 2nd August 2042, The Isarebe Trust Archives, Cambridge, England (Box 108, Folder 3)
110   Isarebe, I, 2042, hand-written note to self dated 3rd August 2042, The Isarebe Trust Archives, Cambridge, England (Box 108, Folder 3)

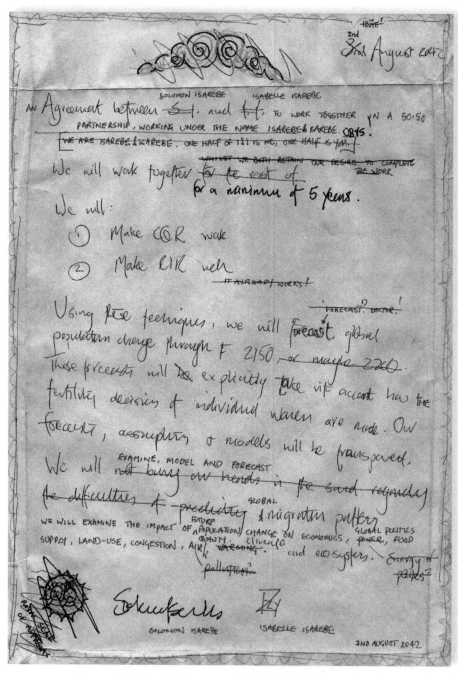

Agreement between Solomon and Isabelle Isarebe, August 2042

They subsequently drew up a more considered business plan for 'Isarebe & Isarebe'; a business partnership it took them some time to formalise. In the business plan, which is still in the Isarebe archive,[111] they assumed the *Future Perfect* project would take them two years to complete. Like many great architects, they were hopelessly optimistic in their time assumptions.

Isabelle resigned from AMRP before the holiday finished, while Solomon called Professor Kamil and asked if it was okay if Isabelle shared his rooms for a while. They arrived in Cambridge to find they had been given a cottage in the College grounds, but within six months they had moved to London, living on the forbidding-sounding Dog Kennel Hill in East Dulwich.

They made rapid progress on the modelling programmes and in finessing the research techniques, and within nine months they felt everything was ready for real-life testing. In a telephone conversation with Hetty Brown, Isarebe was explaining the progress they had made when she asked how much the planned research would cost. Isarebe was stumped: they had made some assumptions in their initial business plan, but had not revisited these assumptions or seriously thought about how they would pay for the programme. Solomon had vaguely assumed The Bates Institute would be willing to support them.

Over the following weekend, he concluded they would need to interview at least 100,000 women around the world and as many potential migrants. He estimated each interview was likely to take at least an hour and these interviews would need to be followed up by a second or even third interview of equal length, with the respondent and members of their family or close friends. He came up with a cost estimate, just for the research phase, that is staggering even in today's money and would have represented The Bates Institute's philanthropic budget for more than twenty years. The eventual cost of the research was nearly three times more than these first estimates.

Isarebe & Isarebe had been surviving on Solomon's dwindling book royalties, income from occasional talks and Isabelle's inheritance. Now, not even twelve months into their project, they did not have enough money to live on, let alone conduct a pilot programme. Solomon noted in his dairy; 'Iz told me she was hungry today. I think maybe we need to rethink.'[112]

---

111   Isarebe, S and I, 2042, *Isarebe & Isarebe Business Plan* dated 24th December 2042, The Isarebe Trust Archives, Cambridge, England (Box 110, Folder 4)
112   Isarebe, S, 2043, diary entry dated 3rd May 2043, The Isarebe Trust Archives, Cambridge, England (Box 113, Folder 3)

2.2 The benefaction of Rita Bortelli

Isabelle and Solomon went home to Garway Hill, physically and emotionally crashing and getting the sleep they had been missing for months, but were soon back working.

Solomon and Isabelle Isarebe, Hilman Cottage, 2043

Jannik cornered Solomon one evening, insisting he tell them how bad their financial plight was. Solomon slithered around the issue, worried that Jannik would offer to sell Hilman Cottage or cash in their pension, or 'make some other crazy parent sacrifice.'[113] Eventually, Solomon could bear Jannik's nagging no longer and showed him his estimates of the money they would need. It was many, many times more than Jannik and Reba had collectively earned in their lifetime. 'Dad's jaw literally dropped open. It was quite funny. He then got up and said he had to go to bed, meaning he needed to talk to

---

113   Isarebe, S, 2043, diary entry dated 12th May 2043, The Isarebe Trust Archives, Cambridge, England (Box 113, Folder 3)

mum. I realised at that moment quite how mad our plans were and the chance we would ever get them off the ground was pretty close to zero.'[114]

In an unexpected resolution, their mother Reba came to their rescue. The audience for her poetry was small, but passionate. She exchanged eLetters with many of her readers and with some had developed intimate relationships built around a shared love of sound and nature. She wrote to one of her correspondents, Rita Bortelli, about the problems of Isabelle and Solomon.

Rita Bortelli was born in Wichita, Kansas in 1998, the only daughter of a pharmacist, Maria S. Bortelli. The identity of her father was never revealed to her and she insisted she had no interest in finding out who he was, although there were rumours he was a senior member of the military based at McConnell Air Force Base. Bortelli had attended Caltech on a fully-funded scholarship, initially studying Computer Science, before starting a second degree in Psychology, eventually obtaining her doctorate in 2026. After university she worked as a practising psychologist in California and then New York.

She gave birth to a son, James Robert, in November 2031 and like her mother before her, kept the identity of James Robert's father to herself. Whilst spending the early months with her newborn son in their small apartment in Brooklyn, she had an idea that was eventually to become Digger Therapy. Digger was one of the first, and certainly the most successful, AI-based psychotherapy apps to be approved by medical regulators. By 2037, it was estimated that nearly 10% of the global adult population had received at least one session of therapy from Digger. At the time of its sale to Mind Soul Life in 2039, it was the 174th most valuable business in the USA. The Digger approach was superseded by others in the 2040s, although Mind Soul Life remained significant in the market for many years before its eventual collapse in 2104.

Bortelli had met Reba Isarebe at the Ledbury Poetry Festival in 2029. Reba's poetry was idiosyncratic, more a series of sounds than coherent words, but Rita became an ardent fan after hearing Reba read some of her work. They were to remain friends until Reba's death in 2058, exchanging eLetters, often hand-written, which 'sometimes ran to over 5,000 words.'[115]

Although Reba Isarebe claimed to have no knowledge of Bortelli's work or fortune, the florid language and pleading tone of her eLetter indicates she knew Bortelli had the financial capacity to help and was seemingly willing to risk her friendship in order to assist her children:

---

114   Isarebe, S, 2043, diary entry dated 12th May 2043, The Isarebe Trust Archives, Cambridge, England (Box 113, Folder 3)
115   Willis, J, 2058, *Obituary: Reba Isarebe, Poet*, The Hereford Bugler, 29th July 2058, p. 45

Janni and I sit like bewildered enraptured fools at Iz and Dizzy's feet. They are totally glorious when they speak to each other. I think Janni understands some of what they're saying, but I feel their words washing over me like a great Hokusai wave, subsuming me, tumbling me, till I can't tell sky from earth. I look up and see Beethoven talking to Picasso, Einstein drinking with Hughes, Barry dancing with Williams. They are on the verge of something momentous, I'm sure, but they seem trapped by something I don't fully understand.

I want you to meet them Rita. Come soon, come tomorrow, come the day after. I don't know why, but I think you must meet them. I have no right to ask, so please forgive.[116]

Rita Bortelli, Portrait by Tito Mannell, 2042

116   Isarebe, R, 2043, e-Letter to Rita Bortelli dated 19th May 2043, The Isarebe Trust Archives, Cambridge, England (Box 113, Folder 5)

Rita flew to the UK two days later and was introduced to Isabelle and Solomon, who were huddled in their pyjamas, dressing gowns and slippers in front of the tiny mid-July fire in the dark living room of Hilman Cottage: 'They couldn't have looked less like the mad geniuses of Reba's imagination if they'd tried.'[117]

Solomon reluctantly started to talk to Bortelli, once he had established she wasn't 'just another of mum's poetry nuts,'[118] while Isabelle stood behind him, nearly lost in the shadows. He talked and then talked faster and faster, according to Bortelli, 'like some Kerouacian-drug-fuelled-beat-maniacal-poet-economist,'[119] explaining their breakthroughs in researching, understanding and analysing individual and group decision-making and its application in understanding the future of women in the world. At some point, Isabelle Isarebe came out of the shadows, kissed Rita Bortelli on the lips and 'escaped like a weightless wraith up the staircase darkness.'[120]

Four months later Isarebe & Isarebe had been given enough funding from Bortelli for the next five years of their research and she was to be a benefactor who stayed loyal to them for life. Bortelli reflected on this moment in a much later interview with the *Washington and New York Post*:

> I put up some money, because I loved their mom. She was my best friend, my mother, my sister, my daughter, my hero, and I had only met her the once until that day in their tiny, claustrophobic cottage on a dripping Herefordshire hillside. Her kids were crazy, I mean crazy, crazy smart, out of this world, and they talked to each other without listening or even speaking sometimes, but understanding everything the other said before the sentence was started. Dizzy was sort of scary, he had something of the Messianic about him, whilst Izzy was a cross between some genius angel and a gypsy princess – she was irresistible and the real clever one, although she hated the limelight that Dizzy seemed incapable of getting away from.
>
> I'll never forget the chaste kiss she gave me on that first night – it was the purest, sweetest-smelling moment of my life and it brings tears to me, even now.

---

117   Bortelli, R, 2070, *The Dizzy Digger*, Manchosens, New York, p. 145
118   Isarebe, S, 2043, diary entry dated 23rd May 2043, The Isarebe Trust Archives, Cambridge, England (Box 113, Folder 6)
119   Bortelli, R, 2070, *The Dizzy Digger*, Manchosens, New York, p. 149
120   Bortelli, R, 2070, *The Dizzy Digger*, Manchosens, New York, p. 150

They could never have succeeded anywhere but around a kitchen table ... their kitchen table ... with no Professor or CEO looking over their shoulders trying to give them unwanted and unneeded advice.

It was the best and continues to be the best thing I've ever done with my money.

You know, there's nothing I wouldn't do for that family.[121]

With Bortelli's money in place, the Isarebes immediately started on the research and modelling programme that was to take them many years to complete and was to result in the publication of *Future Perfect*.

Reba Isarebe and Rita Bortelli, Hilman Cottage, 2043

---

121   Unattributed, 2074, *A Life in a Day: Rita Bortelli*, The Washington and New York Post, 4th March 2074

2.3 Working on fertile ground

There are three determinants of global population change: the stock of people; births and deaths; and for an individual nation, migration also needs to be taken into account. Births, or rather fertility, was the first aspect of population change that the Isarebes examined. It was to be a revolutionary piece of work: in the philosophy of their approach, focussing on the decision making of individual families; in the research and modelling techniques they employed; and in the size of the research study, with nearly 200,000 individual interviews being undertaken in forty countries around the world.

They started this work on fertility with a pilot study to test their assumptions, techniques and approach. This pilot research used conventional qualitative research[122] alongside their research and modelling innovations.[123] This initial work was undertaken in the UK, India, Nigeria and Argentina and was a substantial exercise in its own right, involving over 200 in-depth qualitative interviews and quantitative research[124] with 4,000 women and their partners, examining and testing their thoughts on family size.[125]

After completion of the pilot study, the Isarebes made many changes to their research design. Most of these issues were technical, but some were philosophical, such as how they should interview and categorise transgender people, who had become a statistically significant demographic group in some economically developed nations. Solomon believed them irrelevant to their final fertility projections and advocated not identifying them as a separate group in their research design. Isabelle strongly disagreed, having worked with transgender groups in Botswana. There are many eLetters, emails and scribbled notes between them on this issue. Solomon appears to have been irrationally and dispassionately stubborn and seemed to become more resistant the more emotional Isabelle became:

---

122   Qualitative research is where a relatively informal discussion guide is used with a small number of respondents. There is no formal questionnaire and there is little or no statistical analysis of the results.

123   A description of the technical details of these techniques is given in Appendix 2.

124   Quantitative research is where research is conducted in order to gain a statistical understanding of the issues under consideration, often relying on responses to a formal questionnaire or research design. The research is normally undertaken with a large number of people to ensure statistical reliability.

125   Details of the development path and technical aspects of this fertility research are given in Appendix 3.

I don't understand Solomon D. Isarebe at this moment and I don't like him very much either. He is showing signs of stupidity, which is bad enough, but worse he sounds and smells like a bigot. If we do what he wants, he would realise his mistake one day and be engulfed by shame, as he so often is. I'm not going to let that happen.[126]

A week after Isabelle's diary entry, Solomon came in to find her in his office, together with a woman he was introduced to as Cherrie Mahler and three immaculately behaved young children. Isabelle had previously met Cherrie at a number of family planning conferences, when Cherrie had been Professor Terry Mahler. Cherrie was Research Director for International Conception Choices and Chair of the charity Transgender Family Planning. She was an imposing, charismatic figure and by the end of their meeting, Solomon had enthusiastically agreed to co-present at a meeting Cherrie was having with the UK Office for National Statistics, where they were to explain how and why transgender people should be incorporated into the design of large-scale research studies.

It wasn't until August 2044 that the Isarebes finally felt ready to start the full forty-country study. It was to take them eighteen months just to complete the fieldwork phase. Work dominated the Isarebes' lives, with both Solomon and Isabelle routinely working seventy hours a week. They were rarely in the same country at the same time.

The towering technical achievements of their work on fertility were their development of CQR and CIR and it was these that led to Solomon Isarebe receiving the Nobel Prize in Statistics and Economics. The raw results derived from the application of these techniques are inaccessible and meaningless to the untrained and it is the verbatim records from the qualitative research, carried out alongside the quantitative work, that make more interesting reading and give some insight into the fertility discussions taking place within ordinary families in the 2040s. These qualitative discussions were intended to break the ice and lead to more open and honest responses regarding plans for more children. Many of the interviewers were trained therapists and the relaxed and often humorous nature of the conversations suggest they mostly succeeded in their goal of opening up frank discussions. The transcripts from these interviews run to nearly two million pages.

By this time, the Isarebe & Isarebe central team consisted of eighteen full-time researchers and analysts working alongside the Isarebe siblings. They used the quantitative research results, together with more conventional

126   Isarebe, I, 2046, diary entry dated 18th July 2044, The Isarebe Trust Archives, Cambridge, England (Box 119, Folder 6)

modelling and forecasting techniques, to project forward fertility rates to 2150. They extrapolated their results to the countries not covered by their survey through comparisons of demographics, economic development and cultural norms.

The Isarebes found in countries with a current fertility rate of fewer than two children per woman, their models could explain around 95% of actual behaviour. They tested this by various means, including 'backcasting' lifetime fertility rates using highly disaggregated versions of their models; disaggregating by age, income and cultural background in each country.[127] They found their models had good explanatory powers right back to the 1970s. Their models systematically overestimated the fertility rate by between 1 and 3%, in different countries, together with a random error of between 1 and 2%, with typically just one or two outlying years.[128] This led them to conclude that if they assumed no change in the main determinants of fertility decisions and made adjustments for their models' systematic overestimation, they had a reliable method for forecasting fertility in developed countries.

In countries with higher fertility rates (two children and above) they found they had to put more emphasis on factors such as education levels and access to contraception within their models. These had been widely used as explanatory variables in models produced by other institutions. However, they found these factors became less and less influential as fertility rates edged down towards two.

At the time the research was being undertaken, average global fertility was already below the population maintenance figure of 2.1 children per woman,[129] even though the global population was still rising.[130] The only region of the globe where fertility rates were still marginally above this population maintenance level was sub-Saharan Africa. Most other major institutions producing population forecasts in the 2040s were predicting a relatively slow fall in fertility in sub-Saharan Africa, where the population was still expanding rapidly, and a slow rise in fertility rates in those countries where fertility rates

---

127 Backcasting involves using models primarily designed to project forward, to re-estimate historic data. By comparing this backcast data to actual data, a good measure of model efficacy is obtained.
128 Outliers are results which, due to particular factors or random errors, appear different to other data in a series. These outliers are sometimes excluded from subsequent analysis, as their exclusion improves the explanatory power of the model for the remaining data.
129 The population replacement fertility figure is 2.1 children per woman rather than two children, to account for the number of people who die before they reach their fertility potential.
130 This apparent anomaly occurs when those from a previous baby-boom start having families. Almost irrespective of how many children they have, this cohort will result in population growth for a number of generations. Thus, fertility rates can be falling and population size can still be growing, particularly if life expectancy is also increasing.

had fallen well below the population maintenance level.[131] The consensus was that global fertility would converge at around 1.75 children per woman.

The Isarebes could find no scenarios under which they could replicate these fertility predictions from other institutions. They believed their work showed the prevailing assumptions were almost certainly wrong. They concluded that sub-Saharan countries would almost certainly see fertility rates fall much more quickly than the central estimates in other models, whilst many wealthy countries with already low fertility rates would see a further slow drop in fertility rates through to the end of their forecast period in 2150. In combination, this meant they predicted average global fertility at the end of their forecast period would be closer to 1.4, compared with the 1.75 consensus figure arrived at by many others. This seemingly small difference was to make their eventual population forecasts significantly lower than any previous estimates.

These top-line conclusions, whilst quantitatively different, were not revolutionary in themselves, because it was well known that populations were set to fall if no action was taken. What was new was their conclusion that it was highly unlikely this could be reversed by political initiatives.

Their research showed that for around 78% of families around the world, the decision of whether to have a first child or another child would not be greatly influenced by anything offered to them by governments or employers but would largely be determined by the circumstances of their lives and their cultural environment. 15% of families were only motivated to consider having a child or another child by the most extreme financial or other incentives, and most of these were people with one child, considering whether or not they should have a second. The remaining 7% were more susceptible to financial incentivisation and were in many cases from very low-income households. The Isarebe's work showed that any attempt to influence fertility, whether through financial incentives, coercion or attempts to change cultural norms – known somewhat disparagingly at that time as 'nudging' – would be expensive and largely ineffective in rich countries that typically may want to increase fertility rates, but cheaper and more effective in poorer countries that may want to reduce fertility rates.

Further modelling showed for most of those people where incentives would apparently encourage the decision to have a baby, it would only bring that decision forward rather than fundamentally affecting decisions on family size. This led to the Isarebes stating that for almost all countries, incentivising people to have larger families would be an almost entirely wasted investment.

---

131   Other institutions were mostly only forecasting fifty years out to 2100, rather than the 100-year horizon of the Isarebes.

Their study concluded that falling fertility, which Solomon Isarebe believed was 'perhaps the single most important change in human behaviour since we first set foot on earth,'[132] was not in the hands of politicians, industry or social influencers, but was under the control of billions of individual women and their partners. The Isarebes believed this was 'a new form of behavioural democracy, where individual women's fertility decisions are shaping the future of the planet.'[133]

Aspers[134] had suggested that other unrelated economic policies employed by some countries in the 2040s were negatively affecting fertility rates. Many governments were incentivising women to rejoin the workforce after having a child, in an attempt to maintain the number of people in employment and generate the tax revenue required to support the growing proportion of older people in the population. Thus, some governments were trying to get women to have more children and to undertake more paid work. The Isarebes officially commented that 'These initiatives may further contribute to the lack of effectiveness of policies designed to encourage larger families,'[135] whilst Solomon privately noted that 'This is the most extreme example I have ever seen of politicians wanting to have their cake and eat it, having poisoned it in the first place.'[136]

The Isarebes' work also seemed to answer a question which had confounded many in the field of population research: Why did many women not achieve their desired level of fertility, which had been consistently measured across the world at just over two children, close to the population maintenance level? The answer from their research was relatively unequivocal: after the birth of a first child, the impact of that child on income, time, freedoms and career, combined with a desire to accommodate the concerns and needs of their partners, meant that women on average were having half a baby less than their previously stated ideal. It appeared that when dreams of a certain family size met reality, reality nearly always won.

132   Isarebe, S, 2055, written acceptance for the Nobel Prize in Statistics and Economics, posted to www.nobelcommends.org 1st November 2055
133   Isarebe, S and I, 2046, *Fertility rates in 40 countries to 2150*, Isarebe & Isarebe Publications, London, p. 14
134   Aspers, Z, 2042, *Economic policy and its impact on fertility in the EU*, Journal of Economics, Politics and Geography, 42, 7, pp. 142–158
135   Isarebe, S and I, 2046, *Fertility rates in 40 countries to 2150*, Isarebe & Isarebe Publications, London, p. 310
136   Isarebe, S, 2046, diary entry dated 11th March 2046, The Isarebe Trust Archives, Cambridge, England (Box 117, Folder 2)

Anne Wyeth

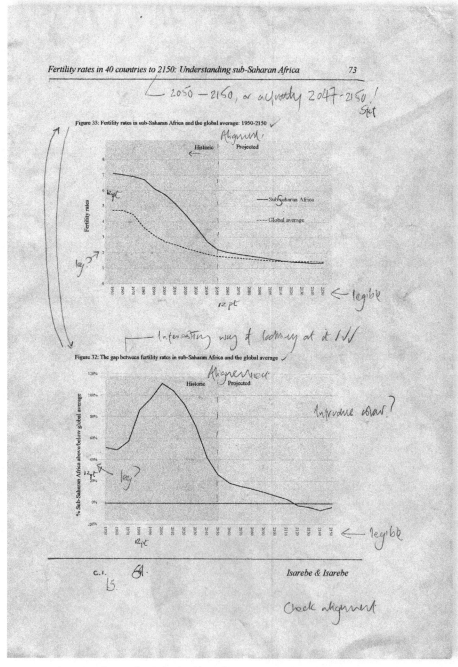

Annotated page from draft of 'Fertility rates in 40 countries to 2150,' 2046

The Isarebes decided to publish their initial results at a press conference in London in September 2046, eschewing the rigours of peer review associated with publishing in an academic journal.[137] As Solomon was reported saying at the time, 'We have no respect for journals that previously published estimates of fertility rates which seemed to be based on nothing more than a finger in the wind – the wind often being generated by a self-styled group of 'experts'. We haven't got the time to waste and luckily we have the wonderful Rita Bortelli behind us, with money other institutions would sell their 1.75 children for.'[138]

History has been kind to this early fertility work of the Isarebe & Isarebe partnership. The conclusions they reached quite closely matched what would come to pass over the next 100 years, even though they made no attempt to assess how cultural norms and attitudes towards family would change over this century, as they undoubtedly have – for example in attitudes to marriage, which is now the exception rather than the rule, and in much lower adherence to formalised religious practice. Despite this, their headline prediction of an average global fertility rate of 1.45 is remarkably close to the actual figure in 2150 of 1.41 children per woman – a figure now reasonably consistent across those parts of the world not in conflict or enduring natural disasters. To put this in context, in 1950 the average global fertility rate was 4.7 and as late as 2000 it was 2.7, not falling below the population maintenance rate of 2.1 until 2032. However, a more detailed review shows the apparent accuracy of their work was more luck than judgement. They made detailed assumptions on changes in age structures, economic growth, education, availability of contraception and female participation in the workforce, but these were as 'heroic' as those of the institutions they were so critical of. They were often significantly wide of the mark in their assumptions of how these individual drivers would change, but the errors miraculously cancelled each other out, leading to eerily accurate predictions. Luck has so often been the shaky foundation of fame and the label of genius.

Their findings on fertility were barely covered in the press, as the media was dominated that week by two events: the murder of two music stars, their bloody and naked bodies having been found together in a hotel room in Mexico; and a minor earthquake in San Francisco. However, the Isarebes received aggressive criticism from some in the normally sober academic and governmental demography community. One of these critics, Casey Ingar, a leading young demographer and editor of the International Global Health Organisation population forecasts, was particularly affronted by their

---

137   Isarebe, S and I, 2046, *Fertility rates in 40 countries to 2150*, Isarebe & Isarebe Publications, London
138   Manda, C, 2046, *New report on global fertility suggests collapse in population*, The Independent Guardian, 17th September 2046, p. 34

conclusions. He appeared on the Isarebe's doorstep at 3 a.m. on the Sunday after their press conference. Solomon answered the door, with Isabelle in the rear.

'The man was beetroot,' recalled Solomon, 'and looked likely to do severe damage to either himself or us. We had no idea who he was. He was standing there, shouting at us, demanding we retract our work "or else". It was farcical, like a 6-year-old whose conker had been stolen. He was worked up into something of a state and I was concerned for Isabelle's safety, so I carefully calculated the likely consequences of my actions before hitting him. I think it was the first time I have ever hit anyone and I must say I rather enjoyed the experience. Casey Ingar is quite small.'[139]

Dons in Sunday morning brawl

NICE!

A fight broke out between two renowned academics last night in Dog Kennel Hill "over the future of mankind".

Solomon Isarebe (pictured), author of Death of the Political Economy, 38, and Casey Ing, an American and a leading figure in the United Nations, came to blows last night outside the home Isarebe shares with his sister.

They told police that they disagreed on methodology for assessing global fertility rates and it had got out of hand. Isarebe said "I was afraid for my safety and for my little sister and felt I had to defend her".

His sister, Isabelle Isarebe, 30, said in a statement, that: "they were both sober and it was over in seconds. No one was hurt and no one was covered in either blood or glory. The police have very kindly agreed not to pursue the matter and both Solomon and Casey are very sorry for any disturbance they caused. They have now decided to work together on an exciting new project."

Neighbour, Marey Deakins, 52, said: "It was disgusting. They were like a pair of animals going at it like they did. We are used to drunks and the odd addict round here, but it makes you worried to go out on the streets when men like that wake you up with their fighting and name calling at 3 on a Sunday morning. I ask you."

CAMBERWELL COURIER 24/09/46

---

139   Isarebe, S, 2067, typed notes for an unpublished autobiography, manuscript dated 24th September 2067, The Isarebe Trust Archives, Cambridge, England (Box 448)

Isarebe and Ingar's violent exchange received more media coverage than the publication of the fertility research, but they were not charged by the police. If Solomon Isarebe had assumed that Ingar would quietly disappear after their fracas, he could not have been more wrong. Solomon woke late the next morning to find Casey Ingar at the breakfast table, deep in conversation with Isabelle, with clearly neither of them having slept. By that evening Casey Ingar was seemingly convinced by their approach and had accepted the job Isabelle offered him, without reference to a stunned Solomon. Isabelle's entry in her diary that day read, 'Met Casey Ingar in somewhat trying circumstances. Dizz and Casey both behaved appallingly, but I thought he was nice anyway and offered him a job. Hope he sticks around.'[140]

They now separated their work into two parts, with Isabelle Isarebe and Casey Ingar managing their work on mortality projections and Solomon taking their CQR research and CIR modelling techniques into the complex field of migration flows, via a research programme they had started a year earlier.

---

140   Isarebe, I, 2046, diary entry dated 24th September 2046, The Isarebe Trust Archives, Cambridge, England (Box 133, Folder 4)

2.4 The discovery of Cheerful Nihilism

Isabelle Isarebe's diaries reveal she was relieved to escape from the claustrophobic and intense atmosphere her brother generated when working and she immediately struck up an efficient and happy working relationship with Casey Ingar, who was only six years her senior. Solomon had been worried about Ingar being sexually interested in Isabelle, but there was no apparent chemistry between them, at least at the beginning of their friendship.

Isabelle Isarebe and Casey Ingar's work on mortality was not ground-breaking from a technical perspective, but it led to the accidental discovery of a previously unrecognised mental health condition. This was a breakthrough of some medical importance, but it also played a part in improving the performance of their mortality models and brought the Isarebe name once more to the public's attention.

Casey Ingar had worked on mortality projections for much of his working life, developing models that isolated the impact of different factors on specific causes of death, from 'snake bites to sexually transmitted diseases.'[141] These factors included: individual behaviours (such as overeating, smoking and drug use); societal impositions (such as work-derived stress, air pollution, food availability and sanitation); medical and pharmaceutical developments; and demographic change. This approach had led him to make predictions of a continued but slowing rise in life expectancy in developed nations, with less developed nations moving towards the mortality level of developed nations. Similar predictions were being made by all the major institutions in the field.

However, a gap had begun to emerge between the predicted and observed death rates in richer economies in the 2030s and 2040s, with a slight and inexplicable rise in mortality. Many casual observers assumed this fall in average age of death was because of the dramatic rise in obesity that had been seen in nearly all countries, or was caused by an increased dependency on opioids and other drugs, or resulted from the impact of a deterioration in air quality and the increased incidence of extreme weather associated with global warming. Isabelle Isarebe and Ingar, along with most other researchers in this field, believed these factors should already be captured by existing models and there must therefore be other unidentified forces at play.

Isabelle Isarebe had worked as a 'Remote Summer Intern' at JB Academic

---

141   Ingar, C, 2047, profile page on the Isarebe & Isarebe website, October 2047–December 2050, www.isarebeandisarebe.com

Research Institute in her teens and had been involved in a project examining ways of engaging the elderly in greater online economic consumption. She had always had a nagging doubt, triggered by watching hours of interviews with elderly people, that it was not technological fear or resistance to change that was the issue for some older people, but a quiet unstated nihilistic lethargy. What she had observed was many of these people, who had been retired for ten, twenty or even thirty years, played no active part in the wider world and had little intellectual or physical stimulus outside of time-passing interest groups and passive media consumption. When this was combined with an increasing list of painful or malfunctioning body parts, she observed a small but significant minority displayed little interest in active living, even though they showed no conventional signs of depression or other mental illness. 'They are alive, but only like moss or lichen. The worst thing is, I sense they think they have no value to others.'[142]

Whilst planning their mortality research Isabelle discussed this with her brother, who said anomalies in his environmental research at The Bates Institute had also suggested to him some older people behaved markedly differently to the rest of their cohort. Isabelle also talked with Rita Bortelli, but Bortelli said she was legally restricted from discussing Digger's research, but hinted she thought there was something in Isabelle's hypothesis. Casey Ingar was also receptive to Isabelle's ideas, having watched his mother wither and die over the previous five years, in a tragic end to what had been a life of adventure.

Isabelle Isarebe and Ingar developed a tentative hypothesis that for some older people their sense of separateness and lack of essentialness in the lives of others, left them silently, secretly, or even perhaps unknowingly, willing for death: a will so strong it affected their ability to respond to health problems. As unlikely as it seemed to them, Isabelle Isarebe and Ingar wondered if this could be the unexplained factor, or one of the unexplained factors, in the slight decrease in life expectancy being observed in the developed world. They were hypothesising a quiet suicide from will power alone.

In one contemporary account of Isabelle Isarebe she was described as 'the quiet light to Solomon Isarebe's roaring darkness.'[143] It seemed her 'rational positivism'[144] lit up any room, argument or intellectual endeavour and many believed the optimism at the heart of *Future Perfect* was 'the distilled essence of Isabelle Isarebe.'[145] Therefore this idea of a mass urge for extinction was an

142   Isarebe, I, 2036, diary entry dated 17th August 2036, The Isarebe Trust Archives, Cambridge, England (Box 76, Folder 4)
143   Knight, D, 2047, *Names to watch: Isabelle Isarebe*, People Watcher, 23rd June 2047, p. 23
144   Bortelli, R, 2070, *The Dizzy Digger*, Manchosens, New York, p. 12
145   Colvin, A, 2099, *The Strange Affair of Isabelle and Solomon Isarebe*, Sheaders, London, p. 93

extremely uncomfortable hypothesis for her to consider: 'I find it an almost unbearable thought that we may have constructed a model for living out old age so awful, such a denial these people ever had a purpose, that some are willing themselves to death, doing all they can to defy medical advances that would give them an extra few years. I hope we are wrong.'[146]

In an attempt to test this hypothesis, Isabelle Isarebe and Ingar started a research programme among the over 65s in three wealthy countries (the UK, Italy, and Japan), three middle income countries (Brazil, Romania and Thailand) and three poorer countries (Uganda, Pakistan and Cambodia).

That there was a strong positive relationship between wealth, health infrastructure and life expectancy was already well known. Their research also showed that 'the young old' in richer countries, defined as those between 65 and 74 years old, were generally happier than those from lower income nations. However, among the 'old old', aged 75 years and over, this was turned on its head. A small but significant number in this older age group in richer nations showed a sudden decline in life satisfaction, which did not correlate with illness or personal circumstances, whereas life satisfaction was relatively stable in less wealthy countries, even as people reached extreme old age, provided their health was reasonable. The research suggested the longer someone had not been an economic participant or had not had some active role in the broader community, the more likely they were to experience this chronic condition. However, whilst there may have been a long gestation period, there appeared to be a sudden cliff over which people fell into this state. Those who had worked for longer into old age – for example, in a family business – or who had retained a meaningful and useful role in the community rather than a token role, were less likely to show these signs.

These qualitative research results, which were eventually independently verified in studies by a number of medical research groups, suggested this syndrome was not about physical health, known mental health issues, wealth, access to medical care, or whether someone lived alone or with someone else.

They called this phenomenon of a sudden deterioration in happiness among some older people 'De-Integration',[147] after the complex set of circumstances it seemed to correlate with. They also observed some of those they classified as 'De-Integrated' (or 'DI') were generally thought of as positive, happy people, even though they had an overwhelming sense of no

---

146   Isarebe, I, 2026, diary entry dated 1st November 2046, The Isarebe Trust Archives, Cambridge, England (Box 137, Folder 1)
147   Isarebe, I and Ingar, C, 2047, *Mortality projections to 2150 and the impact of de-integration on life expectancy*, Isarebe & Isarebe Publications, London, p. 3

longer being a useful part of the world, leaving them 'cheerfully nihilistic'.[148] It was 'Cheerful Nihilism' that seeped into the cultural lexicon, rather than the arguably more accurate, but clumsy, De-Integration.

Isabelle Isarebe and Ingar discussed their initial conclusions with a wide range of mental health practitioners and researchers and many of these thought DI, if it existed, was a synonym for feeling isolated and/or depressed, but Isarebe and Ingar believed it was something different. This difference was important to them, because those other factors were already accounted for in existing mortality models.

Isarebe and Ingar first realised that 'our worst dreams are being realised and our hypothesis seems to have some merit'[149] through their extensive qualitative research, but they found it difficult to quantify this phenomenon, as it was not something that people could, or perhaps more pertinently, wanted to self-identify as. Without this quantitative evidence they would be unable to test whether it was a factor in observed changes in mortality. Whilst they realised that the incidence of DI was correlated with the amount of time since an individual had felt integrated into society and the diversity of an individual's social network, this information was insufficient to determine if an individual was de-integrated or not.

Isabelle and Casey discussed this with Solomon, who thought they may find a solution in some adaptation of the eye-tracking and body movement technology they were using in the CQR research. Isabelle was introduced to Heulwen Gröning, who was still working in the Department of Experimental Psychology at Bangor University. It was already well established that unconsciously we often look first and/or longest at things which are of most interest and pertinence to us, so Gröning thought using eye-tracking in combination with appropriate images may provide some clues as to whether or not someone was DI. Isabelle and Gröning experimented with tracking eye movements of respondents when they were presented with a digital collage of images. A small number of these images were subtly associated with facets of de-integration, such as silence, death, aloneness, power loss, inability to articulate or be heard, and loss of societal purpose. They found that the more subtle the association, the more likely it was those previously identified as de-integrated in the qualitative research would spend time looking at these types of images.

This process was refined in subsequent waves of research, such that they were eventually able to estimate that 4% of 65- to 75-year-olds in wealthy

---

148 Isarebe, I and Ingar, C, 2047, *Mortality projections to 2150 and the impact of de-integration on life expectancy*, Isarebe & Isarebe Publications, London, p. 9
149 Ingar, C, 2047, email to Solomon Isarebe dated 2nd March 2047, The Isarebe Trust Archives, Cambridge, England (Box 140, Folder 2)

countries such as the UK and the US could be characterised as de-integrated, rising to 9% among 75- to 80-year-olds and peaking at 13% in 80- to 85-year-olds, after which the proportion slowly declined.

The proportions were different across the world, but there were people identified as de-integrated in all countries and cultures, although they were less prevalent in poorer countries where older people tended to live in or close to more extended families, and retained an importance in the wider community longer into old age.

When DI was added as an explanatory factor into existing mortality models, it seemed to account for some of the 'errors' that had been observed.

This was an important discovery because it implied that medical intervention and treatment among the de-integrated was less effective than with other groups of the same age, health and economic circumstance. Their state of mind appeared to impact the effectiveness of some treatments. Isabelle and Ingar had no explanation as to why this should be the case and did not pretend they had made anything more than a statistical discovery. It was not until 2083 that Rydal[150] found a link between DI and an area of the brain responsible for some aspects of immune response. By this time DI had been the subject of numerous medical research projects and was eventually characterised as a form of depression which was termed 'Will Suppression Syndrome', a term Solomon Isarebe ridiculed, as 'DI seems to me the ultimate expression of Will Power'.[151]

Although it has now been known about for over 100 years, no effective medical or therapeutic treatment has ever been found for DI once it has developed, and as previously poor countries have become more affluent it has started to become more common in these places too. However, its discovery was important in that it encouraged many initiatives to keep older people part of 'the core societal programme',[152] thereby reducing the numbers going on to develop DI.

This new factor in their mortality models was one of many forecast assumptions the Isarebe & Isarebe team made. One of the other important assumptions they made related to the impact of medical interventions, in particular AI Medical Support systems (AIMS). Primitive AIMS systems had been around since the 2020s, but were still not in widespread use in the 2040s. Artificial Intelligence, the use of machine learning to replicate and/

---

150   Rydal, H, 2084, *Response of the immune system in Will Suppression Syndrome cases*, The New Lancet, 934, 4, pp. 234–312

151   Isarebe, S, 2084, note to himself dated 3rd December 2084, The Isarebe Trust Archives, Cambridge, England (Box 591, Folder 1)

152   US Government, 2063, *Bridging the gaps: Integrating the isolated*, Department of Age and Culture, Washington, pp. 23–27

or advance the activities of humans, was viewed with some scepticism and many at the time rejected the idea of even a partial replacement of people in a medical setting.

The widespread fear of the impact of AI in the early decades of the 21st century seems luddite in retrospect and perhaps had as much to do with the impact of science fiction as available fact. The anthropomorphisation of AI during this period also showed a certain collective arrogance, in that it inferred humans were the model of perfection that robots and AI would do well to replicate. As Professor Magdalene Davis from the Institute for Dissemination of Scientific Intelligence stated as early as 2032, 'Who in their right mind would spend thousands of people years and billions of Euros, designing something based on the human model with all its known flaws: its limited consciously accessible processing power; its irrationality; its recency bias; its ever-evolving, unreliable and fast disappearing memory; its massive loss of computing power in the presence of anything vaguely sexually attractive; its mood swings; and its desire for drug-induced oblivion? The only reasons I can see for modelling anything on a human being would be because we dance so well, are good drivers when we're not singing along to Abba, and have such nice soft skin.'

AI has proved to be little more than a continuation of the straight-line development in the usefulness and application of computing in human affairs that has taken place since the 1960s and has proven to be a good friend to most. That no major institution is now seeking to replicate the human in robotic form is testament to changes in attitudes over the past century. In a recent survey, less than half of people correctly chose 'Artificial Intelligence Systems', when asked what 'AI Systems' meant, with 53% opting for the other choice offered, 'Applied Information Systems'.

At the time of the Isarebes' research in the mid-2040s, AIMS systems had just started to be used in mainstream healthcare. In 2045, the percentage of first medical assessments undertaken by AIMS was around 14% in the USA, which at that time was at the forefront of developments in this area. This compares to a global figure in 2150 of 93%.[153]

It was Solomon Isarebe, who had been assessed by AIMS in a hotel when he had fallen ill on a trip to Seattle, who suggested to his sister the potential impact of this technology on global life expectancy. The ability of AIMS to deliver first-class medical diagnoses to people anywhere in the world, almost irrespective of their wealth, seems obvious to us now, but it was still seen by many at that time as having most potential in more developed economies.

---

153   2150, US Department of Health and Life Transition, www.halt.gov [accessed 14th January 2150]

It's so bloody obvs that AIMS could deliver first world medical care to people from Bangladesh to Benin. All it would need is a medical technician to take measurements and case notes and AIMS could recommend the required treatment – and it is going to be more reliable and accurate than a medic with 10 years' training and 20 years' experience, not even taking into account that a real doctor may have not slept in the previous 24 hours. And it would never get bored, have a hangover, or be having sexual thoughts about the last patient.

Much of the time the treatment is going to be pharmaceutical, rather than surgical or therapeutic, so as long as drugs are available and cheap enough, then the impact on the developing world could be extraordinary. And this would open up new markets to a struggling pharmaceutical industry – so why wouldn't they fund it?

It seems impossible I could be wrong.[154]

Solomon Isarebe rarely thought he could be wrong, but in this instance his belief in his own wisdom was justified. Isabelle Isarebe was sensible enough to realise that such a radical assumption would need external validation, if it was to be seen as credible. She discussed Solomon's ideas with Casey Ingar's old medical colleagues and they put her in touch with high-level contacts in major pharmaceutical companies, as well as some leading medical academics. They too thought it 'bloody obvious' and an inevitable development over the next thirty to forty years. Thus, Isabelle Isarebe and Ingar felt confident in making the assumption of a dramatic rise in the distribution and use of AIMS, which in turn would lead to significant falls in deaths from communicable diseases in the developing world, where they still accounted for a large number of fatalities each year.

AI Medical Support systems took many years to migrate outside of a formal healthcare setting, but they are now available in nearly three-quarters of households around the world. In 2149, 71% of all ailments in the USA were diagnosed and treated by the patient themselves, and it is only when treatment requires less common or more addictive drugs, surgery, or in-hospital care, that professional medical care is generally accessed. This has reduced the real-term cost of primary medical care per capita by 54% in the USA since 2050, although the use of pharmaceutical interventions has increased by over 120% during the same period, with a quarter of this increase said to be because

154   Isarebe, I, 2045, handwritten notes dated 3rd October 2045, The Isarebe Trust Archives, Cambridge, England (Box 125, Folder 6)

those self-diagnosing tend to 'prescribe' more than a medical professional would if examining a patient with the same symptoms.

Isabelle Isarebe and Ingar's mortality models also included a number of other revisions to prevailing assumptions on mortality, including: an improvement in obesity through innovation in food design and a slow trend towards more plant-based food; a levelling-off in drug dependency through changes in pharmaceutical formulations; a reduction in income inequality driven by changes in job demand-supply balance, reducing the proportion of people classified as 'economically health impoverished';[155] an increase in the number of over 70s still working, driven by shortages of people in traditional working age groups, with associated improvements in physical and mental health; and greater migration from poorer nations to richer nations, with associated rises in longevity for those individuals moving to richer countries. Solomon Isarebe's research into migration eventually caused them to revise this last assumption.

When all of their assumptions were incorporated into their forecasting model, they concluded that by 2090 life expectancy in the developing world, even in previously very poor countries in sub-Saharan Africa, would have increased to within six or seven years of life expectancy in the developed world. Their prediction was for a degree of global health equality as miraculous as it was unexpected. History has shown they were optimistic about the rate of roll-out of AIMS and the willingness or ability of the pharmaceutical industry to finance the needs of the developing world, but by the early years of the 22nd century almost all of their predictions had come to fruition. Now, in 2150, with the exception of countries involved in military conflict or having recently experienced a natural disaster, average life expectancy in 98% of all countries lies within the range of 79 to 85 years, with life expectancy in Benin now exceeding life expectancy in Baltimore. Average global life expectancy has now been at or around 81 years for more than half a century.

These results on mortality were first published in June 2047. Whilst their work on fertility rates had caused a small stir in the academic press and among their professional rivals, this work hit the mainstream, although not for their predictions of fast-converging life expectancy, but for 'Cheerful Nihilism'. The press leapt on it and it hit the headlines around the world. It made a minor media star of Solomon Isarebe, whose natural style seemed to suit the message. Headlines at the time suggested 'Mass suicide by old people', far from the intention of Isabelle Isarebe and Ingar, although Solomon Isarebe, whilst never endorsing these headlines, perhaps could have done more to repudiate them. Solomon got the credit for the work, even though he stressed

---

155   There has been a slight increase in income inequality over the past century.

it had been undertaken by Isabelle and Casey Ingar. Solomon flourished in the public arena; his shyness and misanthropy were cast aside and he seemed to find a release and freedom once he stepped on to a stage. His public persona cast long shadows over all those around him. Isabelle was happy to avoid the public's gaze, but for Ingar this was the first in a long line of painful lessons of what it meant to work for Solomon Isarebe and his invisibility 'as one of the dancing girls in Solomon's travelling circus.'[156]

Cartoon by Noj, 2047

The hubbub soon receded, but their work alerted governments and large institutions to a number of potentially valuable ideas: the reduction in health costs that could be achieved through greater investment in AIMS; the possibility of increasing the pension age under the guise of improving the mental health of the nation – an increase which all governments knew would be necessary given the fall in the proportion of people of traditional working age; and a redirection of priorities in health spending.

The Isarebes and Ingar set up a consultancy, III Health, to examine and advise on these issues. III Health was financed by Rita Bortelli and Casey Ingar became its first Research Director. It was successful in its field and employed

156   Bortelli, R, 2070, *The Dizzy Digger*, Manchosens, New York, p. 263

over 800 people at one stage in the late 2050s, with offices in Dubai, Hong Kong, London, Mumbai, Munich, New York and San Francisco. Solomon Isarebe had little interest in III Health and never took an active part in any of its projects. He was happy to be wheeled out for important presentations and client meetings, but he said he felt like 'a buffed-up pig wearing a pink bow at a country fair'.[157] He sold his and Isabelle's 66% shareholding in III Health to Ingar and Bortelli in 2062 for $2. Its estimated value at the time was $900m ($6.8bn in today's money).

Isarebe & Isarebe now had the means to make predictions of aggregate global population growth through to 2150, but they realised such macro-level forecasts would be too abstract and of little interest to the general public. People would want to know what was going to happen in their own country and to do that meant incorporating assumptions on migration. The Isarebes, Ingar and Bortelli made the decision that before they made any further public announcements they would not only complete their population projections for each nation of the world, but also make an assessment of what this meant for the economy, the environment, and land use.

---

157   Isarebe, S, 2058, diary entry dated 27th February 2058, The Isarebe Trust Archives, Cambridge, England (Box 312, Folder 4)

2.5 The world on its feet

The final component in the construction of the Isarebe's nation-by-nation population forecasts was to predict what would happen to migration.

Solomon Isarebe was fascinated with migration and migration law, perhaps catalysed by an unusual personal experience when he first went to the USA as a 19-year-old, accompanying Professor D. Kamil to a conference in Denver. After the conference, Professor Kamil went on from Denver to Washington, leaving Isarebe to fly home on his own. Somewhere between his hotel room and airport check-in, Isarebe lost his cards, his phone and his passport. Unconcerned, he went to the US Border Force office in Denver Airport and asked them how he should get home.

Then, as now, there is a standard process for providing emergency passports for travellers who have lost their documentation. But something went wrong for Isarebe: 'Perhaps I was a bit bolshy from the off, some people say I can be sometimes, and then my head went a bit foggy with all their pointless and repetitive questions, and it didn't help they were all in uniform. Then I noticed and they noticed that my accent had started to go a bit funny and then I accidentally pushed one of the officers who had terrible bad breath and kept getting really close to my face – his breath literally smelt like shit. I only pushed him a bit, more of a nudge, but about ten of them got their guns out and I unfortunately went totally mentaloid as they cuffed me. It was [expletive] awful.'[158]

The situation soon calmed down, but the documentation problem escalated, as Isarebe had literally no identification and in his befuddled state couldn't remember any contact details of his family or friends and for a while couldn't remember his own name or where he lived. The electronic records available to the Border Force officers in the airport showed up his illegal status when he first arrived in London as a 9-year-old, but not his subsequent adoption or registration as a dual British-Swedish national. He was reluctantly arrested as an illegal alien by increasingly sympathetic officials and was put in detention at the airport. At 9 p.m. that night, Professor Kamil arrived back in Denver from Washington, having been alerted by the hotel they had found Isarebe's documentation. The situation was quickly resolved and Isarebe arrived back in London the next day. However, whenever Isarebe went to

---

158   Isarebe, S, 2028, diary entry dated 1st July 2028, The Isarebe Trust Archives, Cambridge, England (Box 24, Folder 2)

America after this incident, he was always stopped, sometimes for hours, at passport control, after his status as 'Illegal Alien' flashed up on the screen.

Migration was the area the Isarebes were most wary of analysing, even though it was a relatively minor factor in their models. Migration only has a small impact on the total global population; that it has any affect at all is because migrants tend to adopt the birth rates of their host nations and their health and longevity after migrating reflects the health infrastructure of where they have chosen to live. However, whilst migration is not critical at a global level, it is of some importance at a national level in determining population growth, and is even more important as a political issue.

Migration forecasts made by other institutions in the 2040s were hampered by the quality of available data, the complexity of the forecasting task and the political emotions that any migration forecasts stirred. As Isarebe said in 2057:

> Only a sucker would forecast migration. You'll be ridiculed and labelled a fascist or a super-wet liberal, depending on what you came up with and who the critic is, irrespective of whether you turn out to be right or wrong. It's one of those areas where rationality and the desire for truth has long since left the building.

> I hate to say this, but I was tempted to stick to the 'business as usual' school of migration forecasting, but then I kept thinking about Nigeria. We knew it was going to go from a medium-sized, slightly chaotic, oil-producing country into an economic giant within a period of fifty years and how could changes on this scale not fundamentally impact migration patterns in some way? Why would people in the future want to move from a dynamic country such as Nigeria to a Spain or an Italy, or any of the old economic powers, who are shrinking in significance at a rate of knots and are often not very welcoming when you get there if your skin is the wrong colour?

> And Venessa, why would the US still be seen as the dreamland destination when it's struggling to maintain economic growth, is no longer the 'world's leader and defender' and after it lost any moral high ground it may once have had in the data disasters of the '30s and '40s?

> And all this was before thinking about the impact of climate change. If there was going to be a literal change in the shape of land masses

because of rising sea levels and new weather patterns were going to threaten old-school crop viability, then surely this would impact on where people wanted to live? It turned out this was a marginal issue, but it was worth thinking about and it'll be worth monitoring in the future.

In the end, my sister and I decided we should at least think about all these things and I'm glad we had a go, despite the crappy ill-informed reactionary response of many of our critics.[159]

Migration was, and continues to be, one of the hardest areas to forecast. There are many reasons for this, but back in the 2030s and 2040s a big part of the problem was poor historic data, making reliable, statistically based, predictive modelling difficult. More fundamentally, the data series showed great volatility, caused by major shocks such as the Syrian and Ukrainian Wars in the early 21st century and smaller shocks such as those felt from politically driven changes in rules, regulations and quotas. This may seem unlikely now, when there is fierce competition for immigrants, but many governments were winning elections at that time on promises to cut immigration and were imposing strict curbs on entry.

Most migration forecasts prepared in the 2040s were based on one of three alternative approaches: the extrapolation of historic people flows, with simple assumptions on whether this rate may grow or decline in the longer term, with little statistical justification; aggregation of 'expert opinion', an approach widely discredited in the 2030s and 2040s; and simple regression models, with socio-demographic indices as the main driver of change. These indices were often an aggregate measure combining income, education and fertility. Many dealt separately with refugees and economic migrants.

The Isarebes were not dismissive of these approaches, as they could see data limitations and the complexity of predicting people movements tied the hands of those producing these forecasts. There were 195 recognised countries and territories around the world in 2040, which meant that modelling flows between all of these countries would in theory require nearly 38,000 models, each constrained by the necessity of the sum of all the migration forecasts adding to zero each year.

The Isarebes wanted to use a different approach, explicitly recognising that migration was about individual and household decisions. These decisions were complex and were determined not only by the collective will

---

159   Venessa, 2057, *Modern Lives with Venessa: Solomon D. Isarebe*, National and Regional Public Media / BIBC Media, 16th August 2057

of the household, but also by the morass of rules and regulations regarding migration and the emotional and financial cost of moving. They wanted to investigate the full complexity of these decisions, but then construct a forecasting system that was simple enough to be workable and credible, whilst being flexible enough to estimate the impact of political decision-making on migrant flows in the future.[160]

Although their research approach appears relatively straightforward in principle, the questionnaire design and underlying modelling were complex, more complex than their earlier fertility study. Once again, they were to complete a forty-country research study, this time involving nearly 250,000 separate interviews.

Their research and subsequent models enabled the Isarebes to predict the movement of people around the world under different conditions. Some of the most important variables in their models were: the immediate economic and cultural differences people would experience after migration from one country to another; what they termed the 'Life Time Differential' (LTD)[161] of living in their chosen host country compared with their home country; and the emotional, financial and bureaucratic barriers people faced moving from one country to another.

As they expected, their models overestimated the numbers migrating, indicating that emotional barriers to moving were higher than people anticipated when looking at the choices in a research situation, when there was no consequence to their 'decision', and also because many respondents underestimated restrictions on entry to their preferred destination. However, the difference between actual and predicted migration was relatively consistent within each demographic group and between countries, such that they felt they could legitimately apply scaling factors to generate realistic forecasts. When they tested the models through 'backcasting' – that is to re-estimate historic levels of migration – they found the models performed much better than previous models with regards both to numbers of refugees and economic migrants.

Their refugee models quantified the migration response to 'shocks' such as war and famine. Despite the extensive and expensive research they conducted with refugees, they did not use the results in their final population forecasts, as they felt they could not reliably predict when or where the 'shock conditions' would occur in the future. However, whilst they could not predict the occurrence of shock conditions, their models fairly reliably estimated

---

160   More details of their approach, which involved the use of CQR research and CIR modelling, are given in Appendix 4.
161   Isarebe, S and I, 2050, *Future Perfect*, Cambridge and Oxford University Press, Cambridge, pp. 119–112

the number of refugee movements catalysed by any such shock. Updated and refined versions of these models are still used by some emergency aid agencies today, perhaps because no one has ever repeated such a large-scale research exercise.

Having decided it was impossible to incorporate their work on refugees into their forecasting model, they instead used the approach adopted by most other organisations, which was to use the historic average percentage of the world population who were refugees each year and then assume they would return to their country of origin within ten years. The Isarebes decided the error this crude approach introduced into their forecasts was insignificant.

They felt under some pressure from environmentalists to conclude climate change would radically impact migration levels; the rise of so called 'climate refugees'. Whilst the Isarebes examined this issue, the data suggested such migrants were practically non-existent at that time, so they were unable to incorporate them into their research and models. History has shown climate refugees have remained a very small proportion of all refugees. There were some people who migrated in the second half of the 21st century at least partly because of climate change, but they represented less than 1% of all migrants. What the Isarebes did not realise, although it would not have affected their forecasts, was there was going to be substantial relocation of people driven by climate change within some countries, particularly in the early decades of the 22nd century.

Their final forecasts of migration differed significantly from those produced by other institutions. They predicted migration would continue to increase from the developing world to the developed world through to 2080, before rapidly falling and then reversing in the first decades of the 22nd century. This anticipation of a reversal of migrant flows was largely a result of their predictions of changes in the Life Time Differential (LTD) between countries, particularly where the homelands of potential migrants had previously been relatively poor. Their modelling showed there was a rapid drop in migration from one country to another if the LTD between the two countries dropped to less than 24%, this 24% roughly equating to the perceived value of the communal, language and cultural ties to their homeland.

The Isarebes predicted that the great homes of migrants in the 19th, 20th and 21st century (in particular Canada, USA, and Australia) would see net outward migration by the end of their forecast period.

They went on to prepare migration forecasts under many different scenarios, assuming different forms of political action to reverse these changes in migration patterns. These scenarios included elimination of quotas, streamlining of application processes and incentivisation of migration – the fabled 'Golden Hellos'.[162] In all of these scenarios, the barrier to migration was reduced. As economic theory would predict, this resulted in an increase in 'demand' and suggested more people would migrate if these incentives were offered. But, what these models also showed was this was likely to be a temporary phenomenon, as many of these migrants would start to return to their home countries within ten years. Their simulations suggested that any financial incentivisation would be expensive and would have little long-term impact. This did not stop many countries from trying to incentivise migration, as they still do today.

Solomon Isarebe became convinced migration, alongside fertility decline, was going 'to get so hot, there will be blood',[163] in a chillingly prescient prediction of the migration wars of the 2090s (see Epilogue).

---

162   Smith-Jai, J, 2101, Presidential address to joint US congress, 21st April 2101, www. potusarchive.org [accessed 3rd January 2150]
163   Isarebe, S, 2047, diary entry dated 4th December 2047, The Isarebe Trust Archives, Cambridge, England (Box 142, Folder 7)

PART 3
Life after Isabelle Isarebe

3.1 The death of Isabelle Isarebe

As they approached the end of their work on migration, the final component needed to prepare their country-by-country population forecasts, it could have been a time for celebration and reflection, but Solomon and Isabelle Isarebe's life together was to come to a terrible halt.

In March 2048, after more than five years of continuous and arduous work and endless travel around the world, Solomon and Isabelle were finally convinced by everyone around them they needed to take an extended break. After months of resistance, they agreed to undertake a short tour of Africa, a continent they both loved. For the first time they left Isarebe & Isarebe and III Health in the hands of Casey Ingar and the rest of the team in London. Isarebe & Isarebe and III Health employed nearly 200 people by this time, with offices in London and New York.

Solomon and Isabelle started their recuperation in South Africa and worked their way up the continent, visiting Mooketsi Mooketsi and his young family in Botswana, and then flying to Kenya, before eventually visiting Alexandria, near their first home together on the north coast of Egypt. After nearly three weeks away, Solomon flew on to Delhi for a presentation for III Health, while Isabelle travelled to Aleppo to visit a cousin, her only surviving relative in Syria, whom she had not seen for many years. Her cousin, Shahd El-Eisaa, was three years older than Isabelle and was a doctor, as her mother and Isabelle's birth mother had been before her.

Shahd was also single and assumed Isabelle would want to experience the single life in Syria. Isabelle politely but unenthusiastically agreed and she was taken on a three-day tour of the nightclubs, restaurants and sights of Aleppo. Isabelle started to feel a little unwell after the second day, but she put it down to alcohol, to which she was unaccustomed. El-Eisaa and her friends were heavy drinkers.

After visiting her cousin in Aleppo, Solomon had arranged for his sister to visit the ruins of Palmyra before returning to London. When they were young they had both been encouraged to think of the Eastern Mediterranean as the birthplace of their family and Isabelle had been read a myriad of stories by Jannik and Reba on Syrian history. Although they had both moaned at 'this endless woke education on our non-existent roots,'[164] they had loved the story of how Palmyra had started to rise from the ashes after its near destruction during the

---

164   Isarebe, S, 2023, hand-written notes dated 3rd December 2023, The Isarebe Trust Archives, Cambridge, England (Box 17, Folder 7)

early years of the Syrian Civil War and they had even built a model of the Arch of Triumph in plasticine, plaster and cardboard, which their mother kept for many years on a shelf in Hilman Cottage.

A car picked up Isabelle from Shahd El-Eisaa's house, with a driver and a security guard, as there were occasional problems with rogue militias in Syria. Isabelle was still feeling unwell and slept for most of the four-hour journey from Aleppo to Palmyra. According to the testimony of the security guard, she had been cheerful if quiet when they arrived at Palmyra and had started to wander the site, with the guard and the driver walking 15 metres behind her.

> She was a lovely woman. Such a beautiful Syrian English woman. She moved quite fast, but with a funny walk, and we had trouble keeping up with her. Near the Temple of Baalshamin there were two small broken-down walls and we saw her climbing one. We shouted to her, because it was not allowed to climb on the monument and she turned and smiled at us and put her thumb up in the air.

> I don't know how it happened, but she seemed to slip and disappeared from our sight. We ran to help her and we found her lying between the two broken down walls, in a small channel, maybe for ancient water or something. She was lying on her back and was sort of laughing. We were so happy she was alright, so we started laughing too. There was not even a tiny bit of blood. She couldn't have fallen more than a metre. I took a photo of her afterwards. She didn't look so good in the photo, but she said to us she was total okay.[165]

After they helped her out, they took her to a café, where she was still talking and smiling, although looking a little shaken, according to the café owner in his later written statement.[166] She went to the ladies' room, but hadn't returned after 15 minutes, so the guard asked the café owner to take a look.

She had collapsed in the toilet and was unconscious. An ambulance was called, but there had been a major road traffic accident that day and congestion meant it took the paramedics 20 minutes to arrive. She was taken to a nearby private hospital, where they suspected her collapse was the result of a heart condition, but they did not have the equipment necessary for a detailed diagnosis. A further 4 hours later she was admitted to the main hospital in the region, by which time Shahd El-Eisaa had arrived from Aleppo.

---

165   Syrian Justice and Security Department, 2048, *Transcript of Coroner's Inquest into the death of Isabelle Isarebe*, 12th – 16th December 2048, pp. 232–3
166   Syrian Justice and Security Department, 2048, *Transcript of Coroner's Inquest into the death of Isabelle Isarebe*, 12th – 16th December 2048, pp. 241–3

Isabelle Isarebe, Palmyra, 2048

Isabelle Isarebe died 3 hours after Shahd El-Eisaa arrived. She was 32 years old.

Her post-mortem concluded that she had been suffering from endocarditis. This is a bacterial infection of the endocardium, the inner lining of the heart. It is a rare infection, particularly in young people, but they found that Isabelle had been susceptible to this infection because of an undiagnosed congenital heart condition – a mild form of pulmonary valve stenosis. In many cases this is not fatal, but it was believed the unavoidable delay in treatment, particularly in administering antibiotics, and Isabelle's poor physical condition after such a long period of sustained work, had contributed to her death from heart failure.

Two days later, Jannik Isarebe, Reba Isarebe, Casey Ingar and Rita Bortelli arrived at Shahd El-Eisaa's home in Aleppo. Solomon Isarebe had sent a text[167] to Rita and said he was too busy to come. Rita arranged through the UK Embassy for a secular ceremony and cremation in Aleppo, before Isabelle's ashes were taken home to Garway Hill where they were scattered on the hillside. At her later memorial service Casey Ingar sang a song to the congregation in a breaking tenor; the song was Bayu Bayushki Bayu, a Russian

---

167   A form of digital communication used from the late 20th century to the mid-21st century.

lullaby her father had sung to Isabelle as a child and which she in turn had sometimes sung to Casey Ingar.

Jannik and Reba Isarebe were desolate, losing their youngest, cherished, 'delicate, brilliant, songbird'.[168] Their loss was made more intense by the disappearance of Solomon Isarebe, who had not returned from India and had not been in touch after his initial message to Rita Bortelli. Bortelli stayed with the Isarebes for two weeks after they returned from Syria, doing the small, practical things needed to keep life going at Hilman Cottage. After two weeks, Reba Isarebe took her to one side and told her to 'go home and do your own crying now'.[169] Isabelle's small, strange, grieving family, were once more flung wide over the world.

Casey Ingar reacted badly to Isabelle's death. Everyone had known he had been in love with Isabelle since the first day they met, back in October 2046. No one but Ingar knew that Isabelle had started to feel some reciprocation of those feelings. It was revealed in her diaries, not published until 2064, that she declared her affection towards him in the spring of 2047, whilst on a field trip together in Italy:

> I told Case how I felt today. A genuine, small love for him. An un-encompassing love. A love I would never mourn, but could enjoy. I don't even know if this feeling can be love, if the term love is defined by the common experience. A romantic love without much sexual desire – what does that mean? I told him all this and said I may be happy with him, but that my first concern, my first thought of the day would always be for Solly and my second for Mooky.

> I have never seen a man's face look like Case's did today. Words won't come to me to describe it. A starving man sat in front of a plate of tainted food, was how he put it. He always thinks in food metaphors. I felt desolate for my honesty. I just wish I'd let him continue his misery of hope.

> I thought better of him for having the pride to reject me. He said he wanted all of me and if he couldn't have all of me, he would have none. It was sweet, but stupid, too Hollywood, too what you're supposed to say. It did hurt a bit too. I've been alone for too long and sort of longed for someone to kiss me, with some affection and a dusting of lust.

168   Isarebe, R, 2054, *Chosen Poet*, O'Daley's, London, p. 167
169   Isarebe, R, 2054, *Chosen Poet*, O'Daley's, London, p. 171

I hope he sticks around though. Sol would kill me if he left.[170]

Casey Ingar did stick around and took on increasing responsibility for Isarebe & Isarebe's work during Solomon's absence after Isabelle's death, despite or perhaps because of his own grief. Solomon Isarebe managed to completely disappear, which was not easy in a time where most citizens voluntarily allowed the state and technology companies to have them under almost constant surveillance.

Although Solomon's diaries and notebooks are particularly sparse during this period and mostly undated, it seems he initially wandered through India, often on foot, sometimes taking trains. His credit records show he stayed in Goa at a retreat for three days, before disappearing again for nearly a month. He resurfaced near Srinagar in Kashmir. From Srinagar, he sent a postcard to Jannik and Reba:

> Sorry. I can't think of the two of you without crying and I don't want to cry any more. I am okay and will be home. You and Izzy sit right in the middle of me. Tell Case I cry for him too. D.[171]

Solomon Isarebe started to access Isarebe & Isarebe files remotely in July 2048 and from records of the times he was logging in, it appears likely he was located in the USA, although his work hours were rarely conventional. He eventually turned up at III Health offices in New York, in a furious temper, angry there was no one there to meet him. The only person there was the security guard. It was 9 a.m., 25th December 2048.

The guard had no idea who he was and was concerned both for the health of the man and for his own safety. He called the police, who took Isarebe, under duress, to New Manhattan General Hospital. Isarebe became more and more agitated at being detained. The doctors were considering committing him to a psychiatric facility, but they heeded his plea to call Hetty Brown.

Hetty Brown was in the middle of preparing Christmas dinner when the call came through. She left her family to complete the preparations and made the journey from Roosevelt Island to New Manhattan General in just 20 minutes, managing to call Rita Bortelli, Reba Isarebe and Casey Ingar on the way. She arrived at the hospital and found the sight of the man the doctors said was Isarebe distressing:

---

170   Kiernan, B, 2064 *The diaries of Isabelle Isarebe; the forgotten genius*, Black and Brown's, London, pp. 312-3

171   Isarebe, S, 2048, postcard to Jannik and Reba Isarebe dated 23rd June 2048, The Isarebe Trust Archives, Cambridge, England (Box 147, Folder 1)

He was almost weightless. I thought of stick insects as soon as I saw this dude, whoever he was. A stick insect with a terrible beard and filthy matted hair. If I'd seen this guy begging on the sidewalk I would've walked round him and hurried on by. But any doubt I had that it was Solomon was gone as soon as he started talking. He was SO Solomon D. Isarebe. Angry, articulate and totally awesome. His normal sane self. I started laughing as soon as I heard him. The doctors must have thought I was mad. Solomon looked up from his rant and saw me. He grinned and jumped over the offending medic and gave me a kiss on the nose – as close to affectionate as I've ever known him. It took me about three hours to persuade them who he was and there was not a thing wrong with him and that he was always rude like this. I then had to explain to the police officer that Ill Health, where the officer had first encountered him, was his business. It wasn't until I said he was English that they finally relented.[172]

By 2 p.m., Hetty and Solomon were in Hetty's car, heading over Queensboro Bridge.

I asked him, 'What you got in your bag, Solster?' He normally hated it when I called him that, but it made him smile. 'Go on, show me, you old bag lady,' I goaded him. He picked up the plastic bag off of the floor. It nearly made me gag every time he moved – he was one bad-smelling dude. Out of the bag he pulled his passport, an enormous wad of money in a million denominations, a pair of spotless underpants, some socks, a huge sheaf of papers and a large notebook of some sort, along with a battered, dog-chewed photo. He showed me the photo. It was Isabelle. Isabelle dead. Dead on the mortuary slab. I had to pull over to the side of the road, where I promptly puked in the middle of Queensboro Bridge. Man, what a start to Christmas.

It turns out he had been in Palmyra within 24 hours of Isabelle's death, before anyone else in the family. He had bribed the mortuary assistant in Palmyra to let him in and had taken the photo of his separated-at-birth no-genetic-link darlink[sic]-baby-sister. I remember looking at him as he showed me the photo. A little smile played around his mouth. I didn't ask why he had taken it. I suddenly wanted to be home and to give my kids a big kiss. I started to feel

172   Colvin, A, 2099, *The Strange Affair of Isabelle and Solomon Isarebe*, Sheaders, London, p273

tears forming inside my nose – I gave a big sniff and punched him on the arm.[173]

At her home they found Rita Bortelli, who had been staying in her New York apartment for Christmas, with her son Robbie and his friend Davi. Isarebe was greeted not by joyful greetings, but by a stunned silence. Dave Brown-Day, Mya Brown-Day, Jonathan Brown-Day, Rita Bortelli, Robbie Bortelli and Davi Hoekstra stood with their jaws hung open. Bortelli said their senses had never taken in a hobo at such close quarters before. Dave Brown-Day broke the silence and walked up and gave Isarebe a kiss on both cheeks. Isarebe stepped back and wiped his face in disgust, which made everyone laugh. Bortelli started crying and kept trying to stroke Isarebe's hair into some kind of normality.

They sat down for Christmas dinner, which Hetty Brown's husband Dave had prepared in her absence and the kids soon started to forget the strange guest and started shouting and laughing and playing silly word games. Isarebe said very little, but smiled at everyone around the table. After dinner, he sat down on the sofa with a very large whisky and was soon deep asleep, his plastic bag at his feet. Like a snake sliding from a charmer's basket, his notebook made its way out of the bag onto the Brown-Day's highly polished wooden floor.

Rita Bortelli and Hetty Brown both stared at it for a while, fidgeting and visibly struggling with the moral dilemma, before Bortelli made a sudden and decisive grab for it, declaring 'Well, I paid for it!'[174] In this book were nearly 280 hand-written pages of what was to become *Future Perfect*. In just over six months, Isarebe had completed his work on the economic impact of population change through to 2150 and had also made substantial inroads into the more complex work on the impact of population decline on climate and the environment.

Isarebe woke around 8 p.m. and everyone insisted he had a wash if he wanted to stay the night. Bortelli went into the bathroom after he had washed and she shaved off his beard, trimmed his fingernails and his curling toenails, and cut his hair. After she had cut his hair, she took the towel from around his shoulders. There across his back was a tattoo of Isabelle Isarebe's face, on the mortuary table.

Isarebe insisted on teaching everyone bezique that night and everyone declared it one of the best Christmases they could remember.

---

173 Colvin, A, 2099, *The Strange Affair of Isabelle and Solomon Isarebe*, Sheaders, London, p. 274
174 Bortelli, R, 2070, *The Dizzy Digger*, Manchosens, New York, p. 124

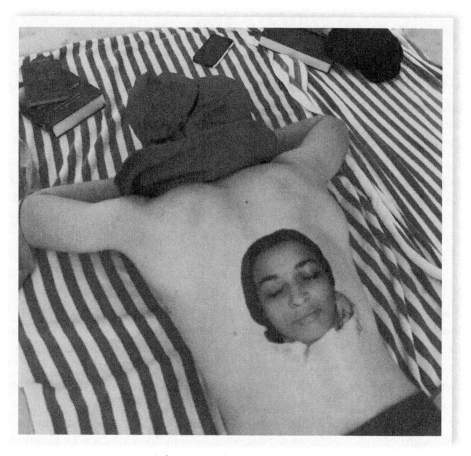

Solomon Isarebe, Tunisia, 2059

Isarebe, Bortelli and Brown stayed up late into the night, discussing Isarebe's new work. Bortelli said that 'despite a deadness in his eyes, there was something desperate but very much alive in his brain. It's not my field, but he was so articulate and the work seemed so convincing. Hetty Brown said that it was the best work he had ever done.'[175] It turned out not only to be the best work he had ever done, but the best work he would ever do.

The doorbell rang just before lunch the next day and the excited but tired faces of Jannik Isarebe, Reba Isarebe and Casey Ingar showed through the glass front door. Bortelli had insisted they hire a private jet at her expense, but Jannik Isarebe had quietly said they had enough money to come see their own son and they travelled economy on the first scheduled flight out of London on Boxing Day. In true Isarebe style, no one mentioned Isabelle, or asked where Solomon had been for the past seven months. Bortelli, her son Robbie and his friend Davi moved into a hotel that night, whilst Casey Ingar stayed with the

---

175   Bortelli, R, 2070 *The Dizzy Digger*, Manchosens, New York, p. 127

Brown-Days. Bortelli lent Reba, Jannik and Solomon Isarebe her apartment overlooking Central Park.

On New Year's Eve, Jannik and Reba Isarebe, together with Casey Ingar, made their way home to England, leaving Solomon Isarebe in New York, for what was to become the final push before the publication of *Future Perfect*.

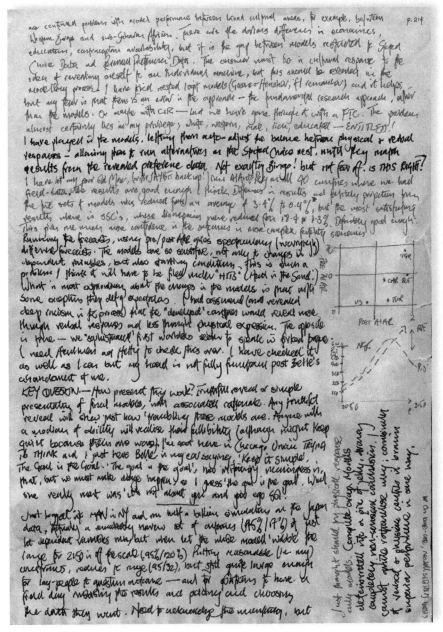

Extract from Solomon Isarebe's notebook, 2048

3.2 Cutting the human world in half

Solomon Isarebe was a different man after the death of his sister: even more insular, more impatient, more difficult to be around. However, his work continued to flourish and in his 'hobo period'[176] he completed their population projections, which combined the results of their work on fertility, mortality and migration. These population forecasts were to shock the world, but Isarebe remained circumspect about these predictions and forecasting in general throughout his life:

> The human world is a phenomenally complex place and making predictions about what we will collectively do next is fraught with danger. Just think about your own life, how you might vacillate for hours over whether to buy Golden Toasty Oats or Toasted Oaty Wonders, but then decide to marry on a whim. We are human and to be human is to be just a little bit irrational and unpredictable, at least at the level of the individual. As a society, we are a bit more predictable, in that for every crazy decision or unexpected behaviour one person might make, there is someone making a more sensible decision next door.

> Politicians play their part too in the uncertain world of forecasting. Something can be functioning perfectly well and then they change the rules with all sorts of unexpected ramifications.

> Perhaps most difficult of all there is cultural change, that slow movement from one set of acceptable behaviours, objects of desire, people of merit and definitions of right and wrong, to another set of equally baseless qualitative judgements. Each generation thinks they have got it right and wonders what on earth their forebears were thinking of, only to find out when they get old they are being mocked by their offspring for their own attitudes and the state they have left the world in. These cultural changes are one of the most difficult factors to account for in long-term forecasting and it's a mug's game to attempt it: you just have to relax and realise you will never get this right, so lose no sleep trying.

---

176   Bortelli, R, 2070, *The Dizzy Digger*, Manchosens, New York, p. 135

Technology is another area of change it is difficult to account for. Things that haven't yet been invented are very difficult to imagine, although sci-fi novelists love to try. However, whilst specific technologies are hard to foresee, technological drift is reasonably predictable and is the main factor behind economic growth. We don't know what it will be, but the effect of technological change at the macro-level is quite straight-forward to account for – most of the time a ruler and a straight line will suffice.

So, what does all this mean? Is *Future Perfect* worth the paper it's written on? Should all forecasters be put up against the wall and shot?

On the latter point, having spent much of my life with fellow forecasters, the answer is debatable, but, even though I am sure none of my forecasts will ever be exactly right – or at least only a little bit more often than luck would have it – I am certain they are worth producing. Our ability to anticipate the impact of our decisions and to modify our collective behaviour accordingly is one of the things that sets us apart from the beasts.

I believe the benefits of modelling and forecasts are threefold: they make us think about what is driving change in our world and where this may take us; they allow us to test ideas that may improve our collective lot, without any real-life consequences; and they let us assess different risks and understand how these may impinge on our future.

Also, although you may conclude I have made it out to be a complete lottery, most of the forecasts in *Future Perfect* are almost certainly correct in terms of direction and scale of change, whilst almost certainly wrong in terms of timing. Thus, I am pretty sure the world's population will shrink and that the change will be dramatic, but I am unsure whether it will take 100 years or 120 years for the population to halve. Looking at the bigger picture, those twenty years are irrelevant – the population is going to halve, have you heard that? – at least halve! That is what it is important to understand and plan for. We also now know that global warming is going to continue, but it will turn the corner, although we cannot be sure if things will start to improve in forty, fifty or sixty years' time. What is certain is we have to be pragmatic and vigorous in ameliorating the short-term effects of global warming, whilst remaining optimistic that in the long-term we will see the earth reach a happy new equilibrium.

So, I urge readers to be rationally critical of our forecasts – understand how they have been constructed and the assumptions we have made, but try to look past the numbers and focus on the implications of the direction and scale of change. My advice is to analyse like a robot and imagine like a poet, although I know I am better at the former than the latter, despite my mother's best efforts. If you can look at forecasts in this way then I hope you will be able to see them as I do, as things of beauty and wonder.[177]

Isarebe's population forecasts are the foundation for the rest of the analysis contained within *Future Perfect* and for Isarebe the population fall they were predicting represented 'the most fundamental change in the collective human condition in 5,000 years of recorded human history.'[178] His forecasts were of a faster fall in population than most other organisations were predicting at that time, but they were also the first mainstream organisation to take their forecasting horizon out to 100 years.

The main assumptions underpinning Isarebe & Isarebe's population forecasts were: the fertility rate would fall faster than previously expected in developing countries, particularly sub-Saharan Africa; the fertility rate would continue to fall slowly in the developed world to an average of around 1.45 children per woman; life expectancy in developed countries would peak at 83 and remain at or fall slightly from this level; life expectancy in developing countries would rapidly improve, partly as a result of improving economic conditions, but also because of a rise in the use of AIMS (AI Medical Support Systems); migration from the developing world to the developed world would continue through to 2080 before decelerating and then reversing in the first decades of the 22nd century.

Isarebe predicted that 2057 would be the peak year for global population, after which it would start to fall, first slowly and then more rapidly from the start of the 22nd century. In reality, it was 19th November 2058 that was chosen by the United Nations as 'Max Pop Day', the day they believed the global population started to fall. The population fell more or less in line with Isarebe's forecasts through the second half of the 21st century, but the rate of population fall from 2100 to 2140 was faster than Isarebe predicted, averaging

177   Isarebe, S and I, 2050, *Future Perfect*, Cambridge and Oxford University Press, Cambridge, pp. 7–9
178   Isarebe, S and I, 2050, *Future Perfect*, Cambridge and Oxford University Press, Cambridge, p. 81

nearly 10% per decade during this period, before starting to slow in the 2140s.

As he stated, he got the timing of key turning points wrong, as well as the rate of change in each decade and many of his assumptions failed to materialise. He would have considered himself lucky that the actual population in 2150 was so close to his original forecasts. His forecast for the population of the world in 2150 was 4.8 billion. The actual figure is expected to be closer to 4.6 billion.

So now, at the time of writing in 2150, the global population is almost exactly half what it was in 2050, when *Future Perfect* was first published. Over the past fifteen years, average fertility rates have slowly risen in Western Europe and the USA from 1.5 to 1.6 children per woman as cultural norms around the ideal family size have finally shown some sign of upwards drift, although the global average is still only just above 1.4 children per woman. The current consensus is there will be a further population decline of around 30% over the next century, taking the population close to 3 billion by 2250, a figure last seen in the 1950s. If these forecasts come to pass, in the 300 years from 1950 to 2250, the population of the world will have trebled and then declined by two thirds to take us back to where we started, and ever closer to the figure of 2.5 billion which most climatologists, ecologists and biologists now believe is a sustainable level for the human population.[179]

Perhaps inevitably, Isarebe's forecasts for individual countries, which were more difficult to construct because of the necessity of anticipating migration and political decisions, were much less accurate, although as he expected, most have seen a population decline of between 40% and 60% over the last hundred years. Some of his original country-by-country forecasts and a comparison with the actual figures for 2150 are given in Appendix 5.

The two countries where his population forecasts were most markedly wrong were Australia and China – a result of the Indochina War in the 2090s (see Epilogue). Australia saw a large increase in inward migration from Asia in the decade following China's invasion of the Indochinese Peninsula. Australia's population had started to fall in the 2070s, but rose again in the 2090s and 2100s, such that it now stands at 26 million, just 24% below its peak. Isarebe thought China would see some of the most dramatic falls in population, at least partly because of ongoing reverberations from the infamous one-child policy imposed from 1979 to 2015. The Chinese population had peaked at 1.4 billion in the early 2020s and he estimated that it would have fallen to 485 million by 2150. The impact of the ultimately disastrous invasion of Indochina and the subsequent cultural and economic

---

179   Global United Science, 2148, *Towards a cool tomorrow*, Global United Science Publishing, New York

turmoil, meant that birth rates plummeted in the early decades of the 22nd century. It is estimated that China's population in 2150 has fallen to a new low of 437 million.

India overtook China to become the most populous nation on earth in 2023 and its population continued to rise until 2042 before starting to fall rapidly, since when it has shed nearly 60% of its population. Isarebe predicted India would have a population of 640 million by 2150, relatively close to the actual figure of 610 million. It is still the most populous nation on earth.

Within Isarebe's original analysis, two major economies stood out from the rest: Japan, which has seen the greatest population decline of a major nation, and Nigeria, which emerged as a significant economic power during the period of Isarebe's forecasts and did not start to see population decline until 2093.

Japan had been experiencing a fall in population since 2010 and was perhaps the most politically mature country in dealing with the issues that came with such a change. Isarebe predicted their population would fall by 73% from the 2010 peak to 34 million by 2150. It is now estimated that Japan's population in 2150 is around 31 million. However, it remains one of the wealthiest nations on the planet, on a per capita basis.

Nigeria's population exploded during the 21st century, from 122 million in 2000 to 603 million by 2093, a rise of nearly 400% and close to Isarebe's original forecast. Its population has since declined in line with other nations and is now down to 395 million. Many people found it confusing that countries like Nigeria continued to see population growth for some time after fertility rates had fallen below population maintenance levels. Isarebe tried to explain this phenomenon during an Eye-Ted Talk given in California in 2051:

> It's an arithmetic thing. I know some of you do not get as sexually excited by numbers as I do, but we have to examine this little piece of maths porn in all its detail.

> First, let's simplify the world a bit. Let's assume there are only 100 people and in year 1 of our little study there are only new-borns, and people aged exactly 20, 40, 60 and 80. There are twenty people in each age group and half of them are men and half are women. You with me? Men, women, babies. Porn, like I promised.

> In this slightly strange world, all women give birth on their 20th birthday and only on their 20th birthday, and everyone dies the day before their 100th birthday. For some reason many dreaded this day,

every twenty years, when babies are born and grandparents die. I think it's a reasonable sacrifice for neatness.

Now, in this world, for eons and eons, every woman had exactly two children on their 20th birthday (there was a mechanism whereby they could choose how many babies they had and luckily they had enormously flexible wombs). The population therefore always stayed exactly the same, with always the same number – twenty – in each cohort. The fertility rate – the number of children a woman had in her lifetime – was always 2.

Then, one year, for no apparent reason, all of the young women decided to have four children when they reached 20. Well, this messed up the demographics good and proper. After they'd given birth, there were now 120 people in the world, with forty of them being babies and half of these being baby girls. The fertility rate had gone up to 4 and the population had of course gone up with it. Just as you expected, you clever people.

Twenty years later, when the twenty female baby-boomers had grown into young women and they were approaching the time they would give birth, many of them realised what an awful time their fathers and mothers had experienced with four children to look after – and collectively decided to have just one and a half babies each – I know, weird.

So, after this cohort of twenty women had given birth, there were thirty babies, forty people aged 20, twenty aged 40, twenty aged 60 and twenty aged 80. The total population was now 130, a rise of 8% from twenty years earlier, despite a dramatic plunge in the fertility rate.

Fertility rate down, population up ... hmm ... I smell arithmetic at play. Sex on a stick my friends.

Twenty years later, when it was time for yet another new generation of babies, the fifteen mothers-to-be collectively decided to stick to the average fertility rate of their mums, 1.5 children per woman – it was a very democratic and disciplined society again by now. There was probably an economist in charge.

So, after they had given birth, there were twenty-two and a half babies – this is the only known problem with arithmetic, it can generate horrible images – thirty people aged 20, forty aged 40, twenty aged 60 and twenty aged 80. This meant that despite two generations of women having substantially fewer than the population maintenance figure of two children each, the total population had still risen, to 132.5 people, a further rise of 2%.

It would not be until a third generation of women had 1.5 children each, that the population would start to fall – and it would be five generations before the population got back below 100 again, although by this point society is in baby free-fall. Sorry, another slightly unpleasant image.

This hopefully demonstrates – has it? – that after an earlier baby boom it can take a long time for a population to fall, even if fertility rates plunge. This is exactly what is happening in Nigeria now and before that in England, Germany and even here in heaven, I mean California.

Arithmetic always trumps common sense. In fact, never trust common sense, it is normally wrong and can land you face down in a whole heap of do-do. [180]

Looking back at the challenges the Isarebes and Casey Ingar faced and the uncertainty inherent in any long-term forecasts, their work on population still stands up as a technical and human triumph. There are many errors in their work, but Solomon Isarebe would have told us to forget these and see the big picture. As he famously shouted in the face of UK Prime Minister Henry D'Aboo in 2051: 'Wake up Mister D'Aboo! The population is going to halve! Don't you get it, man?!'[181]

---

180   Isarebe, S, 2051, Eye-Ted Talk: *The Glorious Baby Bust*, 14th March 2051, www.eye-ted. com [accessed 18th June 2149]

181   Unattributed, 2051, *Boo D'Aboo! Wake Up!*, The British Telegraph, 1st April 2051, p. 1

3.3 Isarebe returns to his economist roots

Solomon Isarebe's diaries from this time suggest a man nearing exhaustion but still forcing himself to work to a punishing schedule. His commitment to work had not changed but when his sister had been with him work had been a pleasure; his only frustrations being the short number of hours in each day and the body's need for sleep.

After completing the population forecasts, Isarebe immediately started on an examination of the economic impact of these predictions. He completed a version of these economic models in his 'hobo period', but when he revisited the work in January 2049 he literally threw his notes out of the window of Bortelli's New York apartment, where they landed on the terrace of the apartment below. The neighbours returned the sodden document to an irate Isarebe, who jettisoned it on the top shelf of the coat closet. It was found there by Rita Bortelli in 2059 and it is now part of the Isarebe archive. It is a fascinating document, written almost entirely without punctuation and with workings and abstruse equations written at all angles on the page. Isarebe may have been disappointed with this first draft, but it is remarkably similar to the final work he produced and its authoritative tone suggests Solomon Isarebe felt he was back on intellectual home ground. However, the economics section of *Future Perfect* is the least coherent and readable part of the book. Whilst his expertise is evident in every sentence, he veers wildly from closely argued thoughts on economic development to pet theories on subjects ranging from income polarity[182] to the role of education in mature economies. It was perhaps his confidence and expertise in the subject matter that resulted in him letting his editorial guard down.

Somewhat perversely, this was the first area of the *Future Perfect* analysis where he sought outside help. He claimed this was because he hoped the endorsement of a big-name economist would improve the credibility of the book, but it is perhaps more likely that Isabelle's death shook his inner confidence.

---

182   See Appendix 6 for more on Isarebe's work on income polarisation.

Extract from Solomon Isarebe's notes on the economy, 2048

He initially started working with Reynard Menning in February 2049. Menning was regarded as one of the world's leading academic macro-economists. By March 2049, Isarebe had dismissed Menning and engaged Akita Smith-Singh, previously Chief Economist at the Bank of Europe, and then within a month moved on from Singh to Maisie Black-Schmidt-Shah, a rising star at the London School of Economics. She lasted three weeks. He was frustrated by the experience, as he wrote in the unfinished and unpublished draft of his autobiography in 2067:

> I really respected Reynard, despite everything he said and continues to say about me, and whilst Akita was a bit (a bit!) pompous, she was spectacularly clever, and Maisie BSS was impressive for someone so young, but they all seemed to suffer from logic failure at the idea of such long-term forecasts. They were rational and confident when we looked out to 2060, a little nervous but still brilliant when we got to 2080, and then they turned into irrational pieces of jelly when we got to the 22nd century. It seems if you ask people to look a hundred years into the future they immediately turn into the unlikely offspring of George Orwell[183] and George Lucas.[184] They suddenly think they need to be imaginative.

> "There will be a catastrophic nuclear war."
> "There will be a virus that decimates the world population."
> "Artificial Intelligence will dominate the human realm."
> "Productivity growth can't possibly keep going for ever."
> "The capitalist model is certain to ultimately fail."
> "Population decline will cause massive deflation and will bankrupt nations."
> "Africa will never be able to grow as Asia did. It just can't."
> "Who would invest in a consistently low-growth economy?"
> "Everyone will be zombies on painkillers."

> I am not making these quotes up and they are not from some inebriated students down the pub, but verbatim notes from conversations with some of the most respected economists in the world. Of course they may be right, but history and rational thought suggests the chances

183   George Orwell was a British author (1903–1950), famous for writing the dystopian political fantasy novel *Nineteen Eighty-Four*, which was published in 1949.
184   George Lucas was the creator of the popular *Star Wars* film franchise in the late 20th and early 21st centuries. Solomon Isarebe was a fan of these science fiction movies in his teens.

are low. I kept assuring them we must do what we have always done and look backwards first – because understanding the past is always the key to unlocking the secrets of the future. Forecasters are historians first and foremost.

Looking back at economic history, there are huge blips in the otherwise relentless upwards progression of the modern global economy: the economic crash of the 1930s; the Second World War in the 1940s; the so-called stagflation of the 1970s; the banking crisis of the 2010s; the impact of the Covid-19 virus; the Ukrainian war in the 2020s; and the Venezuelan oil crisis of '39. During and immediately after these periods of crisis, but rarely before, there are always economists predicting the end of the economic world, but I can't help feeling most of them are just covering their bets and simultaneously seeking a bit of ego-boosting media coverage – the media love a gloomy intellectual, luckily for me – or else they are just suffering from recency bias,[185] which can afflict even the most rational and intelligent people. And yes, these economic crises have brought with them real pain and many personal tragedies, but there has always been a subsequent and complete economic recovery, although sometimes it has taken a decade to achieve. And there has always been a recovery for good reason and that is because some human beings are extraordinarily brilliant and almost all human beings are willing to work pretty hard to look after themselves and their families. This is not a political view and I am not an adherent to any economic 'ism', it is purely an historical observation.

The only assumption we have to bravely make in predicting the continued rise of the global economy is that politicians don't cock things up. Most career politicians in stable democracies – as opposed to the egotistical loons who occasionally emerge – know that economic success more often than not brings re-election, so they generally want to make the right economic decisions. As Bill Clinton reputedly said in 1992 when asked about the key to his US Presidential victory (although, it was actually Carville, his election strategist):

"It's the economy, stupid."

---

185   Recency bias is a well-established cognitive phenomenon, where recent events are given more importance in situation assessment than historic events.

When I asked them to consider long-term growth, these economic superstars started resorting to rhetoric, the last bastion of the nervous academic. They spouted theories, they talked about crises of the nation state (that old chestnut), they adopted gloomy and serious expressions and looked me right in the eye when they quietly spoke of endemic deflation, but it made no sense to me. Why would the rules governing the future be so different to those that applied in the past? The capitalist system, for all its many flaws, has proved very flexible and has always found a way of succeeding – in fact, I'm not even sure it is a 'system', more a description of the human condition, the economic survival gene. The green social capitalism that has dominated Western democracies for the last twenty or thirty years may not survive in its current state, but something will. Of course we need sensible macro-management of the economy, sound governing institutions, trustworthy legal systems and free flow of capital but fundamentally, long-term growth is driven by technological change, which equates to the brilliance and imagination of extraordinary people, because economies are about people and our ability to build on our previous successes. We are never going to forget everything we have learnt and we are never going to stop finding ways to do things better. We stand on a great sedimentary economic rock of innovators and magic makers.

I am often accused of gross simplification, but that is what helps me think, particularly with such a slippery idea as economics and when you look at the long-term, things are remarkably straightforward.

Here is my simple view of economic growth:

> If, every six years, we can each find a way to make 11 very slightly better things in a day, when before we were only able to make 10 very slightly worse things, then we will experience economic growth of more than 1.6% per capita per year.

By the magic of compound growth, that would mean if an individual made stuff or services worth 100,000 dollars in year 1, then 100 years later their grandchild could work the same amount of time and produce things worth nearly 400,000 dollars. Spectacular. This is the sort of growth we have been experiencing in the richer countries of the world for centuries.

But what about less developed (i.e. poor) countries, particularly those who have worked hard to create the conditions necessary for growth and investment? Well, they are starting from a much lower base and they can learn from what others have done, so they have a real chance of catching up fast – they might expect growth of 2.5% per capita per annum. Not a ridiculous idea? If anything, a bit conservative. Well, over 100 years, this would mean if someone made stuff or services worth 20,000 dollars in year 1, then 100 years later they could work the same amount and produce stuff or services worth 200,000 dollars – a ten-fold increase. Now that's incredible.

I can feel the scepticism of the reader ... 'This is just fantasy; it could never happen'. Well, this is exactly what has happened over the course of modern history, from the mid-17th century onwards, when technology started to make a real difference to the economy. In the UK in 1650, it would have taken a year's hard labour in terrible working conditions to make as much as we now make, from the comfort of our desks, in just over a week.

I knew I would be wrong in the details of these forecasts, because I hadn't even attempted to predict the scale or timing of any temporary downturns, even though I knew they would occur: there would be war at some point; there would be a banking crisis; and there would be future viruses to overreact to. I ignored them because they don't really matter in the long term, at least from an economic perspective. What I was certain of was that the direction and broad magnitude of my forecasts would be right. I would have staked my life on it, or even the life of someone I loved.[186]

This more accessible assessment of the economy, written years after the publication of *Future Perfect*, illustrates how powerful Isarebe could be as a writer when he got off his high academic horse.

After Isarebe had discarded three of the most respected macro-economists in the world, he trusted himself to be the best person for the job, although he also employed some bright young quantitative economists, including Jo Qility, who went on to become a highly respected economist in her own right. Although there are a few interesting oddities in this work, it now reads as a fairly conventional piece of analysis, if over an extraordinarily long timeframe.

---

186   Isarebe, S, typed notes for an unpublished autobiography, manuscript dated 24th September 2067, The Isarebe Trust Archives, Cambridge, England (Box 448)

The only contentious parts were his assumptions on the changing structure of the workforce and in particular a long-term decline in investment returns. He shared his thoughts on these issues with Professor D. Kamil in May 2049:

So obvs there will be a sharp drop in the number of people in the trad working age range and a rise in the proportion of older potentially economically inactive people, so it's inevitable older people will be encouraged or forced to work full or part-time. To balance the books it looks like the average retirement age in post-stellar economies will reach 72 by 2100. Most of the billion odd scenarios we have run (I jest not, or at least not much) suggest this retirement age will stabilise in post-stellar and stellar economies around 2100, but will continue rising in proto-stellar economies, particularly in sub-Saharan Africa, well into the next century.

I am not too worried about this, it's just more of the same, but I am worried our conclusions on falling investment returns will create a huge backlash against pop decline. It's not rocket science, but investment returns over the period will certainly fall as a direct result of the drop in the pop (and lower growth in Gss GDP). It also looks like there will be big drops in the value of property in many places, particularly outside of big cities and very low – prob neg – interest rates on savings. It doesn't make easy reading, but all our analysis of historic variations in investment returns – although the data is a bit shaky pre 1950 and positively fluffy pre 1900 – suggests investors will acclimatise to this fall without the capitalist system blowing itself to smithereens, as long as it happens slowly enough. New norms and expectations will assert themselves – won't they? They must. Can you have a look at the technical stuff I've sent you. Is there something missing? None of us can spot it.

The key is we need to make people think in terms of per capita growth, per capita investment returns, per capita happiness! Falling populations make happy people. WE MUST STOP PEOPLE TALKING ABOUT GROSS GDP.

Anyway, the upshot of all this is we think productivity growth will remain at or around 1.5% per capita per annum over the whole period, with a few wobbles on the way. A bit of a dull conclusion, but sort of thrilling too. Let me know what you think. SI p.s. If you have time, look at our work on productivity growth in individual countries. I think you'll like it. We (to be honest mostly Jo Q) have done some neat modelling, incorporating level of economic development, natural and cultural capital, corruption in the local business environment, level of technical specialisation etc etc etc and blah blah blah. Some of her work is so good it makes me laugh out loud. Was I ever this good? I guess I was.[187]

In this communication with Professor D. Kamil, Isarebe makes reference to a new economic taxonomy he had developed. The terms within this taxonomy were designed to reflect the different stages of development of economies around the world, although Jo Qility claimed: 'Solomon came up with this one lunchtime, it couldn't have taken him more than a minute. It was as close as he ever got to making a joke. He loved making fun of the great powers – especially us Americans.'[188] The labels within this classification were linked to his predictions of different rates of growth in different regions over the period 2050–2150. He split the nations of the world into seven groups based on their size, their level of economic maturity and their predicted rate of economic growth. It was a straightforward and unsophisticated segmentation, but the provocative and disrespectful titles he used meant it attained a degree of notoriety. He labelled the USA a 'Post-stellar giant', whilst all the nations of Western Europe were given the moniker 'Post-stellar dwarfs'. China and India were labelled 'Stellar giants', while Nigeria and Indonesia were named 'Proto-stellar giants'.

His labelling of the then developed world as 'Post-stellar' ruffled a few feathers, particular those additionally labelled as 'dwarfs'. These labels are still sometimes referred to, at least in popular economic literature, although they were never taken that seriously at the time.

He was correct in assuming his conclusions on the changing structure of the workforce, in particular his prediction of a substantial rise in the retirement age, would not create much of a stir. The retirement age had been slowly rising throughout the first half of the 21st century and it was accepted by most economists and politicians that further rises, however unpopular, were inevitable. The average age of retirement globally in 2150 has now stabilised at 73 years.

He was also correct in assuming that his conclusions on investment returns would generate headlines and political unease around the world.

---

187   Isarebe, S, 2049, eLetter to Professor Kamil dated 11th May 2049, The Isarebe Trust Archives, Cambridge, England (Box 155, Folder 2)
188   Bortelli, R, 2070, *The Dizzy Digger*, Manchosens, New York, p. 187

including a re-examination of the commonly used Heimlich taxonomy of global economies. Whilst admirable in its simplicity and appropriateness when it was first used in 2034, it is inappropriate for a future where countries such as India and Nigeria, alongside China, will be dominating the economic and political realms. In the Isarebe Economic Taxonomy (IET), the importance of the new economic super-powers is brought to the fore and the starkness of the differences in prospects for the old economic giants and the leaders of tomorrow are made manifest.

Examples of countries within the new Isarebe Economic Taxonomy:

	Giants	**Dwarfs**
Post-stellar	USA, Russia	EU, UK, Canada, Japan, Australia
Stellar	China, India, Brazil, Mexico	Singapore, South Korea, South Africa, Turkey
Proto-stellar	Nigeria, Indonesia	Malaysia, Bangladesh, Egypt, Phillipines
Non-participant		North Korea, Somalia, Afghanistan

Whilst each group within this taxonomy is carefully defined in economic terms (see Appendix 7), the importance of this analysis is primarily as a means of summarising the results of our modelling and presenting them in a way which highlights the global political challenges that lie ahead. Not only will politicians be facing the challenges of a fast falling population, but they will also have to be adjusting to the fast shifting sands of global leadership.

Just as the Romans, the Ottomans and the British amongst others have been forced to reluctantly cede their power over large parts of the world, so will the United States and then China find themselves losing leadership of the global economic eco-system. The challenge then, as now, and in the future, is to allow such inevitable change to occur without the death of millions of politically innocent people. We will come back to these challenges in Chapter 12, when we look in more detail at the new global order and in particularly at the implications of a dominant India.

Excerpt from Future Perfect, 2050[189]

189   Isarebe, S and I, 2050, *Future Perfect,* Cambridge and Oxford University Press, Cambridge, p. 365

That others were also coming to the same conclusion, notably Kruper,[190] Xiao,[191] and Dosticta,[192] only intensified the impact of his work. The analysis itself was not contentious: if a country initially had population growth of 0.5% per annum and then over time this became a decline of 0.5% per annum, then this would roughly take 1% per annum out of GDP growth, with an inevitable impact on investment returns. Whilst almost a logical certainty, Isarebe was worried it would lead to negative sentiments towards population decline, resulting in greater pressure being put on women to have more children, scuppering 'this incredible quiet revolution, brought about by generation after generation of women.'[193]

One of the most credible concerns about falling investment returns was that it would lead to deflation and associated economic crises, such as Japan had experienced in the late 20th century. The country Isarebe considered most at risk from sustained deflation was China and inflation there did oscillate either side of zero between 2072 and 2084. Although this led to a temporary downturn in purchases of goods such as phones and other computing devices in China, their greater reliance on services in the economic mix meant it had a lower-than-expected impact on overall economic growth. China's situation brought about serious discussions in the 2070s at G31 meetings and beyond about mutually writing-off debt but that idea was received with alarm by home audiences. The idea was eventually shelved after it became clear that China had avoided any significant long-term effects from temporary deflation. Sustained deflation has not materialised in any other country over the last century, as increased investment has led to productivity gains that more than offset the slow fall in the population.

At the time that *Future Perfect* was published, some naively argued that with incomes predicted to rise dramatically over the forecast period, individuals would not be worried about investment returns in the future. The opposite has happened: stock market investment in real terms and as a percentage of GDP has increased significantly over the last hundred years, as it has become one of the few places investors can hope for a positive real return on their money, even if absolute investment returns have fallen. In the early part of the 21st century, cash savers could expect annual returns of 2–3% per

190   Kruper, X, 2048, *Models of investment returns in a low fertility environment*, Journal of Investment Economics, 93, 2, pp. 875–931

191   Xiao, V, 2042, *Declines in investment returns for private investors 1960-2040*, Financial Game Play, 32, 4, pp. 145–198

192   Dosticta, P, 2046, *Addressing the supply-demand imbalance: examples from private housing in the US*, The Statistical Social Science Journal, 65, 6, pp. 42–78

193   Isarebe, S, 2051, Eye-Ted Talk: *The glorious baby bust*, 14th March 2051, www.eye-ted. com [accessed 18th June 2149]

annum and stock market returns of 4–8% per annum. In 2150, cash investors are unlikely to get even a nominal return on their cash savings, whereas they can expect real returns of between 1% and 2.5% on the stock market. People have proven to be extremely averse to negative returns on their cash savings, thus increasing the attractiveness of the stock market. Isarebe put it more simply: 'People always want a little bit more – a bit more security, a bit more stuff, a few more experiences. If you can get this through putting your money in relatively safe markets, then why wouldn't a sane person do it?'[194]

The amount of money being invested in stock markets having increased over the last hundred years shows the investment concerns which Isarebe and others provoked in 2050 soon started to decline. As Isarebe had hoped, people, government and businesses slowly acclimatised to new norms of investment returns. It was the snail-like pace of population change that allowed this paradigm shift to occur without upsetting the investment apple cart.

There are nearly forty pages within *Future Perfect* dedicated to the underlying assumptions behind Isarebe's economic forecasts. This perhaps suggests that behind his bravura, Isarebe shared the concerns of his erstwhile economic advisors that continued economic growth was not inevitable. If he was worried, he needn't have been: there was a slight deceleration in productivity growth between 2094 and 2116, before it recovered as bio-computing became more mainstream. He predicted average annual productivity gains per capita of 1.5% over the hundred-year period: the actual figure is slightly higher, at nearly 1.6%.

Much of this part of *Future Perfect* now seems arcane, but it shows Isarebe undoubtedly undertook a lot of research on new and emerging technologies as part of his economic analysis. It was Artificial Intelligence (AI) that he concluded had the capability of maintaining economic growth over at least the first thirty years of his forecasts. The reality is AI, albeit in a much different form, still drives much economic growth today. It was estimated in 2142, by David van Besten from the Erasmus University of Singapore-Rotterdam, that 38% of growth in GDP and 45% of growth in average incomes over the previous 100 years could be attributed to the application of AI, although some believe it has also been an agent in maintaining the gap between the richest and the poorest in many societies. Isarebe saw AI and robotics as part of a continuum of improvements in machines and systems that had started in the 17th century, improvements that enabled us to do 'more and more extraordinary

---

194   Isarebe, S, 2051, Eye-Ted Talk: *Richer, better, more equal*, 21st Jun 2051, www.eye-ted. com [accessed 20th June 2149]

things, faster and cheaper.'[195] His belief was integration of AI into the economy wouldn't decimate jobs, but would enable productivity to continue improving during a period when the number of people of working age was shrinking. His notes on AI and its impact on productivity run to thousands of pages.

His understanding of the potential of AI also led him to conclude new management and technical ideas would propagate much faster in the developing world than they had in the past. Isarebe's assumption was the new emerging economies would go through a much more accelerated period of development than the 'Asian Tiger' economies had in the late 20th and early 21st centuries. He was right in that some countries saw extremely rapid development in the second half of the 21st century (Bangladesh, Malaysia and Vietnam in particular), but others were hampered by slow development of the 'predictable and trustworthy business environment'[196] he identified as necessary for such growth to take place.

He also correctly predicted many large companies from the developed world would start to move manufacturing production to countries in sub-Saharan Africa in the period 2050 to 2100, reflecting these countries' improving infrastructure and their relatively low wage economies. However, as AI and robotics continued making inroads into manufacturing, he concluded that the importance of the cost of labour in determining the location of production would start to diminish, reaching a point where it would become more economical to locate production in the region of consumption, even for so-called 'sweatshop' industries, such as garment production. He believed developing economies would still flourish, but it would be through serving a more local market. His logical conclusion was that in a strict sense global trade in physical goods would decrease in the 22nd century, although international flows of capital would continue to increase. This has been partially realised, but not to the degree Isarebe anticipated.

195   Isarebe, S and I, 2050, *Future Perfect*, Cambridge and Oxford University Press, Cambridge, p. 316
196   Isarebe, S, 2032, *The impact of active economic management on economic growth in 52 countries*, Borcus Economics, 9, 2, p. 76

3.4 A new economic world order

Isarebe predicted GDP[197] across the globe would grow by 179% between 2050 and 2150, very close to the actual growth of 171%. However, after adjusting for population decline, he foresaw GDP per capita growing by more than 400%, such that per capita incomes would be over five times higher in 2150 than in 2050.[198] Actual per capita income in 2150 is almost exactly five times higher than it was in 2050. These global numbers are dramatic, but it was at the level of the individual nation that his predictions were of greater strategic importance, as they implied huge shifts in the global economic and political landscape.[199]

It was his forecasts for the big four economies (India, China, USA and Nigeria) that created the most shockwaves. China was the world's biggest economy in 2050, but Isarebe predicted it would be overtaken by India by 2072 and both would dwarf the USA by 2150. India actually overtook China as the world's largest economy in 2075 and its economy is now three times bigger than the USA's. Nigeria, which had been a relative economic minnow in 2050, was predicted to see its economy grow by over 800% over the period.[200]

---

197   Most of Isarebe's forecasts for economic growth were expressed in terms of Gross Domestic Product, commonly called GDP, which is a measure of goods and services produced within a given time frame. It sums the value added to goods in each part of a supply chain, so avoiding double counting. There are two measures of GDP that can be used when comparing nations: purchasing power parity (PPP), which takes in to account the different cost of items in different countries, and so gives an account of the volume of items produced, reflecting the material quality of life; and market exchange rate (MER) which converts the measurement of GDP in to US dollars, at market exchange rates, giving a comparable measure of the value of goods produced. At the start of the forecast period, in 2050, there was a significant difference between the two measures in many countries. Towards the end of the period, the difference between the two became less significant, as the price of goods around the world converged, aligning PPP and MER estimates of GDP. Both of these alternative measures of GDP were forecast in constant currency terms – meaning that the impact of inflation was taken out of the figures, enabling the reader to consider like for like. It is GDP (PPP) that is being referred to here. Isarebe often used GDP per capita in talks about his economic work, which by-passed the impact of a falling population on total GDP and was correlated to, although not identical to, income growth.

198   Isarebe's economic forecasts covered every nation of the world and through this exhaustive analysis he concluded that GDP per capita would start to slowly converge. For example, he estimated that the ratio of GDP per capita in the USA and Nigeria would fall from 9 in 2050 to 3 by 2150. The actual ratio of GDP per capita in the USA and Nigeria is now 3.5.

199   See Appendix 7 for more details of the forecasts.

200   The growth seen over the period 2050–2150 in developing countries is more dramatic if one considers MER estimates of GDP, as goods were significantly cheaper in these countries at the start of the period.

As Isarebe correctly foresaw, Nigeria has become the fourth largest economy in the world, although its economy actually grew slightly less than Isarebe predicted; 730% between 2050 and 2150. His work suggested that the big four economies would account for 46% of the global economy by 2150, very close to the actual figure of 45%.[201]

By the winter of 2047, Solomon Isarebe had become fascinated by the idea of global hegemony and what this practically meant. He was in China, trying to solve a research problem they were facing in the west of the country, when he asked Isabelle Isarebe in one of his long daily communiques, '... but if, as loads of people claim, the 20th century belonged to America, then who does or will the 21st belong to? China? India? And what does "ownership" mean exactly? What will they own and is it worth having?'[202] Isabelle, facing problems of her own with the resignation of their research manager in South America, gave Solomon an uncharacteristically curt response, saying if he was really worried about it he should try quantifying it.

Isarebe rarely took offence at anything his sister said and decided to accept her comments as wise advice. By the end of that summer, a summer in which he travelled nearly 100,000 miles managing their migration research, he had also completed a short, unpublished paper entitled 'The Silk Road from Hollywood to Bollywood'. In this paper, he presented an outline of his ideas on the quantification of global hegemony and what this might mean for the world in the 21st century. He identified and separated what he termed 'the hegemonic strands': economic power; military assets; media reach and influence; commercial and brand globalisation; investment diplomacy; and technological innovation. He generated metrics for each of these different strands and with some creative but questionable work constructed a data series for each, stretching back to the Ming dynasty (1368–1644). The problem he then faced was that whilst he had 'quantified' each of the likely explanatory variables of hegemony, he had no way of analysing their relative

---

201   Implicit in Isarebe's predictions was a decline in the economic and political power of some of the old economic powers. He believed Western European nations, alongside Canada and Japan, would become 'Post-stellar dwarfs'. Isarebe forecast their combined share of the global economy would fall from 11% in 2050 to less than 7% by 2150. Isarebe predicted Germany, Russia, France and the UK, once partners with the US and Japan at the economic top table, would become minor global players. He believed they would still be very rich in per capita terms, but their global political influence would be minimal. This is broadly what has come to pass. Whilst this political decline was one of the factors that led to the European Consensus War (see Epilogue), it can now be seen to have been a positive step for many of these economies. Once these grand old European nations took the weight of global leadership off their shoulders they seemed to become freer and more economically nimble and have performed well in the first half of the 22nd century.

202   Isarebe, S, 2048, email dated 14th October 2047, The Isarebe Trust Archives, Cambridge, England (Box 142, Folder 3)

importance, because there was no way of knowing, beyond highly subjective analyses, where hegemony had lain at any given time and how dominant a particular culture had been. At this point in his work, he seemed to abandon all attempts at intellectual rigour and rapidly jumped to his conclusions. He determined that whilst China would remain the largest global economy for the first seventy-five years of the 21st century and its investment diplomacy in Africa and Asia would win it many fair–weather friends, the USA would maintain its global hegemony. He believed the USA's military legacy, on-going technological advantage, powerful global brands and continued, if waning, influence in media and gaming would limit the global cultural influence of China, which was still wary about free public expression and unsupervised intellectual curiosity. His hypothesis was that just as there had been a global hegemonic vacuum from 1900 to 1940, when Britain's empire was breaking up but the USA was not yet confident enough to assert its authority, so they were experiencing another hegemonic vacuum in the first half of the 21st century. He foresaw the USA and China engaging in a quiet but intense struggle for domination. He thought these two growling, posturing dogs would not see India walk straight past them and quietly take over. He saw India's hegemonic advantage as being economic, but also cultural and technological: India had a well-established and influential media industry and had long been the outsource provider of choice to tech companies in Europe and America.

Isarebe's conclusions on global hegemony, particularly for work that was little more than an opinion piece with a little statistical stardust thrown in, started to look to Isarebe like 'a racing cert'[203] after he completed his population and economic forecasts. This conclusion concerned Isarebe, particularly the response of the USA:

> I finally finished the last iteration of the economic forecasts tonight and although they paint a wonderful picture of a richer and more equal world, it frightened me to look at them. How will the US respond to India equalling, then surpassing and then dominating Uncle Sam? If a crazy person gets elected, bombs could become the new unit of currency. Thank [expletive] there are no Trumps[204] on the horizon.

> I know it's an elephant I've brought into the room, but I'm not sure I'm brave enough to point it out to everyone and let them see that it's an elephant resplendent in its full Indian rig. I guess I'll have to, but

203 Isarebe, S, 2049, eLetter to Professor D. Kamil dated 3rd June 2049, The Isarebe Trust Archives, Cambridge, England (Box 155, Folder 1)
204 Donald Trump was the 45th president of the United States, known for his strongly held views on American supremacy and democratic procedure.

if in some parallel universe there is a God, please help the wonderful folks in America peacefully accept they are no longer going to be leader of the gang. It'll still be a wonderful place to live. They just have to face it, because it's inevitable and unstoppable. Bollywood's going to [expletive] Hollywood right up the [expletive].[205]

Most cultural analysts now believe that India's global leadership was not established until the final years of the 21st century, but for fifty years now India has been the dominant global force and there is no indication of where any competition for that leadership could come from.[206] Thus, Isarebe's predictions regarding the dominance of India were to come to pass, but the extraordinary story of how relations between India, China and the USA have developed over the hundred years since *Future Perfect* was first published would have been very hard to predict (see Epilogue).

---

205   Isarebe, S, 2049, diary entry dated 5th July 2049, The Isarebe Trust Archives, Cambridge, England (Box 156, Folder 4)
206   Some predicted Nigeria would become the dominant global force, believing their population would exceed a billion or more by the early decades of the 22nd century. Their population peaked at just over 600 million in the late 2090s and then went in to decline. India remains the largest country in the world by population.

3.5 The survival of planet Earth

The 2018 Paris Agreement [from the Intergovernmental Panel on Climate Change] was the biggest political con trick of all time, although the subsequent agreements were not noticeably better. No one who signed that 2018 agreement really believed they could achieve 1.5°C, or even 2°C [mean global temperature rise above pre-industrial levels]. It was one of the most cynical acts of modern political times. Failure was certain, but failure was beyond the next election cycle, so who cared?

The opportunity for climate recovery has been left to three forces: first, technology, through development of low-carbon energy and carbon removal solutions; second, economics, driving the move away from fossil-based fuels and changing land use; and last, and most important of all, the decisions of billions of people around the world to have fewer children.

It's shots, pills, coils and condoms that save planets, my friends.[207]

Isarebe was never a climate change sceptic, but prior to *Future Perfect* it had not been an area of great interest to him, despite pressure from his sister and a commitment in their 2042 manifesto to examine the environmental impact of population change. His passivity, bordering on disinterest towards environmental matters, was an attitude shared by many people of his age and time.

However, the 2040s were a time of great social change and many young people were starting to take a renewed interest in environmental activism. For Isarebe, it was a book entitled *The Negative Herd Effect* that kick-started his interest in environmental issues. It was first published in 2039, but Isarebe received it as a birthday present from Professor Kamil in 2047. It was written by Milo Martine and Kimmi Esposito, evolutionary psychologists from the Universidad Nacional Autónoma de México. They studied cultural change through the lens of genetically inherited characteristics of sociability and cooperation. In particular, their work looked at how pressure groups, seeking

---

207   Isarebe, S, 2065, video: *Lecture to MA Economic Students*, Princeton, 17ᵗʰ March 2065, The Isarebe Trust Archives, Cambridge, England (Box 425, Folder 1)

change around issues where there had hitherto been broad social cohesion, could lead to mass passive-aggression and cultural listlessness among those they were trying to influence. In this book they examined this phenomenon with regards to attitudes to climate change in the 2020s and 2030s. Almost all of the populist voices in the climate debate during this period were apocalyptic in their prognosis for the planet and put the blame at the feet of preceding generations as well as ongoing global consumption habits. Martine and Esposito's analysis showed that despite most people sharing this concern for the environment and accepting that global warming was a man-made crisis, apathy towards global warming grew, not declined, during the 2020s and early 2030s. Martin and Esposito believed activists were a significant cause of this passivity. Their work concluded that aggressive rhetoric and placing blame on society as a whole, as well as on previous generations, created an unconscious closing of ranks, driven by a genetic predisposition to cooperate with and protect an individual's tribe. They suggested this meant people only nominally supported environmental causes, with few making substantive changes in their lifestyles, whilst elections were rarely fought and won on environmental issues. In response to this, environmental tokenism from both politicians and commercial interests became the norm. In his diary, Isarebe recorded his reaction on first reading this book:

> It was like I was watching an intimate scene in a romantic play, with the spotlights focussed on the two lovers, when unexpectedly the house lights come up and I saw everything for what it really was – the scruffy stage, the tare [sic] in the actor's dress, the thick waxy make-up, the scene hand flirting with the chorus boy offstage, the wallpaper hanging from the walls, the carpets stained from endless ice-creams before mine.

> This book turned the house lights on in my brain and revealed my supposedly rational disinterest in all things environmental was nothing more than a shabby societal effect. I was just hanging out with everyone else being deeply ignorant and even more deeply stupid. Ignorance I guess I can do something about, but I suspect I may be hard wired for stupidity.[208]

Once Isarebe became engaged by environmental issues, he became passionate about them and worked at a manic pace to understand the problems. As

---

208   Isarebe, S, 2047, diary entry dated 3rd June 2047, The Isarebe Trust Archives, Cambridge, England (Box 141, Folder 4)

Casey Ingar noted: 'It was typical of him, he had to work something out from scratch in order to really engage with it intellectually and emotionally. Once he saw for himself the scale of the mess we were in, he became the most ardent advocate for change. He was kind of ridiculous, as always.'[209]

In 2048, when Isarebe was starting to try to understand the chemistry, physics, mechanics and biospheric implications of climate change, the average global temperature was already more than 1.8°C above pre-industrial levels and sea levels in the middle years of the 21st century were rising by 5 cm (2 inches) per decade. In 2050, the year of publication of *Future Perfect*, sea levels were 20 cm higher than they had been in 2000, due to thermal expansion of the oceans and melting of glaciers and the polar icecaps. In a few low-lying countries and in particular in many smaller, low-lying islands, rising sea levels were threatening lives and commerce, although the vast majority of countries and people were barely affected. However, nearly all countries in the 2040s were being hit by more extreme weather events. Many countries were experiencing these weather problems on an annual basis and farmers were having to make wholesale changes to the crops they planted, the animals they reared and the farm management systems they employed. Many eco-systems had already been terminally affected by local changes in weather patterns.

It was a complex and enormous task Isarebe was taking on: to understand the impact of population change and economic growth on climate change over the course of the following century. Isarebe made some early decisions ensuring their work in this area was manageable:

1. He decided to only model global temperature change, rather than more localised climate change, which was much more complex, less well understood and subject to more random variations.

2. He decided not to fully integrate his climate models with his economic models, as he did not believe the economy would be significantly affected by changes in climate, even though he recognised climate would be affected by economic change. In his notes he wrote, 'It sounds crass to assume economics and climate are not commutatively related and it appears to belittle the very real problems that small groups of people are experiencing because of global warming, but at the macro-level these impacts are marginal.'[210]

---

209   Ingar, C, 2059, *Interview with Julie Bates of Greenday Research*, 15th February 2059, www.greendayresearch.ie [accessed 4th August 2149]
210   Isarebe, S, 2049, handwritten notes dated 25th September 2049, The Isarebe Trust Archives, Cambridge, England (Box 158, Folder 7)

Isarebe's team ran many economic simulations using different assumptions on climate change, but except *in extremis* his notes show they had little impact on their forecasts of economic growth.[211]

3. He also decided not to fully integrate his climate models with his population models, for the same reasons. He commented on this in his introduction to the section on climate change in *Future Perfect*: 'People may decide to change where they live, in low-lying regions in particular, but there is no reason to suppose that climate change will significantly affect fertility or mortality. There will be more extreme climate events and there will be deaths associated with these events, but the work of Smith, Ping and Xavi-Mason among others, suggests the number of deaths from natural disasters, including weather events, would probably remain under 100,000 people per year even if average global mean temperatures rose to 5°C above pre-industrial levels. In 2020, before global warming was such a major issue, 60,000 people a year died from natural disasters, so even if this figure reaches 100,000 deaths in some future year, those additional 40,000 deaths – we could call them climate-induced deaths – would represent less than 0.1% of deaths at the global level.' [212]

Unusually for Isarebe, his work on climate change was somewhat prosaic and makes dull reading. The work built up step by logical step to its final conclusions. The foundations for this work were the results of his population and economic forecasts, which provided him with a framework for estimating greenhouse gas (GHG) emissions, which in turn were used to predict global temperature changes.

In order to estimate likely changes in GHG emissions Isarebe's first task was to forecast global energy use, as this was the major contributor to global warming. He did this through attempting to understand how both the economic mix and energy efficiency might change over the period 2050–2150.

---

211   Isarebe undertook a substantial survey research programme to help understand the relationship between climate change and the economy. However, this research merely reinforced what was already well known: that whilst people expressed concern about climate change, it made little difference to everyday consumption choices. The research provided strong evidence that unless an environmentally benevolent choice was legally mandated or given tax incentives, people rarely made consumption decisions primarily for environmental reasons. One of the more interesting findings from this research was that many people believed they were making environmentally-based consumption decisions even when objectively they weren't.
212   Isarebe, S and I, 2050, *Future Perfect*, Cambridge and Oxford University Press, Cambridge, pp. 342–3

Even in the late 20th and early 21st centuries, before there was any concerted international effort to contain global warming, there had been substantial improvements in the energy efficiency of the economy. Between 1970 and 2050, global energy consumption per unit of GDP had decreased by 86%. This was partly because of the increased energy efficiency of production and business processes, but also because of changes in the economic mix, with an increasing proportion of the global economy accounted for by services, which generally required much less energy per unit of output.

In a mammoth and well-documented piece of work, Isarebe and his team forecast economic growth at a sectoral level for most economies around the world. Expected changes in the economic mix were particularly marked for developing nations, many of which Isarebe predicted transitioning from being mainly focussed on agriculture and manufacturing to having more mixed economies, with a greater emphasis on the service sector.

Whilst the sectoral forecasts were largely based on historic precedents, Isarebe openly admitted the assumptions he made on the energy efficiency of industrial and business processes were little more than educated guesses, as these improvements would be driven by as yet unknown technological change. Whilst Isarebe showed uncharacteristic modesty in this area of their work, he employed many experts in the field and he himself became deeply engrossed in understanding emerging technologies. Isarebe's final predictions were for a continuing, but decelerating, improvement in the energy efficiency of production processes.

By combining their assumptions on changes in the economic mix and energy efficiency of industrial and business processes, Isarebe and his team predicted a decline in energy consumption per unit of GDP of 44% between 2050 and 2150.

History shows that Isarebe was overly pessimistic in his assumptions on improvements in the energy efficiency of industrial and business processes, particularly heavy industry such as steelmaking, where large improvements have been achieved, primarily through vastly improved heat recovery systems. However, he underestimated the continued importance of manufacturing in the global economic mix, an important factor in overall energy consumption. Using Isarebe's own words, the public have retained a significant interest in 'getting more stuff.'[213] Recent work by Junhui[214] has shown that much of the growth in the manufacturing sector over the past fifty years has been driven by increases in renting or owning second homes, particularly in developed

213   Isarebe, S, 2032, *The impact of active economic management on economic growth in 52 countries*, Borcus Economics, 9, 2, p. 72
214   Junhui, J, 2143, *Quantifying the relationship between home ownership and manufacturing*, Vanguard Econometrics Journal, 256, 7, pp. 456–512

economies. Isarebe himself predicted a massive expansion in second homes, but failed to take this to a logical conclusion in his work on future consumption patterns. Despite these errors in his assumptions, global energy demand in 2150 is only 10% higher than Isarebe predicted in 2050. Isarebe's predictions lagged behind actual energy usage throughout the forecast period.

Energy use: 2020 – 2150 (indexed 2020 = 100)
Predictions within *Future Perfect* and actual

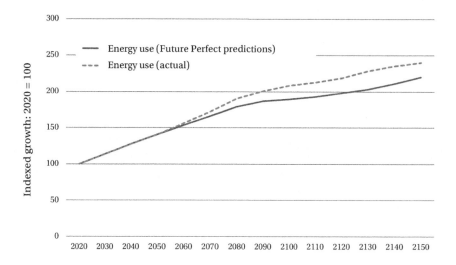

Having made his predictions on energy consumption, Isarebe then examined what this would mean for GHG emissions. This work was complex, because not all GHG emissions come from the CO_2 generated by energy consumption. The other main GHGs are methane, nitrous oxide and fluorinated gases, variously generated from agriculture, fertiliser production and other industrial processes, in particular the production of cement. Many of these other gases are more powerful global warmers than CO_2 but are less prevalent and disperse more quickly out of the atmosphere. Perhaps because of this complexity, Isarebe's work mainly focussed on CO_2 emissions from energy consumption.

The CO_2 generated per unit of energy consumed varies between fuel type, so it was critical for Isarebe to predict how the use of different fuels was likely to change. Fossil fuels produce much more CO_2 than renewables and nuclear, but within fossil fuels, coal is a greater emitter of CO_2 than oil, which in turn is a greater emitter than natural gas. Renewable energy sources produce little CO_2 directly, although there is some produced in the manufacture, installation and operation of facilities. Nuclear produces no CO_2 directly, although again there is some produced in the installation and operation of facilities as well as the mining and treatment of raw materials. Hydrogen produces no CO_2 when consumed, but requires a significant amount of energy to make.

Forecasting change in the energy mix was almost impossible from a modelling perspective, as political, legislative and technological changes were often more influential than conventional economic drivers. The first half of the 21st century saw massive changes in this regard: the Ukraine war in the early 2020s changed many national strategies on energy security; solar and wind technology improved massively, as did renewable energy storage; carbon pricing and permit systems became sophisticated industries; electricity grid management became more efficient through the employment of AI; and state-funded incentives encouraged the development of many new technologies.

As early as the 2030s, solar and wind energy had become competitive with fossil fuels in some situations, but all nations were still highly dependent on nuclear and fossil fuels to fill the energy gap that occurred 'when the wind don't blow and the sun don't shine'.[215] In 2050, renewables accounted for 28% of all energy consumed around the world. This represented a remarkable rise from 2020 when it had accounted for just 12% of energy consumed, but it still fell far short of political promises and what was needed to contain global temperature rises.

The much higher energy density of fossil fuels meant that renewable sources couldn't compete in many situations at this time, particularly haulage, air travel and sea travel. Electricity, whatever the source, was still uneconomic for heating most buildings and heat exchangers remained deeply unpopular and expensive for the majority of properties. It wasn't until later in the 21st century that some of these issues were overcome. In particular, improvements in the economics and energy requirements of hydrogen production, and the addressing of public concerns about its safe use, meant that excess renewable energy could be more efficiently stored as hydrogen, and hydrogen, as a dense energy source, was a practical energy solution for some transport and building demands.

Isarebe knew his work on the energy mix was a 'minefield of error and uncertainty',[216] but he tried to ensure he was well informed on the direction of change. For example, it was clear from his notes that he knew a lot about nuclear fusion, although he made no statements about its future use in *Future Perfect*. Nuclear fusion would not become feasible from either an engineering

215   Jones, J, 2063, *Sitting on the wings of a butterfly*, DRGA Recordings
216   Isarebe, S, 2049, soundnote to Rita Bortelli dated 4th October 2049, The Isarebe Trust Archives, Cambridge, England (Box 159, Folder 4)

or economic perspective until the late 2090s and only started to be widely used in the 2120s. With their far greater efficiency and relative safety, fusion plants are one of the main reasons that nuclear energy has flourished in the past thirty years. Nuclear energy, unlike today, was seen as politically poisonous in 2050, even though there had been very few fatalities ever associated with nuclear energy. In 2049 it was estimated there were approximately 90,000 deaths per thousand terawatt hours associated with coal extraction and use, compared with 33,000 for oil, 3,500 for natural gas and 75 for nuclear.[217] These deaths were either caused during the extraction of the fuel or the use of the fuel, or were attributable to atmospheric pollution.

Isarebe struggled with what he saw as the lack of logic in the deployment of nuclear power. Nuclear energy, despite being relatively safe and carbon free, had been static or declining in many developed countries in the first half of the 21st century, as governments ceded to public pressure:

The public and politicians appear to have an almost wilful misunderstanding of risk. They see a very, very occasional headline-grabbing nuclear accident as more significant and dangerous than the drip-drip-drip deaths associated with the use of fossil fuels. It is fatally senseless. The comparative risk of using nuclear is miniscule, but even sensible educated people seem to want to bite your balls off when you suggest this.[218]

Isarebe was also a strong advocate for greater use of micronuclear plants (MNPs), which, compared with larger plants, were less likely to cause a major catastrophe, were cheaper to build and faced fewer planning objections. This is perhaps why he significantly overestimated the growth in nuclear from 2050–2100, although the fast growth of fusion plants in recent decades has come to his statistical rescue in his forecasts for 2150.

He rightly foresaw an important future role, albeit diminished, for fossil fuels,[219] which have retained a place as a cheap, high density, transportable fuel, with an important role in maintaining electricity supply. They have also retained a significant, but declining, role in household heating, as the transition to the use of heat pumps and hydrogen-fuelled boilers has moved

217   Jaganmohan, S, 2049, *Mortality rates worldwide in 2048, by energy source*, www.statsfora.com [accessed 19th May 2149]
218   Isarebe, S, 2049, typed notes dated 4th October 2049, The Isarebe Trust Archives, Cambridge, England (Box 159, Folder 5)
219   Whilst fossil fuels are still being used, coal production has declined by 75% over the past hundred years, whilst the use of oil and natural gas has more than halved, almost exactly in line with Isarebe's predictions.

at a snail's pace. That fossil fuels are still being used to generate electricity is in large part down to the increased use of carbon capture technologies in electricity generating plants.

Sources of global energy: 2050 – 2150
Predictions within *Future Perfect*

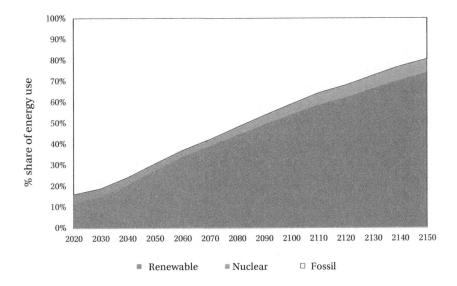

Isarebe's predictions that energy consumption would grow by 56% between 2050 and 2150 and renewable energy sources and nuclear would account for 81% of energy use by the end of the period led him to conclude that CO2 emissions would fall by 37% over this timeframe. Whilst this is a significant fall, it still meant he foresaw significant CO2 emissions continuing throughout the forecast period. However, Isarebe's forecasts, perhaps rather disingenuously, predicted CO2 emissions prior to carbon capture. Isarebe did account for carbon capture, but in a separate part of his climate models.

Isarebe's elaborate and detailed models on CO2 emissions were not matched by his work on other GHGs, for which he glibly stated that 'regulation and alternative technologies will sort them out.'[220] Political focus in the first half of the 21st century had been on CO2 emissions, rather than on these other GHGs and without this political pressure other GHG emissions had continued increasing: methane emissions increased by 46% between 2000 and 2050, whilst nitrous oxide emissions increased by 48%. Isarebe was conservative in his predictions of reductions in future emissions of these other GHGs,

---

220   Isarebe, S, 2049, typed notes dated 30th October 2049, The Isarebe Trust Archives, Cambridge, England (Box 161, Folder 1)

anticipating a slow fall through the second half of the 21st century, before a steeper decline in the 22nd century. The reality has been they fell quite dramatically in the period 2050–2100, following breakthroughs in replacing fluorocarbons in many industrial processes in the 2070s and 2080s, and a barrage of legislation in the 2060s on fertilizer production, which resulted in a sharp fall in nitrous oxide emissions. Methane emissions have fallen more steadily over the past hundred years, as the population has fallen and there has been a slow drift towards a more plant-based diet.

The next component in Isarebe's brick-by-brick construction of his climate models was his assessment of carbon capture and warming defence systems. This was the area where Isarebe made the greatest impact on environmental and climate change analysis, even though his work was technically very straightforward.

Carbon capture had excited many politicians in the first half of the 21st century, as some saw it as a 'way of having their environmental cake and eating it'.[221] It suggested to some they could carry on with energy consumption as usual and let new methods of carbon capture sort out the climate problem. As Pierre-Xavier Baillairge, French Minister for Biospheric Care, stated in an interview with The Financial and Technology Times in 2037: 'We will liberate the skills of the ocean, send the devil's carbon to the depths of the earth and design plants that turn base carbon into gold. We will win this battle with the evil sun.'[222] Even allowing for Baillairge's famously florid language, it was an extraordinary piece of hyperbole, reflecting both a lack of understanding of the science of carbon capture and the political climate.

Isarebe understood the potential for carbon capture and warming defence systems and appreciated the political problems they could bring. He foresaw very different futures for the different means of carbon capture and for warming defence systems.

After many years of development, carbon capture through relatively small-scale, localised applications was already a practical and economic reality when Future Perfect was being written. The most widely used and most effective of these new technologies captured carbon either pre or post the burning of fossil fuels and biofuels for electricity production. The main issue in the early decades of the 21st century had been the storage of CO_2 after extraction, but pumping and storing the gas in spent underground oil and gas fields become a practical reality as early as 2028, before being succeeded by more scaleable carbonate mineral production facilities in the late 21st

221   McMenomey, G, 2141, The fallacy of economic greening, Cambridge and Oxford University Press, Cambridge, p. 128

222   David, L, 2037, Supper with Pierre-Xavier Baillairge, The Financial and Technology Times Weekend, 2nd May 2037, pp. 12–13

century. A second, but equally important issue, which inevitably delayed its widespread take-up, was that carbon capture in power plants reduced the energy efficiency of electricity generation.[223]

Isarebe correctly predicted that capture of CO2 using these relatively small-scale localised means would advance rapidly. These forms of carbon capture were removing or preventing the emission of 200 billion kilogrammes of CO2 from the atmosphere in 2050. Isarebe forecast this would rise forty-fold by 2150 to 8 trillion kilogrammes per year. The actuality has been these forms of carbon capture took off even more rapidly than Isarebe expected and were removing over 6 trillion kilogrammes of CO2 per annum by as early as 2110. However, as carbon dioxide capture by afforestation accelerated, the appetite for further investment in these forms of carbon capture declined and the amount of CO2 they have prevented emission of, or removed from the atmosphere, has been at or around 5 trillion kilogrammes per annum from 2110 to the present day.

There was perhaps even greater political enthusiasm in the early to middle decades of the 21st century for large-scale, global projects to remove CO2 from the atmosphere. These methods of carbon removal perhaps appealed to politicians wanting to be the quick-fix saviour of the planet. There were many such schemes suggested, which included: direct capture of CO2 from the air using chemical means; changing ocean chemistry to encourage phytoplankton growth, which would increase CO2 take-up; altering the acidity of the ocean to increase carbon uptake; and crushing and exposing suitable rocks to accelerate weathering, which would remove CO2 from the atmosphere. There had been experiments of direct capture of CO2 as early as 2016, but at the time *Future Perfect* was first published, they had made little impact on carbon emissions.

In addition to these large-scale carbon capture ideas, there were more high-tech suggestions for setting up 'Warming Defence Systems', a term coined by US president Magda Lane in 2042,[224] which included: introducing aerosols into the stratosphere to increase the reflectivity of the sky, so reducing the amount of energy reaching the earth's surface; seeding clouds over the oceans to make the sky more reflective; launching screens or mirrors into space, to reflect some of the sun's rays; and various schemes to 'whiten' the surface of the earth in order to reflect more sunlight.

---

223   Even smaller-scale schemes, involving the treatment of soil to increase carbon take-up, were also becoming a practical if expensive possibility in the middle of the 21st century, at least in more economically developed countries. This never became a mainstream application, largely because of cost, but also because of concerns about the long-term impact on human health of changing the chemical makeup of soil.

224   Lane, M, 2042, *Taking a walk with James McAvenney*, CBS-A, 20th September 2042

Most of these carbon capture and defence schemes were technically feasible, although complex and expensive. Isabelle Isarebe, in notes she made after a visit to the Clouding Research Labs in Los Angeles in 2045, perhaps captured the mood of the public, with regards to these technologies:

It seems we can't control our desire for control. Arguably without deliberate intent, we have almost destroyed the world we claim to love, through over-population and the rampant burning of fossil fuels and then we have the nerve to suggest we should be trusted with machines and schemes that will sort everything out for us, without really understanding what the implications will be. To put it crudely, it is like putting a paedophile in charge of a Kindergarten.[225]

Isarebe shared his sister's concerns, recognising these global carbon capture and warming defence technologies would have to be employed on a massive scale to achieve their stated goals, and they would be very expensive and would have an unknown long-term impact on the environment. Isarebe believed these considerations alone should prevent their deployment, but he also believed there were additional political concerns that made it essential they should never become a reality. His political analysis was perhaps not as sophisticated as his economic and demographic work (it was once referred to by Dipstang as 'crude in the extreme'[226]), but in long-term strategic assessments such as this his judgement was almost always sound:

The immediate questions that arise are: Who will pay for this technology? Who will decide it's safe? Where will the technology be situated? Who will control it? Who will decide when it is deployed? Who will decide when it should be turned off?

Everything suggests that politics will trump science and when this happens, bad decisions are made. We are talking about the future of the planet and this can't be left to politicians. All we can hope is that some wise minds will inform their political leaders of the dangers of these technologies and the world will be persuaded into inaction.

I don't think it is too strong to say that the dangers of these technologies could exceed those of the nuclear bomb. They may be

---

225   Isarebe, I, 2045, eLetter to Tuesday Willingham dated 7th March 2045, The Isarebe Trust Archives, Cambridge, England (Box 123, Folder 2)
226   Dipstang, W, 2050, letter published in The New Economist, London, 9th August 2050, p. 45

less dramatic than the mushroom cloud and the instant vaporisation of a hundred thousand people, but surely the slow unwitting destruction of an entire planet is worse?[227]

Isarebe was to eventually make the bold assumption that these large-scale projects would not happen, for both economic and political reasons. There were significant trials of such technologies, but they caused such international furore and were so expensive they were all quietly shelved. There was a widespread public belief they 'went against nature'.[228] As mass afforestation became a reality, the political appetite for such schemes rapidly declined.

It was Isarebe's work on land use and afforestation and its impact on CO2 emissions that was to be his most significant contribution to environmental science. The only real differences between his work and that of others at the time were the timeframe of his forecasts, looking 100 years out to 2150, combined with his in-depth knowledge of population change.

Isarebe's team started with an analysis of the efficiency of farming, which had been improving rapidly for many years. There had been a 265% improvement in crop yields between 1950 and 2050, driven by improved farm management, soil science, and use of higher yielding crop varieties. However, this improvement in crop yields had occurred during a time when an increasing amount of land was being used as pasture, as demand for animal protein grew throughout the world. Then, as now, it takes fifteen times as much land to get calories from livestock as it does from plant-based foods, and six times as much land to get protein from meat as it does from plant-based foods.

Isarebe correctly assumed there would be further gains in crop yields, although much less dramatic improvements than there had been historically and there would be a slow drift towards a more plant-based diet in many richer countries. The result of these assumptions on farming efficiency and a decline in consumption of meat-derived protein, was his prediction of a reduction in agricultural land required per person, from 0.52 hectares in 2050 to 0.39 hectares in 2150. The actual figure in 2150 is 0.42 hectares per person, still a drop of 25% per person since 2050.

Given the dramatic fall in population that Isarebe was forecasting, this implied a reduction in the amount of land required for farming from 4.8 billion hectares in 2050, to just 1.9 billion hectares in 2150. Isarebe was predicting a change in land-use unprecedented in its scale and rate of change, with the release from farming of 30% of all the habitable land on earth. This was probably the single most important conclusion he reached in *Future Perfect*.

---

227   Isarebe, S, 2050, eLetter to Professor D. Kamil dated 3rd February 2050, The Isarebe Trust Archives, Cambridge, England (Box 165, Folder 13)

228   Jabber, L, 2047, *Let's cool it: In defence of natural solutions*, Tavistock Print, Glasgow, p. 73

Anne Wyeth

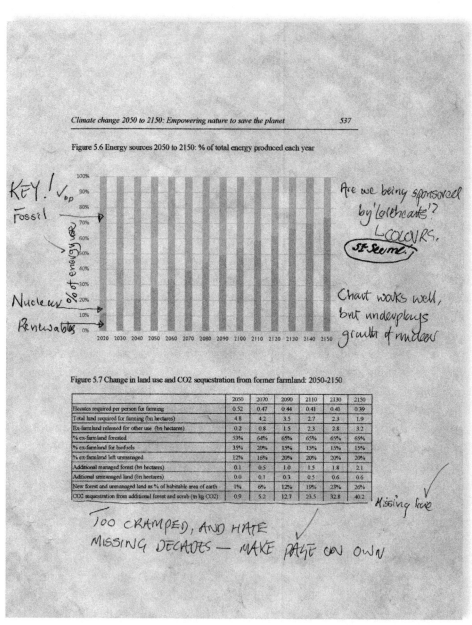

Isarebe's comments on an early draft of the climate section within Future Perfect

Isarebe briefed his team to complete a detailed analysis on what this ex-farmland could be used for, talking to and employing many land economists and dendrologists from around the world. The work was done at a regional level. They concluded most land released from farming was likely to be reutilised for biofuels and as managed forests, or left as unmanaged scrub. They predicted much of the early demand for this land would be for biofuels and then towards the end of the forecast period, when Isarebe expected a slow-down in demand for biofuels, more of this land would be forested or left unmanaged. Their final conclusion was that by 2150, 65% of this released farmland would be managed forests, 20% would be unmanaged wilderness and 15% would be used for biofuels. These forecasts have turned out to be broadly correct. However, many formerly managed forests have now been left to rewild as 'Human Oversight Free Areas'(HOFAs). The afforestation of the planet has had other climatically beneficial effects, in particular the greater use of wood-based materials in construction. 90% of new buildings around the world in 2149 were primarily constructed from wood or other plant-derived materials, whilst just 9% of new-builds in 2149 were fabricated from steel and concrete and these were mostly highly specialist buildings, such as power stations and, perhaps ironically, steel mills. In 2050, at the time of the publication of *Future Perfect*, around 3 trillion kilogrammes of CO_2 per annum was emitted during steel and concrete production. By 2148, this had fallen to less than a trillion kilogrammes.

Having calculated this massive change in land use, Isarebe and his team used the available information on levels of carbon dioxide sequestration by different plants to calculate the amount of CO_2 such newly-formed forests and scrubland would remove from the atmosphere. He was conservative in his estimates, but was correct in assuming that over time forests would be increasingly well engineered with respect to their CO_2 absorption.

On completing this work, Isarebe was reported to have shouted 'think we've cracked it';[229] his more downbeat version of Archimedes' 'Eureka!' By Isarebe's calculation, CO_2 sequestration from these additional forests and newly-formed scrubland would remove over 40 trillion kilogrammes of CO_2 from the atmosphere each year by 2150, compared with human-induced CO_2 emissions of just over 20 trillion kilogrammes. And when this was combined with his assumptions on carbon removal through other means, it meant he anticipated net human-generated emissions of CO_2 into the atmosphere would become negative early in the 22nd century and CO_2 would start to be rapidly removed from the atmosphere from then on.

---

229   Bortelli, R, 2070, *The Dizzy Digger*, Manchosens, New York, p. 192

CO2 sequestration from land released from farming: 2050 - 2150
Comparison of predictions within *Future Perfect* and actual

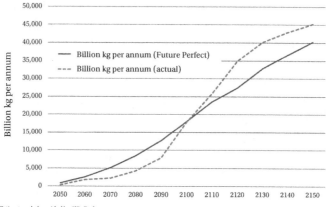

*Estimate only (provided by GlEnFor)

The last piece in this complex jigsaw was to use these forecasts of net GHG emissions to predict what was likely to happen to average global temperatures. Whilst there appeared to be an almost linear relationship between global CO2 emissions and average global temperature, this masked a number of more complex factors: the impact of other GHGs on global warming; the rate of dispersion of different GHGs out of the atmosphere; the slow release of energy from oceans, which have a much higher heat capacity than air; the impact of increased water evaporation as temperatures rise (water vapour is also a GHG); and the reduction in sea ice as temperature rises, reducing the reflectivity of the earth's surface, to name a few.

Net change in CO2 in atmosphere per annum: 2050 - 2150
Comparison of predictions within *Future Perfect* and actual

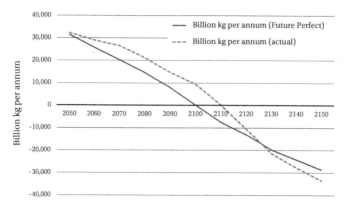

*Estimate only (provided by GlEnFor)

Whilst Isarebe knew these other factors would increase the amount of global warming over and above that which would be generated by CO_2 alone, he was also aware of other feedback loops that would ameliorate global warming, although these were not well understood in 2050. Although this paints a complex picture, Isarebe's models were able to incorporate most of those contemporary understandings.

The main question around which there was still a high degree of uncertainty in 2050 was what would happen when GHG levels finally started to fall: would there be a simple linear fall in global average temperatures; would it take temperatures longer to decrease than they had to increase; or would temperatures continue to rise, through some mechanism not yet understood? Isarebe made the assumption that falling concentrations of GHGs would impact temperatures negatively in exactly the same way as they had positively, but that some of the feedback loops would slow this process down. In particular, his team concluded it would take significantly longer for the oceans to cool and for the polar ice caps to re-establish themselves.

Isarebe's forecasts were built on statistical models, but inevitably were also dependent on assumptions regarding political motivations, public acceptance and technical innovation, which contributed to the considerable statistical uncertainty around the numbers. Despite this, he decided not to publish scenario-based forecasts, but instead only give their best estimate of the future path of change. Isarebe knew scenarios were intellectually and statistically warranted, but his experience was that a lack of understanding of risk meant people picked and chose the scenarios that best met their prejudices. He decided, 'My prejudices are the least bad option'.[230] This suggests he was cavalier, but the work on different scenarios and statistical uncertainty was meticulously completed and these findings were later published in academic journals between 2051 and 2054. His internal struggle on how best to present their results was to the fore in a diary entry from November 2049:

> I imagined talking to Izzy tonight, except that's not true, I didn't have to imagine talking to her, she was there, like she always is. She kept telling me people had to understand what was most likely to happen, rather than be spoon-fed wild stories from politicians about how they would save the planet, or be shouted into submission by the environmental doom-mongers saying we would all be dead in a week, just after the last tiger had been eaten by the last elephant.

---

230   Isarebe, S, 2049, eLetter to Professor D. Kamil dated 19th November 2049, The Isarebe Trust Archives, Cambridge, England (Box 162, Folder 8)

She kept telling me something I already knew – that people don't get risk. They want a clear story, even if they know it is unlikely to be absolutely true. She told me I should stop hiding behind statistical probity. Only Iz could make this sound like a moral crime, up there with murder and rape.[231]

Isarebe's predictions were for a rise in global temperatures from 1.83°C above pre-industrial levels in 2050 to 2.25°C above pre-industrial levels by the turn of the 22nd century. He then forecast global temperatures would slowly start to decline, falling to 1.81°C above pre-industrial levels by 2150. Whilst these predictions utilised the latest available evidence, actual temperatures continued to rise well into the 22nd century, eventually peaking at 2.4°C above pre-industrial levels in 2118. The 1st of February 2118 was named in 2122 as Earth Recovery Day by the United Nations, representing the day when global temperatures officially peaked. This date was somewhat arbitrarily chosen, but it was undoubtedly around this time there were signs global warming had stabilised or even started to reverse. Temperatures hovered around this level through to 2134, when the first statistically significant measurements of a fall in global temperatures were finally confirmed. It is estimated that average global temperatures are now 2.2°C above pre-industrial levels and are forecast to fall by a further 0.5°C by 2200. It is now expected that it will take until 2350 to get back to pre-industrial temperature levels.[232]

Global warming: °C above pre-industrial levels
Comparison of predictions within *Future Perfect* and actual

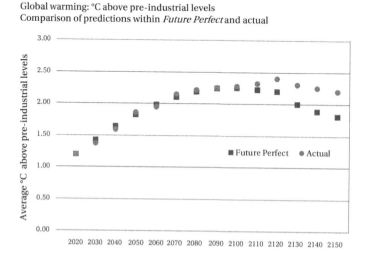

231   Isarebe, S, 2050, diary entry dated 9th November 2049, The Isarebe Trust Archives, Cambridge, England (Box 161, Folder 4)
232   Williams, R, 2148, *Global cooling: A review of models and forecasts 2148*, Energy and Carbon Recovery Science, 184, 1

The current trajectory of global warming in 2150 would have been hailed as a long-awaited triumph back in 2050, but perhaps inevitably there is now a movement opposing further global cooling, with growing numbers calling for increased use of fossil fuels and decommissioning of carbon capture facilities.[233] Their argument is that we have been in a period of relative climate stability for over thirty years and a new equilibrium in the natural world has been established, which should be left well alone. However, unless the new forests are cut down en masse, there appears little that can be done to reverse the current trend, unless political pressures ramp up considerably.

---

233   Mackar, P, 2149, *Still crazy after all these years*, The Independent Guardian, London, 30th November 2149, p. 3

A Collapse in the Global Population by 2150

- ## Population in UK set to fall by 40 million
- ## Prediction of collapse of capitalism

PETER YAN AND KOPI DEES - LONDON

An extraordinary new book, Future Perfect, was published yesterday with all the fanfare normally reserved for a Bollywood Blockbuster or the launch of a new version of ZeeAlphaWar. Its author is a relatively unknown academic economist, Solomon D. Isarebe, who through an admittedly extraordinary feat of research and modelling has produced detailed forecasts of a collapse in the global population and an associated decline in economic growth around the world. He predicts the world population will fall from 9.2 billion in 2050 to 4.8 billion by 2150 and he thinks it won't stop there, with it falling to less than 3 billion within a further 100 years, a figure not seen since the 1950s. His predictions are even more calamitous for the UK, which he believes will shed nearly 40 million people by 2150, with a significant decline in living standards .

When pressed on the impact of this population decline on the economy and house prices in particular, he told our reporter: 'Our models strongly suggest continued economic growth per capita, in line with historic norms, and it looks likely that house prices in major conurbations will remain steady or even grow in real terms'.

Economists and demographers have been lining up to dismiss the conclusions of Isarebe and his team. Professor Rene Dilworthy, Economics Advisor at Mecka Capital and visiting Professor of Economics at Strathclyde & Singapore University, believes: 'Isarebe is in fantasy land if he thinks a population collapse of the magnitude he is predicting would not lead to the end of the capitalist system as we know

it and no one is going to let that happen. There are already signs that the failed experiments of the Beats are leading to a re-evaluation of norms in family size. I think we will start to see the population rise over the next decade, supporting economic growth and protecting investment returns.

Isarebe's renowned and well-respected mentor at Cambridge University, Professor D. Karim, warned: 'You ignore Solomon's conclusions at your peril. He is an exceptional thinker and is taking us in to a new paradigm in demographics, economics and climate analysis. His predictions are not of the end of the world, but the beginning of a new one, a world where through the simple application of family planning we will start to see the world cool and nature reassert its authority over the planet.'

Isarebe insists there is nothing controversial about his population forecasts stating: 'My works shows nothing, except the miraculous planet-saving impact of the self-interested decisions that will be made by billions of women around the world'. He reserves most of his self-congratulations to his work on the impact of these changes on the environment. He predicts the fall in the global population will release huge swathes of land from farming, much of which will be used to grow plants efficient at removing CO2 from the atmosphere, such that human-generated emissions will become net negative towards the end of his forecast period. He believes we can eventually cool the planet just by having fewer children, although he insists we must collectively do all we

can to ameliorate the impact of global warming before his predictions kick in.

Solomon Isarebe, with his adoptive step-sister Isabelle Isarebe, who is named as co-author of the book. Isabelle Isarebe tragically died in 2048, aged just 32, following a sudden heart attack whilst visiting relatives in Syria.

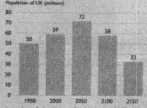

UK population predicted to shrink by 54% over the next 100 years
Population of UK (millions)

1950	2000	2050	2100	2150
50	59	72	58	33

Source: Future Perfect / Solomon & Isabelle Isarebe/ COUP / 2050

FTT view page 24
OPI page 26

For a more detailed analysis see pp7-9

Future Perfect /£49.99 / Cambridge and Oxford University Press

11th August 20

PART 4
The success of *Future Perfect*

4.1 Getting over the finish line

From January 2049 until May 2050 Isarebe kept up a relentless schedule, often simultaneously working on three or four streams of analysis. Once the technical work had been completed and the text written, he insisted on overseeing the process of production, from editing to design, publicity and printing.

The first draft of the population and economic forecasts were completed early in 2049 and Isarebe handed this work over to Casey Ingar to manage a process of review. Although Isarebe had no intention of publishing through the academic press, which insisted on formal peer review, he wanted to ensure there were no fundamental errors in his models and forecast assumptions. Ingar pulled in favours from some of the best economists and demographers around the world, working in academia, public bodies, central banks, global institutions and private firms. Rumours had started spreading about this monumental piece of work and most were more than willing to be associated with it.

The thanks in *Future Perfect* for these reviewers make extraordinary reading: the list includes three Nobel Prize winners, two John Bates Clark Medal winners (including Jeanie DeSoto, Head of Macroeconomics at MIT and former critic-in-chief of Solomon Isarebe), Hughes Davro, Governor of the Bank of England and Pen Legrand, the Head of Population Studies at the United Nations. Isarebe had their comments collated and printed in a private anthology in 2053, which is still held in the Isarebe Trust Archives,[234] but it is the original copies, covered in Isarebe's vitriolic hand-written notes, which make more interesting reading. The reviewer's comments were mostly philosophical, rather than technical, apart from those of Washington Mngo from Beijing University of Technical Advancement, who compiled a detailed critique of their economic modelling, and those from Mark Trainer, Head of Population Studies at Family Health and Longevity International, who completely rejected the approach they had taken to population forecasting, although tentatively agreeing with their assumptions on the impact of AI Medical Support systems on longevity in developing nations. Solomon Isarebe wrote hand-written letters to thank these reviewers and went out of his way to acknowledge their contribution at any chance he could, but privately

---

234   Isarebe, S, 2052, *A Critique of Future Perfect*, Isarebe & Isarebe Publications, The Isarebe Trust Archives, Cambridge, England (Box 230)

he dismissed most of the comments as 'trivial and missing the point.'[235] The exception to this was Washington Mngo's review of their economic methods and forecasts. Isarebe insisted Casey Ingar fly to China and hire Mngo to complete a reworking of the economic models and a testing of all their assumptions. Mngo, realising the strength of his position, negotiated a higher fee for three months' work than anyone else in the organisation earned over the whole year, including Isarebe and Ingar. Mngo identified some minor errors and made a small number of structural changes to the models. The revised models were more elegant, but the resultant forecasts differed little from the original forecasts made by Isarebe and his team.

Isarebe also secured the services of Philo Pili to edit the completed sections. Pili was a renowned American academic, columnist and historian. She was Visiting Professor of Statistical Anthropology at Edinburgh University when Solomon Isarebe approached her to help with *Future Perfect*. As a Harvard freshman, Pili had attended one of Isarebe's legendary lectures at MIT and was undoubtedly a fan. She agreed to work for a nominal fee and within nine weeks had reworked the chapters on Demography and Economics. Although these were not her areas of expertise, she applied her engaging writing skills to what was a relatively dry and technical first draft of the report. Isarebe was so pleased he pleaded with her to edit the rest of the book, which she agreed to, putting aside all her existing commitments. Isarebe commented: 'Phil was perfect. I could barely contain myself when I read what she'd done. It sounded intelligent, rational, indisputable, but more importantly it was so easy to read. You didn't need a heap of letters after your name to get it, just a bit of curiosity and an open mind. And it still somehow sounded like me – a better than real-life version of me. I sometimes can't believe my luck, although whenever I say something like that I think of Izzy and that thought goes straight to [expletive].'[236] The only fight Isarebe reputedly ever had with Pili was when he asked her to be credited as co-author. Pili refused, saying she was 'nothing more than a glorified typist.'[237] What is almost certain is that without Pili the book would not have had the impact it did. Isarebe was a fine and accessible technical writer, but Pili provided the polish.

The hiring of Mngo and Pili were two of many high-level appointments Isarebe made in the first half of 2049. After Isabelle's death, Solomon seemingly lost the need or the desire for absolute control and sought out exceptional

235   Isarebe, S, 2049, email to Casey Ingar dated 3rd July 2049, the Isarebe Trust Archives, Cambridge, England (Box 156, Folder 3)
236   Isarebe, S, 2067, typed notes for an unpublished autobiography, manuscript dated 24th September 2067, The Isarebe Trust Archives, Cambridge, England (Box 448)
237   Pili, P, 2049, email to Solomon Isarebe dated 4th October 2049, the Isarebe Trust Archives, Cambridge, England (Box 159, Folder 6)

people from around the world to help him. Many did not last long, unable to keep up with Isarebe's unrelenting pace or unwilling to deal with his intellectual and personal fury, but for others it was a moment of intellectual creativity they would never experience again. One of these was Merv Ah Ket, Head of Climate Change at ASIRO in Australia, who helped model carbon emissions and energy consumption:

> The man's a bloody animal. Whenever I challenged him on some aspect of his work, he would quote references I'd never heard of, or refer me to some obscure data which when I checked afterwards was almost always right. I was employed as Senatorial Advisor – nifty title! – but to be honest, most of the time I was learning from him. The only area where I added anything to the party was on some of the detailed sub-modelling of carbon emissions and even that small contribution was rendered negligible when Solomon and Hetty Brown started running with whatever I had given them, turning my mundane (if thorough) work into something that was a real beauty.

> Solomon always called Hetty 'Brown Cow' and I'm sure I heard her purr every time he said it. I tried it on her once and thought I was going to catch one round the chops. She called him Solster sometimes, but there was no way I was going to try that – he was paying me big bucks for my six months in NY and he dismissed people like I drink beer – quickly and with no thought for the consequences.

> I loved it. It was a thrill-a-day and in the end we hired five of my best guys in Melbourne to help out. At the end of each day, Solomon and I would write a brief for them for their next working day, which was our night, and then each morning we would find a summary of what they had achieved and so it went on. It all happened so fast. It showed me what you can do if you shed the chains and put a mad bull in charge.

> The funny thing is, I rate it as one of the best times of my life and I guess you could say I have a sort of man-crush on Solomon Isarebe, but I bet you he wouldn't recognise me if he ever saw me again, even if I kissed him on the laughing gear.[238]

---

238 Ah Ket, M, 2067, *Life lived in the happy lane*, Sydney International Media, Sydney, pp. 123–124

Merv Ah Ket's benevolent view of Solomon Isarebe's working style was not shared by everyone. As the end of the analysis for *Future Perfect* came in sight, Solomon upped his tempo further and became an increasingly destructive force, as Rita Bortelli noted in her autobiography:.

> Dizzy was getting out of control. I was told you could literally hear him growling around the office and not a day went by when someone in the team wasn't reduced to tears. One day in '49 I had to go into the Manhattan office for a board meeting. I was early and sat waiting in the one and only meeting room. Ten minutes later Dizzy stormed in, pushing past me, knocking me out of my chair and on to the floor. He looked down at me and after some seconds his eyes appeared to focus and he realised who I was and what he had done. He apologised and picked me up, before locking himself in the restroom.

> I called Reba and the next day Jannik turned up in New York, with no luggage except for the bags under his eyes. Dizzy was passing through reception when Jannik arrived – he stopped and looked at his dad, but not a flicker of recognition passed over his face. He walked on into his office, shutting the door behind him.

> Jannik stood outside the glass door of Dizzy's office like some great immovable Finnish rock. He stood there for hours, or so it seemed to all of us watching and waiting for some great tragedy to unfold. Dizzy eventually came out of the office and put his arms around his dad's neck. Dizzy was at least 6 inches taller than Jannik, but he looked like a little boy that day. He coughed and cleared his throat and on the second attempt said, 'Sorry Dad' and he then turned to us and said, 'Sorry everyone'. Dizzy went back to work and Jannik went home.

> Dizzy still worked 16-hour days and was as intellectually demanding as ever, but after Jannik's intervention few were reduced to tears by the verbal violence of Solomon D. Isarebe.[239]

On Valentine's Day, 2050, the technical work was completed and drafts of the final sections were handed over to Philo Pili. It is reported for the week before he relinquished control to Pili, Isarebe had no sleep at all.[240]

---

239   Bortelli, R, 2070, *The Dizzy Digger*, Manchosens, New York, p. 157

240   Burrage, T, 2050, e-message to Rita Bortelli dated 23rd February 2050, The Isarebe Trust Archives, Cambridge, England (Box 166, Folder 3)

Isarebe left Rita Bortelli's apartment in New York at the end of February 2050. Bortelli had to have the whole place redecorated. It had been home to Isarebe and had been a dorm for visiting 'Senatorial Advisors' for over a year. Isarebe had written ideas on the wall of his bedroom when he woke at night with his head buzzing. Isarebe sent Bortelli five enormous bouquets of flowers to thank her, but she didn't find this out until she took back the keys to her New York apartment in late March. She found them rotting outside her apartment door.

Hetty Brown had been by Isarebe's side for the final sixteen months of the production of *Future Perfect*, as a friend and mentor, but also increasingly as a technical contributor. After finally leaving Bortelli's apartment, Isarebe walked with his two suitcases and carry-on from Central Park to Roosevelt Island to say goodbye to Hetty Brown and her family.

I cried my eyes out. For what felt like the first time in this damned life.

It was BC's endless kindness, her wonderful Dave, her incredible, moronic, accepting kids. But it was something else too. Leaving her meant I had to go home and I wasn't sure I could do it. It meant I had to look at the depression in the bed where Izzy used to sleep. To see her clothes in the drawer and imagine the smell that used to come off them. To see the new lines in Mum's face and to witness Dad trying to happy us all through it.

For the first time since I was a kid I felt beaten.[241]

Solomon went home to the refuge of Hilman Cottage where Reba fed him and watched him sleep and Jannik told him silly jokes while 'Iz sat quietly at the table, watching us all fall apart, tears in her eyes for the death that death leaves behind.'[242]

After three days and without goodbyes to his parents, Isarebe left Hilman Cottage before dawn, driving 500 miles to Philo Pili's cottage on the banks of Loch Sunart in Scotland, where she had retreated for the mammoth task of completing *Future Perfect*. They worked together until the middle of April: Pili writing and Isarebe proofing, checking and urging Pili to go ever faster. They developed a working rhythm, with Pili insisting they work for no more than nine hours a day and they never talk of *Future Perfect* outside working hours.

241   Isarebe, S, 2067, typed notes for an unpublished autobiography, manuscript dated 24th September 2067, The Isarebe Trust Archives, Cambridge, England (Box 448)
242   Isarebe, S, 2067, typed notes for an unpublished autobiography, manuscript dated 24th September 2067, The Isarebe Trust Archives, Cambridge, England (Box 448)

She took Isarebe to the pub each evening for their meal, watching him drink endless whiskies while she sipped on a single Dubonnet.

On Friday, 15th April 2050, the final draft of *Future Perfect* was finished and it was sent to Cambridge and Oxford University Press (COUP) to be prepared for simultaneous online and hard-copy launches. It ran to 662 pages, including 124 pages of technical appendices and 29 pages of references. The introduction was written by an ageing Professor D. Kamil and the book was dedicated to Reba and Jannik Isarebe. The authors were named as Solomon and Isabelle Isarebe. Isarebe refused to concede to any of COUP's suggestions for text changes and ways to edit it down to a more manageable length. There was a stand-off between Martin Haymer, Senior Editor at COUP, and Isarebe, who was ready to self-publish, but a last-minute intervention from Professor Kamil and a financial guarantee from Rita Bortelli got the project over the line.

The cover design was prepared by a young Arem Johns, who was working as a part-time freelancer at COUP. It was a strikingly simple design that gave the book great authority and made it stand out on bookshelves for more than just its size. Isarebe did not meet her and it would be many years before their paths would cross.

Casey Ingar, with the first copy of Future Perfect, Cambridge, 2050

The book was plagued by last-minute delays at the printer, but was finally ready for launch on 10th August 2050. The launch was to take place virtually, in all forty countries where they had undertaken survey research. After a short introduction from the publisher, Solomon spoke by video link for over two hours, without notes, outlining with a cold passion and undeniable logic the main themes of the book. There were no jokes that day, but it was perhaps his most outstanding public speaking performance. People who were present in the studio in New York from where it was broadcast said it was an intense physical experience.

Solomon Isarebe and Rita Bortelli, Launch of Future Perfect, New York, 2050

It was an otherwise quiet summer's news day, but there is no satisfactory explanation for why this quasi-academic tome, presented by this strange sort-of-Englishman dominated international news that day. Isarebe's face was broadcast around the world and the headlines, which focused on the dramatic forecasts of population decline, were predictably negative about its economic impact, despite the contrary evidence contained within the book. However, over the coming weeks more in-depth reviews looked at Isarebe's conclusions on the positive impact of population decline on almost every aspect of human life, as well as for the planet.

For all Isarebe's planning, he was ill-prepared for the sudden and overwhelming media attention and the demands for interviews, comments and appearances. Rita Bortelli called in Maggie Doyle, the former head of her Digger PR team, to manage the interest that *Future Perfect* was generating.

By the end of 2051, Isarebe had appeared on 213 current affairs AV broadcasts, had been interviewed on nearly 820 radio stations, asked to participate in over 2,000 podcasts (he agreed to just twenty-three) and had been featured on the front cover of over 700 newspapers, magazines and websites. He was the most unlikely global media star of 2050–51.

Although it was initially only available in hardback and digital versions, *Future Perfect* became the best-selling non-fiction book of 2050, although as Isarebe possibly correctly surmised 'I bet you less than 10% of those who bought it have actually read the damn thing.'[243] It sold over 8 million copies and was downloaded nearly 12 million times in digital form in 2050 alone.

Maggie Doyle organised a world tour for Isarebe in 2051, during which he spoke in 170 locations around the world, mostly in universities, but also in theatres and concert halls to audiences of up to 2,000 people.

By the end of 2051, *Future Perfect* had sold 42 million copies and after the publication of a paperback version, went on to record sales of 73 million by the end of the decade. It had also been downloaded 124 million times. In 2054, Isarebe prepared a shorter version of the book for high school students and a picture book for younger children in 2055. It was by far the highest selling non-fiction book of the 21st century, outselling the Bible and the Quran, and it was to become a standard text on many undergraduate courses in the 2050s and 2060s.

---

243   Isarebe, S, 2051, eLetter to Rita Bortelli dated 5th January 2051, The Isarebe Trust Archives, Cambridge, England (Box 190, Folder 3)

4.2 A bewildering success

Future Perfect no longer reads as a cutting-edge piece of analysis, but it is still fascinating as a historical document. Many of Isarebe's numerical predictions have proved eerily if fortuitously accurate, as some of the assumptions behind the forecasts now seem laughably inaccurate, stopping just short of predicting we would all be flying to work using jet packs. Whilst it remains a stimulating and enjoyable book, it is not immediately obvious why it was such a success. What was it about life in 2050 that provided such fertile ground for such an unusual book? Even the publishers were sceptical about its likely success, as Graham McDougall-Hines of Cambridge and Oxford University Press explained in his memoir in 2069:[244]

> *Future Perfect* took us all by surprise. We didn't want to publish it at all, but were bullied into it by Prof Kalim [*sic*], who was our most senior Syndic and was also Advocate-in-Chief for Solomon Isarebe. He threatened to resign and make a big noise about it if we didn't publish.

> The draft Isarebe presented us with was long, technical and excessively detailed and was neither a textbook nor a popular guide, although it was beautifully written. We all thought it was a 220,000-word disaster waiting to happen.[245] Isarebe refused to let us edit a single word, apart from a typo we found on page 414. I remember the excitement on finding it, but we suspect it was a joke or more likely a childish insult that Isarebe had left for us to find – he had spelt 'factual' as 'fackuall'. We finally gave in to his demands, deciding it was more bother than it was worth to fight Kalim [*sic*] and Isarebe over a book we were certain would quietly meet its death within a year.

> Within weeks of publication it became clear we were wrong and it was going to be an extraordinary success. We desperately sought reasons for why our calculations were so far out, but we never came up with a totally satisfactory answer.

---

244   McDougall-Hines, G, 2069, *The great publishing coup*, Cambridge and Oxford University Press, Cambridge, 2069, pp. 77–78
245   The main text, excluding the appendices and references, contained 175,000 words.

By 2050, the excitement and energy of the Beat generation had dissipated and there were political turmoils of a largely grubby and domestic nature bubbling up around the world. As a global community, or more accurately as a first world community, we were in a collective funk, the morning after the big party of the 2040s. There were no new big ideas, nothing to rally around and the great droughts and famines of 2049 had engendered a sense of pessimism about the fate of the world. Perhaps *Future Perfect* was nothing more than a big intellectual Alka-Seltzer?

That is a cheap shot, because *Future Perfect* had something elusively magical about it: a magic which, after a while, even old publishing cynics like me came to appreciate. It was perhaps its quiet and rational optimism about the future of the planet and the human race that made you want to hold it close. I don't mean that figuratively: people would literally hold the book close to them. I used to watch them leaving our bookshop in Cambridge, hugging the book to their chests. People wanted the hard copy not the digital; they wanted to smell the words on the page. It was a very strange phenomenon. I think it made people feel better about themselves, about the human condition.

There was also something about Solomon Isarebe. You didn't want to hold him close, for personal hygiene reasons, but he had a strangely mesmeric quality and everything he said or wrote was so convincing. Everyone who met him said the same. I remember taking him out to dinner just before the book launch and without knowing why I ordered exactly the same things he had – I even ordered mussels, which I knew would make me ill. He left me feeling like I had no control over my decisions.

Whatever the reasons, *Future Perfect* started to sell to our core student market and then their younger siblings wanted a copy, and then their parents, and then friends of their parents. It was like some cultish pyramid scheme, where people were paid in warm feelings, rather than money. It was one of those books you had to own, that you had to have an opinion on, that had to be seen on your bookshelf. And if you hadn't read it, then Solomon Isarebe was omnipresent: on TV, on Eye-Ted Talks, on radio, on podcasts. Some said he should take over as James Bond in their new anti-beauty, anti-charisma, anti-sex, anti-humour version of the franchise.[246]

Future Perfect secured the future of COUP, so perhaps eating humble pie followed by some dodgy mussels was a small price to pay.

Many agree with McDougall-Hines, that *Future Perfect* arrived at a moment of collective global uncertainty, division and cynicism after the optimism and cohesiveness of the 2040s. Without understanding the 2040s, it is impossible to understand the success of *Future Perfect*.

---

246   James Bond was a fictional British spy who was the main character in thirty-seven films. The early films were noted for their brutish misogyny and random violence. The franchise was rested in 2058, as the idea of a spy involved in on-the-ground overseas missions became implausible to many. The 37th film, *Two Brains One Gun*, was brought out in 2073 as a supposedly humorous pastiche of previous Bond films. It flopped with new audiences and infuriated previous fans of the franchise.

4.3 Marching to the beat of the Beats

It is seductive to generalise about an entire generation or period in history, but that is to silence both dissenting voices and those who quietly held on to traditional ways, but the period 2037–2048 was undoubtedly a time of great change and collective hope. It was when a more rebellious youth reclaimed their role at the vanguard, after decades of corporately-inspired conformism[247] and they were influential in the break-up of the techno-giants, the introduction of new privacy laws and greater protection of rights of individual expression, as well as a new approach to the environment.

In a small way, Solomon and Isabelle Isarebe were both involved in the early stages of this youth movement. Solomon was never as politically engaged as his sister, but an incident during a lecture he gave at MIT in 2037 led to him taking an interest in the influential 'Turn off the news' campaign group, the precursor of the Beats:

> One of the students stood up at the end of my lecture today, wearing a t-shirt that proclaimed, 'Truth Is All'. He asked me why I maintained economic growth is largely a result of collective human brilliance, co-operation and individual decision making. It was a good question and he had clearly been hanging on my every word. My complacency was shattered when he went on to say '... when everyone knows economic growth is a lie put about by Jewish satanists who are planning to blow up the planet after first escaping to Mars.' I don't know much about religion, the occult, spaceflight or blowing up planets, but I thought it unlikely one could simultaneously be Jewish, a satanist, an astronaut and have access to several billion tonnes of explosives. I assumed he was just mad, so smiled and took another question from the generally rational throng.

> I talked about it with Izzy tonight. She laughed and showed me a video from the Harvard debating society, who had discussed the proposal: 'Satanists will occupy Mars in the next thirty years'. The motion was passed. She then showed me a stream of articles from

---

247   The 2020s and 2030s were mocked by many in song, literature, film and theatre in the 2040s, perhaps most memorably in Paul Dane's 2043 hit, 'The smiling years of fascism we loved so well'.

news agencies, running the same story. It may all be something of a joke, but at least one Mitty student seems to be taking it seriously.[248]

This incident rekindled Isarebe's interest in the power of the media and their exploitation of our evolutionary disposition towards messages of imminent danger. Through discussions with colleagues at MIT, he discovered the 'Turn off the news' movement.[249] 'Turn off the news' shared his concerns and preached turning off all mainstream media channels as a way of finding peace and personal happiness. Isarebe's involvement only extended to wearing 'Turn off the news' t-shirts, but with typical obsession 'Turn off the news' t-shirts were almost the only shirts he wore for the next two years.

The Isarebes, Herefordshire, 2043

---

248   Isarebe, S, 2037, diary entry dated 31st March 2037, the Isarebe Trust Archives, Cambridge, England (Box 80, Folder 1)
249   Isarebe wrote a quote from Mitch Graham's 2034 book *The Last Media Tycoon* (Cornhills, 2034, p. 176) on the front of one of his 2037 notebooks: 'Bad bombs sell, good news bombs!'

Isabelle Isarebe took more of an active interest in politics in the late 2030s, taking part in virtual and real sit-ins against the privacy intrusions of the so-called Information Mega Powers (IMPs), but this was perhaps at least partly because of her relationship with Mooketsi Mooketsi who was heavily involved in the Privacy Movement in Botswana. After their relationship ended, Isabelle adopted the same politically aware but inactive stance as Solomon. However cool, analytical and voyeuristic they may have been with regards to the political activism during this most transformative of decades, they were no more immune than anyone else to the fashion trends of the 2040s, with even Solomon wearing the seemingly compulsory midi-skirts of the day.

The 'Turn off the news' movement, which started at the Berkeley campus of the University of California, morphed into the more organised and politically successful 'Beatified Bohos', universally referred to as the 'Beats', after the movement of the same name from the mid-20th century. The Beats started as a vague coalition of idealists, variously pro-privacy, libertarian, ultra-green and anarchical, while almost all of them were liberal in politics, sexual practices and drug use. This group, which have variously been called The New Hippies, Poppy-Heads, Offliners and Bafflers, were unlike those found in most previous revolutionary youth movements in that they were mostly pro-capitalist, albeit pro-capitalist with an ultra-green agenda. The number who signed up as paid members of the organisation never exceeded 100,000, but they influenced attitudes, behaviour and politics all around the world. They remained influential throughout the 2040s, even after the organisation was formally abandoned in 2046. With the wisdom of hindsight, the extent of their influence was perhaps overstated, as they never achieved political office and they were incoherent and divided on many issues, but they were undoubtedly an important symbol of change, just as the Hippies had been in the 20th century.

> The Beats, led by Earl Lord-King,[250] have power that politicians all over the world crave and CEOs fear. They have succeeded in giving us back nothing less than our personal freedom.[251]

---

250   Born David Jones in Louisville, Kentucky in November 2012, he changed his name to Earl Lord-King in September 2037 whilst a graduate student at The University of California, Berkeley.

251   Unattributed, 2046, leader, The Los Angeles Inquirer, 1st December 2046, p. 45

4.4 The fall of the IMPs

The ascent of the Beats coincided with the break-up and competitive decline of many of the Information Mega Powers (IMPs) that dominated global commerce between 1990 and 2040, and with the rewriting of many privacy laws. These changes represented a cultural, legal and economic socio-quake, the aftershocks of which we still feel today.

It is difficult to pinpoint the epicentre of this socio-quake, but there were arguably two events, alongside the ongoing cultural influence of the Beats, that led to significant shifts in attitudes towards the information giants and the way they and governments treated personal data.

The first of these events seems trivial, almost puerile, through the distorting lens of history, but it was undoubtedly influential. In 2039, there was a meta-review undertaken by SSE[252] on the impact of mobile information devices (MIDs) on health. Their conclusions surprised many, in that they found no link between the use of MIDs and mental health problems, or cancers, which many had assumed was the case. However, they discovered heavy long-term users of MIDs were on average nearly 1.8 cm shorter than light users of MIDs. This was thought to be due to the long-term effect of the use of MIDs on posture and muscle density, although no causal link was established. In itself, this may not have proved significant, but in 2038 there had a been a well-publicised study on the relationship between height and Mating Quotient (MQ), a euphemism for sexual attractiveness. This report, written by Harmin and Harmin,[253] was of dubious merit, but the idea of MQ seeped into the public consciousness and was widely referred to on social media channels. When the SSE report came out, the media and the public joined the dots and concluded heavy MIDs' use led to lower sexual performance and a lack of sexual attractiveness – not the sort of publicity that wins an industry hearts and minds.

The irony was that MID manufacturers had already addressed the problem of the impact of MIDs on posture, through the development of on-face, on-eye and in-eye screens. This didn't seem to matter: the link in the public's mind had become firmly established and sexual attractiveness was obviously more important to many people than 'updates on trivia, virtual

---

252   SSE was the acronym for the Service de Santé Européen
253   Harmin, C and Harmin, A, 2038, *Understanding the physical determinants of male sexual attractiveness in everyday social intercourse*, Journal of Empirical Sexual Studies, 13, pp. 213–311

loves, likes and the state of Murdo Walls' pecs.'[254] MIDs and more importantly the content from IMPs accessed on these devices, started to be seen as a health threat, with parallels often being drawn between IMPs and the tobacco industry in the second half of the 20th century.

Cartoon from SuperG, 2039

This revelation of the possible but unproven link between the use of MIDs and sexual prowess came on the heels of an unrelated event in 2038. Matsi Tempore, a former actress and singer who had forsaken Hollywood in the early 2030s to found Global Childhood Protection (GCP) was arrested for 'sexually damaging children in the care of GCP,'[255] with claims she also suffered from borderline personality disorder and should never have held a

---

254   Unattributed, 2039, The Washington and New York Post, 4th December 2039, p. 2
255   Unattributed, 2038, The Independent Guardian, 17th August 2038, p. 2

position of power in a large charitable institution. What lead to a global outcry about her arrest was there was no physical evidence of either her crimes or her mental condition. All the 'evidence' was derived from predictive profiling based on her Longitudinal Data Record (LDR), collated by IMPs and passed on to Federal government agencies. The FBI stated the LDR-based predictions on Tempore were so conclusive they had to act to prevent further harm being done to children in her care.

At the time of her arrest, Matsi Tempore was the closest thing on earth to a saint and most people refused to accept she was the worst of sinners. At her trial, Tempore's defence team showed the jury anonymised LDR-based profiling reports of all staff and trustees of Global Childhood Protection; 47% had been labelled by the FBI as 'highly likely to be paedophiles'. This included Hope Dawlish, formerly Vice President of the United States, who was Chair of the charity and who agreed parts of her profiling reports could be made public at the trial. Tempore's defence team also revealed the anonymised LDR-based profile reports of thirty-two winners of the Best Actor Oscar and Best Artist Grammy.[256] These profile reports declared nearly 60% of this group were 'highly likely to be suffering borderline personality disorder', compared with an incidence in the population as a whole of less than 1%. The leader of Tempore's defence team, Magnolia Sittingdon, then revealed her own unfiltered LDR to highlight the amount of information IMPs and government agencies held on private individuals. In an act of courtroom drama that was live broadcast around the world, 114 pallet loads of files were brought into the courtroom. Sittingdon then asked for her profile reports from the top 24 IMPs, the FBI, the CIA and the IRS to be brought into the courtroom. To the increasing annoyance of the judge, a further 145 pallet loads of reports were brought in and wheeled out of the courtroom. Every five minutes, for the rest of the trial, a further box-file of new profiling reports was brought into the courtroom and left by the side of the defence lawyers' desk. Matsi Tempore was found not guilty and declared in sound mental health. It was this trial and the response of the public around the world which many believe finally forced the media and politicians to start taking personal privacy seriously.

In 2042, California, Sweden, Australia and Germany were the first states to bring in sweeping new privacy laws. Although each was different in legal detail, they had a common outcome: all institutional and commercial holders of an individuals' information had to destroy this information, unless explicit consent was received from the individual. This excluded information supplied for a specific purpose, such as for health care, where information holders were only allowed to use the information for the direct benefit of the

---

256   These artists had all agreed their anonymised profile reports could be made public.

individual and as originally intended and were not allowed to pass it on to any other organisation, unless explicit approval had been received from that individual. Sweden and Germany went further, in requiring any permission to be renewed on an annual basis. Enormous lobbying pressure was put on politicians to prevent these laws being introduced and the extent of attempted bribery was exposed in a series of trials in the mid-2040s. These lobbyists represented an unlikely alliance of commercial interests, national security organisations, universities and police forces. However, in each of these four states the governments had won landslide elections on promises of privacy law reform and the new laws successfully passed through their legislative processes.

The lobbyists' predictions had been of a collapse in public order, a decline in public health, political infiltration from foreign powers and a drop in economic growth. By 2044, each of these four territories were able to show none of these things had come to pass and each of the governments had record approval ratings. There were also reports of improved mental health in these regions, as some people weaned themselves off social media, although these reports were later shown to be inconclusive. Eventually, nearly every country in the world followed suit, with many going further than these early adopters.

By the late 2040s, most developed countries required social media companies to adhere to existing media legislation. The main impact of this legislative change was that they were required to provide balanced and truthful news reporting and were morally, legally and commercially responsible for the views expressed publicly on their media channels. Some countries also required members of the public who wished to comment on public social media forums to be formally registered by the media channel, with verified proof of address. Therefore, anyone making potentially criminal comments or issuing threats of violence on these channels could be traced by the relevant authorities. Comments on social media almost immediately became less violent and polarised, but most now believe this was not just because of the registration process, but because those making these comments were now required to show their real name on the social media channel. This reduced the perceived distance between the person making the comment and the target of their comments; in a virtual sense it became eye-to-eye. It had been shown many times in academic studies that close proximity in information exchange generally leads to less hyperbole and verbal aggression.

The business models of the IMPs also came under attack from other directions. One of these was the development and public acceptance of 'truth grading'. Ratings on the reliability of information available on the internet had been available for many years, but it was only in the 2040s people started to take 'truth grading' of information on the internet more seriously. There are many logical and practical flaws in all of these systems and these problems remain to this day. However, most truth grading systems in the 2040s claimed to automatically cross-reference statements against many thousands if not millions of sources, each of these sources having a truth rating themselves. Despite the circularity of the logic embedded within these systems, they were used by many in their personal and work lives, with the majority opting to use the auto-redact facility that eliminated the most unreliable sources from search results. These systems were the precursors of the REF systems we use today.

Inevitably, these truth graders were also used to rate institutions and individuals and these ratings are believed to have helped improve the reliability of information on the internet.[257] Despite, or perhaps because of Isarebe's flaws – his cussedness, his spectral directness and his lack of any sense of diplomacy – he was crowned 'Most trusted person on the planet' for eight of the nineteen years from 2050 to 2068. As a result, Isarebe was asked to endorse many things, all of which he refused, although he was sufficiently tempted to talk to Psyqys Mach when they asked him to promote their new auto-fact-presentation eyewear in 2052. This device automatically presented written and visual information via an on-face screen, based on the wearer's known interests and what they were currently looking at. Isarebe was asked to test the device for a week before making a decision on whether to endorse it or not. Two days after receiving the eyewear it was returned to Psyqys Mach with a note, saying: 'It is apparent there is no correlation between what I am thinking and what I am looking at and therefore your product is one of the most irritating inventions I have ever come across. I apologise for the state I return your product in.'[258] Psyqys Mach achieved modest success, but its high price and the lack of relevance of much of the information it presented to users limited its market. Others later exploited this opportunity, with cheaper, higher functionality products.

The IMPs were also hit by the unexpected commercial faltering of predictive algorithms. Predictive algorithms in the 2020s and 2030s presented people with a limited choice of things the IMPs, through their algorithms, believe they 'liked'. This was initially welcomed, but by the mid-2030s people had become bored with the increasingly uni-dimensional offerings

257   Kuchova, K, 2053, *Modelling public factual statements 2010-2050*, Journal of Quantitative Media Analysis, 17, pp. 346-393

258   Isarebe, S, e-mail to Psyqys Mach dated 4th August 2052, The Isarebe Trust Archives, Cambridge, England (Box 228)

they were being presented with and viewing, listening and reading figures started to falter. More people began subscribing to edited programming and recommendations, more akin to the TV channels and radio stations of the 20th century, where a selection of alternatives to 'preferred' choices was provided by panels of editorial experts.

The final existential threat to the IMPs was a global accord on taxing them and a related agreement regarding the collection and distribution of this tax revenue. To many people's surprise, even China signed up to this tax treaty.

By the early decades of the 22nd century most IMPs had been broken up or superseded by new players less wedded to historic systems and practices. In 2030, eighteen of the thirty largest companies in the world by capitalisation were IMPs. By 2080, only eleven of these original eighteen were still in existence and none were in the top thirty. Today only two of these companies still exist in a recognisable form.

4.5 New freedoms, new responsibilities

More important to many people in the 2040s than the curbing of the power of the IMPs were the new privacy laws, which silenced more extreme voices on social media and led to the demise of some of the more invasive uses of big data. These changes were instrumental in bringing about greater social tolerance and perhaps counterintuitively facilitating greater freedom of expression. The Beats claimed this as their greatest triumph and many felt this new sense of freedom directly led to the emergence of some of the greatest artists of the 21st century, including Heylin-Keel and Demisya in the visual arts and Robbie Mansen, widely regarded as the best English-language writer since Dickens.

Part of this new liberality was greater sexual and gender freedom: sexual codes and laws had become increasingly constrictive following the 'Me Too' and 'Time's Up'[259] social media campaigns in the late 2010s and early 2020s. Although Solomon Isarebe was sexually inactive until late in life, many believed his apparent blindness to gender and sexuality was in tune with the times. His diaries suggest otherwise, with Isarebe appearing to have no appreciation of the subtleties of sexual and gender politics and often making statements which individually could be considered either misogynist or misandrist.

A group referred to as Bafflers emerged in the late 2030s, reflecting one aspect of changing attitudes to sex and gender. They initially came out of the strangely acronym-ed LGBTTQQIAAPSA[260] movement in Manchester, England. Bafflers felt they had 'moved beyond the rhetoric of sexual and gender equality'[261] and wanted to live an 'unclassifiable life',[262] disguising their gender and their sexuality. By the early 2040s, the Bafflers were subsumed within the burgeoning Beat movement, which embraced a much wider conception of gender freedom and sexual expression.

Other manifestations of this trend were attempts to de-gender and de-sexualise language, but apart from amongst activist minorities and highly

---

259   The 'Me Too' campaign encouraged women to report sexual harassment and sexual violence, whilst the 'Time's Up' campaign raised money for victims of sexual crimes.
260   LGBTTQQIAAPSA = Lesbian, Gay, Bisexual, Transgender, Transexual, Queer, Questioning, Intersex, Asexual, Allies, Pansexual and/or Sex Avoiders. Solomon Isarebe referred to them as EEMs: Everyone except me.
261   Kel, 2037, *I'm it* [Blog]. Available at http: www.ukblogarchives.org [accessed August 2148]
262   Kel, 2037, *I'm it* [Blog]. Available at http: www.ukblogarchives.org [accessed August 2148]

committed individuals, it never caught on. Comedian Erica Gauphin likened it to being suddenly asked to 'walk backwards and wear inversing glasses', saying that '... you could get used to it, after a few accidents, and you would adapt to a slightly less optimal life, but why bother? Particularly when your mates just think you're being a pretentious prunt.'[263]

The 2040s also saw renewed vigour in the environmental debate and more pragmatism and realism in dealing with the impact of global warming. Most of the Beats were ultra-green, but they were realists above all and advocated a focus on 'symptom management, rather than a silver-bullet cure.'[264]

263   Gauphin, E, 2035, *The dying days of my life*, 10th January 2035 [Blog], available at http: www.ukblogarchives.org [accessed August 2148]
264   Lord-King, E, 2041, speech at the Flower-2-Power-People festival in Portland, Oregon, 23rd June 2041, www.beathistory.org [accessed September 2148]

4.6 The end of the Beats, the end of the world

There were many facets to the cultural, political and commercial revolution of the 2040s and there was barely any aspect of life that was not changed in some way. It therefore seems logical to assume that the success of *Future Perfect* in 2050 must be intimately linked with this most influential of decades. It was, but not with the decade's success, but with the aftermath of the dramatic collapse and fall from grace of the Beats in the late 2040s, which together with climate-events, collectively shook people's confidence and optimism.

Earl Lord-King had been the nominal leader of the Beats since their formation, although it had never been a movement centred on the charisma of its figurehead. Lord-King was less important to the Beat movement as a leader than for his remarkable fund-raising skills and his commercial exploitation of the Beat brand. In late 2047, the year after the Beats had formally closed their operations, rumours started spreading of Lord-King having stolen significant amounts of money throughout the ten years of the Beat's existence.[265] A subsequent IRS investigation claimed Lord-King had passed nearly 20% of all Beat revenue through a series of shell service companies, all solely or partly owned by Lord-King. The scandal was seized upon by the Republican Party in the USA, which had suffered many political defeats over the previous decade and the Beat name was dragged through the courts and the media mud. It was eventually discovered that Lord-King and three more of the original eight founders were guilty of massive corruption, and perhaps more shockingly this fraud had been their goal when they first set up the organisation as students in the late 2030s.

This was not the only scandal to tarnish the Beat name. Demands for the legalisation of recreational drugs had been central to their aims. They had been pushing at an open door, as many wealthy countries had already identified legalisation as the most effective way of improving the health and safety of drug users. In particular, the Beats encouraged the use of ComplaHeX, a mild hallucinogenic and mood enhancer, which had been shown to be short-acting, had few side effects and was non-addictive. In 2049, after the conviction of Earl Lord-King for corruption, a study emerged suggesting ComplaHeX was a contributory factor in the rising incidence of bipolar disorder in developed countries and that Lord-King had been a shareholder in Syzepharm, one of

---

265   The Beats were a registered charity with commercial subsidiaries.

the major manufacturers of ComplaHeX.[266] [267]

By the end of 2049, the Beats had been totally discredited and many started to reflect negatively on the changes they helped bring about through the 'happy sunshine decade.'[268] The confidence and positivity that characterised much of the 2040s was lost as quickly as it had been found: 'It left us feeling like balloons a week after the party had finished; deflated, wrinkled, pointless.'[269]

However, it was not the Beat scandals, but the sudden apparent deterioration in the global climate which led to 1st January 2050 being labelled 'The beginning of the end for planet earth.'[270]

2048 had seen average global temperatures 0.2°C higher than the previous year, with heatwaves in Europe causing the deaths of nearly 3,000 people, most of them elderly people in Spain and Italy. 0.2°C seemed a large increase, but was within the normal range of variation from one year to another. Scientists tried to reassure the public this rise was nothing to worry about and was not indicative of a sudden increase in global warming. However, 2048 was followed by an additional rise of 0.15°C in 2049 and one of the most severe droughts and famines ever seen in Africa, particularly affecting Ethiopia, Sudan, Eritrea and Somalia. Isarebe labelled the subsequent hysteria regarding imminent human extinction as 'one of the worst examples of recency bias and misunderstanding of the nature of statistics I have ever witnessed.'[271] Isarebe's apparent callousness towards the fate of nearly 600,000 people who lost their lives in the drought and subsequent famine of 2049/50, was actually an expression of contempt for the media, who he believed were deliberately misreading the statistics. That the years 2050, 2051 and 2052 turned out to be three of the coolest years of the 21st century came too late to stop a re-evaluation of the rational, calm, global environmental consensus the Beats had been instrumental in creating.

---

266   The Syzepharm ComplaHeX formulation was sold as Haptime SAS (short-acting stimulant).

267   In 2052 it was shown in a meta-review of ComplaHeX by Imperial College, London that it had no significant impact on the development of bipolar disorder and that the 2048 study had been based on a small sample of people, many of whom had lived within thirty miles of Belmont, Massachusetts, the site of McLean Hospital, one of the largest and most respected mental health care institutes in the country. Many people with long-term mental health care issues chose to live within reach of McLean hospital.

268   Unattributed, 2048, *Goodbye Sweet Dreams*, The New London Times Sunday Magazine, 23rd August 2048, p. 31

269   Venessa, 2050, *Really, is that it?*, DC Cardigan, St Pauls, 2050, p. 32

270   Unattributed, 2050, front page headline, The Times Record of India, 1st January 2050, p. 1

271   Isarebe, S, 2049, eLetter to Professor D. Kamil dated 3rd October 2049, The Isarebe Trust Archives, Cambridge, England (Box 159, Folder 2)

By 2050, the golden decade was over. In this, the year of *Future Perfect*'s publication, hope was in short supply: hope for personal and collective salvation and hope for survival of planet Earth. This 'barren land, all that remains after human greed and stupidity has done what it must'[272] was to prove fertile ground for *Future Perfect*. *Future Perfect* perhaps reminded people about all they had, but also that they still controlled their own destiny. *Future Perfect*, amidst all its dry text and stats-heavy pages, seemed to contain an extraordinarily empowering message: it said we could live our small lives and enjoy our small personal successes without guilt, and merely through careful planning of our sex lives and our families, help ensure the planet's survival. It also implicitly stated humans were good and kind and co-operative, if left to their own devices, which was not something often heard in 2050. Solomon Isarebe insisted the future held great promise and people were more than willing to hear that message.

---

272   Jaster, Z, 2050, *The Global Cemetery*, Haskins Press, Glasgow, 2049, p. 121

PART 5
The impact of *Future Perfect*

5.1 The battle for minds and wombs

Isarebe, at least in the first few years after publication, seemed to have little understanding of the scale of *Future Perfect*'s success, or of its political influence. Rita Bortelli sat Isarebe down on the second anniversary of its publication and showed him the sales figures and a dossier on media coverage that COUP's marketing team had prepared: 'I have never seen Dizzy so dumbfounded. I was given the job of explaining it to him because C&O didn't think he'd believe it if it came from them. He was now a very rich man and one of the most influential people on the planet. He started laughing – I'm not sure I'd ever heard him laugh before – and then he called Reba and Jannik but put the phone down before they picked up. And then he started crying in a terrible painful introverted way. I sort of hoped the tears were for Izzy, but I feared they were for himself.'[273]

Whatever the reason for its success, the book's and Isarebe's legacy are undoubtedly political. It is perhaps strange that the only political movement Isarebe ever publicly aligned with was 'Turn off the news' and only then through a t-shirt, as he is now seen primarily as a political influencer; [274] an influencer who for many years effectively restrained political opportunists looking to reverse falls in fertility. Isarebe strongly rejected this label of political influencer, insisting: 'I am not political. I am not advocating anything. I am merely restating research results we have collected from around the world and using these results to build a view on how the world may develop over time.'[275] There is something uncomfortable in reading statements like this, in which Isarebe talks about himself as an academic, when most of his time, post-publication, was spent endorsing the political messages contained in the book. Whether consciously constructed or not, this image of the robustly independent academic was the bedrock of his reputation as a person who could be trusted. For nearly twenty years, until his imprisonment in 2069, Isarebe was arguably the world's most influential unelected political force outside of China.

Future Perfect had given politicians a simple workable environmental idea to latch on to and coalesce around. As President Mbambu of Uganda

---

273   Bortelli, R, 2070, *The Dizzy Digger*, Manchosens, New York, p. 217
274   He was asked to stand for office by all the main political parties in the UK, but he refused each time.
275   Isarebe, S, 2051, *Tomorrow Today*, BIBC Media broadcast and podcast, 11th September 2051

said, 'Wear a condom, get rich, save the planet.'[276] In most democratic countries, Isarebe's popularity, influence and status, particularly among the young, meant most politicians in the 2050s steered clear of any policies that might result in increases in fertility rates. It became an untouchable tenet of a civilized society. Once the initial excitement generated by *Future Perfect* dissipated, Isarebe started to spend more of his time advising and lobbying governments around the world, mostly on fertility and housing issues.

This global consensus on the benefits of low fertility started to come under attack in the 2060s and 2070s, as new generations of politicians saw potential political and economic advantage in increasing fertility rates. Many of these initiatives were introduced in autocratic regimes, but they also occurred in democracies such as the Czech Republic, Hungary and New Zealand. Almost all of these fertility initiatives involved providing financial incentives for people to have more children, along with psychological pressure to 'Breed for the people.'[277] The financial incentives included tax breaks, income support, paid leave from work and free health care. The tax breaks offered to families in the Czech Republic included negative tax rates for those with four or more children i.e. people were paid tax back for every extra pound they earned. Although this was very similar to income support, it was seen as a clever political ploy. It was very popular with the small number of beneficiaries, but was deeply unpopular with other taxpayers.

As soon as a country announced a policy aimed at increasing fertility rates, Isarebe & Isarebe produced an assessment of the likely impact of the initiative, based on their original models and the various updates they produced each year. For almost all these fertility policy initiatives, they predicted an initial increase in birth rates, followed by a period when fertility would drop to an even lower level than it had started at. As Isarebe wrote in *Future Perfect*: 'It appears providing financial incentives for a woman to have more children only brings forward a decision to have a child, rather than fundamentally affecting decisions on family size. This observation breaks down in very poor countries or even among the very poorest in rich societies. For these desperate souls, the offer of a substantial improvement in their short-term living conditions is difficult to resist. Whilst this decision may bring great hardship and unhappiness in the long-term, extreme poverty tends to shorten the time-horizon of decision making.'[278]

276   Mbambu, M, 2056, speech to Ugandan Democratic Conservative conference, 14th December 2055, http://www.ugandanpoliticalhistory.org [accessed December 2149]
277   Unattributed, 2065, headline on a poster that was part of a humorous and highly sexualised advertising campaign in the Czech Republic encouraging people to have larger families, http://old.nacrres.cz [accessed September 2149]
278   Isarebe, S and I, 2050, *Future Perfect*, Cambridge and Oxford University Press, Cambridge, pp. 422–3

Except in the case of New Zealand, Isarebe's predictions that incentives would have little or no impact on long-term fertility rates proved correct. The eventual failure of these policy initiatives further enhanced Isarebe's reputation and successfully deterred most other governments from trying similar schemes for the rest of the 21st century.

New Zealand was the exception to Isarebe's rule. The New Zealand government started providing an additional flat-rate income for all families with three or more children, roughly equivalent to the national living wage. Whilst this was a fairly modest incentive compared to others being offered around the world, the New Zealand initiative worked where others had failed. Most believed it was because it was a small country and one where outward migration had accelerated in the 2040s and 2050s, making population decline an important political issue. In addition, they had a charismatic leader in the 2060s who fervently preached the benefits of large families. Hazel Smith Masdon led the New Zealand government from 2062 to 2069 and births increased by nearly 50% during her tenure. However, in a widely publicised scandal, she was found to have had four abortions in her early twenties and had insisted on her husband's sterilisation when she agreed to marry him. She was voted out of office in 2069, but the New Zealand fertility rate stayed above the replacement level of 2.1 until the 2080s, when it started to fall back in line with international norms.

After the two major wars at the end of the 21st century, there was a second wave of countries who attempted to increase fertility rates through introduction of financial incentives, but by this stage having small families was so entrenched in most cultures that these policies had almost no effect on birth rates and were rapidly abandoned in places such as Japan, Mexico and France. Belgium introduced the most radical financial incentives, providing a lump-sum equivalent to three years' average earnings for every baby born into larger families. It succeeded in raising birth rates, but also resulted in some women being exploited and a rise in children being put up for adoption. The Belgian fertility initiative lasted for ten years in various forms. The policy was finally abandoned after the discovery of a woman who had died after giving birth to her ninth child. She was found chained to her bed with the afterbirth in a tray beside her, with no sign of the baby. She lived in a house with nine other women, six of whom were pregnant when she was found. The other three stated they had given birth within the last three months. They were all heroin addicts. The women refused to give any information on the people behind the 'Bruges Baby Factory'[279] and no one was ever prosecuted.

279　Unattributed, *The Bruges Baby Factories*, The Washington and New York Post, 23rd April 2106, p. 2

Taking a broad historic sweep like this presents a picture of a smooth decline in fertility, with only the occasional hiccup and little resistance from citizens around the world. However, many conspiracy theories developed around it in the mid-2050s. Many were predictable and followed the norm of conspiracy theories in placing responsibility at the feet of Jews, big business, the CIA and aliens. Three of the most persistent conspiracy theories were:

The fall in global fertility was a Jewish plot to take over the world, by reducing the fertility of other races whilst increasing their own, even though statistics showed Jewish family sizes were falling faster than those of many other religious groups.

The fall in the population was due to contraceptives being put into the water supply. These contraceptives were never named, nor was it ever explained why anyone would want to do this.

The impact of the internet and gaming on young minds in the 2020s and 2030s had reduced their fertility, made them gender confused and reduced the sensitivity of their skin.[280]

---

280   Portwain, T, 2034, *The Global Response to Fertility Decline*, Deblick and Zeltman, San Francisco

5.2 Survival versus capitalism

These conspiracy theories spilled over into the arena of economics, with rumours of capitalist cabals, unwilling to accept lower rates of investment returns, attempting to reverse the decline in fertility rates. These groups were variously said to be: plotting to invoke war in order to increase government spending and encourage a post-war baby boom; planning to control the supply of chemicals needed to produce female contraception; and using subliminal messaging in advertisements to encourage women to have more babies.

These fanciful notions were part of a much bigger and more serious attack on the conclusions contained with *Future Perfect*. Many well-respected historians, economists and sociologists put forward carefully constructed arguments as to why they believed there was likely to be a large and potentially violent capitalist, as well as political, response to the predicted drop in the population.

One of the most influential of these was Dr Dawid Marshall, a former colleague of Isarebe at The Bates Institute, who published a book entitled *Normal: Reset*, in which he argued unchecked population decline was likely to destroy social capitalism and decimate financial markets, meaning a capitalist response was both necessary and inevitable. He predicted three waves of response: first, an extensive advertising and PR campaign and the placement and support of influencers to re-set what was seen as 'normal, necessary and desirable' in terms of family size; second, embargoes on countries which encouraged further drops in fertility; and third, sponsored campaigns of violence and intimidation of citizens. Isarebe reviewed this book, published in 2054, for *The Saxon Literary Review*. He had always admired Dawid Marshall and appears to have spent a lot of time examining Marshall's research, claims and assumptions. Isarebe was ruthless in his verdict:

Dawid Marshall has produced a set of apparently well-researched and coherent arguments, presented in an understandable and well-written way, suitable for academics and lay readers alike. He has a formidable intellect and a vivid imagination and on first read I was swept along by his rhetoric. However, upon second read, I came to the conclusion this book is merely a politically motivated opinion piece based on fallacious arguments and a wilfully incorrect reading of the data. This is a shameful piece of work from someone who previously had an impeccable reputation.[281]

This reflects how much of the concern about the predictions within *Future Perfect* were focussed on the economic impact of population decline, just as Isarebe had feared. He spent many hours discussing this with Professor Kamil, whom he always returned to in times of intellectual struggle:

PDK keeps pushing me away from the theoretical and towards the personal. He asked me tonight what I thought keeps bankers and business people awake at night, but he didn't wait for me to answer – I had no idea anyway. He told me it was whether they were going to be made to look stupid, whether others were going to do better than them, and whether they were going to lose their job. He said the two main motivators in finance and business were ego and fear. Full stop. A slow long-term decline in average economic growth – provided it affected everybody equally – would be of no importance to them, however much they might initially squeal at the idea. It wouldn't make them look bad and it wouldn't mean they lost their jobs.

I don't know. Can that really be right? And how would he know? He hasn't left his room in Second Court for the last thirty years.

He also said that strategy and long-term planning, from a practical perspective, is non-existent in most organisations – they might have reams of planning documents, but no one referred to them or acted on them. He insists businesses and banks are largely reactive, not proactive, and this is actually the optimal approach. He thinks if they cared at all about our predictions of lower economic growth, their concerns would last no longer than a day, after which they would refocus all their efforts on a real and immediate crisis or opportunity.

He was probably exaggerating – he was on his fourth whisky and had just beaten me [at bezique], so he was probably a bit light-headed – but even so, it's an extraordinary thought. I don't know whether it's encouraging or disappointing. Why are we bothering with this at all, if it's going to drop off the agenda within a day?[282]

281   Isarebe, S, 2054, *Review of Normal: Reset*, The Saxon Literary Review, 3rd June 2054, London
282   Isarebe, S, 2053, diary entry dated 26th March 2053, The Isarebe Trust Archives, Cambridge, England (Box 248, Folder 1)

Professor Kamil may have been trying to comfort Isarebe in a time of trouble, but he was right to conclude that the ripples of concern among business people would quickly fade, while politicians did much of the work to allay the concerns of individuals with regard to slower economic growth. Most politicians stopped talking about national output and wealth and started talking about OPC (output per capita) and WPC (wealth per capita). It was a simple move that made economics about the individual, where future prospects still looked very rosy.

5.3 Bringing the house down

Whilst politicians were able to deflect concerns about economic growth, many were more worried about Isarebe's predictions of a house price collapse. Falls in house prices had been shown in many psephological models to have a negative influence on support for an incumbent political party, whilst increasing the prospect of deflation, lower consumer demand and a rise in the real value of debt. Politicians were right to be concerned, as it was Isarebe's house price forecasts that most worried private individuals. Isarebe was certain some fall in average house prices was inevitable, given the expected fall in the population, but preached this was a positive development, as property costs had historically represented a significant drag on profits, consumer spending and worker mobility. This was not how it was received, as for homeowners his conclusions meant a potential decline in their main financial asset and even the possibility of negative equity.

Isarebe, on endless visits to political leaders around the world, persuaded many these falls in house prices would happen a long way down the line and would in any case happen so slowly opposition would be minimal. Housing and house prices were an area that was to occupy Isarebe & Isarebe for a number of years after the publication of *Future Perfect*, as they were asked to work as consultants for governments around the world. Isarebe's team helped many states avoid rapid house price deflation, devising strategies of land purchase, social housing demolition, incentives to relocate to major conurbations, debt reduction and targeted quantitative easing. These and other strategies had some effect and the fall in house prices in most countries has been significantly lower than Isarebe originally predicted. Real house prices in the centre of most major conurbations are now higher than they were in 2050, although they are lower as a ratio of house prices to income.

In rural areas and smaller urban areas there was a significant fall in house prices in the late 21st century, but this was at least partly ameliorated by a growth in the number of second homes. In the UK, in 2149, 72% of people rented or owned at least two homes. There was a generation who lost out financially from a fall in house prices and a subsequent generation who lost out on their anticipated inheritance, but a new set of expectations slowly established themselves, with most people in 2150 now seeing property as a cost rather than an investment, with many more now renting rather than buying. Spending on property in the UK, as a percentage of total consumer spending, has fallen from 18% in 2050 to 8% in 2150.

Whilst a large part of Isarebe & Isarebe's income in the late 2050s came from governments, Solomon Isarebe was never afraid to stand up to or contradict the pronouncements of his paymasters. After a big project on federal housing strategy with HURD (the US Department of Housing, Urban and Rural Development), he was asked to attend a press conference at the White House. President Jen Derry spoke first, saying that Professor Isarebe had conducted a detailed research study which confirmed her Small Town Growth Plan would ensure house price stability for generations. She then invited Isarebe to speak, something she almost immediately regretted. Isarebe spoke for less than five minutes, but it took two years for Derry's approval ratings to recover:

President Derry has misunderstood my work. I'm not sure why. Perhaps I was unclear or perhaps it was my strange accent. If I was unclear, I apologise, and I won't charge the people of the United States for our work.

I hoped President Derry had understood that her Small Town Growth Plan would be disastrous and rather than stabilising house prices, if this is what she wants to achieve, the plan would cause house prices to decline rapidly in all areas except the major conurbations.

Population decline is new to America; it's new, but good. As populations fall and as AI further changes and improves our working lives, a greater percentage of us will be living in cities, but cities with less traffic, more open spaces, better facilities and cleaner air. Many more of us will have second homes in the countryside and that will be good. But many of those who used to live in small towns and in rural areas will no longer live there permanently. Maybe not so good in the short-term for those who find they need to move, but in the long-term probably good for them and definitely good for us collectively.

I have always found it deeply refreshing that Americans are so enthusiastic and embracing of change – not like us Brits, who like to moan for a few years before we decide to wait and see. It's one of your greatest cultural assets and it is an asset you will need to draw on in the coming years and decades.

The fall in the population is going to happen, whether you think it's a cool idea or not: people are demanding to have smaller families and it is a wondrous thing for our planet and all our lives, but especially those of women. It is a fantastically exciting new world.

In our work with HURD – and I should say it was a big team of people, not just me, and it was the great people in HURD who did most of the heavy lifting. So, in our work with HURD we think we've found a way to make this change less problematic, by careful federal purchases of redundant land and housing stock, incentivisation of second home ownership and careful repurposing of public housing units.

We hope we have found a way to ensure there will be no significant disruption to the all-important housing market. My personal prediction is that under the plans we have developed with HURD, house prices will be stable – probably grow a little, although not as much as in the past – for the next fifty years at least. Beyond that – well, I'm afraid I just don't know.

So, I'm sorry President Derry, but I think what you have just said is a – what shall we call it – a misunderstanding of everything we told you, less than a day ago. As I say, given your misunderstanding, I will not charge you for this work, but please feel free to use it. I think it will help you.[283]

Derry managed to wriggle her way out of the hole Isarebe politely dug for her and eventually won a second term on the promise of support for people from rural areas moving to city locations. HURD paid for the work and retained Isarebe & Isarebe for many years. Reading this speech, one must conclude Isarebe was either politically fearless, was on the autistic spectrum, or perhaps just had a sometimes self-destructive and painful commitment to the truth. Most concluded it was the latter. It is perhaps why he had so few friends, but was also so widely respected and trusted around the world. He was on nobody's side.

---

283   Isarebe, S, 2059, press conference at The White House, 3rd December 2059, http: www. potusarchive.org [accessed August 2149]

5.4 Holding the climatic fort

Future Perfect came just months after the decline and unfrocking of the Beat organisation, but there were still many environmental youth movements actively campaigning in 2050. Isarebe's prediction of the slow recovery of the planet was cautiously welcomed by many within these groups, although it was not what more radical campaign groups and politicians wanted to hear: they wanted things to change on their watch. This led to some initial criticism, but *Future Perfect* was slowly embraced by nearly all environmentalists for its realism and for its long-term optimism, but also for stressing there was much to do to lessen the impact of global warming in the decades before the climatic corner was turned. Isarebe noted in his conclusion to the Climate Change section in *Future Perfect*:

> We need to reject the desire to return to some romanticised view of the past. We have to adapt to what we have now and what will be in the future. And so does nature. There will be different ecosystems – there will still be animals, birds, plants, insects, invertebrates, fish, fungi, bacteria and viruses, but they will be different and live in different places. We need to look at what we have and not be so egotistical as to imagine we can control it all. The biosphere has always changed over time and will continue to do so. The UK, my home for much of my life, was once primarily forest, home to Robin Hood and wild bears. Those forests are gone and the only bears now are called Pooh and live in the bedrooms of children. It is still a nice place, with an abundant and flourishing natural world, but it is very different from when Robin roamed Sherwood Forest in his tights, dreaming of Maid Marian.[284]

There are many examples of how the global community attempted to deal with the consequences of global warming 'before the climatic corner was turned', but one of the most famous was the building of 'The Great Wash Wall' in eastern England, or 'The Great Washing Line'[285] as it was known locally, which was completed almost fifty years after the publication of *Future Perfect*.

---

284   Isarebe, S and I, 2050, *Future Perfect*, Cambridge and Oxford University Press, Cambridge, p. 412
285   Unattributed, 2095, *The Washing Line Completed!*, Instant East Anglia Times, 2nd June 2095, p. 1

Whilst relatively few parts of mainland Europe were greatly affected by the impact of rising sea levels (sea levels in 2150 are still 68 cm above the level they were in 2000), East Anglia in the United Kingdom, along with vast swathes of the Netherlands and the north-eastern coast of Italy, looked certain to be engulfed by the sea if action was not taken. The Netherlands, with their long history of defending themselves against the sea, adopted a mixed policy of withdrawal and strategic defences, while Italy famously failed to react early enough to stop over 9,000 square kilometres being reclaimed by the sea between Trieste and Rimini, leaving the historic city of Venice a more lonely and vulnerable island receding further and further from the mainland. However, it was The Great Wash Wall in rural East Anglia which captured the imagination of many.

The Wash was an area of sea between Norfolk and Lincolnshire. Much of the low-lying fertile flatlands surrounding the Wash had been reclaimed from the sea from the 17th century onwards and as a result of this drainage and the shrinkage of peat strata, much of the land within the counties of Norfolk, Cambridgeshire and Lincolnshire lay below sea level, only protected by higher land on the coast and just over 100 miles of coastal defences.

This agricultural area – the Fens – was starting to flood regularly by the time *Future Perfect* was published and Isarebe frequently used the Fens as an example of the impact of global warming and rises in sea levels.[286] His interest was not entirely academic. Rita Bortelli had persuaded him to buy a home after the publication of *Future Perfect* and he had bought a house called Hearts of Oak, near Lode, just outside Cambridge, England. His models showed that without attempts to mitigate the impact of rising sea levels in East Anglia, Lode would at best become a seaside village and at worst disappear if sea levels rose by more than 60 cm, even though Lode at this time was nearly 50 miles (80 km) from the nearest coastal town.

The three counties of Norfolk, Lincolnshire and Cambridgeshire, with financial assistance from the UK government, made the decision to build The Great Wash Wall between Skegness in Lincolnshire and Hunstanton in Norfolk as a defensive barrier, creating an inland sea. The barrier was to be over 20 miles long and stand 5 metres above high-water point, with an average sea depth of 5 m. It was one of the biggest engineering projects in the world and turned into one of the most expensive. It was completed in 2095, two years after Isarebe's death and was officially named 'The Isarebe Barrier', but the name never stuck and it has always been called The Great Wash Wall. The enclosed Wash Sea has slowly desalinated and is now one of the great nature

---

286   Isarebe, S, 2051, *Eye-Ted Talk: Population change, global warming and land use*, 3rd September 2051, www.eye-ted.com [accessed 12th June 2149]

reserves of Europe. The Wash Wall is covered by solar panels on its south-western side and is the largest solar farm in Europe.

The social and economic benefits of The Great Wash Barrier (Update 3.1)   ONLINE ARCHIVE

Figure 7.1 The impact of The Great Wash Barrier (2145)

The Wash 2080

The enclosed Wash Sea 2105

The Wash Reserve 2145

Source: Spangle / The Great Wash Barrier Development Company / The Wash Reserve Trust

Chart from 'UK Environmental Engineering 2049'

5.5 Fame, fortune and despair

As well as his consultancy work, Isarebe continued his academic studies throughout the 2050s. Much of this work was focussed on integrating his models of population, economics and climate change at the global, regional and national levels. Most of this research was never published, as it made him question the validity of his original work for *Future Perfect*. These integrated models showed how fragile and unstable the world was, with small perturbations potentially causing large changes in the final results. He called them the 'trembling models'[287] and he was concerned they could damage his reputation, but more importantly they could threaten the growing global consensus around population control and climate change that *Future Perfect* had helped to engender.

His book sales, together with the success of III Health and Isarebe & Isarebe made Isarebe a rich man. It was estimated he was the 575th richest person in the UK in 2061, although Isarebe angrily denied the figures quoted in the press. For a short time, it was reported he enjoyed a lavish lifestyle, but there was no evidence this was the case. He never showed any interest in material things and lived frugally. He gave away large parts of his fortune, including selling III Health to Bortelli and Ingar for $2 and he donated many millions to Bortelli's charitable foundation. She stated Isarebe gave more to her charity than she had ever given to the Isarebes for the *Future Perfect* research.[288] Isarebe bought a lot of land around Garway Hill in Herefordshire, which he called Isabelle Isarebe Moor. In his will he left this land and Hilman Cottage to the National Trust. It is still possible to stay in Hilman Cottage, although there is a long waiting list. Much of his money during his lifetime was given to the Isabelle Isarebe Centre for Women in Botswana, which he set up in the mid-2050s. It was initially run by Mooketsi Mooketsi and it provided family planning advice, career support and educational grants for women. The Centre was the sole beneficiary in his will.

In October 2055, Isarebe was informed he was to receive the Nobel Prize in Statistics and Economics. The citation was for 'development of new research approaches to understanding decision making and incorporation of these into economic and demographic models.'[289] When he went on stage to receive the

---

287   Isarebe, S, 2057, eLetter to Professor Kamil dated 1st March 2057, The Isarebe Trust Archives, Cambridge, England (Box 303, Folder 5)
288   Bortelli, R, 2070, *The Dizzy Digger*, Manchosens, New York, p. 53
289   Details of Nobel Prize winners, www.nobelcommends.org [accessed 4th November 2149]

award, he carried a picture of Isabelle Isarebe in his hand. He was visibly upset and was unable to make an acceptance speech.

In an interview given after receiving his prize, he explained how difficult he found it dealing with public attention. He was one of the few academics ever to have seeped into the public consciousness. He said the question he was asked most often about climate change was 'But what can I personally do to help?' He said his answer was always the same: 'Never have unprotected sex.'[290]

In early 2056, Isarebe was made Professor of the new Quantitative Social Economics Department at the University of Cambridge. After all the adulation he had received around the world, it was not perhaps such a significant event for Isarebe as it once might have been, but it still represented a degree of academic acceptance that Isarebe had long craved. As he noted in an email to Professor D. Kamil, 'It seems I am one of you now, finally! I no longer have to doff my cap to you (although you can be assured I still will). What next though PDK, what next?'[291]

Despite the many flaws in Isarebe's work on population, economics and climate change, it was hugely influential throughout the 2050s and into the 2060s. He worked incessantly throughout this period, ensuring his messages were understood and acted upon, but it took a great personal toll. In a diary entry from March 2057 he stated:

It is now 9 years since Izzy died and I don't know what happened to those years. I feel like I lost them, literally. I can remember odd days, but no continuum. I don't want to go on like this. I am slipping back into the blackness.[292]

290   Shah, S, 2055, *Interview with Solomon Isarebe*, The Times Record of India, 1st November 2055, p. 56
291   Isarebe, S, 2056, email to Professor D. Kamil dated 17th April 2056, The Isarebe Trust Archives, Cambridge, England (Box 299, Folder 1)
292   Isarebe, S, 2057, diary entry dated 26th March 2057, The Isarebe Trust Archives, Cambridge, England (Box 303, Folder 8)

PART 6
Life and death with Arem Johns

6.1 Meeting Arem Johns

5th July 2057

TeePs. Quick weird unbelievable update. I had sex with Solomon Isarebe last night. Yep, that one. Painful, bizarre and briefly exquisite. Buzzing. catch you later.[293, 294]

Arem Johns' record of her first meeting with Solomon Isarebe suggests they shared an immediate physical attraction to each other. It is almost certain this was Isarebe's first close sexual encounter, aged 49, but Isarebe made little mention of it in his normally explicit and comprehensive daily diary: 'Went to Mills Bruceck's ghastly [expletive] party last night, where Di Faustino insulted me in an entirely predictable way, little moron. Met a woman called Arem who pointed at a painting on the wall saying, 'I painted that'. I pointed at an award Bruceck got for selling 50m copies of FP and said, 'I wrote that'. IMO only show off if you're going to win. She had an odd effect on me though.'[295]

Mills Bruceck was Isarebe's American-born editor at Cambridge and Oxford University Press and Isarebe had been attending one of her lavish Independence Day parties. Isarebe rarely attended parties, but the invitation had landed on the same day he completed the purchase of an apartment in the historic Barbican Centre in London and he surprised both of them by accepting. Trevor di Faustino, one of Bruceck's less successful clients, had long been jealous of Isarebe's triumphs. In his blog the next day, di Faustino wrote: 'A famous virgin, misogynist and soothsayer was heard cavorting – I mean violently cavorting – in a cupboard with an unknown ingenue last night – poor thing. Whatever next … something he predicts comes true?'[296]

Arem Johns was 32 years old when she met Solomon Isarebe. She was an artist, barely making a living and largely unknown in the fashion-conscious

293   Johns, A, 2057, Juzz1mo communication between Arem Johns and Talia Player dated 5th July 2057, The Arem Johns Archive, Lambeth School of Art (Box 32, Folder 1)
294   Arem Johns was using Juzz1mo, a communication application mixing spoken, typed and hand-written input, popular between 2048 and 2062 before it was subsumed within the eLetter empire.
295   Isarebe, S, 2057, diary entry dated 5th July 2057, The Isarebe Trust Archives, Cambridge, England (Box 304, Folder 6)
296   Di Faustino, T, 2057, *Diary of some somebody*, 5th July 2057 [Blog], Available at http://www.ukblogarchives.org [accessed November 2148]

art world. Her work, mostly large oil paintings, often referenced the 18th century artist Angelica Kauffmann, reimagining Kauffmann's portrayal of women through a 21st century lens. Johns' work was appreciated by some in academic circles, but over the previous ten years she had been taken up and dropped by three galleries, none of whom could find a niche for her finely constructed, if cool and intellectual works. Johns' heritage was a mix of Welsh and Spanish, with dark almost black hair, light olive skin and brown eyes flecked with orange. She had a strong face and a Romanesque nose. She was nearly 6 feet tall but maintained the posture of a dancer that she had developed as a child.

Arem Johns 2057

Isarebe's appearance had changed considerably from when he was a young man, when he was plagued by skin problems and was 'so thin when he turned sideways he morphed into a line-drawing.'[297] He had filled out and whilst

---

297   Bortelli, R, 2070, *The Dizzy Digger*, Manchosens, New York, p. 18

never athletic was of healthy proportions when he met Arem Johns. He was 6 feet 5 inches tall and his posture had improved as his social confidence and reputation had grown. Physically, he had turned into an imposing man. His face lacked symmetry, in the set of his jaw and in his crooked mouth, but despite his chaste bachelor life many found him attractive.

A week after their meeting, Johns took delivery of a package from Isarebe. In it was a medieval sapphire and gold ring, accompanied by a note: 'I saw this and the blurb said, "In the 14th century it was thought sapphires gave people supernatural powers, protected them against disease and preserved chastity." I thought the magical powers and protection against disease might come in useful. SI.X'[298]

The following day, Mills Bruceck called Isarebe and said a small box had arrived for him – delivered by hand. Isarebe told her to open it. In it was the gold and sapphire ring, together with a hand-made envelope and a note. The note read: 'I'm no whore Solomon. If it's more sex you're looking for go ask someone who likes your particular prelidicktions [sic]. I enclose something to remember me by on your cold lonely nights. Arem.' When Bruceck had stopped laughing she opened the paper envelope. In it was a ring, thickly and intricately woven from many dark hairs, some long, straight and fine, some shorter, wavy and coarse.

At the end of August 2057, Isarebe attended a conference in Geneva, where he gave a speech on the long-term impact of financial incentivisation on fertility and received an honorary award from The DACH Society of Economics, Statistics and Demographics. He left the conference hall at around 6 p.m. to make the short walk back to his lakeside hotel. Outside was Arem Johns.

3rd August 2057

TeePs, I must be [expletive] crazy. I searched online for Isarebe this morning and saw he was giving a speech in Geneva. I spent all of this month's pathetic budget and half of next month's on a flight to Switzerland. We hardly talked, we just ran to his hotel and. just sex. Very, very physical, obvs, but I mean really physical. I have a cut on the inside of my nose – how did I get that? I got the 10 o'clock flight home. He put me in a taxi and that was it. again. Is twice an obsession?[299]

---

298   Isarebe, S, 2057, hand-written note from Solomon Isarebe to Arem Johns, undated, The Arem Johns Archive, Lambeth School of Art (Box 32, Folder 3)
299   Johns, A, 2057, Juzz1mo communication between Arem Johns and Talia Player dated 3rd August 2057, The Arem Johns Archive, Lambeth School of Art (Box 33, Folder 2)

The following week Isarebe knocked uninvited on the door to Johns' studio in Peckham, South London.

9th August 2057

TeePs. Seriously. listen.

Solomon turned up on my doorstep. I guess I'd done it to him, so he felt entitled, if not exactly welcomed. We immediately started where we'd left off in Geneva, but something in me suddenly turned off and I asked him to stop. He didn't or couldn't. I started shouting at him, but he was deaf with sex. Eventually I got him off and he looked at me like a madman. Eyes engorged with blood. I fleetingly wondered if it was to be my last minute.

He didn't say anything, just got up and disappeared into the studio. The next thing I knew a WOMD[300] had gone off. He was trashing the place. Trashing canvases. Trashing my clothes. Breaking pots. Breaking everything, except me. He's no physical specimen, but he's big. I just watched, petrified, wanting to catch him in an embrace, wanting to [expletive] him again. I think I must be sick. He downed a half bottle of whisky I had on the windowsill, slammed the door and drove off, wheels screaming. What a silence that man can leave. The end of something weird and perhaps truly terrible, perhaps love – don't pretend to puke, I won't forgive you this time, because I mean it. I feel like I'm grieving the loss of a husband of fifty years. Serious, TeePs, don't mock.[301] [302]

It was six months later, February 2058, before they saw each other again. Arem was working in the studio she had at the bottom of her parents' garden, to which she often returned when she was struggling for inspiration. Her parents lived in the quietly prosperous town of Leigh-on-Sea in Essex. A former fishing village, it had grown and then declined in the 20th century, before becoming a fashionable commuter town for people working in the East End of London. Her mother called her in from the studio, as there was someone she thought might be Solomon Isarebe sitting on the kerb outside the house.

300   Acronym for Weapon of Mass Destruction.
301   The artist in the studio next to Arem Johns' called the police on hearing the disturbance. Arem Johns made a statement, but said she did not wish to press charges.
302   Johns, A, 2057, Juzz1mo communication between Arem Johns and Talia Player dated 9th August 2057, The Arem Johns Archive, Lambeth School of Art (Box 33, Folder 3)

He looked and smelt like he hadn't washed for a week. He was barely recognisable, with a beard of sorts and disgusting hair. I asked him how long he'd been there. He mumbled something and I thought he said three days. I had no idea what he meant by that – how could he be outside the house for three days and why would he be outside the house for three days? And I couldn't work out how he knew where Mum and Pops lived anyway.

I then remembered the studio had smelt strange yesterday and realised he must have been there. I just lost it. He was quiet, docile, like some beaten kid, but I screamed and screamed at him, telling him what I thought of him and his weirdness and his vile temper. He got up, a bit unsteadily and backed away until he was leaning against the garden wall. I could see he was frightened, or something, but I just didn't care. I also realised he was completely pissed. Never have mum's neighbours been so well served with afternoon drama.

I quieted down eventually and saw some of my spit dripping from Solomon's chin. He looked very large and very small at the same time, if that makes any sense. I suddenly felt a bit ashamed of myself. Dad came out and took me inside and I saw him nod to Solomon to leave.[303, 304]

The police found Isarebe's car parked on the street around the corner from the Johns' house. They told the Johns he appeared to have walked six miles to Benfleet, a town to the west, before stopping outside a house on one of the many estates there. The people who owned the house said he stood staring at the house for about an hour and then ran away. The police rescued him from the Thames some time later, having found him pinned against the bridge traversing the tidal creek between Benfleet and Canvey Island. They estimated he entered the water at around 6.55 p.m. and had been swept along with a floating island of debris and tree branches. Isarebe and the flotsam had got stuck under the bridge. He was spotted by a passing motorist at around 7.10 p.m. He had mild hypothermia and was taken to Greater Basildon Hospital. He was immediately recognised by one of the consultants. Isarebe did not say a word to anyone at the hospital and the consultant, Rose Tinker, assumed he wanted to stay anonymous. The next morning she asked if she could contact

---

303   Three neighbours of the Johns' called the police, but the police took no action.
304   DPP versus Isarebe (5), 2068, CCCt (476) *Arem Johns' statement to the police, made at 11.15 p.m. 13th February 2058*

someone for him. He gave her Arem Johns' number.

Arem's father, Morris Johns, a General Practitioner, arrived an hour later and after a brief discussion with the consultant, took him back to the house in Leigh-on-Sea, where Isarebe was greeted by Lucienne Johns, Arem's mother. He had picked up a stomach infection whilst in the river and spent the day between the toilet and Arem's bed. Arem was no longer in the house. Isarebe recalled these events in his unpublished autobiography:

> Arem wasn't pleased to see me sitting in the street outside her family home. I was so pissed when she came out it was all I could do to stop myself falling in the gutter, even though I was sitting down. I had spent the previous two nights in the Johns' garden shed, which doubled as Arem's studio. It was cold and I hadn't slept, despite the whisky. I remember her shouting at me, but not being able to take in what she was saying. I wasn't thinking straight. I couldn't think straight. In my confusion I seem to have concluded it was better to appear as a deranged alcoholic stalker, than tell her I loved her, couldn't stop thinking about her, couldn't seemingly live without her. In my weak defence, I didn't know how to say these things, simple and everyday as they are.

> Her father, Morris, suggested it might be best if I leave and so I started walking and as I walked, I sobered up a bit. I found a charity shop and bought myself some cleanish clothes. No one recognised me. I kept walking. I walked to Southend-on-Sea, along the promenade, and then turned around and walked back. I went past Arem's house and then up and away from the seafront, [305] through built up street after built up street, the small towns along the estuary melding into a long line of mediocrity. About 5 hours after leaving Arem, I ended up in a nondescript sort of place I later discovered was called Benfleet. There was something familiar about it. At least not exactly familiar, but something about it rattled me. I knew I had walked these streets before, but for all I could remember it might as well have been in another life. I wandered for several hours around Benfleet, which sprawled for miles, unconscious of why and where I was going. Eventually I found myself standing outside a house. It was an ordinary house, a compact 1970s detached house, well-kept and recently

---

305   Leigh-on-Sea and Southend-on-Sea are not technically 'on-Sea', but are located on the Thames estuary. The estuary is 8 km (5 miles) wide between Southend-on-Sea in Essex and Sheerness in Kent.

restored. I stood outside and stared at it. I must have stood there for nearly three quarters of an hour. The people inside stared back, but it was not them I was interested in. I realised, through a memory that kept coming in and out of focus, I had stood here before. It was where I had almost literally first set foot in England, forty years earlier. My 9-year-old self had climbed out of the back of a van, shook the driver's hand and said goodbye. This fragment of memory kept coming and going, odd details but little narrative and I was thankful for that.

I heard a siren and saw a police car approaching so I ran around the corner and then shot down a footpath which led me across a golf course. My head was now racing with fragmented but proliferating memories and I remember half-crying half-moaning like a little lost child, running headlong to who knows where. I couldn't force my thoughts back into their box. I found myself approaching what I thought was a river and I ran straight down the steep bank into the grey water, wanting it all to stop. I immediately sank thigh deep in stinking mud just feet below the surface of the water. The water was running extremely fast and was getting visibly deeper as I stood there. It was one of the ugliest places I have ever seen. The cold of the water snapped me back into the present and I realised I wanted to live as strongly as minutes before I hadn't, but I couldn't escape the mud. I could hear cars going by, but no one could see me. I panicked and started struggling to get my legs free. I lost my balance and I briefly disappeared beneath the foul water. Falling somehow released one leg and the other soon followed. As soon as the second leg came free I was swept away by the current.

The next thing I remember was Morris Johns standing over me, with an unexpected and incongruously friendly smile. A doctor was behind him, talking to him, him nodding, me not hearing a thing.[306, 307]

Isarebe was to spend a week with Morris and Lucienne Johns in their Leigh-on-Sea home, after which Morris took him to his Barbican flat, suggesting he should perhaps not contact Arem again: 'He then held me. He is a round man with fluffy white balding curls and Victorian whiskers and he had an earthy clean musky smell. I sank a little at the knees as he held me. He said they'd

306   Isarebe, S, 2067, typed notes for an unpublished autobiography, manuscript dated 24th September 2067, The Isarebe Trust Archives, Cambridge, England (Box 448)
307   The police charged Solomon with affray and harassment. He admitted guilt and was given a caution.

heard me shouting and screaming in my sleep every night, crying out "no, mum, no, mum!" He suggested I might like to find out why.'[308]

Isarebe returned to work as soon as he got back to London and in the spring of 2058 he left England for a three-month project in Delhi, where he was to work with the Indian government and the Delhi School of Advanced Economics on India's housing and economic strategy. He had been given an apartment for the duration of the project and in the long evenings he started exchanging emails with Arem Johns, emails not of passion but of regretful loss. After some weeks, he asked her to come out to Delhi; she hesitatingly agreed, but said she would stay with a friend who was completing her doctorate at the University of Delhi.

3rd June 2058

Yo TeePs!

How's things? India is [expletive] hot, hotter than Londinium I suspect.

Things have been moving along here. mostly good. It was all service as normal between Solomon and me when I arrived, but in the last few days we've gone from animals ripping each other to sexual shreds to platonic knock-along pals, although to be honest it feels like a pause before it starts again for good.

It's partly because he called me 'Izzy' in the middle of some unusually dreary sex last week. he was mortified, my poor soul. Isabelle was his little adopted sister who died when she was about our age. They were inseparable, apparently. I know there wasn't a sex thing between them but if there was, no business of mine, and I can't find the moral problem in it anyway, but it made me realise there is so much shit in both our heads that we need to find out if we can live with each other's mess before we press the FMF button.[309] So I suggested to him a bit of celibacy might help. I was really sore too and didn't know how much more I could take of Solomon's enthusiasms in all this heat. He wasn't super-chuffed, but he was feeling so mortified about the calling-out-of-sister's-name-during-sex incident that he agreed.

308   Isarebe, S, 2058, diary entry 23rd February 2058, The Isarebe Trust Archives, Cambridge, England (Box 312, Folder 3)
309   FMF, slang for '[Expletive] mates forever', a derivative of the much-derided term, BFF, 'Best friends forever'.

It's been weird and hard, a bit like getting sober (TeePs!) but we've found we can talk, for England, St George, the Universe and beyond!

I told him about Marcus Sympson-Hyde last night.[310] I'm not sure I've ever seen someone listen so hard. He didn't want to believe it. Not like he didn't believe me, just that it wounded him to hear it. I told him in detail about ███████████████████████.[311] I know I have told you most of the gory, but it came back to me in technicolor last night and I unloaded it all on him, down to the meercat and cactus pyjamas I was wearing, ██, and exactly how he held and twisted my wrist when he said I must never tell anybody what I had done. Solomon seemed to understand exactly how I'd felt as a ████████████████████. I know you don't like the sound of Solomon much / very much / at all, but he has some surprising and extraordinary moments of human-wonderfulness, given what an insensitive pig he is most of the time. I told him ████ ██████████████████████████ I drew a little flower on my wall above the skirting board and by the time Sympson-Hyde died – check tattoo: 6.35 p.m., 14th April 2039 – there were 69 flowers growing in my bedroom.

Solomon just nodded and touched the back of my hand with one finger when I told him how Mum and Pops responded when I finally told them about Marcus. It was like he had been there with me, desperate for them to believe me and incredulous they couldn't or wouldn't. I think he might love Mum and Pops, as much as he can love anyone anyway, but he seemed to understand they were capable of this tragic and inexplicable failure as parents – he understood saints can sin. He told me he'd seen the flowers painted above the skirting board in their bedroom – don't know why he was in there, didn't ask – and he assumed these were painted after they chose to believe me. How did he work that one out? He's a bit brighter than us Tee-Pee, brighter than everyone on the planet probably. It's no wonder he has such a big head and no wonder I was desperate for sex by the time we finished talking. I restrained myself, unbeliever.

---

310   Dr. Marcus Sympson-Hyde had been a partner in the practice where Morris Johns worked. He had been Morris's good friend from university and he babysat for Arem Johns throughout her childhood.
311   Redactions in accordance with Child Protection Agency Guidelines MGJ3/23 (2147)

I realised I was leaning on Solomon even harder than I leaned on you all these years TeePs. It was the first time I really appreciated what I put you through, my wonderful love. my wonderful friend. I let Sympson-Hyde sully your childhood as well as mine, just through telling you over and over what evil looked like and felt like. I hope you sensed the relief, through the miles and time zones, of sharing this load for the first time.

Something shifted in me anyway. I painted this morning for the first time in a month. A [expletive] furious bloody depiction of my tiny 9-year-old / 33-year-old ruined body, ruined mind. I have been crying all day, crying like a raging [expletive] bull.[312]

Isarebe and Johns were together in Delhi for nearly six weeks. After the first two weeks, she moved into his apartment. Johns spoke to Isarebe many times about her traumatic childhood experiences whilst they were in Delhi and of her experiences at art school in Wolverhampton. Away from her parents for the first time in Wolverhampton, she had become withdrawn and wanted nothing to do with the 'try-anything-once' fumblings and pretensions of her fellow students. She had never had a girlfriend or boyfriend and had no desire for one. At the end of her first year at university, she got a holiday job in a rock factory in Southend-on-Sea.[313] Whilst there, she had a brief fling with one of the girls working with her on the production line. She had found it a tender, romantic and reassuringly unexciting experience. It heralded a slow awakening of her appetites and by the end of her university life she was sexually and socially very adventurous. Johns insisted to Isarebe that her sudden sexual and social popularity was because people started thinking she was beautiful which seemed to give her unwarranted and unwanted status. It was a label she was to fear and despise for the rest of her life. She told Isarebe if he ever told her she was beautiful she would leave him: 'I'd never thought of her being beautiful or not, before she said this, as it seems a somewhat pointless sort of judgement to make. I then looked at her, with someone else's eyes and realised they were right. She was, in a slightly weird way, the most beautiful thing I had ever seen. I always thought people were staring at me when we were out together, turns out probably not.'[314]

---

312   Johns, A, 2058, Juzz1mo communication between Arem Johns and Talia Player dated 3rd June 2058, The Arem Johns Archive, Lambeth School of Art (Box 34, Folder 2)
313   Rock was a sugar-based confectionery, often sold as souvenirs in seaside locations.
314   Isarebe, S, 2058, diary entry dated 4th June 2058, The Isarebe Trust Archives, Cambridge, England (Box 313, Folder 11)

Johns probed Isarebe on his monastic life before he met her, but he was unable to give her any explanation beyond: 'I'm no peach, Arem.'[315]

Arem Johns was prodigious in her artmaking whilst they were in Delhi. Her new, semi-abstracted forms were literally and metaphorically dark, as well as being disturbingly and violently sexual. They represented an enormous creative leap from the pastel shades, painstaking realism and intellectual formality of her previous work. She posted some of her new works online and they rapidly gathered thousands of enthusiastic followers, with many offers to buy her work, which she refused. By the end of her stay in India, three London galleries said they wanted to meet with her, on her return.

For Johns, this new work was intimately personal and she found she resented much of the new interest, feeling it was at best people superimposing their own experiences and views on her work, and at worst people being voyeuristic and quietly sadistic. Isarebe asked her one night: 'Who wrote the rule that artists have to put all their work online? It definitely devalues the work and it seems to make the artist – i.e. you – miserable and insecure. Economically and personally it's a crazy thing to do. Just take it all down, wondersocks.'[316, 317] Johns took his advice, but the seeds of her subsequent fame had been sown. In particular, a number of radical feminist groups in Germany, the USA and Spain had noisily adopted her as a symbol of freedom from male oppression, despite there being no record of Johns ever making overt political statements.

By the middle of August, Isarebe had completed his work in Delhi. Johns returned to London, while Isarebe went to Beijing, where he was to feature in a series of programmes on creativeness in academia. He then went on to New York, to meet Casey Ingar and Hetty Brown and discuss fieldwork for an update to *Future Perfect*. He was then obliged to fulfil a promise made earlier in the year to visit Botswana in order to open the new Isabelle Isarebe Centre for Women in Francistown. Isarebe disliked visiting Botswana, partly because of his continuing resentment of Mooketsi Mooketsi for breaking his sister's heart, but also because it stirred the ashes of his grief for Isabelle.

Isarebe did not arrive back in London until mid-December 2058. He waited several days before calling Arem Johns and she made no attempt to call him. They eventually met up at The Drama Studio, a restaurant in the City of London, near Isarebe's new apartment.

---

315   Johns, A, 2058, Juzz1mo communication between Arem Johns and Talia Player dated 5th June 2058, The Arem Johns Archive, Lambeth School of Art (Box 34, Folder 3)

316   Johns, A, 2058, Juzz1mo communication between Arem Johns and Talia Player dated 7th July 2058, The Arem Johns Archive, Lambeth School of Art (Box 34, Folder 6)

317   Solomon Isarebe's nickname for Arem Johns. There is no record of why he called her this.

Darling Mum,

Tried to call. Odd, important, mostly happy things going on.

I girded my loins – whatever that means, sounds patriarchal, no? – to confess all to Solomon at the restaurant tonight, assuming a public place would give me some protection.

I still don't know why I did it, but when I arrived tonight I so desperately wanted Solomon to know all the sordid details of my patheticness I was nearly peeing myself with anticipation. I am copying some of this in to my therapist, hope you don't mind, to see if she knows why I felt this urge to prostrate myself before a man and ask for what – forgiveness, hate, contempt, love, pity, humiliation, freedom? I've almost given up trying to understand myself. It's like I wanted him to know I love him – more later – but also wanted him to know I could and would choose to have a destructive, cheap, damaging affair, at any time and with anyone – even with an idiot called Eleven. How can you trust a man who chooses a name for himself like that? I mean, why not an interesting number, if you're going to go down that route?

Or was it I simply wanted to hurt Solomon by having sex with a nobody, for the things he's done, the things he does in my imagination, the things he will do in the future? Get the violence in before he visits it on me. But he's never exactly been violent to me – violence courses through his veins, but not to me. Maybe these paintings I've made recently have taken me over the edge and I'm now so full of hate for anything with a penis I'm not fit to go out in public.

I did tell him about Eleven, but only after he'd told me about the three women he had sex with in Beijing – I suspected he had a thing for Asian girls – the man he tried and failed to get it on with in New York – that was a surprise, although he says he now knows men aren't for him – and the threesome (with girls again, yawn) he had in Botswana. He was very keen for me to know he wore a "thick condom" (?!) at all times and has had tests for all the main communicable sexual diseases, as though he thought we were about to have sex in the restaurant toilet.

He says he doesn't know why he did this and deeply regrets it. Two sick peas in a pod me and him, right?

I wasn't cross, I mean it's his body and his choices right. okay, maybe I was a bit cross and I felt very unattractive all of a sudden. Predictably he went apoleptic [sic] when I eventually made my relatively mild confession. What sick, hypocritical, pieces of weakness us humans are.

We walked afterwards. We're always walking. I don't know if he felt exactly the same thing as me at exactly the same time as me, but we both sort of turned towards each other and it happened. Boom! Some physical metaphysical super real non-existent thing. Did that ever happen with you and Pops? Or you and Derry? It was the weirdest moment of my life. If he'd asked me to marry him, I would have said yes. and said no the next day, obvs, I'm not crazy. In every way except the dreaded deed I feel I am now wed to that man and he says he's wed to me. We had sex later and it was back to the wonderful, uncontrolled, physical thing we had when we first met. Not sure I'll send this bit to the psych, she'll think she has to start again with me from the beginning.

I think we will live a troubled explosive implosive creative life together Mum and who knows, maybe I'll jump in bed with a Twelve and maybe Solomon will want to get it on with a Bonobo, but whatever [expletive]-ups we make, our life is going to be together. I gave him a sort of caveat to the unspoken FMF contract between us – sorry, know you hate that phrase. I said he has to get to the bottom of what happened in his early life. He doesn't have to tell me, or anyone, but he has to understand it. Quite a big caveat actually, I suppose, now I've written it out loud. He asked if I'd mind if he talked to Pops. Blimey, nervous now!

Deep love from your sick, inappropriate and for once happy daughter. AX

p.s. Another surprise. The Femin-I Gallery signed me up today and in my bewildered state of mind I accidentally asked for an advance and they gave me one. Galleries never give advances! Should have asked for more! Yippee!! In love with a self-righteous, supercilious, self-centred, insensitive, wonderful genius, have a mum in a billion and will soon have nearly four figures in the bank (not including decimal places). An average day in the life of A Johns.[318]

The day after Arem Johns and Isarebe made their pledges to each other, Isarebe went to see Morris Johns, waiting for him in the waiting room of his medical practice. At the end of the afternoon appointments, Morris came out and asked him into his examination room. Morris said Lucienne had told him the bones of what happened the previous night and whilst not condoning Solomon's behaviour he was glad they were back together and he knew they had made the right decision. He said he and Lucienne had thought Arem and Solomon had looked 'oddly natural' together, even in the difficult circumstances of their first meeting.

Solomon nodded and said he hadn't come about that. He told Morris that Arem had told him about Marcus Sympson-Hyde and he had spent some time looking into the details of Sympson-Hyde's death. Solomon said the coroner's suicide verdict sounded equivocal and if there was another explanation Arem needed to understand it.

Morris Johns was silent for some time, but eventually started speaking, saying it had been suicide, but Solomon was right, it was not quite what it seemed. Lucienne and he had challenged Sympson-Hyde about Arem's claims immediately after she told them, but Sympson-Hyde convinced them nothing had happened and suggested this often occurred when an adolescent girl or boy had a crush on an older person. They decided to tell Arem she was wrong about what she thought had happened, but immediately noticed a deterioration in her attitude towards them and in her behaviour at home and at school. The only person she ever spoke to was Talia Player.

Morris Johns knew the Chief Constable of Essex through the Freemasons and he decided to tell him about Arem's claims and Sympson-Hyde's response. Harry Lane, the Chief Constable, came back to him the following week. He told him there were rumours about Sympson-Hyde and he had been cautioned for under-age sex when he was a student, but it would be impossible for them to progress with a case, given the lack of evidence and Sympson-Hyde's reputation as an expert witness on child behaviour.

The following year, a family made a complaint to the medical practice about Sympson-Hyde, saying he had inappropriately touched their 10-year-old daughter during an examination. This complaint went down the rabbit

---

318   Johns, A, 2058, eLetter from Arem Johns to Lucienne Johns dated 19th December 2058, The Arem Johns Archive, Lambeth School of Art (Box 37, Folder 3)

hole of the complex complaints procedure, but the family were unwilling to be placated and against their solicitor's advice made their complaint public through the local press. The day after the complaint had appeared in a small article in the Southend Clarion Echo, Morris Johns went to see Sympson-Hyde. He told Sympson-Hyde five other families had come forward with complaints that day and his exposure, social disgrace and the end of his medical career now seemed inevitable. Sympson-Hyde was in a state of turmoil, but believed he could fight the claims, showing no remorse for what he now admitted to Morris Johns he had done to Arem.

Sympson-Hyde had once confessed to Morris Johns at a drunken Christmas party that his mother bullied him and emotionally suffocated him in equal measure and she would punish him if she thought he was seeing another woman. After telling Sympson-Hyde about these new complaints, Morris Johns told him he had contacted Sympson-Hyde's mother that afternoon and told her everything her son had done to Arem and the other young girls. He said they had arranged for his mother to come to their house to meet Arem later that evening and Lucienne was on her way to pick her up now.

At 10 o'clock that night, Morris Johns received a call from Julie McTeer, the head of the practice, informing him Sympson-Hyde had committed suicide. He had left a note saying 'Sorry Mother. It was that bitch Arem Johns.' No other families had made complaints against Sympson-Hyde and Sympson-Hyde's mother was at home in Eastbourne when she first heard the news about her son's death and his crimes.

> Morris looked at me and said they had never told Arem the truth because they didn't want Arem to know the lies her father was capable of telling and with Sympson-Hyde dead, they thought it no longer mattered. I told him he was more of a fool than I was and he should consider whether it was better for Arem to think her parents had betrayed and abandoned her, or that they were flawed heroes, willing to betray their principles to avenge the man who had ruined her childhood.
>
> He called me about an hour later and said he and Lucienne are going to London tonight to talk to Arem. Big tick.[319]

---

319   Isarebe, S, 2058, diary entry dated 20th December 2058, The Isarebe Trust Archives, Cambridge, England (Box 315, Folder 4)

Isarebe had been sincere in his promise to Arem to get help to understand more about his childhood and he went twice weekly, for many years, to see a therapist, 'but we both just sit in silence for 50 minutes before she trousers £500'.[320]

Johns and Isarebe saw each other daily when they were both in London and spent most weekends at Isarebe's house near Cambridge. Johns' work flourished and she had her first solo show in London in September 2059, followed by sell-out shows in New York and Munich. Her reputation spread quickly and she found herself in demand throughout the art world and beyond, having to employ first one and then a second personal assistant by early 2060. As she had feared, her unconventional beauty took her notoriety beyond art and into popular culture, as 'one of the faces of London'.[321]

Arem Johns Exhibition Catalogue, Femin-I Gallery, London, 2059

320   Isarebe, S, 2059, eLetter from Solomon Isarebe to Rita Bortelli dated 6th June 2059, The Isarebe Trust Archives, Cambridge, England (Box 327, Folder 7)
321   Unattributed, 2061, *Art and fashion,* Cosmo London, 10th November 2060, pp. 23–25

In different realms both Isarebe and Johns now regularly featured in the media, but no one beyond their small group of friends and relatives knew they were a couple. This anonymity was to finish when after an interview on Female Identity Hour on BIBC Media, Arem Johns was asked what she would be doing that evening – a question every interviewee had been asked at the end of a Female Identity Hour interview since 2038 – always asked kindly, it allowed even the most serious interviewee to leave on a human and sometimes funny note. Johns said: 'Oh, I think Solomon is taking me ice-skating – his first time, would you believe. I don't know what got into him!' Clare Cutmore, the host, said in a somewhat surprised voice, 'Erm ... would that be Solomon Isarebe, the Nobel Prize winning Solomon?' Arem laughed and said: 'Yes, but I tend not to call him the Nobel Prize winning Solomon, it would make his head even bigger than it already is. It's a very narrow door into my bedroom and I wouldn't want him struggling to get in.'[322]

Johns thought little of it and Isarebe thought she'd been very witty. He had asked her ice-skating on purpose, to give her something to say at the end of the interview. As they came off the ice early that evening, they were laughing and holding hands when they were met by three photographers and two journalists, calling out questions to them: 'When's the big day?; How long have you been together?; Where did you meet?; Isn't she a bit young for you Prof?'[323] It was this last question they least expected and the one that upset Isarebe most. The headlines the next day, in the notoriously intrusive and cruel English tabloid newspapers of the period, mainly focused on this aspect of their relationship.

Isarebe was livid and called Maggie Doyle the next morning to ask what to do:

> She told him there was nothing much they could do. They could complain. They could go to law. They could put their side of the case. But it would just pour gas on the fire. She said they would have to ride it out and hope the papers would get bored. She insisted they weren't big enough for it to last more than a week. And I told him he wasn't that old – which was what he really wanted to hear.[324]

322   Cutmore, C, 2060, *Female Identity Hour*, BIBC Media broadcast and podcast, 14th September 2060

323   Isarebe, S, 2060, eLetter to Rita Bortelli dated 17th September 2060, The Isarebe Trust Archives, Cambridge, England (Box 338, Folder 1)

324   Bortelli, R, 2070, *The Dizzy Digger*, Manchosens, New York, p. 361

Newspaper articles on Isarebe and Johns at Alexandra Palace, Isarebe's scrap book, 2060

However, for some reason, Arem Johns and Solomon Isarebe became a media story that wouldn't go away. Wherever they went, there were photographers waiting. The age difference, which was 17 years, was part of the reason for the fascination, along with Johns' status as a feminist icon and Isarebe being a Nobel Prize winner, but perhaps what really kept the story alive were the nature of the photos, which were gold-plated clickbait. Arem Johns always photographed well and looked very attractive and much younger than her years, whilst Isarebe, who scowled as soon as a photographer approached, looked significantly older than his 51 years, managing to look like a monster in almost every photo.

The spiteful on-going coverage of the tabloid press, almost all of it delivered in a supposedly humorous and mocking tone, was largely but not solely restricted to the UK. Many in the feminist and gay communities were also highly vocal, saying they felt betrayed by Johns, 'for throwing herself at the feet of the controlling patriarchy.'[325] However, it was the comments made by colleagues in the academic community that hurt Isarebe most: some of these differed little in content and tone to the tabloid press, with some colleagues making jibes at Isarebe for 'breaking my duck, taking up babysitting and trying to up my population forecasts.'[326]

Johns and Isarebe started to spend more time in Europe and America, where they received less press attention and any coverage was more curious and less censorious. Johns was not too bothered about the 'ridiculousness of these people'[327], but Isarebe found it disturbing that his most intimate and delicate feelings were being discussed and picked apart by people who had never met him. Johns became the mouthpiece for the couple and defended Isarebe from the most vicious attacks, famously pinning a journalist against a wall at an opening of one of her exhibitions, when he asked her if Isarebe could still perform in the bedroom: 'She whispered something in this bloke's ear. I've no idea what she said, but he went puce and literally ran from the room. It gave me this warm feeling that started in my stomach and then spread over my entire body. W is [expletive] wonderful!'[328]

In May 2061 they made the small step to living together on a full-time basis, splitting their time between Isarebe's London flat and the house in Cambridgeshire, whilst retaining Johns' studio in Peckham, where they both

325   Hisster, B, 2060, *Selling us out, F-me!*, 14th October 2060, p. 21

326   Isarebe, S, 2067, typed notes for an unpublished autobiography, manuscript dated 24th September 2067, The Isarebe Trust Archives, Cambridge, England (Box 448)

327   Johns, A, 2060, note in sketch book 104 dated 31st October 2060, The Arem Johns Archive, Lambeth School of Art (Box 45)

328   Isarebe, S, 2061, diary entry dated 20th May 2062, The Isarebe Trust Archives, Cambridge, England (Box 370, Folder 2)

worked when they were in London. It appears to have been a harmonious life, far from Arem Johns' predictions of turmoil and destructiveness. One of their rare arguments came when Isarebe took up painting:

> Solomon, What is it with you? Do you have to be better than everyone at everything? Can you not leave a small space in this universe for someone else to excel in? You are just about the most famous man on the planet, with a brain acknowledged to be twice the size of Venus, and now you want to be the next Picasso? Leaving me where? And you hate painting, you told me. You [expletive] hate art! I suspect you thought I'd be happy about this, but think about it, what if I suddenly took up econoknobtrics, or whatever it is you do. Do you think we could talk about it together? Do you think we would giggle about the residual values or the r-squareds, ffs? Or would you quite rightly suggest I stick to what I was good at and let you get on with it. I know you're next door, because I can hear you stomping around being bored, but I can't talk to you today, so please don't knock on my door. [Expletive] idjit![329]

Isarebe and Johns at home in Cambridge, 2061

---

329   Johns, A, 2061, email from Arem Johns to Solomon Isarebe dated 28th June 2061, The Arem Johns Archive, Lambeth School of Art (Box 46, Folder 13)

6.2 Exploring the subconscious

In July 2061, whilst Johns and her team were busy working on pieces for her latest show in Singapore, Isarebe went to New York to see Hetty Brown to discuss some ideas she had been developing with Francis Smitherson, an evolutionary philosopher and psychologist. He stayed with Rita Bortelli in her apartment whilst he was in New York.

The techniques Isarebe and Brown, along with Heulwen Gröning, had developed for *Future Perfect* had indirectly been about the role of the unconscious mind in decision making. Brown and Smitherson were attempting to take this further, aiming to quantify the relative importance of the conscious and unconscious mind in different facets of human life and to understand how these roles had developed from an evolutionary perspective. They had some initial success, but their models failed to replicate behaviour in real-world situations. As a favour, Brown asked Isarebe to re-examine their assumptions and their proposed research approach.

Isarebe was still intellectually active both in the academic world and at Isarebe & Isarebe, but his work was mostly in an advisory capacity and he was aware some of his skills had atrophied. This was the first time in many years Isarebe had been asked to examine some fundamental issues and in a completely new area and he was excited at the prospect. After initial discussions with Smitherson and Brown, he called Casey Ingar and said he would be stepping back from Isarebe & Isarebe work for a while. Isarebe immersed himself in books and papers on the conscious mind and its role in human evolution and was surprised by how little was known about its function and evolutionary purpose.

Dizzy spent a couple of months with me in New York that summer, talking to Hetty, Francis, anyone who would give him the time of day and that just about included anyone on the planet. Everyone wanted a piece of Solomon Isarebe and to be associated with some new work from the great man. It reminded me of that last year before Future Perfect was published, when he wrung dry the minds of some of the world's great thinkers.

He went home for a week at the end of July, to get his fix of Arem, and then went to Singapore in early September for her show opening.

They came back to New York together. It was the first time I had met her in person and it was immediately obvious she was an exceptional woman and an extraordinary beauty. They always turned heads wherever they went: Beauty and the Big Beast. How did he get so lucky, hitting the bullseye with his first shot?

They ended up taking over most of my Central Park apartment and I was happy to give it to them. It was just like the old days, except he didn't write on the walls anymore and he'd finally been taught to flush the john.

In mid-September, he got Heulwen over from Wales and presented his findings in an all-day session with Hetty, Heulwen, Francis, their four research assistants and a few hangers-on, including Arem and me, who were allowed to sit in for the ride. He was back to his awesome best and it was great to have most of the team back together – only Casey was absent and he was sorely missed. Arem had never seen Dizzy work like this before and I think she finally got why he is so revered.

His first challenge to the team was to define what they meant by consciousness, because he said without clarity they could draw no conclusions on its role. He thought existing definitions were too complex and "over-facetted" as he put it, as well as being intellectually incoherent and defined with insufficient scientific input. He mockingly showed us a research paper which made reference to early Greek philosophers, which he said was "a crime against science." He didn't hold back.

His second challenge to them was to split the functions of the conscious mind into those with evolutionary survival benefits, those which had developed over a shorter "non-evolutionary timeframe", functions with no apparent benefits – so-called spandrels – and functions which negatively impacted on our success as a species, which he called "super-spandrels." He was very persuasive in his arguments that most of the functions of the conscious mind appeared to be spandrels or super-spandrels and should therefore be ignored. He just loved smashing myths and he made me feel very defensive of my beloved profession, but it takes someone braver than me to stop Solomon Isarebe when he is in full flow.

For each of the "useful" functions of the conscious mind, he recommended Hetty and Francis establish which of these were unique to consciousness, which were entirely duplicated in the unconscious, and which worked in beneficial harmony with the unconscious. For him, the mind was just another analytical challenge.

He provided compelling evidence, much of it derived from the work of the wonderful Juan D'Eath and Seth Ming, that the conscious mind, despite its flaws, was the reason humans dominated the earthly realm, specifically because of its essential role in facilitating cooperation within a group; cooperation being the bedrock of our evolutionary success.

He argued that to successfully cooperate required being aware of self and the impact of self on the health of the group. According to Dizzy, the whole idea of individuality was spurious, because the only reason it is necessary to know we are individuals, to know we exist, to be conscious, is because we are not individuals and we do not exist, that we are just a small part of a superorganism – a human coral reef. I have been in the world of the human psyche all my working life, but it blew my mind to consider individuality an illusion – especially when the idea came out of the mouth of the most individual individual on the planet.

According to the Gospel of St Isarebe, the other great function of the conscious mind was in giving us the ability to communicate with other members of the group and more importantly to record thoughts, ideas and discoveries. Not exactly groundbreaking, although Isarebe seemed convinced he was the new Darwin at this point.

There was loads of other stuff, but my mind was full by mid-afternoon and I stopped taking notes, getting lazy at last in my old age. It was an exhausting, mind-mincing sort of day. I remember thinking if kids were given lessons like this once a week, most of the world's problems would be solved within a generation. He promised more the next day on how Hetty and Francis should test these ideas, but Arem and I looked at each other and nodded – one day was enough.[330]

---

330   Bortelli, R, 2070, *The Dizzy Digger*, Manchosens, New York, p. 386

Isarebe's hypotheses were well researched, but most do not stand up to close examination today, when the roles of the conscious and unconscious mind are much better understood. It was perhaps inevitable that the real value of his input was in his suggestions for the design of the research, for which Brown and Smitherson were to receive many plaudits. Isarebe insisted he should not be named as a contributor to the work, perhaps wanting to pay back the heavy debt he felt he owed to Hetty Brown for her work on *Future Perfect*. Brown and Smitherson went on to reach a number of conclusions broadly in line with Isarebe's initial hypotheses, although critics unkindly suggested this was out of fear of the great man. Solomon Isarebe remained involved in the project through to its conclusion in 2065 in what was to be his last major academic endeavour.

Whilst Isarebe was in New York, he met David Dingle. Dingle was a friend of Rita Bortelli's and a fellow psychotherapist who had worked with her on a paper entitled 'Death of a parent: The secret killer,'[331] which examined the long-term effects of the death of a parent in childhood. Dingle was famously cheerful and had a never-ending line in jokes and stories, usually in extreme bad taste, but delivered with a charm that meant he got away with them, even amongst the intellectuals that were Bortelli and Dingle's friends in New York. They were introduced at a dinner party given in Isarebe's honour in Bortelli's apartment. Isarebe disliked meeting new people, particularly when they 'turn up uninvited at my apartment,'[332] but after a few hours and some free-flowing whisky, 'Davey D had Dizzy in tears of laughter, just as I suspected he would.'[333] At the end of the evening, Dingle invited Isarebe over to his house to teach him bezique. Isarebe went to Dingle's house in Astoria on many evenings until Arem's arrival in New York, after which he saw him less frequently.

In the final week of their stay in New York, Arem Johns could see something had happened to Isarebe during a visit to Dingle's that afternoon: 'He was agitated in a way I had never seen before, pacing the halls. literally pulling his hair out and picking at the scars of old spots. He wouldn't talk to me, so I just left him to it. Somethings going on Mum. no idea if it's good or bad, but it's making my stomach ache.'[334] He refused to go out with the team for a farewell dinner that evening and when Bortelli asked why, he punched a hole in her kitchen wall, narrowly missing Bortelli. Johns called Dingle, to see if he

331   Dingle D, and Bortelli, R, 2049, *Death of a parent: The secret killer*, North American Psychological Review, 198, 2, pp. 640–685

332   Isarebe, S, 2061, diary entry dated 23rd July 2062, The Isarebe Trust Archives, Cambridge, England (Box 375, Folder 6)

333   Bortelli, R, 2070, *The Dizzy Digger*, Manchosens, New York, p. 251

334   Johns, A, 2061, email from Arem Johns to Lucienne Johns dated 19th September 2061, The Arem Johns Archive, Lambeth School of Art (Box 47, Folder 5)

knew what had happened that day, but Dingle just said that it might be to do with his genetic father, whom he had mentioned with increasing frequency over the past few weeks. Isarebe had never spoken to Johns about his birth family, with Isarebe insisting he had no memory of them. Johns decided not to press Isarebe and when Jannik Isarebe called that night, it went to the back of everybody's mind.

Jannik told Solomon that Reba Isarebe had suffered a series of heart attacks over the previous twenty-four hours and it was uncertain how long she would live. Solomon whispered to Arem: 'Izzy, then mum, then you. Moor vill drep all keerlighten.'[335] [336]Arem told her mother she nearly passed out when he said this, even though she did not understand what he had said.

Reba and Jannik Isarebe, Mid-summer 2061

335   Johns, A, 2061, eLetter from Arem Johns to Lucienne Johns dated 24th September 2061, The Arem Johns Archive, Lambeth School of Art (Box 47, Folder 5)
336   It is likely Isarebe said 'Mor vil drepe all Kjærligheten', which translates from the Norwegian in to 'Mother kills all love'.

Isarebe, Johns and Bortelli were in Garway Hill within fourteen hours: Johns clutching a sketch painting of Solomon she had made for Reba and Jannik in New York; Bortelli on the phone, organising transport and food for the coming week; and Isarebe in a semi-catatonic silent state.

Jannik and Solomon sat with Reba Isarebe in The New County Hospital in Hereford for three days, before taking her home, at her insistence: 'She knew she was dying and was quite happy to go, but she wanted to be at home. She wanted to be with Dad and the rest of us, but mostly I think she wanted to feel the hazy presence of Izzy around her. Iz stills hangs out with us sometimes.'[337]

Reba Isarebe died, aged 86, on 1st October 2061. At her funeral, there were over thirty camera crews and photographers, looking for shots of Solomon Isarebe and Johns. One of the headlines the next day was: 'Solomon Isarebe dry-eyed at mother's funeral' showing a picture of Isarebe looking with apparent contempt at his father crying in the arms of Bortelli. Another read 'Arem Johns: Stunning in Black'.

Bortelli and Johns attempted to bring a legal case against these newspapers for invasion of privacy, but were told by solicitors the photos were taken in a public place and it was highly unlikely they would win. They eventually managed to secure court orders forbidding the press from camping outside Isarebe and Johns' homes, where some had been attempting to get photos of them in a domestic setting.

---

337   Isarebe, S, 2067, typed notes for an unpublished autobiography, manuscript dated 24th September 2067, The Isarebe Trust Archives, Cambridge, England (Box 448)

6.3 Taking a step back

When Johns and Isarebe had first met in 2057, Isarebe had been working ten-hour days, often seven days a week, with the bulk of his time spent propagating the ideas within *Future Perfect*. Each year had seen him and his constantly evolving group of analysts and writers producing versions of *Future Perfect* in different formats, for different audiences, in different countries. He had also been managing consultancy projects at Isarebe & Isarebe and since his appointment as Professor of Quantitative Social Economics at Cambridge University, he had recruited a large research group there, although he was rarely seen around the University.

After Reba Isarebe's death, he stepped back from most of his consultancy work and focused his time on occasional media appearances and major speeches on fertility issues, 'although even I'm bored of hearing me banging on and on about the sanctity of condoms.'[338] He continued to nominally head up his research group at Cambridge University, but appointed Jo Qility as Director of the Department and took little interest in the work of the researchers. His only real work at the university were his undergraduate lectures on the last Friday of term, which were still played out to large crowds. They were increasingly attended by students from throughout the university, partly because of a desire to say they had seen the great man in action, but also because the lectures were now a traditional precursor to big end-of-term parties. Many were already 'chemically cheerful'[339] by the time the lectures started.

Isarebe enjoyed the party atmosphere of these lectures and each term offered a prize of twelve crates of vintage wine to the student who correctly identified the three deliberate mistakes he inserted into each lecture. Only once was the prize won, by Professor Jeanie DeSoto, when she was visiting Isarebe from MIT. She offered the wine to anyone in the lecture hall wearing a 'Turn off the news' t-shirt. To great cheers, they found the only person wearing such a t-shirt was Isarebe. To greater cheers, Isarebe gave the wine to Myria Nutt, the youngest undergraduate in the university.

Even after cutting his workload Isarebe still travelled frequently and despite their devotion to each other, Johns and Isarebe were rarely in the

---

338   Isarebe, S, 2063, diary entry dated 16th November 2062, The Isarebe Trust Archives, Cambridge, England (Box 382, Folder 1)
339   Isarebe, S, 2064, diary entry dated 22nd December 2064, The Isarebe Trust Archives, Cambridge, England (Box 421, Folder 9)

same place at the same time. Johns had less time for painting, because of media commitments and exhibitions around the world, so when she was in England she was desperate to spend as much time as she could in the studio.

TeePs,

He's driving me bloody mad. I've got to work, but he's spent the whole day mooning about the studio, making cow eyes and offering me cups of tea every ten seconds.

It's hard to get cross with him, because he's so bloody nice these days, but I sort of long for the days when the man would walk through a few walls before breakfast, knocking me over in the process. Do you want him for a bit? Don't say yes.

He's off again next Monday to Caracas and all countries south and I won't see him for three weeks and then I'll be in bits missing him.

I've turned into a pathetic schoolgirl. HELP!![340]

On 4th July 2062, the 5th anniversary of Isarebe and Johns' meeting, they found themselves 6,000 miles apart, with Isarebe in Edinburgh and Johns in Bangkok. Johns had slipped an envelope full of sunflower seeds in Isarebe's bag as an anniversary present. Isarebe had the medieval gold and sapphire ring Johns had once returned to him sent to her hotel, with a note saying: 'In the blurb that went with this ring, it said they used to believe rings had no special powers, should never be given as presents or payment, were not a symbol of love, couldn't protect you from disease, were hopeless in protecting chastity, but were useful for sending secret messages.'[341] On the inside of the ring in Gothic script was the inscription: 'Wondersocks. Come home.'

Whether because of the ring, or not, they made the conscious decision to spend more time together at home or in the studio, making great efforts to spend Thursday to Sunday, 'the Bigend',[342] with each other.

On 3rd March 2063, Arem Johns was due to meet Isarebe in his rooms at St. John's College, prior to attending an evening event for Nobel Prize winners

340   Johns, A, 2062, Juzz1mo communication between Arem Johns and Talia Player dated 3rd March 2062, The Arem Johns Archive, Lambeth School of Art (Box 50, Folder 2)
341   Johns, A, 2062, undated hand-written note, The Arem Johns Archive, Lambeth School of Art (Box 50, Folder 6)
342   Isarebe, S, 2062, diary entry dated 19th September 2062, The Isarebe Trust Archives, Cambridge, England (Box 379, Folder 3)

from the university. Johns had been in London that day, talking to a curator at Tate Modern about a possible show in 2066 and was excitedly cycling through the congested streets from Cambridge station to the college.

As she neared the side entrance to St. John's she saw the familiar figure of Millicent Bryant, standing on the corner with her placard stating: 'Solomon Isarebe. Baby killer!' Bryant was a staunchly traditional Catholic and had been standing outside the college with her placard almost every day since *Future Perfect* had been published. Millicent was the most kindly of protesters and greeted Johns and Isarebe with a cheerful wave every time she saw them. She even gave them Christmas cards. On this day, as usual, Johns returned Millicent's wave, failing to see the pedestrian who walked out into the road from behind Bryant. Johns veered across the road to avoid the pedestrian and was hit by a taxi coming in the opposite direction.

It was six hours before the hospital managed to contact Isarebe, who had been at Professor Kamil's house. Kamil had died that morning from a combination of pneumonia and an ongoing thyroid condition. Solomon had sat with Megan Kamil and their daughter, Camelia, all afternoon, listening to stories of their husband and father. Isarebe turned on his phone at 6.30 p.m. to find twenty-four missed calls from Eliza Fiorentina, a member of Isarebe's Bezique Club and Senior Consultant in Emergency Surgery at Cambridge University Hospital. Fiorentina told him what had happened, that Arem was going to be okay, but she would probably need surgery on her hip and possibly a hip replacement.

The first thing Arem told him when he arrived at the hospital was she had been pregnant, but had lost the baby.

Mum,

I hope you're feeling a bit better, but please come soon. I really need you here. Pops says there are no flights for 2 days, but surely there's some way of getting back. Solomon says he'll pay, if that's a problem.

I expect Dad told you what Solomon said when I told him I'd been pregnant. was it mine? I don't know if it's some chronic insecurity or if it's hard baked in every man's penis / brain or if he really thinks I sleep around. Once, I have been unfaithful to him, once! I told him it had been his and he said 'of course, of course', but I knew he didn't believe me. I talked to Eliza Fiorentina and she said it was difficult to prove paternity after a loss like this, but she told me if I was willing to say I'd been raped – I literally shivered when she said it – they would be able to do a DNA test on the remains of the foetus straight away. The DNA matched Solomon's of course and he was then cross with me, insisting I hadn't needed to do it. Eliza told me later they had lost the test results and my mention of rape through an administrative error – bless her.

I can't tell you how low I feel at the moment, hormones I expect, along with all the drugs. They now think my hip will mend on its own, but it hurts like [expletive]. Solomon will never be able to look after me when I get out. Talia says she will come, but she has the domestic skills of a skunk. Would you be able to come? Just you. Pops won't be too offended will he? He sounded so upset at 'losing his grandson' that he made me feel bad about what happened.

Talking of feeling guilty, Millicent Bryant has sent me 12 get-well cards in the last 3 days. Poor thing. She even asked Solomon to sign a copy of Future Perfect. She seems to think she is solely responsible and that God went missing at this point in life's proceedings.

I can still have babies apparently, but they have checked Solomon's sperm and the count is so low they say it was a 1 in 10,000 'miracle' we got pregnant. I could immediately see Solomon doing the maths in his head. I suspect he will want us to have sex every half an hour for the next 15 years to give us a decent chance. I don't want a baby though Mum. I never have. You and Pops made the odd mistake doing the parent thing, so what chance emotional and moral no-hopers like me and Solomon.

Hurry home. AX.[343]

Isarebe was hit hard by the loss of the baby, on top of the death of his 'third dad.'[344] Isarebe had known Professor D. Kamil for thirty-seven years, since he arrived in Cambridge as a 17-year-old prodigy. Solomon read the eulogy at Kamil's memorial service, saying 'it was the hardest speech I have ever given in my life.'[345]

---

343   Johns, A, 2063, email from Arem Johns to Lucienne Johns dated 10th March 2063, The Arem Johns Archive, Lambeth School of Art (Box 63, Folder 2)

344   Isarebe, S, 2063, eLetter from Solomon Isarebe to Rita Bortelli dated 15th March 2063, The Isarebe Trust Archives, Cambridge, England (Box 384, Folder 1)

345   Isarebe, S, 2063, diary entry dated 22nd April 2063, The Isarebe Trust Archives, Cambridge, England (Box 385, Folder 3)

Isarebe took Arem from the hospital back to their house outside Cambridge, where Lucienne Johns had set up a bedroom for Arem on the ground floor. Lucienne stayed for the next four weeks, but she found herself nursing Isarebe as much as her daughter. Arem Johns made a rapid recovery from her injuries, but Isarebe spiralled into a depression, the first bout for many years.

TeePs,

I just can't deal with Solomon at the moment and he won't get help. I have never seen him in a state like this. it's not pretty. Mum is carrying his considerable mental weight solo.

But something really weird happened yesterday, on top of all the on-going weirdness. Solomon was in tears as per, moaning about not being a real man, sort of normal low sperm count bollocks, so Mum went to put her arm around him, you know, like she does with everyone. She had a broken nail and she scratched his neck with it as she reached up to him and there was the tiniest amount of blood. Solomon screamed 'No mum!', like a real big piercing I'm being murdered sort of scream and he then collapsed in a sort of ball on the floor. Mum looked at me to do something but he needed more than I could give. It was genuinely scary. God knows what lurks in his head. Fear it may be worse than the crap in mine.

I know it sounds weird, but part of me wondered today if Solomon had such a god-awful childhood that he did away with one or both of his parents. It would explain a lot. Forget that. I think I must be losing it a bit in the head too.

I'm very happy I have you.

AX[346]

Johns was told she needed to exercise every day as part of her physiotherapy and she persuaded Isarebe to try ballroom dancing with her, hoping it would help his recovery, along with her own. Isarebe was a poor dancer, but he reluctantly agreed. Their dancing improved over time and by the end of the

---

346   Johns, A, 2063, Juzz1mo communication between Arem Johns and Talia Player dated 29th March 2063, The Arem Johns Archive, Lambeth School of Art (Box 63, Folder 8)

summer of 2063 Isarebe had a dancefloor installed in one of the outbuildings in the grounds of their house in Cambridge.

One afternoon in September, at the end of their now daily dance practice, Johns held Isarebe by both his hands and they span around in a light-hearted end to the session. Johns was now almost fully recovered and she spun Isarebe around faster and faster, both of them laughing. Isarebe lost his footing and Johns found herself spinning Isarebe around by one arm, for a brief second. She let go and looked down at Isarebe on the floor, immediately realising something was seriously wrong.

Isarebe was lying on the floor shaking, his legs making involuntary cycling movements. Johns said he appeared unconscious, but would then suddenly open his eyes and stare at empty space. He continuously clenched and unclenched his mouth during the whole episode. As quickly as he had gone into seizure, he came back to full consciousness. He immediately sat up and started talking, with no recall of what had happened.

Johns thought he had undergone an epileptic fit, but the medical team were convinced it was a psychogenic non-epileptic seizure (PNES), sometimes associated with anxiety, depression and a history of sexual or physical abuse. They thought it unlikely to have been triggered by the fall. They said the only effective treatments were talking therapies and Isarebe's psychiatrist should be informed.

Isarebe showed no aftereffects of the seizure but refused to dance again.

6.4 Childhood traumas

After Reba Isarebe's death, Solomon went more frequently to Hilman Cottage to see his father Jannik, who was nearing ninety years of age, but was in apparent good health. They would sit together and talk of Reba and Isabelle and Arem. However, after the seizure, it was over a month before he felt able to visit his father.

I told Dad today that my name was Axel. 'Like in a car?', he said, super-calm, as though we were chatting about the price of bread.

I then told him my genetic father was called Jakob and was Norwegian and my genetic mother was called Harriet and I thought she was from Australia.

It was such a relief to tell someone, something. Everything is now all backed up in my head and I know it has to come out sometime. I don't think I can physically keep it in for much longer.

I told Dad how I was feeling and he said he thought it might be easier if I told my story to someone other than him or Arem. Someone with whom I could let it all out in a big ugly rush, before trying to get it in the right order. He thought it might make me feel a bit safer.

I said if I did that it would feel like I was betraying Arem, because she had trusted me with everything and if I couldn't tell her about my childhood then what did that say about me and my love for her.

Dad said I wasn't Arem and she would understand. He asked who I would talk to, if I decided to go down this route. I immediately said Davey Dingle.

I am now on a plane to NY. Arem was so happy when I told her. She cried. It makes me want to cry too.'[347]

---

347   Isarebe, S, 2063, diary entry dated 1st October 2063, The Isarebe Trust Archives, Cambridge, England (Box 392, Folder 5)

Isarebe was back in England in less than a week, but in that time Jannik Isarebe had died from a sudden and unexpected heart attack. Isarebe only found out about Jannik's death as the plane taxied to the terminal at Heathrow Airport. Jannik had died 30 minutes after Solomon left New York on his return journey.

Isarebe wrote the story of his childhood down over thirty times. Arem Johns said each was more refined, harrowing and detailed than the last, 'until he appeared to have nothing left to say.'[348] He then burnt each of the hand-written manuscripts, except for this short, first account of his memories:

I remember Casey telling me once he turns into a normal human being after three or four drinks, and then turns into a monster after seven. I never turn into a normal human being, but after ten drinks I sometimes forget what sort of man I am, a man who killed his mother. No, I was a child who chose to kill his mother and wished he'd killed his father.

Arem tells me to forgive that little boy, but Davey says that will be the last small step and I might never take it. I have told Arem and Davey everything now, at least everything I can remember, maybe there's more. I never got the chance to tell Dad, or Mum, but I'm glad they didn't have to know, although Mum probably guessed. I think maybe Dad decided to die because he thought his job was finally done when I got on that plane to New York. I wish I could have told Izzy. My god I miss them all.

I always thought confession was meant to bring some relief from pain, guilt, sorrow. My confession to Davey, if that was what it was, brought me no relief. It left me feeling so sad and so evil I could not lift myself from his couch. He carried me to bed that first night and hurt his back in the process. The next day it was him lying on the psychiatrist's couch and me in the chair. It was perhaps easier that way.

My earliest memory is of Harriet smoking. I refuse to call her mum or Jakob dad. The smell of the smoke was familiar and comforting, but ███████████████████████████████████ everything changed. I was four years old. Every day from then on, just before Jakob came home, she would give me my tea, usually a piece of bread, then

348   Johns, A, 2064, eLetter from Arem Johns to Lucienne Johns dated 3rd February 2064, The Arem Johns Archive, Lambeth School of Art (Box 75, Folder 1)

██████████████ cigarette, telling me not to tell Jakob or I would be properly punished.

A neighbour commented on a scar on my arm and from then on, she punished me with ████████████████████████ ████. After a while, she started to focus on ██████████████ ██████[349], sticking me three or four times ██████████████ ██████████████████████████ she had just mutilated.

My father was completely under my mother's control. He was made to shower and change when he came in at night, before he was given his chores for the evening. After I went to bed each night, I often heard his muffled cries, as he was beaten. I went downstairs one night, too frightened by the noise to sleep. I peeked through the living room door. Jakob was lying on the floor, blood on his socks and on his underpants. She had a hammer by her chair. I never went downstairs in the night again.

I had to go to school when I was six years old. I don't think I had ever met another child, or worn ████████████████████████. I was given new clothes the day before and my first pair of shoes, and told my name was Axel Solomon Jakobsen-Steiner. When the teacher asked me my name the next day, I couldn't remember. The other children all started laughing. ████████████████████ ██████████████████████████████████ The teacher took me along the corridor to the nurse's room. I was quiet now, waiting for my punishment.

The teacher asked the nurse to give me some new clothes. ████████ ████████████████████████████████████ ████████████████████████████████████ ██████████████████████████████████ The nurse washed and dressed me very gently and kissed me on the forehead. She took me to a small room and left me to play with some toys. I'd never had any toys so I sat on the floor and read a magazine about what was on television that week. Harriet had a television in her room upstairs.

349   Redactions in accordance with Child Protection Agency Guidelines MGJ3/23 (2147)

About ten minutes later, three people came into the room, asking me very nicely where I got the scars and could I remember my name now. I knew not to tell them anything, so I went into the corner of the room and faced the wall. ████████████████████████████████████ ███████

After what seemed like hours, Jakob and Harriet arrived, together with a lady police officer and a man who seemed to be in charge. Harriet said ██ ███ ███ █████████

Jakob eventually convinced them I was okay and we went home. That night, Harriet didn't touch me, but Jakob ██████████████████ ███████████████████████████████, for 'upsetting your mother'.

I never went back to school. We moved into another house in Oslo for a while and then went to Venezuela. Jakob worked as a geologist and had managed to get some work with an oil company in Caracas. Everything was fine for a while and it was warm and the maid and gardener who worked in the house were nice to me. One day Harriet came into my bedroom and told me Jakob was having an affair with his boss's wife. She said I would have to look after her now. ████████████████████ ███ ███████████ After she had finished, she stood up and walked to the window. ███████████████████████████████████████ █████████████████

The maid bathed me that night and saw the cut on my ear. She asked me what had happened but I said nothing. The next day the maid and the gardener had disappeared. Jakob said I had been very naughty 'upsetting your mother' and telling other people about our business. ███ █████████

I was made to ███████████████████████████████████ ███████████████████████████████████████ all over my body now. She now left ██████████████████████████████ ███████████████████████████████

I became used to the routine, but I had stopped crying, because it made things worse.

Jakob's boss and his wife Kirsten came to dinner one night. I was allowed into the dining room to say hallo. They were a beautiful couple and they looked like they liked each other. I couldn't imagine Kirsten letting Jakob do to her what Harriet made me do. She ruffled my hair, although I tried to stop her.

I was ███████████████████████ after they had gone. I saw the next morning that Harriet had bought a new hammer and dad was very quiet.

Kirsten came round unexpectedly a couple of days later. Whilst Harriet was in the kitchen making coffee, Kirsten lifted my shirt and looked at the scars. Jakob ██████████████████ that night.

Shortly after Kirsten's visit, Jakob lost his job and we left Caracas. We went to Iran. It was okay for a while and then the same pattern repeated itself. Within a year we were in South Africa and then we were back in Norway. By now I was eight years old and over 5 feet tall and had only been in school for 1 day. I spent the days reading the books in Jakob's study although I didn't understand them very well.

Just as the other children were starting the new school year at the end of August, Harriet disappeared. I watched her leave with a huge suitcase, soon after Jakob went to work, but she didn't tell me where she was going. I sat at the kitchen table and waited for someone to come home.

Jakob came home at around 11 p.m. He was drunk and happy. I had never seen him like that before. He said Harriet had gone to bury her mother and father and it would just be him and me for a while. He fell asleep on the sofa and I put myself to bed, wondering if Harriet was going to kill her mother and father first before burying them, or whether she was going to bury them alive. I decided she would kill them first with a hammer.

Harriet didn't come back for a month. I learnt to despise Jakob during that month.

The week before Harriet left I had refused ██████████ one day, because I didn't feel well and just wanted to sleep; that night Jakob ████████████████████████, for 'upsetting your mother'. But now, he was behaving like a good father from a happy book: playing, talking, reading, taking me on outings. It was very confusing.

He told me about him and Harriet. The words stuck in my head, even though I didn't understand all he said. Jakob claimed he and Harriet had been happy at first. Very happy. They were married two weeks after they met. He said she started to change about a year after they were married. Harriet was still loving towards him at times, excessively so, lavishing praise on him, but then out of the blue she would start verbally abusing him, mocking his looks, his lack of success, his sexual performance. This was normally triggered by the smallest 'mistake' by Jakob.

Jakob said she also started making increasingly ludicrous demands of him, 'to prove his love', which if they weren't met would result in violence, aimed at Jakob or herself. These included suicide attempts, twice trying to jump out of the car when they were on the motorway on the way to see his mother. He said she would then return to being loving for a while, before the cycle would repeat itself.

After a while she started accusing Jakob of having affairs, with his friends, his sister, his mother, even with the neighbour's dog. She then stopped harming herself and focussed all her violence on Jakob. Jakob said he was forced to cut his ties with his family and friends.

After I was born, Jakob said Harriet was sometimes quite motherly to me, although once ██████████████████████████████████ ████████████████████ and on another occasion he had to take me to hospital ████████████████████████████████, which Harriet said I must have put there myself.

When I was four Jakob said she suddenly turned her violence on me, he didn't know why, maybe because it upset Jakob more than hurting him directly. Jakob said he was sad when this started, but relieved, as it took some of her violent attention away from him. He said he wanted to stand up to her, to protect me, but he was just too frightened.

He said Harriet made him hurt me when she was really upset. Jakob cried when he told me this and I realised I hated this man for his weakness as much as I hated Harriet for her strength. He never said sorry to me.

I found a book I had never seen before in Jakob's room. It was a book of poetry by Reba Desalli. It was called *It is. You are. Let it be.* I asked him about it. He said when he felt low, or bored, or frightened, he would read one of these poems and it always made him feel a bit better. He told me he thought Reba Desalli must be a very good person and a person that could be relied on, even though he had never met her.

He told me I could keep the book. It was the first thing I had ever been given. I couldn't understand very much of it but I took it to bed with me and slept with it under my pillow. I kept reading the title of the book, over and over, trying to understand what it meant.

Harriet arrived home unannounced, the week after I found the book. Jakob was watching me watch television, which he had brought downstairs from Harriet's bedroom. We both froze when we saw her. She said nothing, but disappeared upstairs.

Jakob turned the television off, but I kept staring at it, hoping that whatever was about to happen wouldn't, but nothing happened that night. Harriet was quiet and Jakob fluttered round her, giving her compliments and asking about the trip. I wondered what she had done to her parents.

I lay in bed that night and realised I wanted to kill them both. I didn't fantasise how I would do it, I just knew I wanted to and could see no reason why I shouldn't.

I woke the next morning and Jakob wasn't there. Harriet said he had gone to work. She said I could watch television, but I wasn't to leave the living room. At teatime she told me Jakob was home, but was working on the car in the garage. I hadn't heard him come in.

Just before bedtime a police car arrived at the house and then an ambulance. Harriet came into the living room and told me Jakob was dead. He had died in an accident. The car had fallen off a jack and crushed his skull. She told me to tell the police I knew nothing about it. I was holding Reba's book when she came in. She grabbed it off me and I never saw it again.

At the funeral, all I could think about was my book of poetry; *It is. You are. Let it be.* I knew some of the words in the title were related to each other, but I didn't know if that was important. *Is. Are. Be.* What did this good woman, Reba Desalli, want me to think, want me to do? And why did Jakob give me this book?

The police kept coming back to the house and asking Harriet questions about Jakob. A doctor came to the house and examined me. Harriet broke down crying and said Jakob had made all the scars on my body. That ████████████████████ and she couldn't stop him. I said nothing.

Harriet bundled me into a taxi about a month after Jakob died. We drove to a house on the outskirts of Oslo where she gave a man some money and he handed over the keys to a small Ford, with Danish number plates. We drove to Ystad in Sweden, where we stayed in a rented cottage for three weeks. We then drove over the long bridge to Copenhagen.

Harriet didn't touch me or speak to me when we were in Sweden, or when we arrived in Copenhagen, where she had rented a little apartment. She left me in the apartment each night watching television and went to the bar over the road. About six weeks after we arrived in Copenhagen she came back from the bar with an English truck driver. He came back to the bar and then to our apartment every Tuesday and Wednesday nights.

During the fourth visit from the truck driver Harriet woke me up and took me into her bedroom. ████████████████████
████████████████████
████████████████████
████████████████████
████████████████████
████████████

The same thing happened the next night. Harriet took me into the room, ███
███

The following morning, Harriet gave me a packet of cornflakes and a carton of milk and put me in the hall cupboard where she stored things she couldn't use. She told me to be quiet ████████████████
███
█████████████

I heard her and the man leave. I had finished the milk by the end of the third day and the cornflakes on the fourth day. I knew what I was going to do when she came back. Harriet had bought a new hammer when we arrived in Copenhagen and it hung on the back of the cupboard door.

It was a week before she returned. As she opened the cupboard door, she immediately pulled back ███████████████████████████████.
As she stepped back I stepped forward ██████████████████████████
███
███████████████████████████████████

I knew she was dead. I had a bath and washed my clothes. I then cleaned up the cupboard and took all the filthy cloths and rubbish to the communal bins. It took me nearly two hours to get Harriet in the cupboard, although I couldn't quite close the door. She was heavy and even though I was tall for a 9 year-old, I wasn't strong. After she was in the cupboard, ██████████████████████████████. I cleaned it five times. I then had another bath, washed the new set of clothes and took ███████████████████████████. I then packed my clothes, the only possessions I had, locked the apartment and went to the car park of the bar opposite. The truck belonging to Harriet's English friend was there, as I knew it would be. The cab door was unlocked █████████████████████████

After the bar shut much later that night, the man, David, came back to the truck. ███
███
████████████

I had rehearsed my little speech many times over the previous week. I told him he had a choice: he could take me back to the apartment, ███ ████████████████████████████; he could throw me out of the cab and drive away, when I ███████████████ ████████████████████████ to his employers in England; or he could take me to England and ██████████████████ ██ ████████████████████████. If he took me to England he would never see or hear from me again. He got out of the cab and threw up.

He looked up at the apartment block and then at me. He got back in the cab and told me ██████████████████. He slept in the cot that night and I sat wide awake in the cab, replaying ████████████████ ████████████████████. I felt no remorse. I decided not to think about her anymore. Not to think about any of it anymore. I made the decision no one was ever going to hurt me again. It was like pressing an erase button, except I now find I didn't.

We left Copenhagen very early the next morning. The man still smelled of alcohol. He didn't talk to me, but █████████████████ ████████. We stopped every few hours and David gave me food and something to drink. We went through Germany and stopped that evening near Bremen. The next morning we set off early again and stopped in a deserted lay-by, somewhere in the Netherlands. David pulled back the side curtain of the truck. There was a small space between two enormously high boxes. He cut a small flap in the bottom of one of the boxes and a torrent of small polystyrene shapes fell out, leaving a small space. He told me to get in. I heard him tape the box back up, before cutting two holes in the side of the box as he had promised he would. For air, he said. It was hot and claustrophobic, but I didn't care, even when I was violently sick throughout the crossing of the Channel. David had given me a bag to be sick into. When we arrived in England, he pulled over in the car park of a church and let me back into the cab, giving me some baby wipes to clean myself up. A little while later, he pulled over to the side of the road near a burger restaurant. He gave me some money and told me to wait for him in the restaurant. He said he would be an hour, two at most. I sat in the restaurant, not expecting him to return, but he did. He was now driving a van. He drove me to Benfleet and dropped me outside his house. I shook his hand. He said sorry and gave me £100. I said he would never hear from me again and gave him my word.

It was late in the day. I slept on the veranda of a deserted sports club that night and then walked to the railway station in the early morning. I got a ticket from a machine and got on a train to London, behind a group of teenagers in school uniform. I arrived outside The Poetry Library on the South Bank of the Thames at 10 a.m. and asked to see Reba Desalli. The lady asked me my name. I hesitated and then said Solomon, Solomon Is-are-be, Solomon Isarebe.

I don't understand why no one has ever come after me. I think I'm still waiting for them.[350]

Isarebe in Hilman Cottage, Garway Hill, 2063

There is a photograph of Solomon Isarebe taken by Arem Johns in late November 2063 in the kitchen of Hilman Cottage. It was taken the day after he arrived back from New York to find Jannik Isarebe had died. Solomon Isarebe looks exhausted, dishevelled and older than his 55 years and far from the man

---

350   Isarebe, S, 2063, hand-written undated notes in Isarebe's hand, assumed October–November 2063, The Isarebe Trust Archives, Cambridge, England (Box 399, Folder 4)

in the portrait behind him, painted just three years earlier by Arem Johns.

There was once again a significant media presence outside the crematorium in Hereford, where Jannik Isarebe's funeral service took place. The photos in the press the next day were all of Isarebe, collapsed in the arms of Arem Johns. Around him were many of Jannik and Reba's friends, along with Rita Bortelli, David Dingle and Casey Ingar, who walked with Solomon and Arem, helping Solomon when he seemingly couldn't walk unsupported and Arem could no longer sustain his weight.

These photographs of a loving, grieving couple and of Isarebe as a sensitive, normal man, seemed to change the minds of the general public, who stopped wanting to see Johns and Isarebe portrayed as a long-running joke. The press stance changed to one of benign tolerance for 'this odd-ball, strangely beautiful couple'[351] and would eventually morph into them being portrayed as something of a national institution. When Arem Johns won The Hirst Art Prize in 2066, the headline in the Express-Mail, beside a photo of the couple, was 'Arem and Solomon – Pride of Britain!'[352]

Isarebe and Johns spent much of January and February 2064 in Hilman Cottage, sorting through Jannik and Reba's things and dealing with the detritus of death. They talked of Isarebe's childhood, but Isarebe still found it difficult to relive these moments, and Johns thought he was becoming paranoid, convinced he was going to be arrested for Harriet Steiner's murder.

Arem Johns spent many days whilst they were in Hilman Cottage looking online for evidence of what happened to Harriet Steiner and why no one had looked for Solomon after he had killed her. She had not been able to find anything. She couldn't even find Solomon's birth certificate. She told Isarebe at the end of February she had to leave him for a while as she had a show in Amsterdam, but she would be back as soon as she could.

TeePs,

I'm going to Scandi. Secret mission, although Solomon thinks I have a show in the Netherlands. I'm going to plonk him back in the Barb while I'm away. Can you check in on him occasionally. take him for the odd walk please. Pretend he's a dog, but don't give him a bone. He's not in great shape. poor old mongrel. Thanks TeePs. AX[353]

---

351   Unattributed, 2062, *Arem and Solly: Still Grooving*, The Independent Guardian, 3rd November 2064, p. 13

352   Unattributed, 2066, *Arem and Solomon – Pride of Britain!*, Daily Express-Mail, 3rd December 2066, front page

353   Johns, A, 2064, Juzz1mo communication between Arem Johns and Talia Player dated 16th February 2064, The Arem Johns Archive, Lambeth School of Art (Box 75, Folder 3)

Johns went to Copenhagen, not Amsterdam, where she went straight to the Hovedbibliotek, Copenhagen's main library. With the help of one of the librarians she went through national and local newspapers from 2017 and 2018, but there was no mention of Harriet Steiner's murder. Johns then started looking through *The Copenhagen Morning Bugle*, a Danish newspaper for English speakers. It was only when she was randomly flicking through an edition written almost five years after Solomon's arrival in London that she found a lead. She saw a small article about a woman whose life support had just been turned off. Her name was Harri Stone. The woman had been in a coma since she had been hit by a truck crossing the road outside her apartment block five years earlier. It was nearly 4 o'clock in the morning when she had been hit and the truck driver said she had been crawling across the road and he had only seen her at the last minute. She received multiple head injuries in the accident.

Johns started re-examining editions of *The Copenhagen Morning Bugle* from 2017, now looking for mention of Harri Stone. On page three of the June 23rd newspaper, there were reports of the accident. They said Harri Stone was Australian, single and had been travelling in Europe for some time. They reported she had no living relatives, her parents having died recently. They said there was no sign of foul play. The owner of a neighbourhood bar said she drank there regularly and thought she may have been a part-time prostitute, although she had no regular customers. The police appeared to have little interest in her death.

Johns went on to Oslo and found an original copy of the marriage certificate of Harriet Steiner and Jakob Jakobsen. She also managed to find records of Jakobsen's parents, who both died in the 2040s and through them found the details of Jakob Jakobsen's sister, Ida. She discovered Ida had married an engineer and was still living in Oslo. She was nearing 92 years old.

Ida had been an occupational therapist, specialising in art for young adults who had suffered childhood traumas. Johns approached her, saying she was writing a book on art and sexual violence and she had read many things about Ida's work. Ida Jakobsen was a fan of Johns and was initially awestruck on their meeting. After they had talked of Ida and John's work, Ida probed Johns on what it was like to live with someone like Solomon Isarebe.

Darling Mum,

Hope Pops is on the mend.

I'm in Oslo now and met with Solomon's Aunt today. This is top secret, so don't tell anyone, especially not Solomon.

She is called Ida. I kept wanting to call her Ida Down. Does this incessant and inappropriate childishness come from you or Pops?

She sort of looked like a decrepit Solomon, although that was probably my imagination at work, but she wouldn't stop talking about him, what a genius he was, how good looking he was, how lucky I was. I was bursting to tell her he was her nephew, but I knew Solomon would blow a main fuse if I did.

I left it about an hour before asking her about her family. She said she was the end of the line, that her parents were dead, they had no children and her only brother had died in a tragic accident many years ago. Her husband had been sitting silently in the corner but at this point he got up and said: 'No accident. She crazy murdering bitch. Excuse me lady.' He left the room and Ida looked embarrassed. I asked if her brother had any children. She said definitely not. She said they were very close before her brother met Harriet, who was a little difficult. They didn't see each other after he met her, but he would have found a way to tell her if he had had children. I asked if Harriet had any other names. She looked at me strangely and said she thought her middle name was Dafne. I changed the subject and drew a little sketch of her, which I left as a thank-you. She was very happy with it.

Crazy, huh?! SYS. AX[354]

Johns went on to the Skatteetaten, part of which was the registry office for Norway, and she looked at the registration record of every child born in the greater Oslo area in 2007–2009; nearly 40,000 records. It took her nearly two weeks, looking for any possible combination of their names. There was no record of Isarebe's birth.

On her return, she confessed to Isarebe the real mission of her travels. Johns told him he hadn't murdered his mother, but Harriet Steiner was now dead, and there was no record of his birth, meaning Reba and Jannik were the only people who had ever been his official parents.

---

354   Johns, A, 2064, eLetter from Arem Johns to Lucienne Johns dated 24th February 2064, The Arem Johns Archive, Lambeth School of Art (Box 75, Folder 4)

6.5 The murder of Arem Johns

On more than one occasion, Isarebe referred to the years 2064–68 as the happiest of his life. He said this in a note he wrote to Johns on New Year's Day in 2068, with Johns replying: 'You're setting yourself a pretty low bar there, old man.'[355]

Isarebe was still in demand, but his star was on the wane. He spent more time reading for pleasure, becoming an unlikely fan of P.G. Wodehouse, the early 20th century comic writer. He wrote an autobiography with a working title of *Present Imperfect*, which was never published, although it is a frank and amusing read. Johns' reputation was still growing and she was now seen as one of the leading artists of her day, although there were some in the art world that griped about her style and the sexual nature of her work. Isarebe accompanied Johns on more of her trips abroad, happily playing consort. They both enjoyed this evolution of their working lives.

This peace and happiness came to an abrupt end. On 15th April 2068, Solomon Isarebe was found lying next to the dead body of Arem Johns in their Cambridge house, Hearts of Oak.

They were found by their cleaner, Marie Deedham. She assumed they were asleep, even though it was mid-afternoon and they were both fully clothed: 'I thought they were just doing one of those things artist types do, you know. They were always doing something weird.'[356] She retreated from the room, but called to them from the hallway that she wanted to clean their room. She got no response and after a few minutes she put her head around the door again. It was then that she noticed that Arem Johns was an off-grey colour, except for a small bluish-red circle on her right temple. She also saw there was what looked like scorch marks on Solomon Isarebe's face. She called the police.

The police found them in exactly the same pose that Marie Deedham had described.

Johns was laid out arms folded, eyes closed, like a medieval saint, with no sign of any blood but with a neat bullet hole through her right temple. The medics accompanying the police confirmed she was dead.

355   Johns, A, 2068, eLetter to Solomon Isarebe dated 1st January 2068, The Isarebe Trust Archives, Cambridge, England (Box 461, Folder 3)
356   Unattributed, 2068, *Arem Johns Dead*, Cambridge Morning News, 16th April 2068, front page

Isarebe was lying next to her. He was wearing a crumpled brown pin-striped denim suit, with some brown and magenta stains, which were later confirmed to be his and Johns' blood. On the floor, by the side of his bed lay an old-fashioned gun. On his temple was a cut and what were later confirmed to be burn marks. He was unconscious, but alive. He was immediately taken to Cambridge University Hospital.

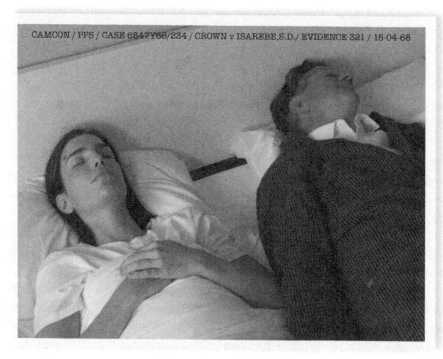

Photo shown at trial of Isarebe, 2068

The police were unable to find any evidence of a break-in and the only DNA traces on the gun and on Johns belonged to Isarebe.

Isarebe soon recovered from his wounds which were relatively superficial and he was arrested for the murder of Johns. In a packed press conference, Sarah Winders, Chief Constable of Cambridge Police, said they were not looking for anyone else in connection with the case and the initial evidence suggested it may have been some sort of failed suicide pact, but they were not ruling out other possibilities. The newspapers and TV news channels gave the event enormous coverage, with most referring to it as a 'failed lover's pact'.[357] The assumption was that Isarebe had killed Johns but had been too cowardly to follow through on his own suicide.

---

357   Unattributed, 2068, *Arem Johns Found Dead*, British Telegraph, 16th April 2068, front page

In a second press conference, 48 hours after the incident, Chief Constable Winders stated Solomon D. Isarebe had been arrested for the murder of Arem Johns and no suicide note had been found. The media could now almost literally smell blood and they turned their full vitriolic force on Isarebe, who they now claimed had 'always been a suspicious and deeply untrustworthy character'[358] and 'a dangerous and unstable pervert'.[359] There were soon reports that the police had previously investigated other instances of Isarebe's violence towards Johns and there were cries for a public inquiry to discover why these earlier crimes had not been followed up by the police.

Rita Bortelli came over to Cambridge from the USA as soon as she heard the news and Casey Ingar rushed back from a trip to Malaysia. Isarebe told them 'I don't care what happens to me',[360] but they organised an experienced legal defence team, led by Sir Hester Dalrymple. The defence team made a press statement on Isarebe's behalf to prevent Isarebe 'being convicted by public opinion, before the trial had even started'.[361]

The statement, read by Hester Dalrymple, said that Isarebe, on the morning of Arem Johns' death, had taken a trip into Cambridge where he had intended to buy a present for Johns. However, he had been distracted by an idea for his autobiography and had spent the morning sitting in the Fellows' Garden in St John's College, having let himself in the back gate. He then returned to his and Arem Johns' house, Hearts of Oak, around midday, where he found Arem Johns in the kitchen, dead, with a gun on the floor beside her. In his grief he had carried her body to their bedroom, where he had cleaned her and dressed her. He had then tried to take his own life, but had failed in his attempt to do so. This suicide attempt had resulted in cuts and burns to his face.

The public and the press took an immediate dislike to the 'plummy voice and supercilious manner'[362] of Dalrymple and what many saw as the highly unlikely nature of the story. The Express-Mail said: 'Smug lawyer tells tall story about the tallest storyteller of all'.[363]

The trial started on 9th November 2068 at Cambridge Crown Court. The court was cordoned off by the police, after many thousands of people surrounded the building. Most in the crowd were feminists, mourning the loss of their hero. Many were demanding a life sentence for Isarebe and there were even calls for the return of the death sentence.

358   Unattributed, 2068, *Nobel Prize Winning Murderer*, The Morning Sun, 19th April 2068, front page

359   Unattributed, 2068, *Isarebe kills wife*, Daily Express-Mail, 19th April 2068, front page

360   Bortelli, R, 2070, *The Dizzy Digger*, Manchosens, New York, p. 382

361   Bortelli, R, 2070, *The Dizzy Digger*, Manchosens, New York, p. 383

362   Unattributed, 2068, *Guilty as charged*, Morning Shine, 22nd April 2068, front page,

363   Unattributed, 2068, *Isarebe faces life*, Daily Express-Mail, 23rd April 2068, pp. 1–2

There was little evidence to support Isarebe's version of events. There was no CCTV footage indicating Isarebe had been in the centre of Cambridge that day and no one had seen Isarebe in the Fellows Garden in St. John's College. The college's CCTV showed someone entering and leaving by the back gate of the College at about the time Isarebe said he had been there and his lawyers insisted this was footage of Isarebe. However, many people had been in and out of the college that day and the person in the CCTV footage had been stooped, with the hood of his coat up, despite the warm weather. Under cross-examination, Isarebe said he couldn't recall owning such a coat.

The only substantive evidence apart from the testimony of Isarebe was forensic. Isarebe was in the middle of a period of profound grief and the recordings of the trial show him in the witness box looking like an old man, bent over and unkempt, giving monosyllabic and barely audible answers to the prosecution's questions. His demeanour caused The Real Daily Mail to label him an 'unreliable witness'.[364]

Halfway through the trial the prosecution lawyers, perhaps sensing a groundswell of public opinion behind them, went from presenting the case as murder within the context of a suicide pact, to straightforward murder. Although they could show no motive for murder, they attempted to demonstrate it was unlikely to have been a suicide. They brought forward medical records showing Johns had never been diagnosed as depressed[365] and no one had noted Arem Johns ever saying she was unhappy with Solomon Isarebe or any other aspect of her life. Both Lucienne Johns and Morris Johns took to the stand and said their daughter would not have committed suicide and was happily in love with Isarebe. The prosecution said it was extremely unlikely they would have made a suicide pact without leaving a note, given Johns and Isarebe were both prolific professional communicators. This circumstantial evidence was at the heart of the lawyer's argument that this had been 'murder, plain and simple'.[366]

Given the lack of other evidence, the trial was short, lasting only three days. The jury took less than four hours to unanimously find Isarebe guilty of murder.

Prior to sentencing the judge made it clear he thought it was a failed suicide pact, describing Isarebe as 'a coward certainly, but not a devil'.[367]

---

364 Unattributed, 2068, *Evidence mounts against Isarebe*, The Real Daily Mail, 10th November 2068, pp. 1–2
365 This was one of the first times confidential medical evidence had been presented in a criminal trial in the UK. This followed a change in the law that required doctors to provide medical records in rape and murder cases, when asked to do so.
366 DPP versus Isarebe (1), 2068, CCCt (476) *Prosecution summary*, 11th November 2068.
367 DPP versus Isarebe (4), 2068, CCCt (476) *Judge's summary*, 11th November 2068.

He gave Isarebe a sentence of 12 years, the minimum possible sentence for murder, but recommended he be considered for parole 'within 5 years'.[368] There was public uproar at the apparent leniency of Isarebe's sentence and on appeal, and under pressure from Prime Minister Faith Oxenby, the sentence was eventually increased to 25 years, with a minimum of 15 years to be served in prison.

Rita Bortelli and Casey Ingar replaced Dalrymple and his team after the trial, but the new lawyers did not believe there was anything further that could be done without new evidence. Isarebe was 61 years old when he was imprisoned. Within a year of his imprisonment he was stripped of all his honorary professorships and his Fellowship at St John's. His Nobel Prize was rescinded, with demands for return of the prize money. The UK Government, in a move indicating a desperate desire to get on the anti-Isarebe bandwagon, said Isarebe would never again be considered for a Knighthood and wished this 'evil man had never been offered one in the past'.[369] [370] There were reports of public burnings of copies of *Future Perfect*. One of the most decorated economists in history and author of the highest-selling non-fiction book of the 21st century had become a pariah.

---

368 DPP versus Isarebe (4), 2068, CCCt (476), *Judge's sentencing*, 11th November 2068
369 Reynolds, P, 2068, *Statement from Prime Minister's Office re Solomon Isarebe*, 13th November 2068, London
370 Until this statement, no one knew Isarebe had been offered a knighthood.

PART 7
Incarceration, freedom and exile

Isarebe was imprisoned in Gloucestershire. He had been declared a medium risk prisoner and was given access to the internet and to books. Isarebe reportedly did little in the early years of imprisonment except write letters to Arem Johns. 'He just sat there most of the time, sometimes in the garden, sometimes in his cell. Not talking. Not reading. Nothing. Just writing endless bloody letters to that really fit woman what he murdered. He was seriously weird – not like most of the other murderers on the block, who were quite decent blokes.'[371]

In 2073, five years into his sentence, Isarebe asked to talk to David Dingle. In those five years he had received no visitors and had not written or spoken to anyone on the outside, despite many attempts from Bortelli and Ingar, among others. He had also stopped writing his diary or making notes, leaving no evidence of what he had been thinking during this time. He would burn the hand-written letters he wrote to Arem Johns at the end of each day.

David Dingle arrived from New York in late July 2073 and spent just 40 minutes with Isarebe. Shortly after he saw Dingle, Isarebe stopped writing to Arem Johns. By the end of that year he had re-established contact with his friends. He wrote almost daily eLetters to Casey Ingar and almost as often to Rita Bortelli and David Dingle. Ingar now visited Isarebe every Tuesday afternoon, having retired from III Health. Bortelli and Dingle came over from New York to England every couple of months, specifically to see Isarebe.

Ingar and Bortelli communicated with each other about their visits to Isarebe. They both said he looked well, partly because of having his teeth capped. His natural teeth had decayed after he refused to look after any aspect of his personal hygiene in the first few years of imprisonment. Apart from that, the most notable thing about their correspondence and Isarebe's letters was there seems to have been so little to be said. Isarebe had been hollowed out. He had seemingly lost everything that had previously defined him: gone was the intellectual curiosity; gone was the burning impatience; gone was the passion of his love for Arem Johns. He reportedly smiled at Ingar, Dingle and Bortelli's stories and touched them frequently when they visited, but said little and hardly ever made reference to Johns or his family.

He started to teach in the prison school, not advanced economics, but simple arithmetic, with many of the prisoners going on to pass their secondary school level exams, 'which has given me as much pleasure as the Nobel Prize, to be honest.'[372]

---

371   Unattributed, 2072, *Isarebe writes to murdered lover*, Daily Express-Mail, 20th March 2072, p. 4
372   Isarebe, S, 2079, eLetter to Casey Ingar dated 14th October 2079, The Isarebe Trust Archives, Cambridge, England (Box 543, Folder 7)

In an unexpected twist, Bortelli and Dingle found love on their visits to England. They were formally married in California in 2075, but also had a blessing in the garden of Hilman Cottage on Garway Hill. Isarebe was allowed day release from prison to attend the event. Bortelli was 77 years old and Dingle was 75 years old and neither had been married before. Isarebe seemed to find some emotional release at their wedding. He wrote to them the day after the event:

You two made me happy yesterday. You both looked so beautiful – well, you not so much Davey – actually I was pleased to see you still look older and uglier than me.

For this to be a world of justice, you are certain to be happy together. That it is not a world of justice will not prevent you living a great and interesting life, just because the two of you are the wonderful people you are. But, please don't have any children, which I understand is what newly-weds normally do. It would be weird and news of it would ruin the wafer-thin sales of Future Perfect.

I was so touched you decided to have the blessing in Hilman Cottage. It is such a magical place and has been so important in our lives. Not just mine, but yours too I think Rita. I wandered the rooms and felt love from you, from Izzy, from mum and dad. It was unbearable and wonderful. I was almost delirious with anticipation before arriving there and have managed to keep the memory of it going, like when you were a kid and you kept a sweet in your mouth for as long as possible. I sit here with stupid tears on my cheeks, but stupid happy ones I think.

I have failed throughout my life to express love as I have felt it. Arem helped me change a little in this regard. But I have never told you how deeply I love you Rita, which sounds a bit inappropriate, seeing as you've just got married, but there you are. You have never been anything but wonderful and giving and loyal and kind to me and I know I didn't deserve it. I used to think it was because of mum, because you loved her so, but I now know it is because in this weird and random world of being human you loved me too. It is so hard for me to say that.

I am so sorry I wasn't able to be the same person to you, but it wasn't because of a lack of love. A lack of the necessary character traits I suspect.

We talked about you all the time Rita – me and Izzy, me and mum, me and dad, me and Arem. They all loved you too. Arem blessed you for keeping me in one piece, in readiness for her she seemed to think. Rita, I have been so lucky with the people around me, protecting me, helping me, loving me, until it seemed there was just you and Casey left from my old rickety made-up family, but then you brought Davey along, to keep up the numbers.

Davey, on more than one occasion you have saved me from the pit of despair. These phrases seem so cliched and trite, but it was a deep pit of despair I kept falling into. You tell the rudest of jokes and I think there must be a rule that says psychiatrists can't do that, but they and you were of life-saving importance to me. I always wondered if you had a bit of a thing for Rita and I assumed for many years you just pretended to be my friend and saving my soul was just you trying to impress the girl you loved. This may have been the reason you cared for me at the start, but I realise now you are my friend and I am yours.

I was never the sort to have a gang of mates, to go out together and keep secrets, have 'tour rules' as you once told me, but if I was to have a gang, it would be with you and Casey. What a vision, possibly the dullest gang in history – you would be cracking jokes and having a great time – me and Casey would be looking bewildered and trying to find an academic paper to read. You would be on a Harley and we would be on pushbikes. I would still want to be a member of that gang, though. Thank you David Dingle for being a buddy. A buddy I love. I wish I could save your life sometime, just to even things up a bit, but I don't think I am the life-saving sort and current circs probably make it even more unlikely I would be up to the task.

I just had a thought. Maybe my life-saving you was getting imprisoned, which meant you and Rita had to keep coming over here to keep my chin up, which in turn led to you getting your evil way with Rita, which saved your life. What a selfless wonderful guy I truly am!

I don't know if you saw the papers before you went home, but there was only one small mention of me attending your wedding, on page 18 of the Real Mail. Something along the lines of 'Evil monster goes to boozy wedding. Now safely back under lock and key.' I laughed with joy when I saw it. David Mare from The Washington and New York Post had let me know it was common knowledge I was going to escape from prison for the day to go to your wedding and all the papers were sending photographers, camera crews and the whole works to Hilman Cottage in order to ruin your day and establish their moral superiority over perverts and monsters such as myself. I asked David to spread rumours the blessing was going to take place in the barn at Hearts of Oak and not at Hilman Cottage. He owes me – another story – and he paid that debt off big time. My old neighbour at Hearts of Oak, Dustin Beaker, took the trouble to email me to let me know the reporters and film crews had parked on his lawn and ruined some of his rhododendrons and to tell me he hoped I would rot in hell for making his life so difficult and for writing my anti-Christian diatribe and for killing my wife (in that order). What a splendid result.

Thank you. And thank you. And well done for being in love.[373]

Although Isarebe had been emotionally revived by his friends' marriage, over the next six years his interest in external events diminished and his correspondence returned to being a polite but loving exchange of pleasantries and nothings. Casey Ingar had a small stroke in July 2078 and visited Isarebe less regularly from then on. Bortelli and Dingle still came over to see Isarebe from New York, but less frequently than they initially had.

Isarebe spent most mornings reading and in the afternoons he ran a small, informal school for other prisoners, now on a wide range of subjects. In the evenings, he started to write to Arem Johns once more, although he now kept these letters in a box, where he was allowed to keep personal possessions. They are painful to read, lamenting the loss of their love and his bitterness with the world. The margins are filled with drawings and endless writing of Arem Johns' name. Most of the letters are incomprehensible, with incomplete sentences and indecipherable handwriting. In some he writes short poems in the style of Reba Isarebe, with noise motifs and references to the natural world. It would be easy to assume that Solomon Isarebe was slowly losing his

373   Isarebe, S, 2075, eLetter to Rita Bortelli and David Dingle dated 4th August 2075, The Isarebe Trust Archives, Cambridge, England (Box 510, Folder 4)

sanity, but Bortelli's letters to Ingar suggest otherwise and that 'deep down, Dizzy is still there – the awkward, rude, brilliant son of a bitch we have always known and once in a blue moon loved.'[374]

In May 2080, an old head camera was found by Christopher and Karen Evans, under the insulation in the loft of a house they had recently purchased. This house was just two miles from Isarebe and Johns' house in Cambridgeshire. Christopher Evans was an electrical engineer at the university and out of curiosity managed to get the camera working. As soon as he realised what was on it he handed it over to the police. Recorded on the camera was a video taken by the wearer as he entered a house through an unlocked back door. The house was Hearts of Oak. It shows the figure approaching a surprised, but smiling Arem Johns, who said 'Hi Dave, I didn't know you were coming today – want a coffee? What on earth are you wearing a camera for – twit!'[375]. As Johns started to make coffee, the man came up behind her and shot her through the temple. This happened within a minute of him entering the house. There is then a halt in the filming. The next recording shows Arem Johns lying on the floor, bleeding from her temple. Although this part of the video was never released to the public, the court records indicate the man had filmed himself loosening her clothing and removing his own clothing. He approached her dying body on his hands and knees, naked apart from plastic gloves and appeared to be preparing himself to have intercourse with her. He could not achieve an erection and after three or four minutes he got dressed and the filming stopped.

After further searches of the house where the camera was discovered, the police found workman's overalls beneath floorboards in the downstairs bathroom, which on analysis had traces of Arem Johns' blood on them.

The house where the camera had been found had previously been rented by David Staveson. He was a sometime academic, who had scratched a living as an odd-job man and gardener since his late twenties. He had done various jobs for Isarebe and Johns during the three or four years before Arem Johns' death. Isarebe's diaries suggest employing him had been an act of charity by the couple.

Two days after the discovery of the camera, David Staveson was found. He was living in a two-room flat above a take-away restaurant in Sleaford, Lincolnshire. He immediately confessed to the crime. When interviewed by the police, he said: 'I love Arem and she loves me. I know she does, even if she never said it. I had to save her from that ignorant insensitive [expletive] and

374   Bortelli, R, 2079, hand-written birthday card sent to Casey Ingar dated 4th October 2079, The Isarebe Trust Archives, Cambridge, England (Box 543, Folder 6)

375   DPP versus Isarebe (1), 2081, CCCt (217) *Defence presentation*, 3rd June 2081

I'm not sorry for what I did. She is happy and at peace now and I know we'll soon be together in heaven.'[376]

Staveson committed suicide before his trial commenced.

Isarebe was pardoned, although due to legal complications it took a further five months after Staveson's confession for him to be freed. He was released from jail in June 2081. Isarebe was 73 years old and had spent over twelve years in prison.

Isarebe on release from prison, 2081

He went to live with Bortelli and Dingle in their Manhattan home, before they all moved to Bortelli's ranch near Big Sur in California. Bortelli and Dingle lived in the main ranch house, whilst Isarebe lived in the guest house, which was still a 5,500 square foot behemoth. Isarebe rarely spoke in public again and was never to return to England. His jobs, his titles and his medals were all offered back to him, but he declined them all.

---

376   DPP versus Isarebe (1), 2081, CCCt (217) *Defence presentation*, 3rd June 2081

David Dingle died in 2083, aged 83. Rita Bortelli and Isarebe continued living in separate houses on the ranch for several years, before they were joined by an ailing Casey Ingar in 2087. They decided to all live together in the big house, with live-in carers for Ingar.

Many people in the public eye fight to ensure history recalls them in a favourable light. Isarebe showed no interest in what anyone thought of him after his imprisonment and signed away the rights of *Future Perfect* to the Isabelle Isarebe Centre for Women in Botswana almost immediately after his release from prison.

Isarebe's reputation recovered and if anything was given a special sheen by the story of his wrongful imprisonment and the tragic death of his beautiful and talented young partner. *Future Perfect* was republished and sold nearly 500,000 copies in 2082. It was now being bought less as a prophecy of the future and more because it was part of the story of the man.

Bortelli and Isarebe were to live together for nearly twelve years on her California ranch. Almost nothing is known of their life together, but it seems to have been peaceful and for the large part healthy. Rita was in her eighties when Isarebe moved to the USA and there is no suggestion of any romantic attachment having developed between them.

Solomon D. Isarebe died, aged 85, in August 2093. He had learnt to ride a horse in his years on the ranch and died having fallen from his mount on the outer reaches of the Bortelli ranch. He had broken his neck and doctors determined death was almost instantaneous. Bortelli agreed to be interviewed by *The Washington and New York Post* for Isarebe's obituary, her last ever interview:

Dizzy somehow managed to get to the end of his life living how he wanted to live. He loved that horse and would hold no ill will for having been shipped the way he was. I think he had been longing for the end to come, as long as it was on his terms.

We talked about dying often. He always maintained death was a nothing event. He used to say it's no different to when you have anaesthetic for an operation, you try to count to ten, but never get past 4 and then there is nothing. It's just that when you die, you never come to. He said all this rational stuff in true Dizzy style, but I wish he'd retained a little hope that he would be reunited with Arem when he died. Boy, they were a couple. If there was a God and he was mid creation, wondering what Adam and Eve should be like, he could have done worse than model them on Dizzy and Arem. The world would have been a much better place if he had.

I will miss the old bugger, something rotten, as they might say in England. He was one hell of a man and one hell of a friend.[377]

At his request, his ashes were scattered on Garway Hill in a ceremony only attended by Bortelli.

Casey Ingar died from cancer of the liver, shortly after Isarebe passed away. Rita Bortelli outlived them all. She was 99 years old when she died in July 2097.

---

377   Unattributed, 2093, *Solomon D. Isarebe: Legendary Economist (2008–2093)*, The Washington and New York Post, 25th August 2093

EPILOGUE

After his release from prison, Isarebe may no longer have cared about the fate of the world, but, if anything, *Future Perfect* became more pertinent as the century reached its cataclysmic climax, as illustrated by this extract from the Preface to *Future Perfect*:

> Our work and the work of others has shown population decline is both inevitable and in the long-term a miracle that will ensure the survival of the planet. The miracle is that it will be brought about by the self-interested decisions of billions of women around the world. Self-interested decisions are the ones we can rely on most.

> I have been mocked for entitling this work 'Future Perfect', being called a hopeless optimist, a dreamer, a peddler of fantasy. I can't help thinking I am being teased when people say these things, as I don't believe I have an optimistic, dreamy or fantastical fibre in my body. The title 'Future Perfect' is meant to encapsulate the possibilities offered to us by these momentous changes in fertility rates. We have before us the potential to thrive, to live in glorious abundance, and simultaneously reverse the harm we have done to the atmosphere, the biosphere, the hydrosphere and the anthroposphere. We have an opportunity to make peace with the Earth and with ourselves.

> Even as my pen wrote the words 'Future Perfect', I was imagining the many ways in which we might make an almighty mess of this opportunity. I am hopeful we will eventually get there, but it seems inevitable there will be painful and violent tragedies along the way. We have a media that only succeeds through peddling misery, conflict, hate and disaster, sneering at any sign of truth, hope, goodness or sincerity. We also have an evolutionarily honed survival instinct that quakes and responds violently to any sign of change, of the strange, of the stranger. And we have politicians and political systems that scavenge on these instincts. A rapidly falling global population, even though rationally a good thing, is going to excite these potentially destructive forces unless we forearm ourselves.

> The area that represents the greatest risk of catalysing conflict is migration. In some nations, migration is going to be seen as a simple palliative to the falling number of people of working age. For many centuries politicians have seized on immigrants as the source of a country's woes: the dirty, dangerous, lazy, cheating, lying, violent

stranger in our midst. In this new paradigm, the immigrant will be portrayed as the saviour, the hero of the people. The fight will be on to grab as many migrants as possible: to grab the brilliant scientist; grab the domestic operative; grab the ground-breaking engineer; grab the retail worker; grab the wonder manager; grab the beautician; grab the teacher; grab the call-centre operative; grab the dentist; grab the sex worker. And the irony will be that as the fight for migrants intensifies, the less the potential migrant will want to come. The reversal, or at least stalling, of income differentials across the globe will mean the brave and the desperate, who for so long have been the source of migrants around the world, will increasingly say: 'Why should I leave, when I have it so good at home? Why should I forego seeing my family, my friends, my faithful dog? What makes them think that culture in Baltimore is so much better than culture in Benin?'

My fear is instead of politicians realising falling populations and economic decline are not synonymous – they will fight the inevitable and tell their people that without more immigrants they will all go to the dogs. When you have nations fighting over a dwindling resource – in this case, people – these are conditions that could lead to war. It may sound incredible, but I can see American soldiers forcibly stopping Mexicans leaving the US; I can envisage China invading Korea in order to make Koreans work in Chinese factories; I have even dreamt of Germany annexing Poland to make Poles fill the gaps left by fleeing Turks.[378]

During most of Isarebe's lifetime, the relative global peace that characterised much of the 21st century held firm, but tensions started to mount throughout the 2080s before erupting into the bloody migration wars of the 2090s. The European Consensus War (2094–2096) and the invasion and occupation by China of the Indochinese Peninsula (2096–2097) are covered in detail by other commentators and historians, but it is worth recapping on these events in the context of Isarebe's work, which represented his worst fears come true. They were the two bloodiest conflicts of the 21st century and whilst neither descended into nuclear conflict, the threat of global destruction was real.

In 2086, Germany was still the most powerful economy in Europe, but the rise of Turkey to the south-east was shaking its confidence. Germany had experienced a fourth consecutive year of GDP growth of less than 1%, which

378   Isarebe, S and I, 2050, *Future Perfect*, Cambridge and Oxford University Press, Cambridge, pp. 14–16

the political opposition led by Dietmar Aydin likened to the economic crisis of 1929–1933. This was not a valid comparison, as the German economy was not in recession and GDP per head, which for many years had been used as the most reliable indicator of economic health in countries with falling populations, had grown at an average of 1.6% p.a. over the previous decade. Germans had never been richer: the average couple had one child, two cars, three homes, peerless medical care, and travelled around 12,000 miles each year during their seven weeks of holiday. Aydin, however, wanted to use the ebbing self-confidence of the country to his own advantage. His likening of the situation to the years before Hitler came to power in the 1930s was no accident.

Germany was seeing small but increasing numbers of people of Turkish and Syrian heritage returning to their homelands, even though many were second, third, fourth or even fifth generation immigrants. Turkey had a vibrant economy and had been experiencing population growth as late as the 2060s; by the 2080s it was the largest country by population in Europe and was nearing Germany in its economic power. Many German Turks owned second homes in Turkey and some were now returning to Turkey permanently on a wave of nostalgia and the expectation of Turkey's future economic success. At the margins, this small outflow of people was exacerbating the challenge of coping with falls in the number of people of working age in Germany.

Aydin himself was of Turkish descent, but this did not stop him taunting those returning to Turkey, suggesting they were traitors to Germany, although his real ire was reserved for Syrians, whose families had mostly come to Germany as refugees between 2017 and 2024. Aydin claimed they had abused 'the incomparable hospitality of the German people' and those leaving were 'despicable fleeing rats'.[379] His campaign against these Turks and Syrians leaving Germany exacerbated the problem, as many in these ethnic groups started to feel unwelcome in Germany after many decades of peaceful and successful assimilation into German life. There were increasing incidences of violence against these ethnic groups, particularly in the poorer eastern regions of Germany.

Alongside this stoked-up racial tension was a more real economic concern: German companies were finding it increasingly difficult to attract new investment. Capital flowed ever more freely around the world, with more of it finding a home in the dynamic economies of Africa, such as Nigeria, Zimbabwe and South Africa. Over the course of the 21st century, Germany had not followed other European economies in becoming more

---

379   Aydin, D, 2086, *Aydin speech to parliament on election as Chancellor*, 1st October 2086, Reichstag, Berlin

specialised in particular high value technologies as had been seen in the UK (AI health systems) and Sweden (bio-computer design and production). Germany's largest companies, with interests spread across many traditional industries, were no longer seen as having the appeal to investors they once had. Germany's long held claim to be the global centre of manufacturing technology and engineering was losing its credibility. 'Designed in Germany' was no longer synonymous with excellence.

Difficult economic and social conditions have often led to the rise of extremist populist politicians. Dietmar Aydin, who in another time may have been recognised as the immoral opportunist he was, succeeded in sowing racial discord in Germany, but he also tapped into these concerns over Germany's economic future. He was elected Chancellor in 2086 in an openly racist campaign. After being elected, and with some irony, he introduced huge incentives for new migrants to relocate to Germany and made it almost impossible for those wanting to leave to realise their financial assets; freezing their bank accounts and seizing their homes. This provided a short-term reversal in population decline and he and his Social Liberal Nationalist party were re-elected with a vastly increased majority in 2090, with promises of returning Germany to its former position as a major global power, 'ruling a new Europe, with German women the most fertile in the world.'[380]

After his re-election, Aydin started to make economic threats to his weaker neighbours, in particular Poland, Czechia, Slovakia, Austria and Hungary. He claimed they were stealing German jobs and unless this was reversed, they would face economic reprisals. None of these countries could rationally respond to these obvious untruths and they received nothing but platitudinous support from France, Italy and the UK, who had no desire to pick a fight with Germany or risk a military conflict they were unable to adequately respond to.

Every time one of Germany's near neighbours made some capitulation to Germany's demands, Aydin raised the stakes. One by one, each of these countries started to allow German 'advisors' into the highest echelons of government and the armed forces. By 2091, Germany had established military bases in each of these countries and by 2092, their armies were effectively incorporated within the German army, under the banner 'Strength in Partnership.'

After the Ukrainian war in the 2020s, many European countries invested heavily in military equipment and capabilities, but prolonged peace had led to a reduction in military investment. Twenty years earlier, in the late

---

380   Aydin, D, 2086, *Rally speech to party members in Nuremberg*, 10th October 2090, Die NeueLuitpoldarena, Nuremberg

2060s and early 2070s, the US had vacated most of its bases in Germany, as the perceived threat from Russia had declined and developments in weapon technology and advances in intelligence gathering meant the US felt it could respond to any aggressive Russian activity from their American bases. These two factors left a military vacuum in Western Europe which Aydin was happy to fill, rapidly increasing military investment as soon as he was first elected. Most European countries were culturally, organisationally and militarily unprepared for this newly aggressive Germany.

In 2093, Aydin announced he had reached 'consensus, with our neighbours in Greater Germany'[381] and from now on they would 'be equal partners in a great new era of German leadership in Europe.'[382] This coup by decree was swiftly followed by his army taking control of government buildings in Prague, Budapest, Bratislava, Warsaw and Vienna.

In was perhaps the greatest bloodless coup in history: 'the construction of an instant Fourth Reich'[383] as Aydin's political opponent Hannah Schmidt put it.

It was also the greatest example since the Russian invasion of the Ukraine of major powers such as France and the United Kingdom doing nothing whilst a monster fulfilled his megalomaniacal ambitions. The wider international response to Aydin's audacious move was also muted. 'Greater Germany' was not recognised diplomatically and there were muffled complaints of Germany breaking international treaties, but no one in Western Europe was willing to raise their heads above the parapets and the Americans, although incensed and concerned about what this meant for them in terms of trade and defence, were unwilling to act unilaterally. Russia was vocal in its opposition to the formation of Greater Germany, but following their rapid economic decline after the Ukrainian war, Russia could now speak but few listened. Turkey was very concerned at these developments, but whilst it was now an important economic power it had limited military resources and was unable to respond except through economic sanctions.

Political cronies favourable to Aydin were soon installed in governments throughout 'Greater Germany' and the official news coming out of the region was of a people happy to be part of 'a great new country, with government and administrative regimes unchanged but functioning with increased efficiency with help from colleagues from Berlin.'[384]

---

381   Aydin, D, 2093, *Chancellor speech broadcast across all terrestrial and satellite channels across Greater Germany*, 7th June 2093

382   Aydin, D, 2093, *Letter to Leaders of the G31*, 7th June 2093

383   Unattributed, 2094, *The mythology of Dietmar Aydin*, The Financial and Technology Times, 2nd January 2094

384   Bartek, J, 2093, *Speech to press upon appointment as Czechia Prime Minister*, 7th December 2093

In February 2094, just six months after Isarebe's death, Aydin introduced New National Service, whereby anyone aged between 25 and 45 was obliged to work in Central Germany, as he now called the original German territory, for at least five years. 'This is for the good of Greater Germany. It is an honour all Germans, whether they hail from Berlin, Budapest or Brno, will be delighted to undertake.'[385] Whilst portraying it as a common sacrifice required of all Germans, it was no hardship for people from Central Germany, whose life carried on as normal.

After the establishment of New National Service, the disparate resistance movements within 'Greater Germany' had an influx of new volunteers and started sniping attacks on German military bases, as well as more actively lobbying for military help and financial support around the world. By August 2094 they had formed a single coordinated group called The European Consensus Opposition (TECO), under the leadership of the charismatic former Czech military leader Tomas F. Havel. Whilst they did not get official support from any foreign government, they started to receive covert military and financial help.

Aydin responded with sustained and ruthless violence against these emboldened rebel groups. In October 2094 he summarily executed nearly 15,000 rebel fighters, with a further 34,000 killed in action. These atrocities proved impossible for the international community to ignore. Havel, who was based in Paris, secured the formal military support of France, Italy and the United Kingdom, starting a war that was to last for two years. Once more mirroring the experiences of the Second World War, this war was to continue until the Americans landed an estimated 250,000 soldiers on the European mainland in the summer of 2096. By September of that year, the allied forces were marching on Berlin, having liberated Austria, Hungary, Czechia, Slovakia and Poland. Aydin made his escape and was never seen again. It is believed he spent the rest of his life in Colombia.

After this bloodiest of 21st century European wars, Germany was left economically and culturally devastated and the reconstruction of the German economy took around thirty years to complete. The return of people of Turkish and Syrian descent to their original homelands accelerated and Germany was never to recover its lustre as one of the best destinations in the world for economic migrants. The birth rate in post-war Germany fell to a new low of just 0.9 children per woman in the early 2100s, but has since recovered to 1.5, slightly above the global average.

---

385   Aydin, D, 2094, *Chancellor speech broadcast across all terrestrial and satellite channels across Greater Germany*, 14th February 2094

The Consensus War, as it became known, shook the complacent assumption of perpetual harmony across Europe, as Tomas Havel noted in a remarkably forgiving speech after his election as President of Czechia in 2097:

> The rise of Dietmar Aydin took place in Berlin, but it could have been here in Prague, or in London, or Paris, or Washington, or Abuja, or Delhi. We must not demonise the German people. It could so easily have been us.

> We are all finding our way in these new times. We need to look around and ask for help. We must not be afraid of asking for directions. There is a chance of something wonderful happening in the coming decades, but we need to keep our nerve.

> As Solomon Isarebe once said: *Only a fool would predict the future, but it could be wonderful, as long as we don't let politicians mess it up.*[386]

Whilst Isarebe had predicted in remarkable detail what came to pass in Germany in the 2090s, he had always been less vocal about the risk of conflict in China. Despite his oft-stated belief in the primacy of empirical analysis in decision making – 'Data always trumps debate'[387] – his views on China were undoubtedly influenced by his personal love for the country and the people, first noted on his visit there in 2037. Professor Kamil's granddaughter, Joan Gameshin, had written to Solomon Isarebe throughout his imprisonment and was one of the few he kept in touch with after his release. In a letter he wrote to her in December 2092, he said: "You mustn't worry about China – you sound just like your grandad who always thought the Chinese had something nasty hidden up their sleeves – you must trust me, they will come good, as they have for the last 2,000 years.'[388] This may have been nothing more than an old man trying to sooth the fears of someone he was fond of, but also reflects his rose-tinted perspective on China.

China was in a uniquely difficult political position in the mid to late 21st century. It had become the largest economy in the world in 2040 and its global cultural and military influence had increased as the Communist Party had

386   Havel, T, 2097, *Speech to nations upon appointment as Czechia Prime Minister*, ČNM1 broadcast and online, 1st November 2097
387   Isarebe, S, 2056, lecture to student body after receiving Honorary Fellowship at MIT, 10th October 2056, The Isarebe Trust Archives, Cambridge, England (Box 297, Folder 4)
388   Isarebe, S, 2092, eLetter to Joan Gameshin dated 4th December 2092, The Isarebe Trust Archives, Cambridge, England (Box 591, Folder 2)

gradually liberalised and introduced democratic reform at a regional level. However, it had one of the most rapidly shrinking populations in the world, falling by 10% per decade over the second half of the 21st century. It was struggling to support the growing proportion of older, economically inactive people and was fearful its global influence would decline as rapidly as it had grown.

Whilst these were the concerns of the ruling classes, there was little unease amongst the Chinese people, most of whom were enjoying the benefits of over a century of rapid economic growth. Many compared this period in China to the 1950s in America, before any overt disillusionment with materialism had set in. Yan Xiangyu, General Secretary of the Communist Party (2074–2097), was renowned as a man of little charisma, but great organisational and planning capabilities. As early as 2085 he had privately concluded that to maintain the stability of the nation and defend its global dominance he needed to massively increase inward migration and this was unlikely to be obtainable by peaceful means. In the late 80s and early 90s he gradually increased military spending to 16% of GDP, a figure normally only seen in times of full-scale war: this compares to the US which was spending 6.2% of GDP on its military in 2086. This rapid and unprecedented military build-up in China was achieved whilst externally maintaining a position of appeasement and peace. The US was aware of an increase in China's military spending, if not the scale, and responded by increasing its military presence in South Korea. However, by 2092, international political attention was firmly fixed on Germany and the war in Europe.

Through late 2093 and early 2094, China started a small-scale military build-up in North Korea, which had remained an important ally of China despite significant liberalisation in the second half of the 21st century. These forces, ranged along the border with South Korea, excited the diplomatic interest of the US and India. China insisted they had no strategic military interest in the area and were just helping North Korea with manoeuvres. In November 2094, the US and China both agreed to reduce their forces in the Koreas, to the lowest level seen in over 140 years. With the US realising they may have to intervene in Europe, they were more than happy to sign this military pact with a friendly and compliant China. The US Pacific Fleet withdrew all but a handful of vessels from their base in Japan, with many being redeployed to the 2nd and 6th Fleets in Europe, ready for a possible offensive against Germany.

The withdrawal of US forces was largely complete by September 2095 and by June 2096 nearly all the US's military assets had been allocated to the war in Western Europe. Yan Xiangyu had anticipated each of the US's moves and in July 2096 he started one of the largest military movements of all time, taking all the major global powers by surprise. Five and a half million personnel and associated weaponry moved through the Indochinese Peninsula, occupying Vietnam, Laos, Cambodia, Thailand and south-east Myanmar, down to the border with Malaysia. This invasion, predominantly by sea into Thailand, Cambodia and the south of Vietnam, by air into southern Laos, and by land into northern Vietnam and rural northern Laos, took less than three weeks. The Chinese reported the loss of only 300 personnel during this campaign, of which only fifteen had been killed in military action. Most of the other fatalities were from road accidents involving the 530,000 vehicles they took into Vietnam and Laos, together with losses from friendly fire. They met some resistance in Vietnam and Thailand, but the overwhelming odds were with China. China had knocked out all but its own communication satellites in the region, making coordination of defence strategies impossible; theirs were the first low-level satellites with ultra-stealth technology. The Chinese forces were brutal and sadistic throughout the short campaign and combined deaths among civilians and opposition soldiers in the five countries were nearly 170,000.

In less than a month the occupation was secured and a combined population of almost 400 million had been brought under Chinese control. The US was the only country with sufficient military might to respond to the plight of its former allies in Southeast Asia, but they were committed to the European Consensus War and made the ineffective decision to respond economically rather than militarily. The economic sanctions applied by the United States and its allies were largely token; China still produced 42% of the world's manufactured goods and any greater sanctions would have resulted in devastation to already stretched economies in the West.

Yan had taken on the United States, under its ailing President, Malcolm McDonald, in a game of military chess and had won without losing a single piece. However, whilst Yan's organisational strengths led to him conquering a vast, complex and difficult territory, it was his lack of understanding of his people and his lack of charisma that would eventually lead to his and China's downfall in the region.

After the success of his invasion and occupation, Yan immediately instigated a nationalisation programme in the occupied territories. He found many of the corporations in his new territories were more efficient and well-funded than those in China. He declared this a great triumph and the solution to many of China's problems, believing the peninsula would be able to meet the funding shortfall for China's ageing population:

The people of Vietnam are the hardest working, friendliest people I have ever come across and they have welcomed the People's Army with open arms. I am humbled by their attitude and the superiority of their industry in producing high quality goods at low prices and all delivered with a smile. We have a lot to learn from them.

I have invited ten million of their finest young people to return to China with me, to invigorate our economy and teach us the secrets of their success.[389]

The people of Vietnam and elsewhere in the Indochinese Peninsula may well have met Yan Xiangyu with a smile, when they saw over five million soldiers behind him and the largest collection of war machinery the world had ever seen, but that didn't mean they were happy. Their only remaining weapon was their labour and whilst seemingly cooperative, they operated a silent war of slow working and feigned incompetence. Within a short time they turned factories once the envy of the world into basket cases.

There were almost no volunteers for migration to China and many of those who were 'invited' disappeared into the rural bosom of their families. Yan started a violent campaign against these migrant dissidents, leading to mass killings of both the dissidents and their families. This campaign, mostly conducted in rural areas, was dubbed 'The China Killing Fields' by a horrified international community, making a historic comparison to the genocide committed by the Khmer Rouge in Cambodia in the 1970s. Whilst there are no official records of deaths in the China Killing Fields, it is estimated at being close to a million people.[390]

Meanwhile, back in China, Yan's negative comparisons of Chinese workers to those in the new regions in the Republic and the reports of killing of ordinary civilians throughout the Indochinese Peninsular, created an unprecedented backlash. There was a populist uprising, which was well-funded by those Chinese corporations who had been criticised by Yan for being inefficient and incompetent. There were a series of marches in cities across China against Yan's actions in the peninsula. In early March 2097, there was a march of nearly ten million people in Beijing, which ended in a sit-down demonstration in Tiananmen Square that was to last for nearly a week.

---

389   Yan, X, 2096, live internet broadcast across the region, retrieved from www.
chinahistoryarchives.com, 6th September 2096
390   Roserman, N, n.d., *Deaths in conflict* (data file), The Universe in Data, Viewed 4th
August 2149, (www.theuniverseindata.com)

Yan could literally not understand why people were demonstrating against him, when he had 'delivered a momentous solution to a long-standing and growing problem in China.'[391] After five days of occupation of the square, with wall-to-wall international media coverage, he debated with his colleagues on the State Council how they could resolve the crisis. He was convinced the solution was military force and against the advice of his colleagues he ordered the army to clear the demonstrators.

The army command, following their extraordinary success in the peninsula campaign, were ready to follow Yan anywhere and the tanks duly rolled into Tiananmen Square. They were accompanied by nearly 40,000 troops, but the operation was hampered by the vast numbers in the square and the refusal of the crowd to back away. The demonstrators had claimed the plum blossom as the symbol of their protest. This was the national flower and it had enormous importance to ordinary people in China. As the soldiers moved into the square, each was met with armfuls of plum blossom. Within four hours, many of the soldiers were sitting alongside the demonstrators and the guns of the tanks had been turned away from the people.

It was one of the more extraordinary moments in history and one of the most significant in the modern history of the Chinese nation. The 'Plum Blossom Revolution' did not change things immediately, but it was one of the factors that led to the removal of Yan Xiangyu and the withdrawal of China from the Indochinese Peninsular, and arguably it was instrumental in the introduction of greater democracy in China in the 2130s.

Whilst this is often romantically portrayed as the moment ordinary individuals stood up for the rights of others and defeated the greatest army ever built and one of the greatest military leaders of all time, there was another force at play. The US, fresh from triumph in the European theatre, seized on this popular uprising as an opportunity to be the 'saviour of a downtrodden people.'[392]

The US military was not the well-equipped but inexperienced force it had been two years earlier. After the successful campaign in Europe, it was now composed of battle-hardened soldiers, sailors and aircrew. The US fleet came en masse across the Pacific, bristling with conventional and nuclear weapons, and even before they arrived in the East China Sea, Chinese military leaders were advising withdrawal from the peninsula and the removal of Yan from power.

---

391   Yan, X, 2097, *Statement to National People's Congress*, 15th April 2097, retrieved from www.chinahistoryarchives.com

392   Smith-Jai, J, 2097, *Presidential address to nation* (all networks and news channels), 5th July 2097, retrieved from www.smith-jai.org.

The US fleet anchored off Yokosuka in Japan, Pattaya in Thailand and Busan in Korea, but never engaged in combat with the Chinese Navy. It was arguably a war the US would have lost, or destroyed the world in trying, but neither China nor the US had the desire for a fight to the death. China had its tail between its legs after the domestic rebellion and the people of the US wanted their boys and girls back home after fighting 'other people's battles'.[393]

Yan was quickly and quietly removed from power, although he was still officially hailed by the government as a national hero. He was informally put under house arrest and was to spend the rest of his life on his family farm near Qingdao.

These wars in Europe and the Indochinese Peninsular, alongside the Covid-19 pandemic of 2020–22, were perhaps the greatest tragedies of the 21st century and the wars were both caused by the political desire for more immigrants as a result of falling populations, just as Isarebe had feared.

The US, for all its resources, was brought to its knees, psychologically and financially, by its role in these two wars and China lay bloodied and distraught. This was a time when India could have played its hand and laid the groundwork for military as well as economic dominance of the 22nd century. It could have gently crushed its competitors for global power. Instead, a woman emerged who, with extraordinary vision and determination, brought about the most extraordinary reconciliation.

Samira Sharma was of Indian Chinese descent, born in Shanghai, but raised in Boston, USA. The daughter of radical academics Sonil Sharma and May Chen, she relocated to India with her family in 2072, aged 17. She went on to study engineering at the Indian Institute of Science and Technology in Mumbai. She says she was 'forced to be interested in politics'[394] by her parents and after a short career in consulting was elected a Member of Parliament. She was the youngest Member of Parliament, aged 27, and she quickly rose through the ranks, becoming renowned as a master negotiator, forging alliances and deals in the fast-moving sands of Indian politics. Following the death of Reyansh Donhi she was elected leader of the New Congress Alliance and after the conclusion of the Indochinese War her party won the 2098 election and she was duly named as Prime Minister. She was called 'Maan'[395] by her followers, Hindi for mother, reflecting her steadiness, compassion and desire to seek consensus.

---

393   Unattributed, 2097, *Bring them home*, Washington and New York Post, 6th July 2097, front page

394   Sharma, S, 2112, *No time for diplomacy*, Bayjun House, Mumbai, p. 46

395   This has echoes of Angela Merkel, Chancellor of Germany from 2005–2021, who was widely known as 'Mutti', German for mother.

With her strong links to America and China, she realised India and indeed the world was at a crossroads. Members of her newly elected government were demanding the US and China be brought into line with India's interests, but her instinct was for global interaction, the free flows of ideas, and harmonisation of social and work conditions. Ten weeks after her election as Prime Minister, without consulting her party or the Indian Parliament, she flew to Beijing with a small security detail and without official announcement turned up at Zhongnanhai in the Imperial City in Beijing to speak to Deng Xiang, the new General Secretary of the Chinese Communist Party.[396] News of her unofficial mission spread quickly around the world and her arrival, smiling and alone, at the door of Deng's official residence was covered by over fifty of the world's press. Chinese bureaucrats were reportedly furious at her apparent disregard for diplomatic protocol, but there is a famous picture of Deng opening the door, laughing as he greeted Sharma with a hug. They were of similar ages and had met many years before in a cultural exchange programme between their universities: there were persistent unsubstantiated rumours they had been involved in a brief romantic entanglement. She stayed in Beijing for 48 hours and whilst there are no formal records of what was discussed, many claimed to have been there and witnessed Sharma and Deng talking without respite for the entire period. There are many myths about what happened that week.

She left the Imperial City without making a statement to the press. There was now a trail of some 600 reporters and camera crews behind her as she made her way to Beijing International Airport, where she flew back to Mumbai on a scheduled Air India flight.

Her actions had inevitably created headlines at home and abroad, with the media portraying her both as crazy woman and superhero, but what was not in dispute was that her actions had the world watching on in amazement and anticipation. In Mumbai, she got straight onto another commercial flight to Washington. US President John Smith-Jai was there at the airport to meet her, with a forty-vehicle security cavalcade.

Two days later, Sharma was back on a plane, still having made no statement to the press. This time, however, it was John Smith-Jai who made the headlines, as he walked up the steps of Air Force One[397] beside her. They flew together to Beijing.

Three days later and just a week after Sharma had first left Mumbai, Smith-Jai and Deng emerged to make a joint statement, with Sharma standing

---

396   Although the mythology suggests she literally walked unannounced up to Deng Xiang's front door, records released in 2148 show that she had called him daily in the previous week and they had agreed to meet.
397   The name given to the US President's aeroplane before it was renamed Commander 1 in 2124, following the unification of the US's armed forces.

quietly behind them, a diminutive figure almost out of view. The statement they made, subject to the approval of their governments, was that they had agreed a new free trade arrangement between the three countries, allowing free movements of goods, people and ideas, and in addition there would be military cooperation on intelligence matters and a joint military response force to ensure global peace.

Smith-Jai and Deng got to make the statement, but 'Maan' got the credit and paved the way for a smooth transition to India becoming the leading force in the world it is today. It took three years for the deal to be finally agreed and signed and it was inevitably somewhat watered down from their initial agreement, but most analysts agree 'The Beijing-Washington Accord' has played a major role in ensuring a global peace that has now lasted for over fifty years. It also helped Smith-Jai get re-elected for a second term, Deng to remain General Secretary until his death in 2123 and for Sharma to be named by Time Crake Media as the most important global figure for twelve years in a row. It also meant T20 cricket would become the dominant world sport it is today.

Even with all Isarebe's imaginative and intellectual powers, he couldn't have predicted this and without The Beijing-Washington Accord the world may have looked very different to how it does today. Was Isarebe just lucky, as his many critics continue to say, or did he just understand that the economic and political necessity of smooth and free-flowing global trade meant that a Samira Sharma, a mother for the world, had to come along?

In the early years of the 22nd century, a new global consensus was reached around population decline. Most governments stopped offering ineffective and expensive incentives for women to have more children and there was a new managed approach to the global movement of people. Perhaps most importantly, there was a renewed pragmatism in the long walk towards a cooler climate. It was India that led the way to this new world political consensus: a consensus that mostly holds to this day.

Isarebe played a small but important part in bringing about the miraculous changes that have occurred in the world over the past hundred years, but he also showed how it could end in tragedy and failure, as it so nearly did.

APPENDICES

Appendix 1: The Venezuelan oil crisis

Despite international agreements on cutting carbon emissions, global energy use had continued to rise throughout the economic boom of the late 2020s and 2030s. There had been substantial state and private investment in renewable energy in these early decades of the 21st century and by 2038 renewables accounted for nearly 20% of global energy use. This may seem low by today's standards, when renewables account for over 70% of energy use, but there had been strong growth within a relatively short period of time and it should be remembered that the global population was nearly twice the size it is now, making energy and carbon management more challenging.

The corollary of this rise in the use of renewable energy was fossil fuels had seen their share of the energy market fall, from 87% in 2010 to 77% by 2038. This was not yet an existential threat to the once mighty global oil giants, as non-energy use of oil was still growing, but this period of flat demand for oil as an energy source, combined with the first Micro Nuclear Plants (MNPs) coming on stream, had put sustained downward pressure on oil prices. Between 2028 and 2038, nominal oil prices had fallen by 10%, but in real terms, after accounting for inflation, oil prices had fallen by 38%.

Despite significant lobbying at both the national and international level, oil companies seemed impotent in their attempts to reverse this decline. In many wealthy democracies, governments, wary of the very active and powerful environmental lobby, did not want to put their weight behind any initiative that would result in an increase in demand for oil, particularly as China had very publicly made the environment its top priority, despite many reports of China regularly flouting international environmental agreements.

Publicly listed oil companies had seen their share prices fall and were finding it hard to raise funds for exploration. Even state-owned enterprises had found it difficult to justify investment when there was no immediate prospect of a return to growth in the oil market. Known and economically accessible oil reserves, which as late as 2020 had been estimated at 47 years at prevailing consumption levels, were estimated to be down to 26 years by the mid-2030s, as oil companies could no longer afford to extract much of the remaining known reserves.

OPEC, a confederation of oil producing countries, had once wielded great power on the international stage and had been held responsible for the oil crisis and global recession of the early 1970s. Although less powerful than they had once been, in 2038 they still accounted for 78% of known oil reserves and many argued they were less a confederation and more a cartel.

Venezuela was a member of OPEC and was the country with the highest share of known oil reserves. Throughout the late 20th and early 21st century it had squandered its oil riches and in 2038 was suffering the latest in a series of political crises. The state's finances were historically dependent on oil revenue and since the drop in demand for oil, they had been experiencing localised violent uprisings as a result of high unemployment and rising taxes. The Venezuelan government put enormous pressure on the powerful Gulf State members of OPEC, who were already experiencing high existential angst over this prolonged oil price deflation, to take action. In September 2038 OPEC members agreed to cut production by 40%. This was unprecedented: in 1973, a 25% reduction in production had triggered a major global economic recession.

A rapidly developing crisis ensued. Non-OPEC oil producing nations ramped up production, but there was inevitably a significant shortfall. Oil prices sky-rocketed, at one point peaking at five times their pre-crisis level. Manufacturers were also hit with severe supply problems for oil-based materials and the world started slipping into an economic chasm. Global GDP fell by nearly 7% in the first quarter of 2039, a fall only previously seen in the early months of the first Covid-19 pandemic in 2020.

The international community were united in their condemnation of OPEC's actions and the crisis fostered an unheralded pact between the US, China, India and the EU, known officially as The Four Powers, but referred to by many at the time as 'The Flower Powers'. They put in place economic and diplomatic sanctions against OPEC members, ramped up their own oil production and agreed a near doubling of state investment in renewables and nuclear energy. Despite this aggressive public stance, there was vigorous behind-the-scenes diplomatic activity, as the potential for a major global war seemed higher than at any time since the 1960s and there was great public anxiety. There were also concerns that the free trade agreements that had proliferated in the previous twenty years, which many believed had been partly responsible for the sustained economic boom, would be imperilled, as calls for isolationism from those on the political right in the US and EU increased.

An agreement was reached by The Four Powers with UAE, Saudi Arabia and Kuwait in July 2039 to increase oil production with immediate effect. In return, The Four Powers agreed to invest in tourism, renewable energy and renewable energy storage in the three nations over the next fifty years, whilst these Gulf States agreed to withdraw from OPEC. Once this agreement had been reached, OPEC was finished and other member countries soon came into line, with Nigeria in particular obtaining favourable terms in return for a short-term increase in oil production and long-term greening of their economy. The one country that The Four Powers refused to deal with was Venezuela, as the US had made this a non-negotiable condition of the terms reached with other nations. Venezuela was hung out to dry for its role in starting the crisis, with some economic sanctions remaining in place as late as 2047. In 2047, amid increasing international concerns for the plight of the impoverished Venezuelan people, a pact was finally agreed with the new centrist government and Venezuela was once more given access to world markets.

Within six months of The Four Powers agreement with the Gulf States, much of the lost economic ground had been regained, and it was the start of the end of the oil-producing nations having such influence on the global stage as ironically it had provided more impetus to growth in renewables and nuclear. A reflection of the failure of OPEC's attempts to reverse the prospects for oil producing countries was that by January 2040 oil prices were 17% lower than they had been before the crisis.

Appendix 2: Research techniques developed for *Future Perfect*

Collective Quantitative All-Cue Preference Research was one of the technical cornerstones of the Isarebe's work and it addressed some of the problems survey researchers were facing in the middle of the 21st century.

Quantitative survey research had become increasingly discredited in the 2030s and 2040s; the quality of responses, particularly in online surveys, had been shown to be very poor. More importantly for the Isarebes, explicitly asking people about past or future behaviour had been shown to have little correlation with actual behaviour. This was because most survey research attempted to measure conscious reasoning, whilst experimental psychologists and neuroscientists had shown it was unconscious thinking that dominated the majority of people's decisions and actions.

A technique developed in the second half of the 20th century at least partially bypassed conscious thought in the context of researching and understanding decision-making. This technique, Discrete Choice Analysis (DCA), required respondents to make choices between alternatives without asking for an explanation of their choice. Respondents were then presented with other alternatives and asked to make another choice and so on. Their responses could be analysed to determine how important different factors were in making a particular choice, i.e. what trade-offs were unconsciously being made. When results were normalised with real-world data, DCA models gave reasonable predictive accuracy in simple decisions.

Isarebe, Brown and Gröning realised DCA was less effective when used to examine complex decisions. There were two particular problems they felt had to be addressed:

i)   In more complex or emotionally important situations, respondents became more concerned about revealing their underlying desires and motivations and were more likely to consciously choose answers that portrayed them in a good light.

In Isarebe, Brown and Gröning's work they found measuring certain unconscious body and eye movements when respondents were shown alternative choices, generated better predictions of real-life behaviour. This was termed All-Cue Response Analysis.

ii) When people were asked to make choices in a research environment where they were insulated from the conditioning effects of society, they gave responses that differed significantly from the choices they would make in real life.

Solomon and Isabelle Isarebe realised this was particularly pertinent in decisions about family size, where either consciously or unconsciously decisions involved parents, partners, children, friends and others, including religious leaders.

They developed an approach which consisted of a multi-phase interview, with the individual alone, and then with the individual and key people in their lives. The complexity of this method was in the modelling of the combined responses. Solomon Isarebe termed this Collective Research, which when used in combination with All-Cue Response Analysis, became known as Collective Quantitative All-Cue Preference Research, or CQR.

These advances greatly improved the predictive power of resultant models in many social research situations. The research method and models were complex, particularly the analysis of non-verbal responses, and were not superseded until late in the 21st century. However, CQR would not have become a practical research technique if it weren't for Isabelle Isarebe's development of Continuous Inference Revision (CIR).

CIR is a programme that continuously analyses and models an individual's responses in a complex survey research study. It continually learns, both within studies and across studies, in real time and draws heavily on Artificial Intelligence Learning Techniques (AILT). It is now an area of study in its own right and is perhaps the only lasting technical legacy of the Isarebes' work.

Appendix 3: The development of Isarebe & Isarebe's research into fertility decisions

The Isarebe's initial qualitative research and pilot studies indicated there were five dimensions influencing decisions on family size:

i) Personal identifiers: age, gender, family size when growing up, education level, ethnic influences, strength and nature of religious views

ii) Personal circumstances: marital status / living arrangements, number of existing children, household income, personal income, working hours, local support network, working status of partner, stability of relationship, stability of job, ability to conceive naturally, ability to conceive with technical intervention

iii) Personal attitudes: views on gender roles, views on ideal family size, views on personal independence, aspirations for life outside family and work

iv) Employment terms: level of maternity pay, length of maternity pay, level of paternity pay, length of paternity pay, flexibility of hours

v) Institutional and personal support: fertility incentives, childcare subsidy, school fees, university fees, childcare fees, health provision, and the legality, availability and cost of contraception and abortion

The fourth and fifth dimensions were the main focus of the CQR element of their research.

After the pilot studies, the Isarebes reduced the interviews for each family from three to two: with the woman alone and then an interview with the woman and her partner, eliminating the separate interview with the partner. They found this made little difference to the predictive capability of their models, whilst significantly reducing cost and time.

The main phase of this research programme, involving research in forty countries, was to take the Isarebes eighteen months to complete. The fertility surveys were complex to set up, particularly when ensuring the right locations could be found to set up the body and eye monitoring equipment, and the researchers needed to be given significant training before the research could begin.

They weighted the final results to ensure they were representative of the whole female population in terms of age, education level, marital status, religious views, family size when growing up and ethnic influence.

Appendix 4: The Isarebes' approach to forecasting migration

The Isarebes adopted an innovative approach to predicting migration movements, basing their models on survey research into individual and household decisions on migration.[398] After an initial programme of qualitative research they developed a hypothesis on the factors most people considered, often unconsciously, when they had made their decision to migrate. They separated these into 'Net Benefits of Migration' and 'Transition Costs'. There were three subcategories within the Isarebes' definition of Benefits of Migration:

i) Net Community Benefits: associated with family, friends, language, acceptance, religion and cultural familiarity.

ii) Net Short-term Personal Benefits: associated with immediate differences in income, living costs, job satisfaction, cultural amenities and access to new experiences.

iii) Net Long-term Personal Benefits: associated with differences in career prospects, education, cost and availability of health provision, pension provision and the cost of maintaining relationships with people in their country of origin.

The Transition Costs included: the complexity and cost of visa applications; the cost of travel; the cost of language acquisition; the cost of realising existing assets; the cost of visiting prior to migration; the time and cost of arranging the basics of life in their new home prior to migration; the process of saying goodbye to friends and relatives; the time and cost of closing formal agreements; and the safety and legality of the move, particularly for refugees.

The Isarebes decided to adapt the CQR and CIR methods they used when they examined fertility rates, launching a second large-scale study across forty countries. Quotas were applied on age, education, wealth, income and

---

398   Isarebe, S and I, 2047, a draft paper, entitled *The Impact of Differentials in Perceived Benefits of Home Country and Potential Host Country and the Cost of Transition on Economic and Refugee Migration Decisions*, 14th July 2047, The Isarebe Trust Archives, Cambridge, England (Box 141, Folder 9)

household type. The sample included a boosted sample of those who were actively considering migrating in the next three years.

Four of the countries were chosen because they had been a recent source of refugees. Research in areas experiencing war, famine, or natural disasters always involves a degree of personal danger to those involved in the research programme. Rosemary Mai and David Tsonga, subcontracted researchers working for Isarebe & Isarebe, were kidnapped and ransomed by insurgents during their work in the Democratic Republic of the Congo. Mai was released after payment of the ransom, but Tsonga was found dead by the side of a road near the border with Rwanda and Burundi. DRC was not a refugee region at this time.[399]

Within the CQR element of the research, respondents were presented with pairs of choices. In each case, one option was to remain at home, given certain conditions, and the other was to migrate, with another set of conditions. The real-life decision on whether to migrate or not is complex and emotional, so the choices presented to people were also complex. Although the choices were presented on screen, the research was done in the presence of a researcher, who helped respondents to understand the options.

One or both of the choices presented to respondents may have included an incentive offered to encourage or discourage migration. The government incentives examined included: subsidy of travel costs; subsidy of moving costs; financial incentives to migrate / remain; reduction in visa requirements; reduction in visa costs; language training; contribution to healthcare; contribution to education; pension provision; and subsidy of annual travel to and from their country of origin.

The aggregated models were adjusted to ensure net global migration in each forecast year was zero, i.e. migration had little impact on overall global population, just the location of that population. These migration forecasts built on their forecasts of births and deaths and also incorporated their assumptions on economic growth. These forecasts were subject to Monte Carlo simulations, to estimate the uncertainty of their predictions for each country.[400]

---

399   Although Isarebe & Isarebe were insured and David Tsonga was not an employee, they provided a lifetime pension to his wife, equal to his annual income at the time of his death.
400   Monte Carlo simulations allow the impact of uncertainties within a model to be assessed. The uncertainties are allowed to vary randomly, within a pre-defined distribution, in any particular simulation. Many thousands or even millions of simulations are typically run for a model in this type of analysis. The result gives the most likely outcome, given the uncertainties and assumptions, but also a distribution of other possible outcomes.

Appendix 5: *Future Perfect* population projections

A sample of some of the original population projections contained within *Future Perfect*. This facsimile was made from Solomon Isarebe's proof copy and includes his handwritten comments:

Figure 3.5 Population forecasts (1): Major economies : millions of people

	1970	1980	1990	2000	2010	2020	2030	2040	2050	2060	2070	2080	2090	2100	2110	2120	2130	2140	2150
Global	3,683	4,433	5,280	6,114	6,922	7,753	8,520	8,970	9,180	9,140	8,926	8,640	8,100	7,400	6,700	6,100	5,600	5,200	4,800
India	555	699	873	1,057	1,234	1,380	1,520	1,555	1,520	1,460	1,360	1,220	1,060	915	820	760	715	680	640
China	818	981	1,135	1,263	1,338	1,402	1,419	1,360	1,260	1,135	1,097	887	782	710	650	600	560	520	485
Nigeria	56	73	95	122	159	206	282	361	438	497	545	575	582	565	530	480	430	390	360
USA	205	227	250	282	309	329	342	352	351	344	335	320	305	285	260	232	205	180	160
Indonesia	115	147	181	212	242	274	288	293	290	281	266	248	228	207	186	168	155	145	136
Brazil	95	121	149	175	198	212	223	228	228	219	205	188	169	150	137	126	116	107	100
Mexico	51	68	84	99	114	129	142	152	154	152	146	136	124	110	110	99	90	82	75
Russia	130	139	148	147	143	144	143	137	129	121	112	104	97	90	84	77	70	63	57
Turkey	35	44	54	63	72	84	92	100	104	104	102	99	93	86	77	69	62	56	50
Japan	104	117	124	127	128	126	121	112	101	90	79	70	61	55	50	46	41	38	34
Germany	78	78	79	82	82	83	84	83	87	78	74	69	63	57	51	46	42	38	34
UK	54	56	57	59	63	67	71	72	72	71	70	67	63	58	52	47	42	37	33
France	52	55	58	61	65	67	68	69	68	66	63	59	54	49	44	39	35	31	28
South Africa	22	29	37	45	51	59	64	66	68	69	68	66	63	58	53	48	43	38	34
Italy	54	56	57	57	59	60	59	55	51	45	40	36	32	29	26	24	23	21	20
Canada	21	25	28	31	34	38	41	42	43	42	41	40	38	36	33	30	27	24	21
Spain	34	37	39	41	47	47	45	43	40	36	32	28	24	21	19	17	16	15	14
Australia	13	15	17	19	22	26	28	30	32	33	33	33	32	31	29	26	23	21	19

Figure 3.6 Population forecasts (1): Major economies: % growth in each decade

	1970s	1980s	1990s	2000s	2010s	2020s	2030s	2040s	2050s	2060s	2070s	2080s	2090s	2100s	2110s	2120s	2130s	2140s	2050-2150
Global	20%	19%	16%	13%	12%	10%	5%	2%	0%	-2%	-3%	-6%	-9%	-9%	-8%	-7%	-8%	-8%	-48%
India	26%	25%	21%	17%	12%	10%	2%	-2%	-4%	-7%	-10%	-13%	-14%	-10%	-7%	-6%	-5%	-6%	-58%
China	20%	16%	11%	6%	5%	1%	-4%	-7%	-10%	-11%	-12%	-12%	-6%	-8%	-7%	-7%	-7%	-7%	-62%
Nigeria	30%	30%	28%	30%	30%	37%	28%	21%	13%	10%	6%	1%	-3%	-6%	-9%	-10%	-9%	-8%	-18%
USA	11%	10%	13%	10%	6%	3%	0%	0%	-2%	-3%	-4%	-5%	-7%	-9%	-11%	-12%	-12%	-11%	-54%
Indonesia	28%	23%	17%	14%	13%	5%	2%	-1%	-3%	-5%	-7%	-8%	-10%	-10%	-8%	-6%	-6%	-6%	-33%
Brazil	27%	23%	17%	13%	7%	5%	2%	0%	-4%	-6%	-8%	-10%	-11%	-9%	-8%	-8%	-8%	-7%	-56%
Mexico	33%	24%	18%	15%	13%	10%	7%	1%	-1%	-4%	-7%	-8%	-11%	-10%	-9%	-9%	-8%	-8%	-55%
Russia	7%	6%	-1%	-3%	1%	-1%	-4%	-6%	-6%	-7%	-7%	-7%	-7%	-8%	-9%	-10%	-10%	-10%	-56%
Turkey	26%	23%	17%	14%	17%	10%	9%	4%	0%	-2%	-3%	-6%	-8%	-10%	-10%	-10%	-10%	-11%	-52%
Japan	13%	6%	2%	1%	-2%	-4%	-7%	-10%	-11%	-12%	-13%	-13%	-10%	-9%	-9%	-9%	-9%	-9%	-60%
Germany	0%	1%	4%	0%	1%	1%	-1%	-2%	-4%	-5%	-7%	-9%	-10%	-11%	-10%	-9%	-10%	-11%	-19%
UK	4%	3%	4%	7%	6%	6%	1%	0%	-1%	-2%	-4%	-6%	-8%	-10%	-10%	-11%	-12%	-11%	-54%
France	6%	5%	5%	7%	3%	1%	1%	-1%	-3%	-5%	-6%	-8%	-9%	-10%	-11%	-10%	-10%	-10%	-54%
South Africa	32%	28%	22%	13%	16%	8%	3%	3%	1%	-1%	-3%	-5%	-8%	-9%	-9%	-10%	-11%	-11%	-50%
Italy	4%	2%	0%	4%	2%	-2%	-7%	-7%	-12%	-11%	-11%	-10%	-10%	-8%	-8%	-7%	-7%	-8%	-62%
Canada	19%	12%	11%	10%	12%	8%	2%	2%	-1%	-2%	-3%	-4%	-6%	-8%	-10%	-11%	-13%	-13%	-51%
Spain	9%	5%	5%	15%	0%	-4%	-4%	-7%	-10%	-11%	-13%	-14%	-13%	-10%	-8%	-8%	-8%	-6%	-60%
Australia	19%	13%	12%	16%	18%	8%	7%	7%	3%	1%	-1%	-3%	-5%	-7%	-9%	-10%	-10%	-10%	-41%

Handwritten note (left margin): I still think these are too small. Do you think people have superpowers or something? WHO could actually read this without magnifying

Handwritten note (right margin): Cassy – D find numerous check – I've gone nuclear blind!

Handwritten note (bottom): HATE the colours

Annotated tables on population projections from Future Perfect proof

A comparison of selected population predictions within *Future Perfect* and the actual estimated population in 2150:

Population projections: 2050 - 2150
Comparison of predictions within *Future Perfect* and actual

	Future Perfect	Actual			
	Population 2150 / millions	Actual population 2150 / millions	Peak population year	Population in peak year / millions	% fall from peak population
Global	4,800	4,630	2057	9,210	50%
India	640	610	2042	1,557	61%
China	485	437	2025	1,432	69%
Nigeria	360	395	2093	603	34%
USA	160	162	2044	355	54%
Indonesia	136	142	2042	295	52%
Brazil	100	106	2042	231	54%
Mexico	69	72	2051	155	54%
Russia	57	54	1992	149	64%
Turkey	50	58	2063	108	46%
Japan	34	31	2010	128	76%
Germany	34	31	2032	84	63%
UK	33	36	2054	73	51%
France	28	29	2040	69	58%
South Africa	34	37	2063	69	46%
Italy	20	19	2014	61	69%
Canada	21	22	2058	44	50%
Spain	14	15	2023	47	68%
Australia	19	26	2074	34	24%

Global population: 2050 - 2150
Comparison of predictions within *Future Perfect* and actual

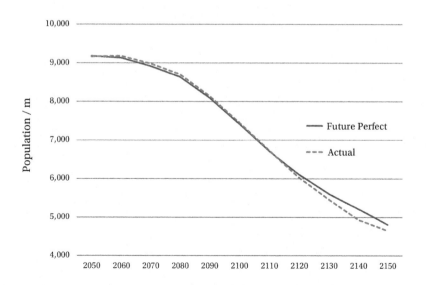

Appendix 6: Isarebe's work on income polarisation

History only tends to remember the successes of futurologists, but there are always areas where they get it wrong and Isarebe was no different. One of these was his prediction of a reversal in income polarisation that had occurred in most countries from the late 1970s through to the date of publication of *Future Perfect*. His arguments on income polarisation were mainly focussed on the impact of Artificial Intelligence on different types of jobs:

> AI is going to change things. For example, it will be tough for some of the previously protected professions – lawyers, bankers and doctors in particular – whose roles will be significantly de-skilled. Although it will be difficult for them as individuals, society will benefit from a vastly improved service at a fraction of the price.

> There will still be an 'elite', but it will be smaller and restricted to innovators, knowledge holders, researchers, entrepreneurs and those with significant capital, i.e. those with exceptional brilliance, exceptional knowledge, exceptional judgement or exceptional wealth. Below this much smaller elite, there will be a more egalitarian society, with people in previously low-paid service jobs being in great demand.[401]

As he predicted, Artificial Intelligence has decimated the old middle-class professions; in the UK, the number of professionals in law, medicine and architecture fell by 82% between 2050 and 2148, while high-level jobs in computing, technology and research rose by 480%.

He proposed a new method of measuring income polarisation, which he modestly entitled 'The Isarebe Coefficient'. This was a bizarre measure showing implicit generosity towards 'a meritocratic and necessary elite'[402] that he obviously believed he was a member of. The Isarebe Coefficient gained no traction. This is perhaps lucky for Isarebe's legacy, as his predictions on

401   Isarebe, S, 2051, Eye-Ted Talk: *Richer, better, more equal*, 21st Jun 2051, www.eye-ted. com [accessed 20th June 2149]
402   Isarebe, S and I, 2050, *Future Perfect*, Cambridge and Oxford University Press, Cambridge, p. 343

income polarisation were almost entirely wrong. Whilst there have been some changes in the income distribution profile, there has still been an overall increase in income polarisation, although this trend has decelerated in the past forty years.

Appendix 7: *Future Perfect* economic forecasts

A sample of some of the original economic projections contained within *Future Perfect*. This facsimile was made from Solomon Isarebe's proof copy and includes his handwritten comments:

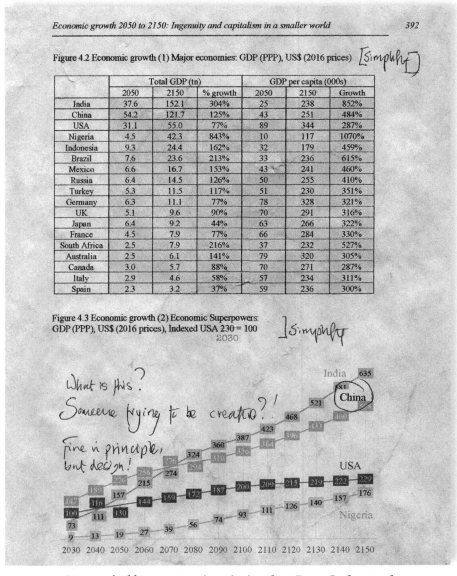

Figure 4.2 Economic growth (1) Major economies: GDP (PPP), US$ (2016 prices) [Simplify]

	Total GDP (tn)			GDP per capita (000s)		
	2050	2150	% growth	2050	2150	Growth
India	37.6	152.1	304%	25	238	852%
China	54.2	121.7	125%	43	251	484%
USA	31.1	55.0	77%	89	344	287%
Nigeria	4.5	42.3	843%	10	117	1070%
Indonesia	9.3	24.4	162%	32	179	459%
Brazil	7.6	23.6	213%	33	236	615%
Mexico	6.6	16.7	153%	43	241	460%
Russia	6.4	14.5	126%	50	255	410%
Turkey	5.3	11.5	117%	51	230	351%
Germany	6.3	11.1	77%	78	328	321%
UK	5.1	9.6	90%	70	291	316%
Japan	6.4	9.2	44%	63	266	322%
France	4.5	7.9	77%	66	284	330%
South Africa	2.5	7.9	216%	37	232	527%
Australia	2.5	6.1	141%	79	320	305%
Canada	3.0	5.7	88%	70	271	287%
Italy	2.9	4.6	58%	57	234	311%
Spain	2.3	3.2	37%	59	236	300%

Figure 4.3 Economic growth (2) Economic Superpowers: GDP (PPP), US$ (2016 prices), Indexed USA 230 = 100 [Simplify] 2030

Annotated tables on economic projections from Future Perfect proof

A comparison of selected economic predictions within *Future Perfect* and the actual economic outcome in 2150:

Economic projections: 2050 - 2150 (GDP PPP, US$, 2016 prices)
Comparison of predictions within *Future Perfect* and actual

Territory	GDP 2050 / $tn	Future Perfect GDP 2150 / $tn	Actual GDP 2150 / $tn	% growth	Forecast error (%)
Global	288.2	805.1	780.3	171%	3%
India	37.6	152.1	145.3	286%	5%
China	54.2	121.7	108.3	100%	12%
USA	31.1	55.0	57.8	86%	-5%
Nigeria	4.5	42.3	37.2	730%	14%
Indonesia	9.3	24.4	25.9	178%	-6%
Brazil	7.6	23.6	22.3	196%	6%
Mexico	6.6	16.7	15.0	127%	11%
Russia	6.4	14.5	13.8	115%	5%
Turkey	5.3	11.5	12.3	133%	-7%
Germany	6.3	11.2	9.9	57%	13%
UK	5.1	9.6	9.8	94%	-2%
Japan	6.4	9.2	10.1	58%	-9%
France	4.5	7.9	8.2	83%	-3%
South Africa	2.5	7.9	8.2	229%	-4%
Australia	2.5	6.1	6.8	168%	-10%
Canada	3.0	5.7	5.6	85%	1%
Italy	2.9	4.6	4.9	67%	-6%
Spain	2.3	3.2	3.3	41%	-3%

Economic growth (% change GDP-PPP): 2050 - 2150
Comparison of predictions within *Future Perfect* and actual

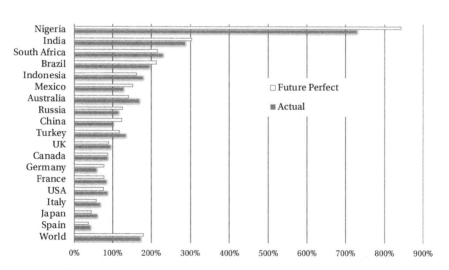

Chronology

1998	Rita Bortelli born in Wichita, Kansas, USA
2008	Solomon Isarebe born in Oslo, Norway, as Axel Solomon Jakobsen-Steiner
2016	Isabelle Isarebe born in Egypt, as Inessa Denikin
2017	Solomon Isarebe arrives in London, England, aged 9
	Reba Desalli and Jannik Nieminen adopt Solomon Isarebe
2018	Reba Desalli and Jannik Nieminen change their family name to Isarebe
2019	The Isarebe family move to Egypt
2020	Start of the Covid-19 pandemic
2022	Inessa Denikin formally joins the Isarebe family and becomes Isabelle Isarebe
	The Isarebe family move to Germany
2023	The Isarebe family move to Garway Hill in Herefordshire, England
2024	Arem Johns is born in Basildon, Essex, England
2026	Solomon Isarebe goes to study at Cambridge University, England, aged 17
2030	Solomon Isarebe receives his doctorate from Cambridge University, aged 22
2032	Solomon Isarebe publishes *The Demise of the Political Economy*
2033	Isabelle and Solomon Isarebe move to Cambridge, Massachusetts, where Isabelle studies and Solomon lectures at MIT
2034	Isabelle Isarebe meets Mooketsi Mooketsi
2037	Isabelle Isarebe moves to Botswana
	Solomon Isarebe starts work for The Bates Institute

2038	Venezuelan oil crisis and global recession
2039	Solomon Isarebe made Research Director of The Bates Institute
2040	Isabelle Isarebe receives her doctorate from the University of Botswana
	Isabelle Isarebe becomes pregnant
	Isabelle Isarebe's biological father dies
	Isabelle Isarebe has a termination, before taking a job with AMRP in Dublin, Ireland
	Solomon Isarebe has a mental breakdown and returns to Garway Hill, England
2041	Solomon Isarebe works as a part-time assistant at Cambridge University
2042	Solomon and Isabelle Isarebe start to work together on *Future Perfect*
2043	Rita Bortelli becomes a benefactor to Isarebe & Isarebe
2046	Casey Ingar joins Isarebe & Isarebe
2048	Isabelle Isarebe dies, aged 32, in Palmyra, Syria
	Solomon Isarebe disappears before surfacing in New York, USA
2050	*Future Perfect* published
2055	Solomon Isarebe receives the Nobel Prize for Statistics and Economics
2056	Solomon Isarebe appointed Professor of Quantitative Social Economics at the University of Cambridge
2057	Solomon Isarebe meets the artist Arem Johns
2058	Max Pop Day, when the global population started to fall
2061	Reba Isarebe dies in Garway Hill, Herefordshire, England

2063	Jannik Isarebe dies in Garway Hill, Herefordshire, England
2068	Arem Johns is found murdered in her and Solomon Isarebe's home near Cambridge, England
	Solomon Isarebe is imprisoned for Arem Johns' murder
2081	Solomon Isarebe is pardoned and released from prison
	Solomon Isarebe goes to live with Rita Bortelli and David Dingle in the USA
2093	Solomon Isarebe dies, aged 85, near Big Sur, California, USA
2094	The European Consensus War begins
2096	China invades the Indochinese Peninsula
2097	Rita Bortelli dies, aged 99, in Rockport, Massachusetts, USA
2102	India, China and the USA sign the Beijing-Washington Accord
2118	Earth Recovery Day, when global temperatures officially peaked
2150	The 100th anniversary of the publication of *Future Perfect*

Printed in Great Britain
by Amazon